Argent Blade:
Plague Carrier

Luke Courtney

First published 2021
by Rowanvale Books Ltd
The Gate
Keppoch Street
Roath
Cardiff
CF24 3JW
www.rowanvalebooks.com

A CIP catalogue record for this book is available from the British Library.

Paperback ISBN: 978-1-913662-57-8
eBook ISBN: 978-1-913662-58-5

To Sean, Roger and Katherine for helping make this a better book, and to my parents and the always wonderful Becky Finch for supporting me and always being willing to listen.

"Loathsomeness waits and dreams in the deep, and decay spreads over the tottering cities of men."

—H.P. Lovecraft, *The Call of Cthulhu*

Prologue: Dark Salvation
Lincolnshire, England, 1348

He did not need a physician to tell him he was dying.

Another spasm tore through him, and he vomited up blood so dark it was almost black. He didn't even have the strength to wipe the filth from his mouth.

"No, not like this," he whispered, struggling to stand. His legs gave out.

He thrust out a hand, the tips of his fingers already turning black, to keep from falling face first into the dirt. He breathed in the air of the barn, heady with the stink of sweat and rot. He could see his fellow knights shivering and shaking as they fought against the pestilence ravaging their bodies. When the villagers had learnt that one of the men in his company had black boils upon his neck, the surest sign of the pestilence, they'd insisted that the knights isolate themselves in the barn to prevent the spread of the sickness. Unfortunately, even as they tried their best to tend to their brother's sickness, it had spread to them in turn.

Their breaths rasped. He looked around at one of his men, neck and face covered in black blotches and boils, coughing up bloody phlegm. He tried to crawl over and join those he could hear in desperate prayer, beseeching God to heed them, to forgive them their sins and the sins of all those who had brought His wrath down upon England in the form of this plague, but he was too weak.

The crunch of soil underfoot caught his attention. Glaring at his companions for silence, he crawled to the door of the barn. He pressed his ear against it and heard voices outside.

"We sure they're not all dead?"

"The food they paid for is taken in when we leave it outside."

"If they've got gold to pay for food, then they may have more in there."

A mocking burst of laughter. "Go ahead. Gold won't do you much good when black boils are popping up all over you."

"Then we better burn it down, along with those wretches, 'fore they spread the pestilence to the entire village!"

"One more day, then we talk to the alderman."

The villagers left, their footsteps fading into silence.

The diseased knight spat a wad of bloody filth in disgust, then muttered to himself as he crawled over to join his brothers. "Bloody peasants! Is this our reward for loyal service? To die in some godforsaken fleapit? No, no—I won't let it happen. I am a knight, a scion of a great house. I will not die in this wretched sty, stinking of sweat and shit, breathing in the odour of my own body rotting!"

Weak groans and calls of agreement came from his companions. Sinking to his knees, the sickly knight scratched his neck. His fingernails punctured the swollen boils there, and he winced as streams of blood ran down his front and back, seeping into his clothes and chest hair. Another coughing fit overtook him.

Flies buzzed around his head. When he'd had his full strength, he could easily have snatched them out of the air and crushed them in his fist, but now he barely had the energy to bat them away. Their incessant buzzing in his ears, his fury at the villagers' treachery, his self-loathing over the betrayal of his own disease-ravaged body, made a rasping growl of impotent rage escape between clenched teeth… and then he heard the voice.

At first he thought it was a hallucination, but then it was unmistakeable: a voice made from the buzzing of thousands of flies' wings—harsh, echoing but understandable.

"You seek salvation from this plague? I can give that to you all. Accept the gift that I offer, and you will rise again, stronger than you can ever imagine. No disease will hold you, no blade will slay you. You will walk shrouded in death yet never need fear its touch."

It was dark in the barn, the only light from the moon piercing the holes in the roof, but he swore he could see a shadowy, man-shaped figure standing over him, watching, waiting for his decision. He remembered his father's warnings, repeated again and again as he watched over their tutelage in the ways of the Order, in preparation for the day they were initiated into its ranks and mission.

"Remember always, my sons, that demons never offer anything for free. Their power comes at a price, and always a heavy one."

"And what must we give in return?" he said, raising his head.

A buzzing laugh came in answer. "You will forswear everything that it means to be human. You will all become my foremost servants in this world, and until the end of days, you and your brothers will wander this earth, enlightening the dupes of the false and empty idols of my beneficence, until all are like you: infested, empowered and basking in the light of my glory!"

He shook his head, trying to clear it, to think. He knew this was damnation, but across the length and breadth of England, priests were already preaching that anyone who died of the pestilence was damned to hell for their sins. *If I must choose between one form of damnation or another, I will take the one that lets me live.*

He looked up at the shadowy figure looming over him and nodded. "Then I will serve."

Red pinpricks burned in the air in place of eyes, and then something bit into the back of his neck, stabbing like a dagger. Agony erupted in his chest like a half-dozen bone skewers had been driven between his ribs, into his lungs. He coughed up blood as they drove deeper, but to his amazement, as the pain grew stronger, so did he. The flies buzzed ever louder. The shadowy figure turned its gaze on his sickened comrades, and he threw back his head and laughed, a gleefully maniacal sound as he felt his face split and peel like a serpent shedding its skin.

***

The demented laughter coming from the barn woke the village. The menfolk quickly dressed and grabbed scythes, pitchforks, sickles—anything that could be used as a weapon. They advanced on the barn doors. Fearful of what might be happening within, the villagers clustered together, hoping for safety in numbers.

The knights had stopped here for supplies on their way to the Scottish border, supposedly on a mission assigned to them by King Edward himself. The alderman had insisted they be confined when one of their number had proven to have the pestilence.

That had been a week ago. The insane laughter was the first sound any of the villagers had heard from them in days.

"Wat, open the door," a muscular villager snapped, gesturing with the blade of his sickle.

Wat, a spindly lad leaning on a pitchfork balked at the demand. "Why me?"

"Because I said to, that's why!"

But as Wat started forward, the barn doors were smashed open from the inside with a thunderous crash. Between them stood a figure from the depths of hell.

A grinning skull leered out from beneath a stained and tattered hood. Its swollen body was covered in diseased skin like melted candle wax, stretched so far in places that rotten flesh and yellowed bone could be seen. Burning green lights blazed in its empty eye sockets, and it smiled, its teeth scraping together. It was clad in armour red-brown with rust, an equally rusted sword clutched in its gauntleted fists. Gasps rang out from the crowd as they saw the bloated flies clinging to the side of the monster's neck, swelling and turning a brighter shade of red as they fed upon the abomination's blood.

The once-man laughed and spread its arms wide. "Look upon me and awe! I am the Great Mortality made manifest. Bow down before me, embrace the pestilence, and it will spare you its ravages!"

The villagers answered with screams of terror. They ran in all directions, though some of the men stood their ground as the monster hefted its sword and advanced. Wat charged forth, his pitchfork aimed at the beast's gut. He drove it deep, the rusty breastplate easily giving way to the tines, but the monster didn't even flinch. A gauntleted hand darted out, seizing Wat by the throat. He choked as his feet left the ground. Over his captor's shoulder, he saw five more such figures emerging from the shadows in the barn, while a sixth lay on the floor, unmoving.

"Get off him!" the big man with the sickle shouted, pulling back his weapon to swing at the elbow joint of the arm holding Wat, but before he could, another brutish monster thrust a rusty shield between the two. Chunks of rusted metal broke off as the sickle collided with the shield, but the big man was sent staggering back, long enough for one of the diseased knights to drive a corroded sword through his belly.

Wat watched as his would-be saviour pitched face first to the ground, guts spilling out. A low growl pulled his eyes back to the death's head grin of the creature holding him aloft.

"The pestilence will spread, and you will all assist, in this life *and* the next!" the monster growled.

Its jaw distended and black froth erupted from between rotten teeth, enveloping Wat. He screamed as it burned his skin, running down his face and neck and carving furrows into his flesh. Just before the slimy vomit melted his eyes, Wat saw the lifeless body in the barn explode, an immense swarm of flies erupting from its gut and smashing their way out through the barn's roof.

The village died to the sound of fly wings buzzing and the laughter of the damned.

Chapter 1: Dark Pact

Northern Iraq, close to the Syrian border, November 2016
Two weeks after the Samhain incident

The gurgling choke was cut short as the gauntleted hand around the neck of the Iraqi militant tightened its grasp and the man's neck snapped wetly. The bloated figure let the body fall from its grip. The rest of the man's patrol lay scattered about, their blood staining the sand crimson amongst the bullet casings. The men had tried in desperation to put down the monsters that had come shambling out of the desert, howling and moaning and impervious to all attempts to bring them down.

"A fine kill, Brother Pestis," said another swollen figure in rusted armour, raising a hand in acknowledgement even as it drove a red-brown sword through the belly of another man desperately pleading for his life in Arabic. The rust-clad monstrosity pulled its blade free and began rooting around in his belly.

"Indeed. From what they have endured in this wilderness, these fighters are hardy specimens. We will need more, though, if we are to complete the great work, Brother Ebolae."

Pestis irritably drummed his fingers against the rotten haft of his mace. Centuries had passed since their induction into their master's service, but the great work—the spreading of the glory of infection and contamination that He might breach into reality, had not yet come to pass.

A distant rumble came, and the two demonic knights looked up.

"Americans, maybe?" Pestis suggested. They hadn't seen any signs of US troops, but they'd learned to keep at least one eye on the sky for their metal machines. The captives they'd taken had referred to such as "drones". Though they had long since left their humanity behind, the plague knights could not help but be amused by the ever-continuing efficacy of men at developing new ways to kill one another.

If they devoted as much effort to saving lives as they do to taking them, our work would have been thwarted and our master defeated long ago, Pestis thought as one of the militants tried to crawl away.

The man began bleating in Arabic and then in pidgin English as the armoured monster stalked over.

"No, no, have family, don't kill, don't kill—!"

His pleading ended abruptly as Pestis kicked him onto his back and drove a rust-riddled dagger through his neck. Blood vomited from his mouth and the ruin of his throat, pale white forms writhing in the spreading dark puddle. The knight didn't bother to clean the blood from his blade; it would add to the corruption already seething through the weapon.

The rumble came again and suddenly, the air began to spit red sparks, an unnatural wind whipping up the desert sands. The two plague knights raised their weapons and went on guard as a sphere of crackling scarlet energy began to form in mid-air, growing until it was tall enough for a man to walk through.

As the two warriors watched, several figures emerged from the glowing portal, the first a lean man, dark haired and dressed in an expertly tailored suit, his face a patchwork of healing cuts, a pair of sunglasses covering his eyes. Despite the heat of the desert, he showed no signs of discomfort. Next came a dozen men and women dressed in clothing more suited to the environment, while two twisted and deformed women in tattered black clothing brought up the rear. Witches who'd embraced dark magic to the point where it had corrupted them entirely, body and soul, judging from the spider-like mutations that protruded from their flesh.

The knights snarled at this intrusion, warily watching the advancing party, when the man in the suit removed his sunglasses and inclined his head.

"Greetings, good knights. I humbly beseech you for an audience; I am bound to deliver a message to you and your master."

The eyes burning in the man's face were a pale yellow, with jagged reptilian slits for pupils. Pestis and Ebolae lowered their swords. This newcomer was one like them, an entity that had long ago made a bargain with dark powers.

"You have our attention, creature. What business do you have with our blighted brotherhood?"

The once-man shook his head and replied, "Not with you. My master and mistress would speak with yours: Nergal, Lord of the Flies, the Putrescent King. They would offer him an alliance."

The knights studied him for a moment, then nodded. The malefic green fire burning in their eye sockets turned a deep red, and their jaws opened.

"You have our attention." Rasping voices speaking as one addressed the interlopers. "Speak."

***

Nathaniel Danvers went to one knee. Technically, his status as the Emissary of Typhon and Echidna positioned him above most of the lesser demon lords that dwelt within What Lies Beyond, perpetually vying for influence and the favour of their betters, but certain courtesies had to observed. The cultists he'd brought with him, most of them survivors of the debacle in London, followed suit. Beneath their hoods, their faces were painted with smears of green, red and black, like claw scratches. They were a gaggle of discredited doctors, struck off-nurses and medical volunteers from around the world, having grown disgusted with trying to stem the tide of disease and infection while mankind's brutish, destructive nature unleashed all manner of new wars and disasters, letting disease run rampant across the world every single day. Small wonder so many had become disillusioned to the point they were willing to help destroy their fellow men. The irony never failed to amuse Danvers.

But then, this little war has been full of ironies, he thought, blinking rapidly as a fly darted across his face. His vision had all but completely healed since Halloween, though the scars left by silver blades, fangs and talons remained. As far as the world at large knew, Nathaniel Danvers was away on business in America, transferred there after the disastrous failure of the Phoenix Initiative's London branch.

"Great Nergal," Danvers spoke with both his and the Emissary's voice, his words and tone ritualistic, "I bid you greetings, mighty plague bringer! On behalf of Lord Typhon and Lady Echidna, I offer you the gifts of flesh and bone, a token of the pact my lord and lady wish to make with you."

"A pact?" enquired the demon speaking through the plague-ravaged throats of its disciples, amongst numerous grating clicks and hisses.

The buzzing of insect wings was growing louder, and several of Nathaniel's acolytes made noises of disgust. He understood why; the wind was picking up, whipping sand in their faces, and the already palpable smell of rotting flesh was growing stronger, as if something long dead were using the bodies of its hosts to draw as close to them as the veil between their worlds would allow.

"Of course, great lord," Danvers insisted, his arms spread wide in supplication, his own voice echoing as the Emissary pushed its way to the fore to address one of its own kind.

It was a great risk dealing with such a creature—while technically one of their ilk, Nergal owed no allegiance to the Pantheon, being a capricious and individualistic creature, but it had more than enough reasons to hate the Order of the Argent Blade, and its overwhelming desire to infect, contaminate and poison every living being in its path would be to his advantage.

"I, who speak for Lord Typhon and Lady Echidna and all who kneel before their aegis, would remake our ancient pact with you, Lord of Pestilence. With our aid, your power shall grow mighty until your greatest works are surpassed, and the Black Death you wrought will seem a summer cold compared to the magnificence you will unleash!"

"You wish to use my knowledge and that of my disciples to further your goals," the burbling voices said. "You wish to strike at mankind with the blades of virus and bacteria, all of which I have at my command. Force of arms has failed you, so now you come crawling to me, seeking my aid. And tell me, what benefit is in this venture for me? I will not be satisfied with some meagre scraps from the table of Typhon and Echidna this time! What can your little cult and its acolytes give to recompense me?"

The Emissary used Danvers' flesh to smile as it raised his head. "The chance to complete your great work. Enough human flesh riddled with disease and contamination for you to shatter the barrier and bestride this earth in physical form, a worthy addition to my master and mistress's court, and lands and subjects to bestow the bounty of your great gifts upon when this world falls!"

The rotted knights rubbed their chins thoughtfully in unison as their master used them like marionettes, clearly weighing up the benefits of such a pact, trying to find some kind of catch. Nathaniel waited on tenterhooks, hoping against hope the demon lord would see the benefit of such an alliance. He needed something good to take back to his patrons; his standing with them was in tatters after the debacle in London.

At long last, Pestis removed his right gauntlet and spat a wad of black blood into his palm. Overcoming his revulsion, Nathaniel spat in his palm and extended his hand, finely manicured fingers grasping diseased claws as dark powers united in pursuit of a common goal.

The burning red light in the eye sockets of both plague knights receded, becoming bilious green once more as Pestis and Ebolae returned to themselves.

Pestis took charge. "It would seem we have an accord. What facilities do you have for us to do our work?"

"My agents are some of the finest medical staff on this earth. They have a comprehensive laboratory set up, and we will acquire suitable test subjects to use for your master's…" Nathaniel fell silent as Pestis raised a gauntleted hand for quiet.

"Ebolae, you will go with our new allies and see what they have prepared for us. I will wait here. You will leave one of your pet witches here until I am ready to depart," Pestis explained, using a bony claw to puncture an oozing boil at his wrist.

Thick pus stinking of rot spilled forth. The cultists struggled not to gag at the stench. Pestis sifted through the filth, pulling out a maggot the length of his little finger. He repeated the process with three other boils, until four fat white maggots writhed in the palm of his hand. Nathaniel and the Desolated cultists watched in confusion as Pestis strode over to one of the dead militants and inserted a maggot into the gaping wound in the corpse's chest. The plague knight then proceeded to do the same with three more of the dead.

"And what will you do?" Nathaniel asked, only to start in shock as one of the corpses started twitching and thrashing, then scrambled to its feet.

The corpse's head was bent at an angle, but with a hideous crack of bone, the neck snapped back into place, the flesh around the lower jaw splitting apart as insect-like mandibles protruded, snapping hungrily. More bodies with similar such mutations were clawing themselves upright. The watching men and women gasping as fragile wings pushed through the mutants' spines, completing their resemblance to humanoid flies. The cultists looked stunned, but Nathaniel couldn't stop grinning at what he was seeing.

Last time was a setback, but with the gifts these new allies could bring to our cause, the Order of the Argent Blade will find us a much greater challenge.

"I will stay here and wait for my brothers." Pestis snapped his fingers and motioned for the monsters to head out. With a series of keening screeches, their wings started beating and they took to the air. "They have gone hunting in all directions. Cholera and typhus are running rampant in this area, and those we can capture will be of great use in spreading the infection," Pestis explained to Nathaniel as the maggot-born monstrosities became dark specks in the sky that separated and flew off, east, west and north. "The messengers will bring them back, and when they are here, you will have six of the greatest minds on every disease, every infection, every contamination in existence, ready to fight your war."

Chapter 2: Blood in the Canals
Venice, Italy
December 26th, 2016

"Come on, Joshua! Run!" Rosa yelled as she dragged the dark-skinned boy out of her uncle's church.

Her uncle was dying in front of his altar, his blood flowing from a trio of slash wounds from collarbone to groin. Even the sanctity of his church had not protected him from the killers.

"Run, Rosa! RUN!" had been his last words, and she had done that, taking with her the refugee boy her uncle had taken in at the request of an old friend. The boy had all but ignored her while she'd been staying with her uncle, only really conversing with the priest in rapid Swahili, but when Rosa had seen the monstrous figure looming over her supine uncle, heard the bestial snarls coming from the church, she'd known she couldn't leave him to such a fate. Grabbing Joshua's hand as he'd looked up in shock, she'd pulled him to his feet, thrown the door open and run into the streets.

Chancing a look behind, she saw their pursuers closing the gap as they fled towards Venice's old Jewish quarter. The three creatures were running on all fours, with narrow, dog-like faces and long-limbed, rangy bodies, their near-hairless skin marked with long scars and tattoos. They sprinted down the streets after her, their claws clicking on the cobbles.

Suddenly, there was a howl from above. Rosa looked up and screamed in horror as two more of the dog-like monstrosities dropped down from the rooftops, blocking their escape. They barked and snarled, forcing Rosa to retreat, as the three that had chased her and Joshua rose up on their hind legs, towering over their quarry.

Breathing rapidly, trying to get her heartrate to slow, Rosa pushed Joshua behind her as they retreated into the doorway of a long-abandoned house. As the monsters encircled them, Rosa brandished a table knife, the closest thing to a weapon she'd managed to grab before fleeing. The quintet of monsters threw back their heads and howled at the sky, clearly psyching themselves up for the kill.

"Don't look," Rosa whispered, and she stepped forward, desperately jabbing at the circling monstrosities.

She heard sounds like rocks grating together and realised the monsters were laughing at her. Her defiance *amused* them. Her anger flared.

"Laugh at this, you freaks!" she shrieked, and charged at the nearest beast.

The creature caught her knife-hand inches from its right pectoral. Its muzzle of a face twisted into a cruel smile as it bent her wrist back. Crying out, Rosa lost her grip on the knife, which clattered to the ground. The wolf-man turned its head towards its pack, who nodded, more cruel laughter escaping between their fangs. It slammed Rosa against the wall, forcing her head back. Feeling the werewolf's hot breath on her neck, she closed her eyes, braced herself for—

A crossbow bolt slashed through the air, sending the monster staggering back, its claws releasing her in shock. It screeched in pain, clutching the bolt buried halfway in the meat of its chest, before a second punched out of its throat in a spray of blood. The monster collapsed. Its limbs thrashed in spasms as it bled out, painting the cobbles scarlet. The werewolves snarled angrily, and another staggered, a crossbow bolt jutting from its back. They turned to face this new threat, and Rosa looked between them to see where the shot had come from. What she saw was quite a surprise.

The shooter was a young woman in black body armour, her head hidden beneath the hood of a long coat. Rosa could see silver details engraved into the body armour and piercing blue eyes that stared at the unusual scene before her. Rosa felt uneasy. While the newcomer had saved her in the immediate, there was no proof her situation had got any better.

What is going on? Why is this happening to me?

"Unless you ugly mutts want to die here, back away from them now!" the woman bellowed in a voice that demanded obedience.

Rosa raised an eyebrow. Speaking English, the newcomer was clearly British, another insane addition to the proceedings.

Again came the grating laughter of the werewolves, overconfident and dismissive… and suddenly there was a flash of silver and the closest werewolf was on all fours, whimpering and clutching its chest. Rosa gasped as it turned and she saw a long, deep wound cut diagonally across its chest. She looked at the hooded woman, who dragged a long silver whip along the cobbles, its segmented metal length rattling ominously.

"Last warning," she snapped.

The werewolves, however, weren't listening. Two of their number were injured and another dead; their blood was up. With a bitter sigh, the woman pulled something from within her coat, and then flung it, a flash of silver darting through the air.

The closest werewolf looked down. A small knife jutted from its biceps. It chuckled darkly as if amused by such a pitiful effort, then reached up to pull the blade from its arm with clawed fingers.

"Take cover!" the British girl screamed as she darted into the shelter of a doorway, protecting her head with her hands.

Confused, Rosa did as she was bidden, pressing herself and Joshua, who watched the tableau with wide eyes, against the door behind them.

As the werewolf ripped the knife from its arm, the blade suddenly exploded and the monster's guttural laugh became a sound somewhere between a howl and a scream. Blood and metal sprayed in all directions. Rosa cried out as a silver shard clipped her cheek, and she clutched the bleeding slice in her face.

The shrieking was making her ears hurt, and when she looked, she felt her gorge rise. The werewolf was on the ground, clutching its maimed arm close to its chest, its grey fur smeared with blood. Its hand was blown to pieces, the mangled limb studded with silver shrapnel. The rest of the pack were disorientated by the blast, left trying to pluck bits of shrapnel from their bodies.

God almighty, Rosa wondered, looking at the devastation around her. *What the hell is going on?*

As she watched, the hooded woman advanced on the injured werewolf, pulled a shotgun from a holster on her back, racked the slide back and planted a booted foot on the monster's chest. The werewolf snarled and snapped its fangs, about the most violent thing it could do. The girl jammed the shotgun's barrel between its jaws and pulled the trigger. At such close range, the monster's head came apart. Rosa goggled in horror, then her stomach churned and she emptied her dinner into the street.

She heard a roar of fury and managed to look up from vomiting as the remaining werewolves charged at the hooded woman. The woman pulled the trigger again, and a werewolf staggered back, howling in pain as its shoulder took the hit, but the other two pressed their attack. She blocked the slash of claws with the gun's stock and kicked out at her attacker, a precise blow to the knee that drove it back. She ducked under the next blow, aimed at her head, but Rosa, still struggling to get her stomach back under control as Joshua patted her on the back, had to wonder how long her luck would last.

And then two unexpected things happened.

Another lupine howl rang out from the rooftops, this one deeper than the jabbering cries of her attackers. The werewolves looked up to see a hulking, dark shape, tall and broad shouldered, glaring down at them with golden eyes, but Rosa's gaze dropped as she heard something hit the floor. She saw a silver sphere, about the size of an apple, rolling past her and Joshua, coming to a stop as it hit the back of a clawed foot. Oily grey smoke spewed forth, but the smell told Rosa it wasn't smoke.

It was gas.

"Come on!" Rosa shouted, adrenaline invigorating her as she shoved Joshua into the relative safety of a doorway, shielding him as the grenade went off with a thunderous bang.

The werewolves screamed as the explosion ignited the gas cloud surrounding them, setting hair and flesh ablaze. With a roar, the dark figure on the rooftops leapt, hitting the ground in a roll and flinging itself into the pack. Rosa felt a hand on her shoulder. She raised her fists, only to lower them at the sight of a fearsome-looking man, maybe Kenyan or Zimbabwean, dressed in the same dark body armour as the young woman—who was still alive, judging by the periodic gunshots. Rosa's mouth went dry as the man said in a firm baritone, "Stay behind me. I will keep you safe."

A bestial scream came from the fighting. She chanced a look and saw one of the werewolves on its knees, its back still on fire, its clawed hands desperately trying to stop long ropes of intestines from spilling over the cobbles. Looming over it was a black-furred werewolf, its broad, heaving chest worthy of a bodybuilder, the pectorals criss-crossed by thin white scars; its right hand dripping with blood. With a roar, its left hand lashed out, and its dying enemy's head went flying, blood spraying from the truncated corpse. The body and severed head began to regress from wolf to human, the fur and snout receding until the decapitated corpse of a woman was left on the ground.

The black-furred brute suddenly roared in pain as two others attacked it, one leaping onto it from behind and sinking its fangs into the right shoulder while the second sank its teeth into its foe's hip. Bellowing furiously, the black-furred werewolf tried to throw off its attackers, but their jaws would not let go.

Fortunately, the black-furred monster had help. The warrior woman, whose hood had fallen down to reveal a wild mess of dark hair, pulled a knife from her belt. Its silver blade gleamed in the moonlight.

"Hang on, Liam!" she shouted as she charged in and buried the knife in the closest werewolf's spine.

It let go with a howl of pain, and the black-furred Liam grabbed it by the throat, pulling it off his back and flinging it into the side of a building.

The werewolf biting Liam's hip yelped as Liam pulled its jaws free of his side, then jerked its head back and bit its throat out. Blood spurted everywhere as he pulled back, flesh and fur between his fangs. His enemy vainly tried to staunch the gaping wound, Rosa again retching at the overpowering smell of copper. The last werewolf gave a panic-stricken whimper, turned and bolted on all fours. With a snarl, Liam dropped his victim and gave pursuit.

A wraith-like figure, long strawberry-blonde hair streaming behind it like a banner, came charging out of nowhere and shoulder-barged the fleeing werewolf, knocking it down. Liam came to a halt, watching as his prey scrambled to its feet and tried to attack this new threat, but the newcomer, another woman, spun and seized the outstretched arm. There was a crack and the werewolf staggered back shrieking, its right arm twisted at an impossible angle. It tried to slash out with its left, but she easily caught its wrist, and then drove her clenched fist into its chest. The werewolf pitched forward with a weak moan.

The redhead stood over it, a heart still giving its final frantic beats clutched in her blood-red grasp. The woman flashed her a dazzling smile—and Rosa felt a chill as she saw the long canine teeth gleaming in her mouth—and squeezed the heart's blood into her open mouth like an orange.

What the fucking hell is all this?!

She stared in utter disbelief and shock—Joshua alongside her with wide eyes, though otherwise oddly calm—as the warriors and monsters congregated. They stepped over the carcasses of their enemies without a care in the world. The black-furred werewolf stalked over to the redhead and began to shrink. Its fur receded back into its skin, its long snout shrinking back to form the handsome, if rugged and unshaven, face of a man in his early thirties, well-muscled, with a short black beard and curly black hair, a few tattoos scattered across his upper arms and legs. He turned around so they wouldn't get a full look at his privates, the vampire pulling a pair of pants out of her coat for the purpose.

"I had it under control," the werewolf, or rather the man he'd turned back into, said over his shoulder in a thick Irish brogue as he quickly preserved his modesty.

The redheaded vampire gave him a peck on his shaggy cheek, and said with a sly smile, "And why should you have all the fun?"

"Thank you for the help, Liam," the dark-haired woman chimed in, patting him on the shoulder.

"Happy to be of assistance, Lucy." He raised a hand in acknowledgment.

"Well, that was a fun night's work." The vampire smiled, picking at her teeth with a long, claw-like fingernail. "Thank you for the invite," she added with a nod to the young woman, who holstered her shotgun and gave her a suspicious look.

None of them paid Joshua and Rosa a bit of notice.

"What do you want, Siobhan?" Lucy asked. "I'm fully aware that you didn't hand us this information out of the good of your heart."

Siobhan smiled at the pun, baring her fangs. "Oh you know me so well!" Her expression grew serious. "I need a meeting. With Lawrence. Face to face, in Paris. A friend of mine wishes to speak to him."

"He doesn't trust you."

"And I don't trust him not to put a stake through my heart, but this is serious." Siobhan pulled an envelope out of her coat and placed it in Lucy's hand.

"Give your fellows my regards, and tell Larry if he wants to run down Mengele after what happened on Halloween, I have a few leads on where the good doctor has gone to ground. Most of what he'll want is in that envelope. Tell him if he wants more to meet me in Paris at the enclosed address on January fourth. Until then."

With a snap of her fingers, Siobhan and Liam began to run. In seconds, the night had swallowed them.

Broaching the silence, Rosa turned to Lucy and asked, "What's going on?"

Lucy sighed as she wiped her silver blade clean on one of the dead creatures. "Never thought I'd have to go through this again," she muttered to herself as she sheathed the kukri at her hip. "We can explain everything," she said, turning to Rosa, "but this is not the time or place to do so. You need to come with us."

"Why?" Rosa demanded. "What is going on here? Why did those things kill my uncle? And how are they even real?!"

"It's complicated," the big African man intoned, his baritone voice firm but understanding, "but it all revolves around him."

He pointed towards the boy she'd been trying to shield.

***

Two hours later

Rosa sat in silence, drumming her fingers on the armrests of her seat, feeling completely out of place. A few rows behind her, Joshua talked in Swahili to the African man, who in turn translated the boy's answers to a priest who'd been waiting for them aboard a private plane at the Marco Polo Airport. Within minutes of them arriving at the airport, they'd boarded the aircraft, an exchange of documents between Lucy and security officials expediting their passage.

"Here," a woman's voice interrupted her thoughts.

She looked up and saw Lucy offering her a glass of whiskey. Rosa had never been much of a drinker, but she hastily swallowed it down, glad of something to help calm her nerves. It didn't work. In her head, she still heard the bestial shrieking, the gunshots, her uncle dying on the floor of his church…

This can't be real. I'll wake up soon. Maybe I overdid it a little yesterday…

Lucy nodded sympathetically as she poured Rosa another glass. "I remember that feeling well. Your mind trying to process it all, make sense of what you've seen. About a year ago, I was going through this."

"What did you think of it all?" Rosa asked.

Lucy gave a helpless shrug. "Honestly, when I first saw a creature like that, I thought someone had spiked my drink. Seemed a perfectly logical reaction to your flatmates turning on you and trying to kill you with a pack of hell hounds!"

Rosa raised an eyebrow at this, but then shook her head. "Those things can't be real."

"I'd say the blood on my coat and blade says otherwise," Lucy joked, only to fall silent at the look on Rosa's face, one so glacial it could have frozen mercury. "Sorry, we've all got our coping mechanisms. Mine seem to be sarcasm and shitty jokes." A serious look crossed her face as she took on a sympathetic tone. "I know it's hard to take in at first. I honestly thought I was having a nervous breakdown. Hell, some of the things I've seen in the time since then, I still keep hoping I'll wake up in bed with the mother of all hangovers!"

"So where are we going?" Rosa asked.

Lucy smiled. "London. We're taking you both to the safest place on the planet after what you've just witnessed… and where you can both get some answers."

***

Kensington, London, four hours later

"What's so significant about the kid?" Lucy whispered as the two newcomers helped themselves to breakfast.

Gillian sat in a corner of the kitchen, gnawing on a crumpet, while Lucy had purloined a croissant. The young Italian woman, Rosa, was sitting in mute silence. Charles glowered in a corner, Claire pored over her laptop, while Anne, Father Peter and Lawrence stood together. Zuberi had left them at the airport, insisting he was needed back in Nairobi.

The kid in question was slowly working his way through a bowl of cereal, utterly oblivious to the fact that all those present were discussing him. It was a relatively informal briefing, but it had been early morning when their flight had arrived into London, and the delayed drive from Heathrow to the Chapterhouse meant they were back in time for breakfast. Lawrence had decided it was futile trying to make them abandon the kitchen for the conference room when their minds were on toast and coffee.

"He's a Bane," Anne explained with a look towards the priest. After they'd arrived, she'd taken Joshua to her study, where she'd run a number of medical tests with Father Peter's assistance. Lawrence had checked on them several times, and each time he'd left with expressions ranging from disbelief to jubilation.

"A what?" Lucy asked, nonplussed. Her eyes went from person to person, gauging their reactions. Claire and Lawrence looked awestruck; Gillian was giving the boy a wary eye, sliding away from him as if he were contagious;

Charles, as per usual since Halloween, looking away, indifferent—but nothing gave away why that word mattered.

"Banes are unique in that they are born with a genetic condition that makes them anathema to demonic presences," Father Peter explained. "Possessed creatures die in their very presence, dark magics fuelled from What Lies Beyond weaken and collapse at their touch, and they can heal those afflicted by demonic corruption. Not to mention, witches and spell-casters in the presence of a Bane suffer complete failure of their abilities."

Lucy raised an eyebrow, understanding the look Gillian was giving Joshua. "So why isn't it more publicised? It's the first time I've heard of such a thing…"

"Oh, I beg to differ. This condition, while not named as such, has been recorded in the Bible of all things—one of the few examples of our shadowy war that has made it into the historical record."

"You don't mean…"

"The best known Bane was, of course, Jesus. The Bible is replete with stories of how demons recoiled from him. You're familiar with the story of the demon that referred to itself as Legion requesting that Jesus let it take refuge in a herd of pigs, rather than endure his presence?"

Lucy nodded. She might have been a lapsed Catholic, but she remembered enough from RE to recall that.

"Unfortunately, we have no confirmed records of Banes turning up after the death of Jesus. Their rarity and value make them a prime target for the disparate enemies we face—regardless of their personal allegiance, they will always make a Bane a priority target, even collaborating to ensure the individual's elimination. Banes are too dangerous to them to be allowed to live. All we have had to go on regarding Banes post-Jesus have been fragmentary tales, urban legends, folklore passed down by word of mouth, nothing concrete… until now."

"How did you find him?" Lucy asked.

"A rumour from an old colleague of mine back when I was doing missionary work in Tanzania last year. He told me tales of villages being terrorised by attacks from a leopard that appeared… wrong, twisted, an unnatural beast—clearly something touched by What Lies Beyond—and how it had collapsed and died in the presence of a young boy. I knew then that it had to mean something important. My friend, a Venetian priest called Father Pablo, did a bit of investigating for me, and he confirmed the veracity of the tales. We knew then—"

"We?" Lucy asked.

"Not all amongst the priesthood are ignorant of the shadow war and those who fight it; men and women from all denominations have assisted your Order and others like it around the world in the battle against evil. We knew this boy's abilities could be of invaluable use, and since the Argent Blade are those I deal with most closely, I felt it was best to transport him from Africa to a safe haven here, hence why I asked you to provide some support."

"Good thing too," Lucy muttered. "So now he's here, what do you plan to do? We may have fended off one bunch trying to kill him, but if they know we've moved him here, surely others will come. I don't doubt for a minute that the bunch me and Zuberi killed in Venice were working for someone. Nathaniel Danvers and his ilk would be my prime suspects…"

"Nathaniel Danvers, Lakshmi Varsani and what little of the Desolated that survived Halloween seem to have dropped off the radar," Claire interrupted. "They know there's a price on their heads now; I doubt they'd risk resurfacing so soon. That's assuming, of course, they're still alive. The Pantheon are not forgiving of servants who fail them."

"Well, I won't break out the champagne just yet," Lucy replied. "Not before I see their heads on spikes. Even so, the Desolated aren't the only ones we have to fight; whoever those werewolves were working for might show up again.

And I'm sure there must have been trouble getting this boy out of Africa?"

"Not as much as we feared, but we need to keep him safe."

Lawrence cut in before Father Peter could continue. "A Bane's abilities have never been fully understood or studied. If we could find some way to artificially replicate them, it would be an unparalleled advantage. There are artefacts in the vault that might only be awoken, according to legend, by his touch. This is an opportunity we cannot afford to let slip by—"

"And does *he* get a say in what happens to him?" a voice cut in. All eyes turned to the speaker; most of them had forgotten Rosa's existence.

"I'm sorry, who is this?" Lawrence asked.

Rosa puffed up angrily. "The woman who watched her uncle die and nearly died herself keeping him safe. I think he deserves a chance to make his own decisions."

"We're not even sure he can speak English," Anne said. "But you're right, my dear. I also don't think anyone's taken the time to acknowledge the bravery and courage of your actions, but I think it's fair to say that it is in our remit to protect him. Our organisation's resources will keep him safe for a time, and our war effort could utilise his abilities. We will not put him on the front line," Anne insisted at the outraged look on Rosa's face, "but until we can confirm you and him are both safe, we need to keep him out of sight. The one who sent those assassins in Venice is likely still out there, and until they are dealt with, we need to keep Joshua, if that is his name, out of harm's way."

"And what do you plan to do with *me*?" Rosa asked, her English good but slightly accented.

Lucy smiled a little behind her hand, remembering her own hostile attitude when she'd woken up in this mess, what seemed like a lifetime ago.

"Well, that depends entirely on you," Lawrence replied. "You're a civilian. Gillian confirms you have no ability to channel power from What Lies Beyond, so unless you have any skills we may have use for—"

"What Lies Beyond? What are you talking about?"

Lawrence sighed and rubbed his temples. "Someone give her the basics, if you're prepared to waste about thirty minutes of your time. I'm not entirely sure we shouldn't just wipe her memory and put her on the first flight out of Heathrow."

"It might be useful to keep her here," Anne spoke up, Rosa's head turning to her. Lucy hid a smile at how the young woman appeared to warm at Anne's tone, remembering how Anne's maternal attitude compared to Lawrence's standoffish manner had helped ease Lucy into her own introduction to the Order of the Argent Blade.

"She's a nurse, or at least that's what Father Peter said," Anne argued. "I could make use of that. Plus, the boy knows her, she's a familiar face. Keeping her around might make him feel safer here."

Lawrence looked displeased but couldn't argue with his old friend's logic. "Fine, you and Claire can give her the rundown. Gillian, fix her and the boy up a couple of the guest rooms; if they're going to stay here, they may as well be comfortable. Lucy—" But before Lawrence could complete his command, his mobile rang. His face tautened as he checked the number.

"Something wrong?" Lucy asked.

"No, but I need to take this." He left, answering the call.

Lucy watched him go. Until he told her otherwise, she'd help Gillian, she decided. The spellweaver, with her father distracted, would be the one debriefing her on what had happened in Venice.

Plus, the sooner she's finished, the sooner she and I are free for other things, Lucy thought with an impish grin.

As she rose to leave the room, she heard Claire start to give Rosa the same speech Lucy remembered from when she'd been unceremoniously introduced to the shadow war.

"What you think you know about this world is wrong. Unbeknownst to most of mankind, since the earliest ages of Earth's history, a war has been fought for the survival of humanity against those allied with fell powers determined to destroy it..."

Chapter 3: Aftermath

Lucy Murray desperately struggled against her bonds, but the bindings keeping her arms tied behind her back resisted her efforts. The soft whisper of footsteps crossing the floor told her that her captor had returned, and suddenly cold ran down from the nape of her neck to the small of her back, an icy claw traced along the bare skin. She winced as the same touch ran down her neck, going lower, lower, lower...

"Okay, we can stop with the ice now," Lucy insisted.

Gillian sat in her lap, biting at her lips, neck, belly and more as both women enjoyed the first night they'd had together since Lucy's return from Venice. Gillian coquettishly popped the ice cube in her mouth, running her tongue over it with a playful grin before swallowing it and bending her head to Lucy's stomach. Lucy gasped as Gillian's ice cold lips kissed her naked skin.

"Oh, you want something hotter, do you?" Gillian teased, a small flame kindling to life in her fingers.

Lucy raised an eyebrow, giving her girlfriend a pointed look. "I know I said I was up for experimenting, but this is *really* pushing the boat out!"

Gillian's eyes had grown darker, something hungry burning in her gaze as she stared at Lucy.

"You alright, love?" Lucy asked.

Gillian cocked her head like a bird of prey seeing a mouse in the grass. A firm hand placed itself between Lucy's breasts, resting over her heart, then shoved her hard to the mattress. Lucy winced as her full weight landed on her hands, but before she could readjust, Gillian was straddling her, shrugging off the corset she was wearing, leaving nothing between their bare skin.

"Gillian, what's—?" But before Lucy could complete her sentence, Gillian's lips were forcefully pressed to hers. She moaned in pleasure; it had been too long… but then she felt Gillian's tongue pushing its way between her teeth, one of her hands pulling her head forward as the other tore at her breasts. It was pleasurable at first, but then the pain overtook it.

Lucy had to tear herself free from Gillian's lips. The redhead looked askance at her, her lips peeling back from her teeth in a snarl, before she descended on Lucy's neck, kissing her way down, and Lucy winced as she felt teeth sinking into skin.

"Ow, that hurts!" she hissed, a note of anger entering her voice, but Gillian didn't stop, and Lucy, for the first time, felt a sense of fear.

"Okay, that's enough! Spire! Spire!" Lucy said with increasing insistence as Gillian's grip on her thighs became firmer, as if she were trying to force them apart…

"Spire!" Lucy shrieked, and at long last, Gillian came back to her senses.

The hands that had been clamped like manacles around Lucy's thighs flew to her mouth as she gasped in horror. "Lucy, oh my god, I only—I'm sorry!" Gillian gushed, quickly freeing her lover's hands.

Lucy rubbed circulation back into her wrists as Gillian stepped back from the bed, head shaking, looking on the verge of tears.

"I'm sorry, I'm so sorry, I didn't mean—I mean, I just— Oh gods!" Gillian slumped against the wall and sank to the floor, trying and failing to not cry.

Lucy scrambled to her feet, scooping up a dressing gown and wrapping it around Gillian as she curled up in a ball.

"I'm sorry, I just got carried away. I'd never… I never would, you know that," Gillian insisted, looking anywhere but Lucy.

Lucy didn't say a word; she just held her girlfriend. She knew exactly what was at the heart of the problem, but she paused, uncertain of how to proceed for fear of either driving Gillian to deeper misery or worse, causing her lover's anger to return and make her lash out.

A knock on the door made Lucy look up.

"Lucy, Gillian! Are you two alright in there?" Claire's concerned voice asked from the other side of the door.

"We're alright. We just got a bit carried away, but we're fine!" Lucy called back. "Nothing to worry about," she added, willing Claire not to investigate any further.

"You sure?"

"Yeah, it's all fine!" Lucy hoped she sounded confident enough that Claire wouldn't come in.

"Alright, if you insist." Claire didn't sound convinced, but her footsteps faded away and Lucy let out a sigh of relief.

Turning her attention back to the sobbing Gillian, she pulled the blanket off the bed and draped it over to them as Gillian cried into her chest.

"I'm sorry, I didn't mean, I just lost control…"

"It's okay, it's okay," Lucy whispered, holding Gillian close, even though she knew that was the furthest thing from the truth.

***

Down in the kitchen, Claire poured herself a glass of water and looked up at the ceiling. She had clearly heard crying coming from Gillian's room, and knew the reason why. She, too, still felt a sense of empty sadness when she walked past Valerie's room.

"Everything alright, love?" a voice asked her from behind.

Claire turned to find her mother looking tired.

"Working late, Mum?" Claire asked, offering her the water.

Anne shook her head and went rooting around in the cupboards. "I need something stronger than bloody water!" she said over her shoulder. "Ah, here we are! I knew Larry didn't have it all squirreled away in his study!" With a grin, she pulled out a bottle of Glenfiddich and poured a sizeable glass for herself.

"Yeah, that's something we need to talk about," Claire remarked.

Her mother looked over the rim of the glass. "What do you mean?"

"Larry's drinking like a fish, Gillian's upstairs sobbing in her room, despite Lucy's best efforts to tell me otherwise, and Charles is violent, taking his anger out on any Desolated stragglers or Othersiders who break the rules. They're not coping with their grief, Mum. You need to talk to them, try and—"

"And what? I'm a nurse and a researcher, not a bloody counsellor. Believe me, I've tried, but none of them will talk to me about it."

"Well, you've got to do something, because I've talked to Lucy. Larry's had to put her in charge of field operations because Charles is too unpredictable. The violent tendencies he's exhibiting have their uses for scaring dissidents straight and ensuring no Desolated will come back to this city for another century at least, but it's making him liable to screw up plans. She's afraid that if we don't try and help him— help all three to come to terms with what happened to Valerie—one, or all of them, might do something stupid."

***

Camden, London, 11.17 p.m.

Screams. Gunfire. Pleas for mercy. It all washed off him like rain off stone.

The information Moira and Edmund had given was accurate. What they'd at first assumed was an illegal brothel hiding in Camden was something far worse. They'd seen the withered corpses, chopped up and dumped in the river, fodder for the rats. Only two creatures left a body in such a state.

This was an Othersider smorgasbord.

The police might have dismissed the handful of cut-up corpses as random acts of drug- and gang-related violence, but this was something more sinister and predatory.

Charles had wasted no time with preamble, kicking the door almost off its hinges and charging in, accompanied by several thralls, a mixture of former gang members and hired thugs loyal to the Daltons, trained and conditioned to fight. With their greater speed, Moira and Edmund would ensure no one escaped. Lawrence's orders were simple; put all inside to the sword. Make an example.

The madam came storming out of a side room, hastily throwing a red bed robe about herself. Her pretty face twisted in a moue of anger. "What is the meaning of this?! Who are—"

Her demands were promptly cut short as the Champion's Blade punched through her belly. The stink of burning flesh filled Charles's nostrils. As she gasped in disbelief, her eyes flashed from hazel to electric blue. She was one of them.

Charles kicked the dying succubus off his zweihänder and stepped over her as one of Moira's thralls moved to finish her off. A keening screech came from his right. He darted back as an incubus's clawed hand slashed air where his throat had been. Standing naked in the doorway, the incubus was quite attractive, with muscular arms and legs, a flat chest and lustrous brown hair curling around his shoulders, all the better to seduce unwitting prey… but his eyes were narrowed, the irises electric blue, the pupils jagged slits, his screeching mouth full of needle fangs. He lunged for Charles's throat. Charles kicked out, driving him back before he slashed high.

As the incubus's headless body collapsed, Charles stormed down the hall and kicked open another door. The succubi within shrieked in fright, hastily trying to cover themselves. Charles took one look at the withered bodies of the men they were straddling, snarled and promptly shot them both in the head. Blood sprayed the walls.

It was over swiftly. Floor by floor, the brothel was cleansed. By and large, incubi and succubi didn't pose too great a threat to the Order; most, like vampires, knew how to stay below the radar by predating on those unlikely to be missed. Most fed on abusive spouses, child molesters, human scum they could drain dry and who would disappear without suspicion. These, however, had overstepped their bounds, and for that, there was no mercy.

A final scream petered out as the succubus making it parted company with her head, and Charles planted his zweihänder in the ground beside her corpse. Moira and Edmund's thralls looked shocked at the scale of the butchery they'd just witnessed; most hadn't even had a chance to bloody their weapons. Charles took a deep, shaking breath, a moment to let his emotions, always running high now, calm, and then it was straight back to business.

"You have your orders from your master and mistress. Get these out of here," he snapped with a gesture to the inhuman corpses around him. "Take them somewhere private, burn them and destroy anything that's left."

"And you?" one man asked.

"When you're done, I'll torch this place. As far as the police will know, just a house fire," was the brusque reply.

As Charles turned away, the thrall who'd spoken asked another question. "I've seen the rage that drives you before, the fury fuelled by loss. Does it help, what you do, to cope?"

"Never."

"Why do you do it then? If it doesn't help, why do you let your Grand Master use you as an attack dog?"

"Why do you let Moira and Edmund do the same with you?" Charles asked curtly. "Because it's the only thing we both know how to do."

He didn't bother to look back as he left the thralls to their work.

Chapter 4: Bug Bites
Guy's Hospital, London
January 2ⁿᵈ, 2017

"I'm sorry, Mr Templeton. It's terminal," Doctor Khatri said.

Lawrence took it in stride. "How long do I have?" he asked, sounding almost ambivalent about the fact his life was swiftly coming to an end.

"Nine months. Maybe a year at the outside. We might be able to extend that timeframe with—"

"No." Lawrence refused, adamant. "I have no intention of dragging out a few more months of painful existence at the cost of my hair falling out and myself withering away to nothing. I have more than enough time to set my affairs in order."

"I'm truly sorry, Mr Templeton." Doctor Khatri, to his credit, did sound genuinely regretful. "If you like, I could arrange for you to see one of our counsellors. You may find it beneficial to—"

"Thank you, but no. I came to terms with my own mortality when I was a much younger man."

"If you're certain, but in my capacity as your physician, I must advise that—"

"Thank you, but I've taken up enough of your time, Doctor Khatri, and if you'll excuse me, I need to make the most of mine."

Lawrence picked up his coat, waved aside the doctor's well-meaning but ultimately futile efforts to convince him to endure further treatment; Lawrence had meant what he said. He had no intention of dying weak and feeble in a hospital bed. This would give him enough time to set his affairs in order, and then… find some way to make an end.

He made to exit the hospital, but as he pulled out his phone to call his solicitor, then the others who needed to be informed, he heard a commotion at the front entrance.

"Medic! I need a medic!" a dark-haired man in a long black coat was bellowing as he ran in, carrying a young woman bridal-style.

The woman looked to be in her early twenties, either British-Iraqi or Iranian from her complexion and torn hijab. She'd clearly been savaged, judging by the state of her clothing and the dried blood around her neck… but the identity of the man shocked Lawrence far more.

"Edmund, what are you doing here?" he asked, but before the vampire could answer, a couple of receptionists and a nurse came racing over.

"What happened to her?" the closest of them, a shaven-headed man, asked.

"A gang of thugs started laying into her. I think one of them set a dog on her; they ran off when I intervened," Edmund explained, perfectly conveying the impression of a panicked bystander as he pulled back the girl's hijab and they saw a set of bite marks in the side of her throat.

"Okay—don't go anywhere, sir. We're going to need you to give a statement. Can I get a team here?"

The medics took the girl from Edmund's arms, laying her on a gurney and shouting for antiseptic dressings and to get her blood type, but Lawrence's gaze was burning into Edmund. He'd seen bite marks like this, and he knew full well the culprit was standing right in front of him. With a wordless jerk of his head, he motioned for Edmund to follow him outside the hospital. The second they were there, Lawrence didn't hold back.

"You've started feeding on innocent people?! She doesn't look anything like your usual prey, so I trust you have an exceptionally good reason for attacking her, Edmund."

The vampire looked affronted. "I did not attack her! The injuries she's sustained were as I said; she was set upon by a pack of racist thugs—my usual prey, as you put it. They would have killed her, or at the very least left her badly hurt, had I not moved to intervene."

"And how do you explain the fact you clearly had a taste of her?" Lawrence replied, eyebrows raised.

"Because my bite will ensure her memories of what truly happened to her will be irretrievably muddied, and believe me, the last thing you need is that poor girl causing a panic, screaming about what she saw tonight."

"What are you talking about?"

"I had to get something out of her. A mutual acquaintance wanted to pass along a message…"

***

"Back off," Edmund had demanded as he stepped into the alleyway.

The terrified girl was backed into a corner like an animal, while her tormentors whirled round to confront the interloper. Edmund's lip curled; they all had the look of Britain First or some other racist band of knuckle-draggers. Racism was a facet of human behaviour that utterly escaped vampires. *When are they going to learn that skin colour and race make no difference? Caucasian and Arab are both human, as Clydesdale and Friesian are both horses.*

Edmund didn't think, however, that reasoned argument was going to work with this bunch. Fortunately, he had other methods that might.

"Who are you?" demanded one of the louts, ugly and flabby, the result of a lifetime abusing alcohol.

"Call me a concerned citizen," Edmund replied with a blasé shrug of the shoulders.

"The fuck do you want?" another yob, this one younger, with dark hair and a beard, snapped.

"Just wanted to compliment you on your bravery. I mean, four of you ganging up on a girl who looks like she weighs thirty pounds soaking wet? Truly, an awe-inspiring sight! How dangerous she must be if you four brave souls are risking your necks to confront her! Bravo, truly bravo!"

Slowly, it began to filter through into their skulls they were being mocked.

"You trying to be funny, mate?" a third man growled, bloated belly straining against his Union Jack T-shirt.

"And so intelligent as well," Edmund sneered. "What are you doing wasting your time here, when such brain power is needed elsewhere in the world?"

The yobs turned away from their quarry and began to advance on Edmund, the vampire slowly backing towards the exit of the alley, keeping their attention on him. He tried to keep from showing his fangs; he had to put these bastards down without attracting attention.

"You some kind of Muslim lover?" said the thug in the Union Jack T-shirt. "You look like a poofter; you like towel-heads and ISIS bitches too?" The brute made to shove Edmund's shoulder, only to be forced to his knees, squealing, as the vampire seized his outstretched fingers and bent them back with an ominous crack.

"This is your only warning," Edmund snarled, his teeth bared, fixing the other three with a warning glare. "If I find you menacing girls again for no better reason than their skin colour—"

Before he could finish, something went terribly wrong.

Edmund heard a fly-like buzzing, but much louder, coming from above. He chanced a look up and then dived for cover, throwing his captive back. The brute screamed as a monstrous insect the size of a lion seized him by the throat. The thug's wails were silenced by the creature's mandibles tearing his throat out with a single bite.

The dark-haired man seized a discarded beer bottle and swung at the monster. The bottle smashed atop its carapace and the giant insect spun round, wings buzzing angrily. It lunged and the man was knocked down. He desperately threw his arms up to protect his face as the monster's snapping mandibles descended on him.

Edmund's eyes went wide. Strips of flesh and skin sloughed off the thug's arms as gobbets of acidic saliva left behind with every bite took effect, blood and loose chunks of human meat smearing the pavement. The girl, backed in a corner, screamed in horror.

The man's thrashing and struggling as he tried to crawl away, even as the flesh of his arms dissolved, were abruptly ended as the monstrous insect darted forward and its mandibles snapped closed around his neck. The cries from the wretch—*Not so brave now*, Edmund sneered—were cut short by a wet snap, and the monster let the body fall, head near-severed.

The third thug bolted, only to find Edmund blocking his path. The vampire gave a smile, baring his fangs, his blue eyes narrowed in utter contempt, then seized the side of the man's skull and slammed him into the nearest wall. The bone gave way like glass.

"Impressive as always," a familiar voice chuckled from behind.

Distracted for a second, Edmund let loose a leonine roar, feral glee gleaming in his eyes. It seemed too good to be true—he wouldn't be so stupid as to come back to London—but that didn't matter, nor did the scuttling horror feeding off the dead behind him or the girl shrieking at the top of her lungs in terror. All that mattered was that Nathaniel Danvers was standing at the end of the alley. The bloodthirsty beast within Edmund surged to the forefront of his mind, bellowing at him to tear, shred, kill.

With a roar, Edmund lunged, clawed hands outstretched, reaching for Danvers's throat... only for his talons to pass through the man's neck as if it were smoke.

A projection.

Edmund cursed, snarling in fury. Nathaniel Danvers, or at least the simulacrum of him, laughed mockingly, shaking his head.

"After Halloween, did you honestly think I'd let you get this close to me?" Danvers sneered, tapping the side of his skull. "No, Edmund, I'm in a very safe place, far from you, your lovely wife and your annoyingly persistent associates. I just wanted to pass on a little message."

"Which is?" Edmund snarled, willing his fangs and claws to retract.

"You and all your kind are going to go hungry. What we are about to do to this world will ensure there will be nothing left for your parasitic ilk to feed on, save what scraps we deign to toss them. Rest assured, when their food supply begins to dry up, my agents will make sure the rest of your species know *exactly* who's responsible!" The cultured, elegant tone became a snarl as the Emissary made itself more present through its host.

The false Danvers removed its glasses, showing the ruin Edmund's fangs had made of its face. "Consider this repayment for Samhain... and other insults."

"And how do you plan to do that?" Edmund sneered.

"Oh, you'll find out soon enough, but I won't spoil the surprise." Danvers smiled cruelly, even as he began to pale and fade away like smoke, whatever spell had let him project himself ending.

The girl's screams made Edmund whirl around. The monstrous fly had its legs wrapped around her waist and was trying to escape with its quarry. The only thing stopping it was the thrashing woman in its grasp, making its flight wobble. Without thinking, Edmund sprinted and leapt, seizing the girl by her thighs, holding on tightly. The extra weight unbalanced the demonic insect. With a frustrated buzz, it reluctantly let go of its prey, and both Edmund and the poor woman came crashing to the ground. The girl was sobbing incoherently, but the bug was not going to give up its meal.

It dived, wings buzzing frenziedly, but with supernatural speed, Edmund leapt into the air, his arms wrapping around the insect's neck. Both of them crashed to earth. The monster lashed out with its front claws. Edmund cursed as the hooked barbs tore open his shirt, carving an ugly red trench across his pale chest.

They both saw movement out of the corner of their eyes. It was the girl, trying to run. With a buzzing growl, the demonic insect flung Edmund aside and attacked. The girl turned around, frozen in terror, and its mandibles sank into her arm, drawing a spurt of blood and a scream as they clamped down.

With a roar of fury, Edmund shoulder-charged the insect, smashing it hard into the closest wall. As it lay stunned, Edmund leapt onto its back. The monstrous fly reared up to throw him off, but Edmund's claws extended and stabbed into the spongy flesh beneath the head.

The insect's buzzing became ever more desperate, but Edmund clung on, his fangs lengthening as he began to bite and bite, aiding his claws in their tasks. Repulsive, stinking ichor spilled forth onto his tongue, and he fought down the urge to vomit, remaining focused on his task. Pulling his claws free of the monster's maimed neck as its struggles got weaker and weaker, Edmund seized its frantically clicking mandibles and pulled with all his might.

The insect's head came free in a spray of stinking white ichor, its limbs twitching in spasms before finally curling in on themselves. The girl gave a scream of utter horror and then passed out, everything she'd seen too much for her. Edmund dropped the severed head and advanced on her, his fangs still bared. His oath to the Order forbade him from killing her, but she was a civilian and she'd seen evidence of What Lies Beyond.

Edmund pulled back the hijab to expose her neck, hating himself for what he was about to do, but seeing no alternative. She would play no further part in the shadow war. He had to free her of that cursed knowledge, and vampire saliva had amnestic properties, to ensure those they fed from had no recollection of it.

It's for the best, he told himself as his fangs pierced skin and his world filled with red. The taste of copper flooded his mouth, but the sweet taste turned bitter and foul. Edmund pulled away and spat out the blood in his mouth in disgust.

And then he saw it. There was a bulge at her elbow, about as long and thick as his middle finger, and it was moving, slithering under the skin. Edmund grimaced; it had to be what was tainting the girl's blood. He could think of only one breed of demonic insect that implanted its larvae in living flesh, and they did it for one purpose. He had to act now, before the girl succumbed.

Edmund extended his claws and sliced above the slithering bulge beneath her skin, then clamped his mouth over the wound, ignoring the disgusting taste, and sucked like an old prospector drawing venom from a snakebite. He felt the intruder in her body trying to anchor itself in her flesh, but it wasn't in a position to resist, and Edmund pulled his head back as he felt a squidgy mass fill his mouth. He spat it out, as far away from the unconscious girl as he could. He lapped up the blood from the wound and licked it—vampire saliva was both anaesthetic and anti-bacterial, since they didn't like their food to be tainted—then turned his attention to what he'd removed.

It was a maggot, pallid white and covered in long spines that it would use to anchor itself within its victim's body once it reached the appropriate organ. As it thrashed on the floor, Edmund brought his foot stomping down, crushing the larva to paste beneath it.

His ears pricked up as he heard movement behind him. He turned to see the two racist thugs the monstrous fly had killed were, somehow, staggering back to their feet, their movements erratic and unsteady, as if they were marionettes being jerked by an unskilled puppeteer. It should have been impossible, given one man's throat had been ripped wide open and the other's was barely hanging on by a few scraps of muscle and damaged bone, but Edmund was all too familiar with how it had happened.

He snarled, baring his fangs and extending his claws as the two once-men shambled towards him, bitter, bloody memories of a night he'd rather forget foremost in his mind.

***

Lawrence listened intently. He wasn't pleased about the vampire's method of keeping secrets, but he couldn't deny it was better than having an unsanctioned civilian starting a panic.

"Please tell me you got rid of the evidence."

The look Edmund gave him was unimpressed. "I was a Knight long before you were born; please don't tell me how to do the job. Besides, I didn't have to. The insects all dissolved into black sludge, and I made sure the bodies were safely disposed of before I left... all except this." The vampire reached into his coat and pulled out a small glass jar. Inside it, a white, maggot-like creature as long as Lawrence's little finger angrily thrashed and squirmed. Along its sides, long, fibrous fronds stretched and flexed, vainly searching for purchase on the glass.

"Hell-fly larva. I haven't seen this since 1940, back when I worked with your father before Dunkirk." Edmund shook the glass jar, baring his teeth in disgust as the creature within futilely tried to get free. "It would seem our friend Nathaniel is racking the brains of his past incarnation for something to throw at us. He must be desperate if he's reaching out to Nergal, given that creature owes no loyalty to the Pantheon."

"Typhon and Echidna *are* desperate," Lawrence reasoned. "The Desolated's failure to free her on Halloween, not to mention the destruction of the Einherjar army she was to lead, was a major setback. They need to turn the tide against us and their other enemies. Nergal has always wanted a seat at their table; now he can demand whatever concessions he wants from the Father and Mother of Monsters in return for the aid of his fetid brood."

"What could he want?"

"If Echidna and Typhon come through, the world is theirs. No doubt, Nergal would only want a small token of appreciation, maybe a continent to spread his pestilence, not enough to rob Typhon and Echidna's children of their food supply. If he succeeds in helping the Desolated, they'll be more than willing to be generous."

"What could his plan be?"

"I don't know, but half the world is on fire, thousands of people displaced from their homes, desperately trying to find safety, flooding into refugee camps not suited for so many. Such places are breeding grounds for disease, a perfect place for his disciples to do their work, and I dread to think how much worse it could be with the Desolated's resources to help..."

***

The Mediterranean, 100 miles off the Italian coast

Ahmed was terrified. The rickety fishing boat, currently holding sixty people, refugees from Libya, was taking on water; it would sink long before they got anywhere close to dry land. Some of the stronger refugees might be able to swim for it, but the vast majority were sick or carrying small children. They'd never make it.

"Ahmed, Ahmed, come quick!" Ibrahim shouted.

Ahmed ran to the boat's prow, weaving between panicking women and screaming children as the boat sank ever lower, and saw what Ibrahim was indicating.

A black shape in the distance, growing larger. A helicopter, heading straight for them.

Ahmed let out a gasp of relief. He had no idea who the helicopter belonged to, but he didn't care; all that mattered was that it offered salvation. Ahmed, along with Ibrahim and many others, realising this might be their only chance to survive, began shouting and waving his hands, trying to attract the notice of the pilots.

The helicopter was jet black, save for a white insignia on its side: a snake eating its own tail. The craft descended towards the ocean. The side door slid open, and a dark-haired man leant out, a megaphone in his hands. Lifting it to his mouth, the man started speaking in flawless Arabic.

"Please, remain calm. There is a ship making its way to your position right now that should be here within the hour. Please remain calm. We will provide you with flotation devices, and food and medical aid will be made available to you when you are on board our medical ship, after which you will be conveyed to a safe harbour. Please remain as calm as you can."

A number of flotation devices were tossed out of the helicopter. A relieved cheer went up from the boat as the passengers grabbed the kernel of hope they'd been given.

***

Nathaniel Danvers closed the helicopter door and motioned for the pilot to move on, his lip curling in disdain.

"Take us back to the *Siren.*"

"Yes, sir," the pilot replied.

As the helicopter pulled away, the passenger in the cabin's rear seats smiled gleefully. "I trust these will be made fit for my work?"

"Once Nergal has begun the initial work, they are yours, Josef." Nathaniel sank into the chair facing the doctor. "You will need to ensure full conversion of the subjects; our associates want as many of these parasites bred as possible so we can carry out preliminary strikes to test their effectiveness before proceeding to the main event. I expect your best work for this."

After he'd been evacuated from London before Echidna's arrival, the undead doctor and his staff had been transported to a secure location, where they'd begun to lay the groundwork for the new plan.

"You still wish preliminary tests to be in London?" Mengele asked, surprised despite himself. The revenant doctor did not feel the same sense of rage and humiliation as Danvers and the Emissary, even despite the loss of his arm to that dark-haired bitch and the hand-shaped burn branded onto his face. *Perhaps he fears a second run in with the Order, and losing some other body parts in the process?*

"Of course." Danvers smiled cruelly. "The Order will be complacent after their victory. I intend to make them pay for it."

Turning away from his chief scientist, Danvers seized the helicopter's radio. "Hunting Hawk to Siren, Hunting Hawk to Siren. Come in, over."

"Siren here. Go ahead, Hunting Hawk."

"We've got new materials ready for you. Sending you the coordinates now. You have about an hour before they're lost. Get here before then. Neither I, nor our guest, will be happy if you lose these, over."

"Understood, Hunting Hawk, we're on route now. Siren over and out."

"Dare I say what happened in London is making this a bit too personal for you, Nathaniel?" Josef said calmly. "I think we should distance ourselves from England a little, focus our operations in areas where the Order does not have such a large presence—"

"Afraid, Josef?" Danvers looked over his shoulder, an eyebrow raised. "Have no fear—the Mediterranean will keep you safe from losing another hand—but I want the first strike to be in London. I want the Order to know we are still out there, still breathing, still devoted to our cause, and that as long as the sun continues to rise, every day that passes with humanity not in its rightful place beneath our master and mistress's heel, we will always be a presence looming over their shoulder."

Chapter 5: War Makes Monsters
Redacted location, northern France
June 1940

Alfred Murray's eyes widened at the sight that greeted him. Separated from the rest of his company after a German ambush, he had done the only thing that made sense: try and get back to Dunkirk, and hope there might be some escape by sea. With the rain getting heavier, Alfred had spotted the village in the distance and quickened his pace, hoping it was devoid of Nazi occupiers and that he might be able to wait out the night. He wasn't sure of his exact location—when the tanks had hit them, it had been chaos. Alfred had been lucky to get out alive.

Hopefully, I can find someone who might be able to point the way, he thought as another rumble of thunder came, the rain growing heavier and heavier.

As he drew closer to the village, he was surprised to see it was relatively intact, though there were signs of fighting—dried blood smeared on the walls and cobbles, smashed windows and doors battered down, but no bodies. He proceeded through the centre of the village. Though it was better preserved than others his unit had fought through, it was clearly abandoned. There were no lights on in any buildings, the only illumination coming from fires burning in a handful of severely damaged structures, resisting the rain's effort to extinguish them.

"What happened here?" Alfred muttered to himself.

Suddenly, there was a clatter from behind him. Alfred spun, raising his rifle, only to see a glass bottle roll across the ground. He lowered his rifle and let out a sigh of relief, dismissing it as the handiwork of a stray cat or a fox scavenging for leftovers while no one was there to chase it away. He turned back to continue looking for somewhere to wait out the night, and got the shock of his life.

He was no longer alone.

Standing in the street a good metre or two away was a young woman. A local who had seen better days, her clothes were ragged and torn, exposing an array of cuts and scrapes on her pale skin. Her bare feet were black with dried mud, as if she'd been shambling through the muck for days, and her rain-damp hair was plastered to her face. It was a wonder she could see anything.

The woman was staring off into the distance, oblivious to his presence, and Alfred cautiously advanced, not wanting to scare her.

"Hello? Er… Bonjour, mademoiselle?" Alfred asked, trying to remember the little French he'd picked up before being deployed. "*Je m'appelle Alfred Murray. Je suis un soldat anglais. J'essaye d'arriver à Dunkerque*—oh, careful!"

The woman shambled towards him, throwing her arms out and grabbing him by the shoulders. Despite her wasted appearance, her strength was surprising, her fingers digging into his arms, almost painfully.

"It's okay, it's okay, I can help you," Alfred insisted, forgetting to speak French as the woman pulled him towards her mouth as if about to whisper something in his ear, revealing horrendously stained teeth…

"Get off him!" a strident voice shouted.

A pair of extremely pale hands seized the woman's shoulders and pulled her off him. He watched in awe as the newcomer slammed her hard onto the cobblestones, putting himself between her and Alfred as the woman scrambled back to her feet and shrieked like an animal. Along with her blackened teeth, her eyes were so bloodshot they were almost red, and there were black blotches and angry yellow pustules on her cheeks and neck.

She looks ill. Alfred gasped, about to extend a hand to offer help again when the newcomer slapped him back. With a rabid snarl, the woman charged. Impossibly fast, the newcomer backhanded her, spinning the woman around. As she staggered, the man seized her head and twisted hard. Alfred grimaced as he heard bone snapping, fighting down the urge to vomit when he saw that the other man had twisted her head around completely.

"What the bloody hell did you do that for?!" Alfred demanded angrily, raising his rifle level with her killer's shoulder blades. "She was sick, she needed help—"

"There's no cure for what she's infected with," the man muttered as he turned to face Alfred. He was lean, dark haired and pale with piercing blue eyes. There was something about him that made the hairs on the back of Alfred's neck stand up. His uniform was tattered and heavily ripped, marked with dark red splotches that could only be blood.

Bastard must have been in some brutal fighting, Alfred thought as he studied the man. He didn't lower his rifle though.

"You'd better start making sense, buddy, or I'll—"

Whatever else Alfred might have said was lost as they heard a gagging sound. Both men looked and saw it was the woman, or rather her corpse. Her jaws snapped and heaved, as if she were trying to expel something from her throat. The stranger pushed Alfred behind him as he goggled at what was happening.

"What the bloody hell—?!"

Something pale white and stinking slithered from her mouth. It landed on the cobbles, a maggot, as long as his middle finger, squirming and trilling angrily. It started to crawl towards them, but the dark-haired man stormed over, hastily squashing it under his boot.

"Disgusting," he muttered, only for a cacophony of bangs and crashes to shatter the moment.

Both men whirled round to see more figures emerging from houses and buildings down the street behind them.

As well as French villagers, Alfred could make out men in British and French military uniforms, along with a few Wehrmacht troopers, their exposed flesh covered in what looked like bug bites, all moving towards Alfred and his companion, with herky-jerk movements that reminded him of crawling insects.

"Stay back!" he shouted, raising his rifle.

It had no effect; they just bared their blackened teeth and continued staggering forward. Alfred could start to make out horrific injuries on some of them—a fellow Brit whose throat looked to have been bitten out; a German soldier whose lower face had been destroyed by a close-range gunshot; a big man with a moustache and mutton-chops, perhaps the local mayor, who'd had his arm torn off at the elbow; and a teenage girl whose legs were gone at the knees, dragging herself forward by her hands—but their injuries didn't seem to impede them.

"Come any closer and I'll fire! I mean it!" Alfred levelled his rifle at the moustachioed man's chest.

"Don't talk about it, do it!" the pale stranger bellowed.

Alfred chanced a look to his left, starting in shock as the man hefted a Browning Automatic Rifle as if it weighed nothing and pulled the trigger.

In the silence of the abandoned village, the gunfire was like a dragon's roar. The man aimed high, shrieking like an animal, and dozens of heads exploded into red mist, but the pack continued to shamble towards them. Alfred followed his lead, training and instinct overcoming shock and disbelief, and he fired. His first shot took the moustachioed man in the chest. The man was spun around by the force, but turned around and kept coming. More figures emerged from houses and buildings, moaning and chittering as they came.

"Don't waste your shots! Shoot for the head, it's the only way to put them down!" the other man shouted over the thunder of his weapon.

Taking the hint, Alfred reloaded and fired again. This time, his shot took the man in the centre of his forehead.

The back of his skull exploded in a red spray. To Alfred's disgust, another of the white maggots slithered out of the bullet hole, looking around desperately for a new body to ensconce itself in.

A series of crashes came from behind them; Alfred and his ally turned to see they were on the verge of being surrounded as more of the deranged villagers advanced on them. Trapped between two advancing crowds of these lunatics, Alfred heard his ally's gun click empty, and the man flung it into the advancing pack, smashing several off their feet. Alfred pulled his gun back to stab the bayonet—

"COVERING FIRE!" a new voice bellowed from above, followed by the roar of gunfire. Alfred risked a glance towards where the shout had originated, and saw at least a dozen men perched on rooftops firing down. Their shots thinned out the edges of the horde, forcing them to disperse from forming a circle around the two in the middle of the street.

"Edmund! Rendezvous point beta! Move!" one of the figures on the roof bellowed.

"Got it!" Edmund shouted back, before seizing Alfred's wrist and pulling him. "Come on, boyo! Before they regroup!"

Alfred followed Edmund, too confused and shocked by all he'd seen to resist. The pair raced into a house whose door had been smashed down. They heard a screech. Acting on instinct, Alfred slammed the butt of his rifle into the face of another red-eyed villager, sending the bearded man staggering back. Edmund kicked open the back door and charged out when a black shape tackled him from the right. Alfred raced out, intending to help, only to find Edmund was on top of his attacker and bringing his fist down. The punch disintegrated his enemy's head into red mush, and Alfred stared in shock.

"How the hell did you—"

"No time! Move!" Edmund shouted, the pair of them hearing the moaning of the villagers following them. It could have been Alfred's imagination, but he swore he could hear something else: a buzzing, like that of a fly, but almost as loud as a plane engine…

The pair darted down alleys deeper into the town, Edmund overturning wagons and tossing rubble to make it difficult for the villagers to give chase, before they came to a well-proportioned house in the centre of town. Edmund led Alfred round to the back, where a pair of doors leading down into a cellar remained amongst the grass. Edmund seized Alfred's rifle, knocked the butt against the doors thrice, then tossed it back to Alfred as the doors opened from the other side.

"In, quick!" a man in a British Army uniform snapped.

The two of them hastened down the steps as the soldier quickly locked the doors behind them. Alfred sank against a wall to catch his breath, trying to process everything he had seen. None of it made sense; it was like something out of a nightmare.

Maybe it is. Maybe I died in that ambush and these are my last thoughts before darkness claims me, or perhaps I'll wake tomorrow and everything, even this whole bloody war, will have been just a nightmare…

"Name, soldier?"

Coming back to himself, Alfred saw Edmund looming over him, staring expectantly. Alfred couldn't deny the feeling of unease the pale man exuded, but he pushed it down and got back to his feet with a hasty salute.

"Sorry, sir. Murray, Alfred, private with the 42nd Infantry."

Edmund nodded in satisfaction. "Dalton, Edmund. Sergeant assigned to the 52nd Highlanders."

"You don't sound much like a Scotsman."

"I'm not, but my wife is Scottish, I've lived up there for several years now, and it was a recruiting office in Edinburgh I signed up at."

"What's going on? What was wrong with all those people? Why—" Alfred started to ask, but Edmund cut him off.

"Not yet. I'm not in charge of this outfit. When the CO gets here, he can brief you in full. Get some rest, soldier. You'll need it."

The sounds of fighting outside had begun to recede. For want of anything better to do, Alfred looked about his surroundings. The cellar might once have belonged to the town's mayor—who he suspected he'd just shot—but where once it might have stored wine and beer, now it was a makeshift armoury. A wooden table was in the centre of the cellar, a map of the town pinned to it with silver knives, while on the far wall, a defaced red and black banner bearing the swastika encircled by a pair of fanged jaws hung in rags and tatters. Boxes of ammunition and more rifles had been stacked against the wall. Alfred opened one and frowned as silver gleamed under the meagre light from the lamps dotted around the room.

Besides Edmund, who was helping himself to a nip from a hipflask, there were three other soldiers in the room; aside from the lad who had let them in, there were two men who looked like Gurkhas, talking quietly amongst themselves and sharpening their knives.

Suddenly, all heads in the cellar pricked up, hearing cautious footsteps above them. They waited in silence before three knocks came on a door up a short flight of stairs, no doubt leading up to the house. Edmund grinned and opened the door. The soldiers who'd saved them in the street headed down into the cellar, Edmund clapping them all on the back in gratitude as they passed him to gather round the table.

"Who's the new meat?" one of the soldiers, a dark-haired man with an upper-class accent, asked as Alfred stood to attention.

He saluted again, and noticed the soldiers were all armed to the teeth.

They clearly came here expecting a fight, but what is so special about this place?

"Private Alfred Murray, sir. 42nd Infantry. I got separated from my company. I thought it best to pull back, join up with the withdrawal at Dunkirk. I got lost, stumbled upon this place by accident, and then everything went to hell."

"Major Dominic Templeton, on secondment to the 43rd Infantry from SIS," the man who'd addressed him replied.

Alfred lowered his arm from his salute. "Major, what's going on here?"

Templeton sighed. "About a month ago, a team of German scientists accompanied by a detachment of Waffen-SS turned up. They turfed the locals out and started doing some digging in the catacombs beneath the church. The Germans up and left a few weeks ago, so the locals came back, hoping to re-establish their homes and livelihoods. Unfortunately, some of them went into the church, thinking perhaps the Nazis had uncovered buried treasure in the catacombs."

"What happened?"

"My regiment stumbled upon a survivor from this village while we were retreating back to Dunkirk. He said the Nazis had opened the gates of hell under their church, and that its demons were coming out to hunt. I volunteered to investigate, as part of my duties from the SIS and the War Ministry, taking what men my commanding officer could spare. We've been encountering soldiers and civilians all along the way here, all bearing the same symptoms and behaviour as those you encountered tonight. Whatever is wrong with them, whatever that thing inside them is, it spreads with one bite. If those things make it to Dunkirk and infect our lads waiting for extraction, it'll be disastrous. The last thing we need is an unknown infection ripping through England while we're trying to prepare for an invasion. I don't know if this is something the Germans have specifically created, or just something they found and seek to take advantage of, but if those parasites make it back across the Channel, our defences will be decimated, and the Germans will easily overwhelm what little we can put in front of their invasion."

"So, what's the plan, sir?" Alfred asked. He had no idea what he was in the middle of, but it sounded severe, and he very much doubted he was going to be allowed to go on his merry way to Dunkirk given what he'd seen. Nor did he feel he could.

I've got parents, a brother, a girl I care about back home. I won't see them, and however many others, suffer to whatever Hitler's goons have unleashed here!

By way of an answer, Templeton motioned at the map on the table. The rest of the group fell in as the major pointed to a specific point at the far west of the town.

"All our intelligence, and our observations of the behaviour of these creatures, indicates that they're nocturnal. In the daytime, they retreat to the church, to sleep, hibernate, digest what they've eaten—we're not sure. Our contact told us the infections started after whatever work the Nazis were doing in the catacombs concluded. Whether it's a nest, a hive or some kind of laboratory, it's the source of what's happened to everyone who's stumbled on this place. To ensure it doesn't spread any further, we need to strike while all the infected are in one place, kill the infestation in one fell swoop. We wait until daylight, and then we go into that church, level it to the ground, and kill anything that tries to stop us."

Chapter 6: Evil Rears Its Head Again

Lawrence sank into a chair in the briefing room. Lucy and Gillian sat to his left, bright and alert. Charles, looking somewhat hungover, as he usually did these days, was to his right, grim and red-eyed.

Father Peter was to Charles's right. With Joshua and Rosa a constant presence in the Chapterhouse, the priest had been working with Anne to try and understand what the boy was capable of, as well as providing a sympathetic ear to Rosa. Anne's ongoing studies had allowed her exemption from the meeting. To his right, a seat that had once been occupied by Valerie remained empty. Lawrence tried not to stare at it too long.

Claire, the last to arrive, took a seat at the end of the table, and Lawrence began the meeting, depositing a mason jar in the centre of the table. Inside it, a squirming maggot-like creature, pale-white and covered in thorny spines, battered its head against the glass as if trying to smash its way free. Gillian spitefully jabbed a finger at the jar, and the larva retreated as if it had been burned.

"What is that thing?" Lucy said in disgust.

Lawrence picked up the jar and the creature inside it curled up, trying not to touch the sides of the jar, lest it be burnt again.

"Edmund Dalton pulled this from the skull of a man who died at his hand last night… for the second time." The Order's Grand Master paused for a moment to let that sink in, then carried on. "He also killed two similar creatures, one that was puppeteering another corpse and one implanted in the arm of a civilian. He also had to destroy the adult form of this creature, which was how these larvae were transmitted.

Ladies and gentlemen, we face the possibility that someone has helped summon and establish a hell-fly nest within this city."

All eyes around the table went wide at that bombshell. Hell-flies were dangerous and powerful demonic entities, but rare. They were drawn to rich concentrations of dead bodies, where they could feed and spawn, growing in number before spreading out to find others to infect with their pestilence. It took huge amounts of death to bring them out, usually in the wake of wars or epidemics. The biggest outbreak the Order had had to deal with in its history had been not long after its foundation, when the Black Death had swept across England in the late 1340s, but others had come during the First World War and the Spanish flu pandemic, the Second World War and numerous other conflicts across the world.

"The only prospective source of death that could have attracted it was what happened on Halloween, and if that were the case, then a hive would have made its presence known much sooner," Claire protested. "Also, these creatures do not hunt alone, so either this one Edmund killed is deeply erratic… or it was deliberately released."

"I'm inclined towards the latter," Lawrence replied. "It would be easy enough to transport a single specimen from the main hive's location. We may have killed a great many of our enemies on Samhain, but I don't doubt there are more still out there. Edmund claims to have seen a familiar face directing the creature, but I don't care if it's the Desolated taking another stab at us or some other pack of amateurs looking to fill the void—we find them and we destroy them. I won't let more degenerates get a toehold in my city."

Everyone sat around the table knew why his anger was so strong.

He blames himself, Lucy thought. *He thinks his complacency is the reason the battle on Samhain was so brutal… and why Valerie died.*

The mention of Lucy's name brought her out of her reverie. Lawrence was looking straight at her.

"Lucy, I'm putting you in charge of this hunt. Take Gillian, liaise with Edmund and start investigating. Wherever the hell-fly he killed came from, I want to know. If there isn't a hive within the city, then we need to know if it was shipped in from somewhere else… what?" Lawrence demanded, noticing that Lucy and Charles were both staring at him like he'd grown an extra head.

"I've always been the one to lead hunts for information," Charles muttered sullenly.

"And I thank you for it, but now I wish to see how another fares in taking the lead," Lawrence replied bluntly, before addressing Lucy. "Use any method you see fit. If some new threat is trying to establish itself in London, I'm not going to sit and let it do so uninterrupted!" Lawrence finished, the memory of the battles fought on Halloween clearly still fresh in his mind.

"And then what am I supposed to do?" Charles didn't bother to hide the hostility in his voice.

"You're coming with me," Lawrence replied curtly, giving his tone some bite to remind Charles who was in charge. "I'm headed to Paris, and I need an escort."

"You're going to meet with Siobhan?" Claire sounded genuinely surprised.

"I won't overlook potential information simply because I don't like where it's coming from. I've not forgiven Siobhan for what she did, but I'll admit her warning about Venice proved accurate, so I don't mind hearing her out. But I'm not going into her territory alone… assuming you can manage to be alert and sober for this, Charles?"

"Of course." Charles sat upright. "What do you need from me?"

"Pack a suit and some weapons. We fly to Paris tomorrow."

Charles nodded and got to his feet, sketching a salute that still managed to convey sarcasm, before leaving the briefing room.

"You sure that's wise?" Claire asked.

"He needs something to help him focus. Besides, he's still the best warrior we've got, so I'm taking him with me. The rest of you will assist Anne and Father Peter. The boy's safety remains our priority, and his abilities, if there's more than one of those flies about, could be a great advantage, but we need to know more."

"Consider it done. I'll ensure the jet is prepared to get you and Charles to Paris. Anything else?"

"No," Lawrence replied as he got up, the others all doing likewise. "I need to deal with some personal matters before I leave."

Claire looked at him askance, but Lawrence showed no sign of giving an answer. All those present exchanged confused looks, but Lawrence exited the briefing room without a backwards glance, heading downstairs and out the front door.

The moment he was outside, Lawrence began walking in the direction of South Kensington station, his mobile phone already out of his pocket. The number he dialled was one he hadn't called in a long time, but his time was running out, and there were a few matters that had to be dealt with. The person on the other end of the line picked up on the third ring.

"We need to talk. Meet me in about an hour," Lawrence said bluntly before hanging up.

He knew she'd be there. The secret was as much hers as his.

***

The Stables Market, Borough of Camden, London

Lawrence studied the statue of Amy Winehouse, taken before her time. *Far too many fall too young. I know that all too well. My wife, my daughter, my father, all gone too soon. If truth be told, that's been the way of the Order throughout its history. We sacrifice the comforts of long life so that others can have them and be kept ignorant of the war raging all around them.*

Soon enough, my part in that war will be over. But it won't die with me, and I must ensure there are others able to continue the struggle when I am no longer here to fight it.

A familiar perfume wafted to his nose, and Lawrence gave a rueful smile. There had been a time when he and its wearer had been a lot closer, before her insistence otherwise. He'd kept his distance, out of respect for her wishes and the feelings of the children who would have been affected had he disobeyed, and they'd always feigned ignorance of their past closeness to hide that, but with time running out, there were things that had to be addressed.

"What do you want?" she asked brusquely.

"Lovely to see you too, Angela."

"What do you want, Lawrence?" Angela Drake repeated. "Are you on a recruitment drive? I'm not going to deny, I'm proud of how my girls handled themselves on Samhain, but I can't believe you're even asking—"

"I'm dying."

Angela's stony visage softened a little. "I'm sorry, Larry. If there's—"

"I'm quite sure, as talented as you and your girls are, you don't know a spell that will undo terminal cancer. No, I want to set my affairs in order."

"Your affairs? Of course, this is about those weeks in the nineties, isn't it?" Angela scowled. "You feel a sudden urge to be a father now? You've never shown an interest in her before."

"At your insistence, I might add. I respected your people's customs that a mother would raise her daughter by herself without interference from the father, but she's a grown woman now, and I'd at least like her to know of me before it's too late." Lawrence took a deep breath, knowing Angela was not likely to be happy with what he said next. "And I'd like to extend her an invitation. She's smart, powerful, able to work as part of a team—"

"Bullshit! You want another girl to replace the one you lost, but I will not have you take mine! She's not Valerie, and it's a bit late for you to be showing paternal instincts."

"That's not why I'm doing this. I won't deny, part of me would like that, though," he admitted. "Two members of the Order died that night, and our numbers continue to decrease. In less than a year, I will join Valerie and Amelia. I need more to fill the ranks, and I need to know those who will remain after I'm gone are up to the task. I've heard the whispers: Danielle is one of the finest girls your coven has to offer, you've done a fine job nurturing her talent to the fore. People of lesser talent have been inducted into the Order before now…"

Angela's seething eased a little at the compliment, but then she got defensive again. "I have other girls nearly as talented as her. I know you're still dubious about the loyalties of the coven after so many supported the Emissary. If this is what it takes to prove otherwise, I can offer three of the most talented—"

"Your daughter is the best I've seen."

"Why witches? Why not soldiers? Having a high number of mages will mean nothing if they're torn to pieces because they didn't have enough bodies to protect them. What guarantee do you have that if I let you take her, she won't be torn limb from limb in a week by some monstrosity?"

"Believe me, I know all about that," Lawrence replied grimly. "I have over two dozen files from some of the army's best personnel to look over… In any event, the decision is not yours to make. I could invoke the old pact and compel you to hand her over, but I'd rather not."

Reaching into his pocket, Lawrence pulled out a business card and handed it over to Angela. "Give that to your daughter. Tell her to be at the Chapterhouse in three days. The rest will be out on their patrols, so there should be no one to disturb us. Whatever she chooses, in *all* regards, I will respect."

Still wary as a cat, Angela looked at him askance as she took the card.

"Not today or tomorrow? As I recall, you weren't one for letting time slip away."

"I have business to attend to outside the country. An agent in Paris has warned me there may be something big on the horizon."

Chapter 7: Whispers of the Dead
Paris, France, 7.30 p.m.

The group exited their rented car, and Siobhan led Lawrence to a secluded warehouse, with Liam bringing up the rear and Charles at Lawrence's shoulder, clean and sober for once. The Knight and the werewolf exchanged glares, sizing each other up. Lawrence could see the Eiffel Tower in the distance, but they were not in town for sightseeing; this was a far more secluded part of the city, away from prying eyes.

At the warehouse entrance, Siobhan rapped on the steel shutters thrice. There was a rapid exchange of French between the vampire and whoever was on the other side.

As the shutters rose, a man in a finely made suit beckoned them to enter.

"Ah, Mademoiselle Siobhan Dalton! A pleasure to see you again, and your *loup charmant*," he said, clearly a local from his accent.

Lawrence and Charles studied him but could see nothing to indicate what sub-species of Homo sapiens he was.

"I'm here on business, Phillipe. These two are here to see your boss regarding the rumours from Athens."

"Ah, of course." Phillipe motioned them to follow as the shutters closed behind them.

"What's this about Athens?" Lawrence hissed at Siobhan. "If this turns out to be a trap—"

"Are you ever going to trust me?"

"—then I've got a sharpened length of hawthorn with your name written all over it!" Lawrence snarled, talking over her.

Liam growled at the threat, and Charles's hand went to the kukri hidden in his coat. Lawrence raised a hand to calm Charles down, seeing Phillipe watching the spectacle with amusement.

Normally, Lawrence would have said Charles would win that fight, since they were out in public and the werewolf couldn't use his natural abilities to tip the scales in his favour, but in his current depression, Lawrence wasn't so sure. He reluctantly motioned Charles to stand down and followed their guide.

Inside, crates and boxes were piled up under tarpaulins. Charles caught a glimpse of the contents of one as a burly man picked up a lid to nail it down.

"Sig Sauer P320, looks like about a hundred of them. I also think I can see what look like Barak 8 surface-to-air missiles, presumably acquired from suppliers to the Israeli military. You didn't mention your associate is an arms dealer," Charles snapped at the vampire.

"The international arms trade is my employer's primary source of income, but he does it primarily to keep an eye on mankind's warmongering ambitions," Phillipe interjected, "and to ensure more dangerous items remain out of the hands of those too unstable to possess them. Privately, he's also an information broker on the darker elements of this world."

"So if he prefers to deal with the human world, why is he wanting to speak to us for the first time?" Lawrence asked.

Phillipe shrugged. "I'm not completely privy to my employer's secrets. I'd suggest you ask him."

He started up a flight of metal stairs to an office at the rear of the warehouse. Siobhan followed him, Lawrence and Charles next, while Liam remained at the foot of the staircase.

Halfway up, Siobhan looked back at Lawrence and added, "Konstantin's extremely private, but in the years

I've worked with him, his information's always been good. Just don't react if you get a glimpse of his face."

Inside the office, a figure sat in shadow behind a desk, face completely hidden by the darkness.

"Lawrence Templeton, Grand Master of the Knights of the Order of the Argent Blade, and Charles Pryce, heir and wielder of the Champion's Blade." A Russian accent coloured his voice.

"You have us at a disadvantage," Lawrence replied coldly. "You know who we are, but we don't know you."

"Of course, where are my manners?" the Russian replied. "Konstantin Sokolov, at your service." He extended a hand covered by a black leather glove, but Lawrence didn't take it.

"I make it a habit not to get into business with people who hide in shadows. Too often I find they're hiding secrets from me, ones that come back to bite me."

Siobhan tensed and two guards on either side of Konstantin cracked their knuckles, but he chuckled. "You've got balls, I like that. I understand the necessity of knowing what you're dealing with, so… Dimitri, raise the lights."

One of the guards flipped a switch and the lights came on. Konstantin leant forward, and Lawrence did his best to keep his face neutral. The Russian was no longer human, and judging by the state of his visage, he hadn't been for a long time. The upper left side of his face still looked human, albeit covered in parchment-thin skin and greying hair, but the right side and the lower jaw were decomposed to the point that bone was visible beneath wasted and rotted muscle, the teeth grinding together. The left eye was a brilliant blue, but the right was an empty socket, though a green glow from within told Lawrence the creature could clearly see him. Lawrence knew necromancy when he saw it—Gillian's abilities had made him familiar, along with numerous battles against death cults in his youth—but he suspected this creature was far older and more powerful than the undead he'd encountered before.

"Revenant…" he whispered without thinking.

Siobhan gave him an irritable look, but Konstantin inclined his head, as if amused.

"How long?" Lawrence asked.

"August sixth, 1915," Konstantin rasped. "Osowiec Fortress. I remember the burning as I inhaled, my lungs filling with fire, collapsing amidst black grass, feeling bits of my body come away inside, dragging myself through the dirt, crawling like an animal… and never stopping."

"Who raised you?" Lawrence asked, but the revenant shook his head, the exposed vertebrae of his neck creaking with the motion.

"All I remember is thinking so strongly about what I was going to lose—a wife, pregnant with our child, an old mother and father—and then being so angry that it would end like this, rolling around in mud and blood, choking for breath like a pig with its throat cut. As I breathed in, I felt something filling me the angrier I got, pouring strength back into my failing limbs. I remember getting back to my feet, following my comrades as they pursued German soldiers panicking at the sight of dead men attacking. When the battle was done, I walked away, with no idea of what I was or how I was still moving."

"So how did an undead man killed by chemical weapons go on to become an arms dealer?" Charles asked. "I'm not judging, I'm just genuinely curious."

Konstantin's features twisted into a death's head grin. "When I died and rose again, it changed everything. I had to learn what I was, what I could be, what I was capable of. Plus, never dying gives me a lot of time on my hands to learn new things, and not just about what I am or the otherworld I find myself a part of. I discovered I had a flair for business, and given my, shall we say, military past, the arms trade seemed a sensible line of work. I must say, mankind has come a long way from when my countrymen and I were crawling through mud, and the computer age makes it a lot easier for me, since obviously I don't really have the look for doing business face to face," he concluded with a wheezing, self-deprecating chuckle.

"I take it, since you deal with Siobhan, your employees are all like you?" Charles remarked.

"Of course. Not all who walk in the shadows wish to be embroiled in the war you fight, good Knight. And who am I to deny others who share the same 'disadvantages' as myself the chance to enrich themselves? Some of us just want to make a living as best we can."

"Fascinating as your entrepreneurial ideals for your fellow undead are, we're here on business," Lawrence cut in. "You invited us here, so clearly you want to talk. What about?"

Konstantin's voice became curt and professional, all business. "I don't deal in bio-weapons; they bring back bad memories." His rotted features contorted into a grimace as he spoke. "But my contacts in the black market whisper something big is about to become available, something that will make what was used on me look like nothing."

"Who's selling?"

Konstantin shrugged. "I don't have a name or a location yet, but my contacts say they're hiring medical professionals and epidemiologists in bulk and that they're promising to show a demonstration of what they're working on soon. And once they have confirmation their product works, they'll start selling."

"What makes you think this is of interest to me?" Lawrence said, feigning disinterest.

Konstantin slid a Polaroid photo across his desk.

Charles picked it up and snarled. "A familiar face." He passed the photo to Lawrence.

It was a shot looking down on the deck of a cargo ship. A grey-haired man stood in front of a crate, talking to someone out of frame. It was unmistakeably Josef Mengele. Lawrence growled in fury.

"I thought you'd recognise him," Konstantin remarked. "Believe me, most of my agents in the Mediterranean are eager to get their hands on that bounty you lot put on his head after London. They get a sniff of him, they'll be more than happy to pass it on to me, and I'm more than obliging to pass it on to you."

"Where was this taken?" Lawrence asked.

"Port of Piraeus, Athens. Other agents who trade intel to me also imply he's been seen around a number of hospitals in the city, trying to acquire medical supplies."

"What's his goal?"

"I don't know," Konstantin admitted, "but that ship he's aboard is the *Siren,* owned and operated by Brizo Shipping. They're a European front for Ouroboros Industries," he explained at their blank faces. "As I understand it, there were suggestions that the incident in London in October was traced back to another of their subsidiaries, yes?"

As Lawrence nodded, Konstantin suddenly slapped his brow, as if unable to believe he'd forgotten something. "There was one other thing that might interest you, if you know your history, Grand Master. Anyone who wants to bid on this new weapon is being instructed to send a specific code to indicate their interest." His gloved hands scrawled something on a scrap of paper, then slid it across the table to Lawrence.

The moment he saw what was on it, his blood ran cold.

Four numbers. *1348*.

"You cannot be serious," he whispered.

The revenant smiled, his rictus grin sending a chill down Lawrence's spine.

"In this world, Grand Master, information is my business. As I understand it, your family has a bit of a grim history with that year, don't they?" Konstantin asked with another ghoulish smile.

Lawrence nodded dumbly, feeling stunned.

Chapter 8: Betrayal

Northumberland, England, 1348
45 miles south of the Scottish border

The village was a gutted ruin. Robert Templeton saw dilapidated buildings, wagons and stalls either torn down or thrown on their sides, as if a whirlwind had ripped through the village. The stench of death hung over the place, and his men-at-arms hastily made the sign of the cross as they looked at the devastation.

"Spread out!" Robert shouted, dismounting and tossing the reins of his horse to his squire. "Look for survivors! My son and his men should be here!"

The rasp of steel being drawn was an odd comfort to Robert. He was no longer a squire trying not to shit his britches before his first battle, but the silence that hung over the village made him feel that long-forgotten fear. He and two of his best men stalked past abandoned houses, all of them marked with white chalk crosses on their doors. They wrinkled their noses in disgust at the stink.

"Try not to breathe in the foul vapours, my lord," Godwyn remarked as they passed the sprawled body of a man. "I heard an apothecary say even breathing in the air from a corpse can spread the disease."

"Thank you for the warning, soldier, but I am well protected," Robert replied, unconsciously rubbing the mark tattooed into his wrist, hidden beneath the armour. The plague was clearly demonically touched, so the blessing of the ancients worked into the mark would keep him safe.

He only hoped his children were safe too. Marian was fortunately with her young husband, the son of a lord of

Wessex, and she had received the mark of the Order as well, so hopefully she would be safe. His sons, however, were too young to have been initiated. His eldest and heir, Thomas, had been assigned by the king to watch the northern border in case the Scots decided to take advantage of the chaos to raid, while Edward remained at court, watching over the king and providing his father with forewarning of any threats.

He had been concerned by the lack of news from Thomas, but three nights earlier, a harried-looking page boy had stopped him at court and delivered a hastily scrawled missive written in his son's hand.

Father, we must speak face to face. The pestilence is emboldening the Scots. We've heard rumours that they are amassing an army, seeking to raid and plunder while the pestilence ravages this land, and what is worse, they have help. Our enemy is whispering in the ears of Scottish lords close to the border, goading them on, seeking to sow death and terror that will weaken the walls between worlds. My comrades and I managed to capture one of the cultists, who claims to have sorcerous knowledge of how his brethren are spreading and worsening the disease, and what the next part of the cult's plan is. You need to hear his words for yourself, and Grand Master Sigismund needs to know too.

Come as fast as you can and bring only those you trust to the location marked on the map I have enclosed. The fate of England may hang upon your swiftness.

Your son, Thomas.

"Where are you, Thomas?" Robert muttered, stepping around the corpses of a woman and child. Other than the signs of the plague, the bodies were untouched.

"Never known wolves and crows to turn their noses up at such plentiful carrion," the other man-at-arms with him, a youth by the name of William, remarked.

"Scavengers know better than to touch such filth," Robert said as they approached an inn, the largest building in the village still standing. More of his men were congregated outside, though, reluctant to go in.

"Any survivors?" Robert asked.

Brother Talbot shook his head. "Nothing but ruined building and corpses that, judging by the stink, have been dead for days."

"Did you find my son amongst the dead?"

"Not yet, milord," the sergeant replied. "But we haven't checked any of the houses or the buildings yet. By your command, we'll start searching."

The men around him saluted as they awaited the command.

"Thomas, where are you?" Robert called out.

"I'm right here, Father," a gurgling voice replied.

Robert whirled round, and saw something monstrous emerge from a ruined house.

It was tall and broad, clad in a knight's armour, the metal a dirty green where it wasn't stained with red-orange patches of rust and dried blood. The blade of its heavily damaged sword was notched and covered in rust. On its left arm, a monstrous fly with a skull-like head capered on the rotten wood of a kite shield. In place of a helm, a rotten cloth hood covered the figure's head, its face hidden behind a veil of rusted chainmail.

"Who are you?" Robert demanded, drawing his sword as his men raised their weapons.

By way of an answer, the interloper lowered its hood and removed the veil. "Don't you recognise me?"

Robert's lip curled in disgust. His son had been handsome, with short red hair and pale blue eyes, features that had caught the eye of so many maidens at court. This creature's hair had fallen out, leaving a bald pate threaded with pallid skin, veins black with rot, sickly yellow eyes and a gaping crevasse where a once-aquiline nose had been. Pale red worms slithered beneath the skin.

It smiled, baring jagged yellow teeth jutting from diseased gums, and spat a wad of filth at Robert's feet.

Robert's lip curled at the sight of white maggots, as long as a man's finger, writhing on the ground. Robert levelled his sword at the monster's chest, when he heard Godwyn whisper, "Milord?"

Footsteps came from all around them. He chanced a look behind him, and saw the dead villagers begin to twitch and struggle to their feet, moaning and gnashing their teeth.

"What are you?" Robert asked, his tone one of revulsion.

"Reborn as one with the great pestilence, free from the sickness," the Thomas-creature growled. "Now I, and my new brothers, serve the will of my new lord, to make this world one with the plague."

"You betrayed us, Thomas. You betrayed me, your family, the Order," Robert snarled, his fingers clenching around his sword's hilt.

The Thomas-monstrosity laughed cruelly, as if amused by his outrage. "Not Thomas, Father. Thomas died, weak and pitiful, begging for help. I have a new name for a new life," he declared. "I am Falciparum of the Blighted Brothers, and together, we are the sword of the great one. The Lord did not save us while the pestilence devoured our flesh, robbed us of our strength and will... but *he* did. In the darkest hour, he came and offered us deliverance. The priests call this pestilence God's punishment, but for what? Why punish me and my brethren? We were loyal, faithful, penitent... and still it took us! So when the priests and the nuns saw us upon our resurrection, tried to banish us with their worthless prayers and false relics, we split them open as they begged their silent god for mercy. This is the cleansing, Father, the winnowing of the wheat from the chaff! The weak will be purged and the strong will emerge, purified, made new, ready for the order that is to come."

"To arms!" Robert heard his sergeant bellow somewhere in the village and the moaning and groaning getting louder. The monsters the villagers had become were getting impatient. *It won't be long now*, Robert knew, feeling the tension building.

"Join us," Thomas, or rather Falciparum, entreated, slamming his rusted sword into the ground and extending a hand. Pallid, diseased skin extruded from holes rusted in the gauntlet's metal. "Once the infestation takes hold, it burns away everything weak, everything human! You become stronger, impervious to pain; sickness holds no sway, you can walk off wounds that would slay a lesser man! Join us, Father. You, Marian, Edward—we can be a family again, under the aegis of a new god! Accept the great Nergal's gift, and he will forgive your sins against him!"

"I have done nothing that requires forgiveness!" Robert snarled at the diseased thing claiming to have been his son. "Your god is just a parasite, Thomas, like everything this sickness has birthed, glutting on things you do not deserve!"

"I am Falciparum, Father! A new age is coming. Nergal will usher it in! Man and demon combined—together, we will possess power greater than anything we were denied in Eden! And when the barrier falls and the rightful king and queen step through—"

"Nergal is not a part of the Pantheon! Typhon and Echidna will never suffer a rival!"

"A rival?" Falciparum laughed, a hideous wet gurgling that set Robert's teeth on edge. "Nergal doesn't want this world, just a small piece of it... and a seat at the Pantheon's table. When Typhon and Echidna find this world on its knees, sickly and weakened, just waiting for them to reclaim their thrones, they will have to hear him out, and my brethren and I will be at the vanguard of the armies that will pour from What Lies Beyond! When we secure their victory, the rewards for our aid will be unimaginable! Why settle for bowing and scraping to a king when you could be one yourself?"

Robert raised his sword and spat at Falciparum's feet. "A king in service to the Pantheon is just a slave play-acting with a crown! I'd rather die than submit to that... as you should have done."

"If death is what you want, then you can have it," Falciparum snarled, hefting his own blade. "I regret this, Father, but those who will not accept the purification Nergal brings must die!"

With that, Falciparum threw back his head and howled, a sound echoed by the shambling horde encircling Robert's party. With a war cry in answer, Robert and his men raised their weapons. Silver steel clashed with rusted iron.

Robert's longsword bit through the monster's corroded pauldron, black ichor leaking from the wound, then he leapt back to avoid being gutted as Falciparum's sword swung for his abdomen. He retaliated with his own blade, dipped in holy water blessed at the shrine of St Thomas Becket. The monster that had been his son growled as the sword cut deep into its shoulder. Robert pulled it free with a snarl, only to freeze as he saw the wound close up with preternatural swiftness.

His surprise almost cost him his life. With a snarl, Falciparum slashed out, and Robert dodged, narrowly avoiding the sword's blade. Thomas's new shape had not retained the skill with the sword the youth had possessed; instead, he swung out with heavy, sweeping blows of incredible power. Robert was able to dodge aside from most of them—fortunate, as he feared the damage that could be done if his enemy's blade connected.

Every time the monster's swing left it open, Robert dived in, stabbing and slicing the creature's torso and arms, chipping away at armour and exposing diseased, pallid flesh. Every strike he landed opened a fresh wound, but to his horror and frustration, they closed up almost as soon as he hit. Robert let loose a growl of frustration, staying focused even as he heard the moaning cries of the other monstrosities and screams and cries of frustration as his men found their foes near impervious to pain.

Falciparum gave a phlegmy roar, and Robert gave ground as his foe swiftly hobbled towards him, pulling its arm back for a stabbing thrust at his gut. Robert twisted aside and brought his sword up. The monster shrieked angrily, and Robert grinned as its rusted sword clattered to earth, accompanied by several bony, rotted fingers.

Falciparum staggered back, staring at his maimed hand... and then laughed. Revolted, Robert watched as bony, chitinous digits, like an insect's limbs, grew from the severed stumps. The monster gave a cruel smile as it flexed its new fingers.

"You see, Father? Your god silently ignores you, but with the favour of mine, I can never die! Join us and worship a god who answers your prayers!"

"Never!" Robert spat back, trying not to show fear.

It did not matter how many blows he landed if this creature shrugged off every wound. In addition, Robert was not a young man, and he was already breathing hard from the exertion. Unless something changed, Falciparum would just continue swinging at him until he grew too tired to dodge.

Screams came from behind Robert, and he risked a look. At least half a dozen of his men were dead, dragged down and butchered by foes that refused to fall. Most of the undead villagers had clearly lost limbs and regrown insectile substitutes in the fighting. One of his men-at-arms buried a falchion between the neck and shoulder of what had once been a woman, her face all but rotted down to the bone in places. She just looked at the sword for a moment, then sank her teeth into the man's neck. Another man struck her head off, but before Robert could see how it played out, he heard lumbering footsteps, and turned back just in time to block a swing at his chest.

He went low this time, and his sword bit through the rotten flesh of his once-son's hip, catching on the bone. Falciparum growled, genuinely angry this time, but when Robert tried to pull his sword free, it stayed stuck, and Falciparum laughed at him mockingly. Snarling, Robert punched, his right gauntlet smashing into the monstrous visage, once, twice, thrice, until the creature staggered back and Robert pulled his sword free. The insectile monster snarled, its jaw broken badly, until flesh and chitinous growths began to emerge from the split flesh and broken bone. Robert's stomach churned as his son's already deformed face grew mantis-like mandibles from the side of his jaw.

"In the name of God, die!" Robert heard Brother Talbot roar.

Forbidden by his vows from carrying a blade, the friar swung at one of the resurrected villagers, once a portly tavern wench, with the closest thing to a weapon he had: an oil lantern. It smashed into the side of the woman's mutated head, and her oily, pallid skin ignited. The monster thrashed and howled, staggering into others of her ilk, who also ignited as the flames touched them. The sergeant charged forward and the woman raised her arms to defend herself, but his blade bit clean through the elbow joint. This time, the wound didn't heal. The sergeant's sword came up again, and this time it was her head that was cut off.

"The fire harms them! We can burn them!" Brother Talbot cried out triumphantly, only to then land flat on his backside as another diseased monstrosity knocked him off his feet. Another of Robert's soldiers drove a spear through its chest before it could finish the friar off, but by now, there were only ten of them left, and they were badly outnumbered.

Robert had his own problems. With a roar, Falciparum charged him again. Robert's sword stabbed out, punching through the rust-riddled breastplate, but the monster barely acknowledged the sword erupting from its back. It grinned and backhanded his father, knocking Robert flat on his back. Robert rolled away from Falciparum's sword as it stabbed down, piercing the place his heart had been a second before.

Ripping a dagger free from its sheath at his waist, Robert stabbed upwards, his blade biting into the monster's thigh. With an angry roar, Falciparum kicked Robert's jaw with a booted foot. Dazed, lying on his back, Robert felt steely fingers around his throat, lifting him off the ground.

"Ssshhh," his enemy whispered as those fingers began to tighten and it became harder to breathe. "One should know when it's time to submit. You rejected the only power that could save you from the fate of all flesh, Father, so now you will feed its strength, that it might claim others who will accept the putrescent gift. Rest, Father, you will still serve a purpose. I just hope my brother and sister are wiser in their choice than you when the time comes…"

Robert desperately fought against his once-son's grip, punching and kicking to no avail, his struggles steadily growing weaker. As his vision started to darken, he thought he heard the sound of hoofbeats and tried to laugh, even as Falciparum's throttling grip tightened further.

Did the Church have it wrong? Were the Vikings of old right? Will it be the Valkyries, rather than the angels, to take me to Valhalla, not Heaven?

Suddenly, there was a blinding white flash, the sound of a sword biting into flesh, the crackle of flames, a scream of utmost agony, and abruptly the hands around Robert's throat were released. Gasping as he sucked down air like a babe at its mother's breast, Robert rolled over and saw salvation.

A force of heavily armoured knights rode towards the insectile undead assaulting the last of his men-at-arms, their swords aflame. At the head of the charge was a man wielding a broadsword wreathed in white fire. As the rest of the knights rode through the undead, setting them ablaze with strikes of their swords, their leader dismounted before the last of the Templeton men-at-arms, pulling a flask from his saddlebags. The men held out their blades as the knight uncorked the flask, pouring oil over their weapons, then pressed the Champion's Blade to their swords. Their swords ignited at the touch of the holy weapon, and with a reinvigorated war cry, the soldiers followed Grand Master Sigismund Wildegraf of the Knights of the Order of the Argent Blade into battle.

"Sever and destroy the heads!" the Grand Master bellowed. "It's the only way to put them down for good!"

Robert Templeton had his own battle to fight. He struggled back to his feet, recovering his fallen dagger, which Falciparum had ripped out before throttling him. The same white flames on Grand Master Sigismund's blade chewed the creature's flesh, the monster shrieking in agony as it desperately tried to pat out the holy flames. Its attention was no longer on him, and the old knight seized his opportunity.

Robert charged forward, his dagger in hand, and with a roar of fury, drove the blade into the back of Falciparum's neck at the base of the skull. This time, he got the reaction he'd hoped for. Pain.

Robert forced the dagger deeper into the swollen creature's spine, heedless of the heat and pain from the flames, and then he felt the blade touch bone. Falciparum thrashed his arms to ward Robert off, but he wouldn't be denied. At that moment, two of Sigismund's men attacked, swinging low with battle-axes into Falciparum's knees, toppling him.

As the soldiers hacked off Falciparum's limbs, Robert stepped back and recovered his sword, ready to put an end to this.

The diseased knight raised his head and snarled mockingly, "Killing your own son, Father? Whatever would Mother say?"

"My son is dead," Robert replied coldly, raising his sword. "I will remember him as the good, brave lad he was, not the diseased thing you are. If there is something left of Thomas Templeton, then I hope he goes free with this act. You, like all your diseased brethren, will be consigned to the only thing you deserve."

"And what is that?" Falciparum sneered.

"The flames." Robert Templeton brought the sword down.

When it was done, he cleaned the blade and walked away, wishing the flames consuming the corpse could burn away his own fears and regrets. A gauntleted hand was placed on his shoulder. Robert turned to find it was Sigismund Wildegraf, his sword driven into the ground, the white flames dancing along its edges guttering out.

"I am sorry for your loss, my friend, but you must gird yourself to face him again. Sooner than you might expect."

"What?" Robert asked, incredulity in his voice.

Sigismund waved a hand towards the village, where his men were hacking off the heads of the resurrected villagers then smashing them into paste with hammers, while others set fire to the houses. As he watched, one of the long white maggots he'd seen his son spit out slithered out of the mouth of a woman's severed head before the hammer fell, but a booted foot stamped down, grinding it to paste.

"This is the third such village we've found. We've faced these creatures in Scotland, with entities like what your son had become leading them. This pestilence may have been a natural sickness, but something from What Lies Beyond is using this as an opportunity, seeking to use the death unleashed to free itself, and your son and his former companions are part of it. Whatever they're doing, we need to find out and end it before this goes beyond our ability to stop… or to keep our shadow war hidden."

Chapter 9: Incubators

"Scent trail is strong," Edmund muttered as he explored the alleyway where he and the girl had been attacked.

Standing a distance away with Gillian, Lucy wrinkled her nose. The stench of stale urine, rotting garbage and a melange of other disgusting odours was bad enough to her nose; she could only imagine how much worse it was to the vampire's superior senses. Fortunately, Edmund and Moira's agents had cleaned up the blood and got rid of the bodies of the thugs the demonic insect had torn to pieces, to ensure no one learned a monster was on the prowl.

"The hell-fly attacked from above, but it wasn't full size. My guess is it only hatched recently," Edmund explained as Gillian crouched down over a small puddle of green slime, making gestures above it with her fingers and muttering to herself. "That means during the incubation period, someone would have had to have hidden it while it pupated. That would have to be somewhere close by. It would have been hungry, driven to attack the first thing it could; the transition from larva to adult consumes a huge amount of energy, so it would have needed to replenish what it lost. Too bad it ran into something even more dangerous…"

"Any idea where it might have been housed?" Lucy asked. "I mean, you're the only one who can track scents through the air—"

"Not necessarily." Gillian moved forward to examine a patch of sickly green slime on the ground, her fingers shimmering. "All creatures touched by What Lies Beyond leave a trail that can be tracked, imperceptible to the human eye, but for those of us who bear the mark…" She whispered an incantation, and a thin green mist began to rise from the slime and away from the alley.

"A spoor trail to follow," the spellweaver said with satisfied relish as they started after it. Gillian took the lead, with Edmund and Lucy following behind.

"The girl who was attacked, was she one of your people?" Lucy asked as they exited the alley, referring to the people living close to the Daltons' residence, offering the vampires information about what was going on in the area in exchange for protection and support.

Edmund shook his head. "No, but we'll keep an eye on her once she's been discharged from hospital. The thugs threatening her, however, are familiar faces and I have no intention of letting small-minded, racist scum like that threaten my flock."

"Your flock?" Lucy replied with a raised eyebrow. "And there was me thinking you gave people protection for altruistic reasons."

"You imagine me like a farmer, fattening my livestock up and driving away the wolves so they don't eat what I'm keeping for myself?" Edmund scowled. "Neither Moira nor I feed on those we protect; there's plenty of those more deserving of that fate. If you know anything of my history, you'll know I still hold true to the same ideals you fight for: to keep mankind safe from an enemy that threatens to devour everything. I haven't forgotten that, and I call the people my flock in the same way Jesus did, protecting them from the threats and snares of evil and ensuring they live good, healthy lives in safe pastures."

"A vampire comparing himself to Jesus? That's a bit blasphemous, isn't it?" Lucy gave an amused smirk.

Edmund didn't rise to the bait. As they continued through the streets of Whitechapel, all three ignoring the strange looks from the locals, Lucy found herself grateful for his company. A few men, either too drunk or stupid to know any better, catcalled Lucy and Gillian.

"Oi, gorgeous, you got anywhere else pierced?"

"Airport security must just love you two, eh!"

"Whose funeral was it?"

"You're a bit late for Halloween, aren't you?"

The pair didn't bother to respond, and when Edmund turned his gaze on them, the nasty little men quickly lost their bravado and scurried off.

If I had more time, I'd show them a few things I'm into, though I doubt they'd like it, Lucy thought to herself, idly fingering the handle of the whip hidden under her jacket. She had to admit, although she knew she did good in the Order's ranks, when confronted with people like those misogynistic oafs, she did wonder if her oath to protect mankind from the demonic horde that dwelt in What Lies Beyond required her to step in if one of those louts ever found themselves with an Ammut's fangs snapping at their throat.

As Gillian followed the magical trail down the high street, shouldering aside anyone who got in her way, Edmund dropped his voice to a whisper and asked, "How is she doing? Her and her father?"

"I don't know," Lucy admitted. "They don't talk about Valerie, no matter how we try to broach the subject. Charles makes his feelings plain on the matter; he's harder and crueller now, shows no mercy to any who crosses the Order… and he drinks far too much. Gillian and Lawrence keep their thoughts to themselves, no matter how much I and Anne and Claire tell them we're willing to talk about it if they want."

Edmund nodded sympathetically. "Grief's a distant memory to me. I haven't mourned for anyone close to me for more than a century, but when the last living member of my family died, it took me years before I even mentioned Bethany to Moira. She waited until I was ready. All I can suggest is just wait and be patient—"

"You two, over here!" Gillian's shout interrupted them.

She was standing in front of a shop with its shutters down. The name above the door read '*Junaid Halal Meat*'.

A laminated notice had been stuck on the shutters: '*Closed until further notice by order of the Department of Health.*'

A convenient place to hide, Lucy thought to herself. *Certainly means no one was likely to come nosing around.*

"Is there another way in?" Edmund asked. "If we want to have a look around, probably best not to make a scene out here."

The trio followed the road around to the alley behind the shops; the back door was locked. With a swift kick, Edmund smashed it in, and strode into the derelict shop, both women trailing in his wake.

"Glad to see that old shtick about vampires needing an invitation isn't true," Lucy joked, before the nauseating stench of rotting meat, faecal waste and sewage assaulted them. She felt her gorge rise and choked back the urge to vomit.

Edmund's mouth twisted into a snarl of disgust, and Gillian was pale as a sheet.

"No wonder the Department of Health closed this place down," Lucy muttered, taking a step forward.

"Watch yourself!" Edmund warned, throwing out a hand to stop her.

Lucy looked down. A gaping hole had been torn into the floor of the butcher shop, the horrific stench rising up from it. Gillian extended her hand over the edge of the pit, a ball of fiery light kindling to life in her palm. She let it drop into the void below. The hole was at least ten feet deep, with no handholds or easy way of climbing down without breaking something.

"Powerful dark magic was used to make this," she muttered. "Something old, and extremely dangerous."

"I take it we need to investigate what's down there?" Lucy said. "Any ideas how we get down without breaking our legs... at best?"

By way of an answer, Edmund took off his shoes and coat and handed them to Gillian. The unmistakable sounds of bones cracking and tendons popping came as his arms and fingers elongated into wings and his feet lengthened into grasping talons. Before the pair could say anything, Edmund leapt into the air and grabbed Lucy and Gillian by their shoulders. His wings beat as he descended into the hole, the two women suppressing the urge to vomit as the foul stench of rot and decay grew stronger.

Edmund's talons released them when their feet were an inch from the ground. Their boots sank into murky slurry the deep red of raw meat. Edmund snatched his shoes out of Gillian's grasp and put them back on before setting foot on the sludgy ground.

The two women looked at him askance.

"What? Just because I'm a vampire, you think I'm going to go wading through this muck barefoot?" he remarked as he indicated their surroundings. "Now come on! The sooner we find out what's down here, the sooner we can get out of here."

All around the rock walls of the pit, sickly white mounds of chitin and flesh had been fastened by sickly green resin. One had been torn open from the inside. Edmund reached into the shattered cocoon, and the girls made a noise of disgust as he pulled out a forearm and a skull, only partially denuded of flesh.

"What the hell did that?" Lucy whispered.

"Hell-fly larvae gestate inside human corpses," Gillian explained in a tone of utter revulsion. "The adults immobilise the bodies their larvae have been laid in, while the creatures use the warmth provided by decomposition to keep them alive while they pupate, and then when they hatch, they have a nice meal ready and waiting for them."

"Well, then, that means the adult laying these eggs is still out there and we need to find out where it is before we have a nest of these creatures to deal with," Lucy whispered, horrified.

"I think it might be too late for that," Edmund said from the far side of the room.

Lucy turned, raising her torch as Gillian kindled fire to life in the palm of her hand. There were at least a dozen more such cocoons, leaving an overpowering stench of rotting meat. As the trio eyed them with disgust, a chitinous claw broke the surface the surface of one.

"Burn them," Lucy snarled.

The orb of fire in Gillian's hand turned into a whip, and she lashed each of the cocoons, setting them and the growing monstrosities inside aflame. Keening screeches, albeit muffled by the cocoons, came as the demonic insects desperately tried to get free. Fire ran down the back of the one that had started to tear its way out of the cocoon. It had just managed to get its thorax clear of the burning, fleshy morass when Edmund's claws seized the head, heedless of the snapping mandibles that tried to drive him back, and pulled.

It came away in the vampire's grip. Stinking white ichor spilled from the stump as Edmund tossed the severed head aside and retreated as Gillian intensified her spell to incinerate the others. Lucy watched in surprise as Edmund angrily stamped the fly's severed head into stinking grey mush. He noticed she was staring at him and gave an idle shrug.

"I hate bugs. Always have."

"Can't fault you for that," Lucy muttered. The mark upon her wrist was burning; the air of the pit was saturated with demonic energy. "Have you ever encountered these demons before?"

"A long time ago. One on one, as you saw, they can be dispatched easily enough, but they usually come in swarms that can number in the hundreds. What makes them truly dangerous are the diseases they carry. In times when the Desolated and other cults the Order has fought have resorted to open war, they like to bring forth swarms of these creatures to infect those who would stand against them with all manner of hell-spawned plagues, as well as provide them with soldiers who can be quickly replenished. The Order's knights are protected from such things, but I've seen diseases carried by these things decimate entire armies."

"Is there any way to cure people infected?" Lucy asked.

"Only a handful of things work for certain." Edmund had to raise his voice over the crackle of flames as Gillian utterly incinerated the cocoons. "Vampire saliva, for one. We prefer what we eat to be untainted."

"Can your kind even get diseases?" Lucy asked, intrigued by the thought.

Edmund shook his head. "No, but we prefer the blood we drink to be pure, for the sake of our digestion. Drinking the blood of a man in the prime of health, with a good diet, who looks after himself, is a lot better than drinking the blood of a smoker or an old woman with leukaemia. It won't hurt us, but it does leave us experiencing something akin to what you call heartburn. Unfortunately, there aren't enough of my kind out there to inoculate all mankind with our saliva, and the side effects outweigh the benefits. Other solutions are kept under lock and key in places I can't reach. The only certain way I know is to remove the parasitic larvae before they can reach the brain. Unfortunately, given how rarely the Order has encountered these, we have little in the way of research to try and develop a vaccine for the diseases hell-flies carry—"

"Sorry to interrupt you," Gillian cut in, "but I think I know how Mummy got in to lay these eggs."

Their eyes followed her pointing finger to a small hole at the base of one of the pit's walls, clearly dug by something that had crawled its way in from below.

"Hole's only big enough for something small. I think the poor bastards were caged here, left to wait until the bug came from wherever it was hiding, got the larvae put in them and were left to rot. Not a good way to go."

"Is there any way to make that hole bigger?" Lucy asked. "Because I am not crawling through that muck to find where Mummy Fly came from!"

"Pansy," Gillian muttered with a wink, before unleashing a bolt of lightning that shattered the wall, leaving a hole tall enough for them to walk through.

"What's below us?" Lucy asked.

"The sewers… and the District Line," Edmund answered. "Plenty of places for a lone insect, even one that big, to hide. They like damp, dark places. Believe me, I speak from experience." He grimaced.

"Gillian can help us track it, but we don't need distractions." Lucy tapped her earpiece as Gillian began incanting the spell that would illuminate the hell-fly's spoor for them to follow. "Claire, can you inform Transport for London there's been a terrorist threat on the District Line in the vicinity of Stepney Green station? We're tracking something demonic down here, and the last thing we need is to be dodging trains while we follow it…"

Chapter 10: Extermination
Northern France, June 1940, 10.30 a.m.

The town church had been left in ruins. The doors had been smashed to splinters by a blow of great force from the inside. As the party of soldiers stalked into the vestibule, Alfred and several others gagged at the stench that hit them: an overwhelming miasma of rotting meat and faecal matter. Major Templeton looked at him sympathetically as he passed.

"Revolting, isn't it? The stench of utter corruption. No matter how many times I breathe it in, it still sickens me."

"You've seen this before?" Alfred goggled at him.

Templeton gave a shrug. "Not exactly like this, but sights like these are becoming more common for me and my organisation. The Führer and his inner circle are meddling with dark and dangerous powers that watch mankind with hateful eyes; the chaos and carnage of this war is like blood in shark-infested waters. Hitler and his cronies will turn them loose without a second thought for a chance of winning this war, not realising these things care nothing for his goals. Allies or Nazis, we are all the same to them, meat to be stuffed down their gullets."

"Why haven't I heard of this?" Alfred asked, utterly confused.

Templeton bit his lip, as if unsure how to procced. He was saved from an answer when Edmund Dalton shouted out, "Dominic, you need to see this!"

The major made his way into the nave of the church, Alfred following behind with the soldiers. Alfred thought he'd seen all manner of horror in the desperate fighting as the Nazis had steamrollered through everything in their path, but this was beyond any manmade abomination of war.

The church looked more like an insect hive than anything else. Back at school, his science teacher had shown them the cocoons of moths and butterflies, and Alfred had to admit, the fleshy structures pinned to the walls and pillars in the church resembled those, although far bigger than anything he'd seen—and formed from rotting corpses. Chunks of human skeletons and tattered clothing protruded from the fleshy wreckage. Pages torn out of Bibles and hymnals were scattered all over the ground, and the altar and pews had been smashed to pieces. Smears of blood, slime and other substances splattered every wall, adding to the fetid reek.

But the worst thing was in the centre of the church. Directly below a massive hole torn in the church roof, a gaping cavern in the floor led into the catacombs below.

"Well, I guess that's how the bugs got out into the village," Alfred muttered. "We got to worry about them dropping in on us?"

"Not at the moment," Edmund Dalton replied, causing Alfred to jump. He'd been talking in a whisper, and the soldier was a good distance away at the front of the group—Alfred didn't see how he could have heard. The man was wearing a hood, a helmet and a scarf about his face despite the summer heat, which made it even more surprising.

"These creatures detest daylight; it causes them pain," Templeton said, clapping Alfred on the shoulder. "In the daytime, they become torpid, or at least the adults do; the larvae are steadily making the carcasses they puppet more suitable for the final stage of their infant cycle. They're what we're most likely to encounter down here." As he spoke, he made sure his gun was ready, and all the rest readied their own weapons.

"This is the only way in or out of this nest. We plant the explosives at a place that'll bring the roof crashing down on their heads, we set the fuse, and we run like hell. Beyond this point, anything that moves is to be considered hostile.

Moore, Clayton, be ready for anything," he added to two soldiers clutching appropriated German flamethrowers, the Wehrmacht details on them hastily painted over.

One by one, the soldiers descended into the pit. The oppressive atmosphere and the stink of rotten meat only grew more palpable as they made their way through old tombs, following a trail of stinking slime through medieval tunnels.

"How far do these catacombs go?" Alfred muttered, his rifle ready at any sound of movement ahead. He was the seventh in the party, the catacombs only wide enough for two men at a time. Suddenly, he saw a flicker of movement to his left.

"Contact!" Templeton bellowed.

Alfred spun in time to see a figure lunging through a broken wall behind a medieval sarcophagus. It looked like a woman, but her face was so rotten that the skull was starting to punch through the skin, snarling like a rabid animal. Before he could take a shot, she'd grabbed him in a vice grip, pulling him closer to her snapping, rotten teeth…

Suddenly, impossibly, Edmund Dalton was there, seizing the monster's head and slamming it into the wall. Her skull came apart in pieces. Edmund tore out something white and squirming from the messy remains, than squashed it in his fist. Alfred tried to get his breathing under control at the shock as Major Templeton walked over and investigated the hole the creature had emerged from.

"Looks like she tunnelled her way up from below; there might be another way down into the main nest. If we can use it to attack there from a distance, it might save us having to fight our way down any further."

"Works for me," Moore, one of the soldiers with the flamethrowers, said. "But I don't think any of us are fitting down there to see how far it goes."

"Out of my way," Edmund griped, stripping out of his clothes until he was standing only in his underwear.

Alfred couldn't help but admire the man's physique. Despite his pale complexion, he looked like a statue of a

Greek god. With a grimace, Edmund clambered face first into the hole and crawled into the darkness.

"Isn't it a bit dangerous sending him down there alone?" Alfred protested. "I mean, what if there's more of those things down there?"

To his surprise, Templeton dismissed his protest with a wave of his hand. "Relax, he can take care of himself. He's been in far tougher scrapes than—"

"Major, we've got incoming!" another soldier at the front of the group shouted.

At the far end of the chamber they were in, the wall had collapsed, and beyond it a tunnel led deep into the earth, wide enough for five people to walk through side by side. In the distance, Alfred could hear a mixture of sounds: moaning, buzzing and clicking of the sort insects might make, and footsteps coming closer.

"Form up!" Templeton shouted, readying his pistol. "Two lines! Six men in each! Phillips, stay back with Caxton and Walters. The moment Edmund tells you we can use the tunnel he's down, flood it with all the explosives we brought! The rest of you, shoot anything that comes up that passage. Once we have confirmation from Edmund, toss the charges down there and seal it up, then we burn it!"

Alfred was in the first rank, down on one knee, levelling his rifle. The soldiers had supplied him with plenty of ammo for the fight ahead; he only hoped the silvery bullets were as effective as Templeton had claimed.

"Nervous, soldier?" one of the men to his left muttered.

"No," Alfred said, but the quaver in his voice gave away the lie. "You?"

"Shitting myself," the man said with a shrug. "I'll watch your back if you watch mine."

"Deal," Alfred said with a nod as Moore bellowed, "Contact!"

Alfred turned his gaze back to the tunnel. A half dozen shambling figures appeared around a corner, with the shadows of more behind.

"First rank, fire!" Templeton ordered, and Alfred added his bullet to the others.

The creatures staggered, but even as they fell, none stayed down, trying to get back to their feet as more of their ilk stalked up the passage, trampling over them.

"Second rank, fire!"

Bullets flew over their heads as Alfred and his fellows in the first rank reloaded. These shots were more successful. At least three of the shambling once-men toppled, holes blown in their skulls. Pallid, finger-length maggots slithered out of bullet holes and gaping mouths, the rest of the horde trying to avoid trampling them under foot.

"First rank, fire!"

Alfred and the first six shot again. He aimed a little higher and was rewarded with the back of a skull exploding. At closer range, more of the creatures toppled, but only metres separated them, and the once-men had the advantage of numbers...

"Covering fire!" Moore shouted from the second rank, and those around Alfred scattered to the right.

Heat erupted behind him as Moore's flamethrower opened up. The first four ranks of shambling monsters turned into blazing torches as they were doused in flame. They staggered back, keening and wailing, into more of their kind, who in turn ignited. The shambling horde suddenly retreated, even as Moore advanced and bathed them in fire. The soldiers shot after them and as the walking dead fled out of sight back into the depths, they all let out a cheer.

"Can the noise!" Templeton snapped, slamming a fresh clip into his pistol. "They'll be back before long and—"

The major's protests were silenced by a loud, fly-like buzzing from the tunnel.

"I think I have movement," Moore said from his position at the tunnel mouth.

"Moore, get out of there!" Templeton raised his pistol.

The buzzing got louder, and Alfred heard the roar of the flamethrower again, the crackle of flames and screeching, and then something huge hit Moore like a thunderbolt.

It was a monstrous fly, nappy-grey and stinking of rotting meat, the size of a lion, that smashed Moore to the ground. Before he could recover, the monster's snapping mandibles, as long and sharp as swords, bit his throat out. Blood sprayed across the walls and floor as the insect and another that came fluttering up from the tunnel started fighting amongst themselves to feed.

"Get the fuck away!" Alfred shouted, jabbing out with his bayonet, but the closest monster screeched and swatted at him with a forelimb covered in jagged spikes.

The limb connected with surprising force, and Alfred was smashed off his feet, his rifle cut in half. As he landed on his arse, the creature crawled towards him, mandibles clicking. Alfred tried to scramble away, but the thing was much faster, and...

"Fucking die!" a voice bellowed.

There was a flash of silver and the creature shrieked as a long, slender blade stabbed through its thorax. Major Templeton planted a foot on the creature's back, forcing it down, and emptied his gun into its head.

"You're not dead yet, soldier." Templeton pulled a second gun from within his jacket and handed it over. "Until you take your last breath, you keep fighting!"

"Yes sir!" Alfred replied as he turned around.

The battle had taken a worse turn. Although one hellish fly was dead, two more of the creatures had stormed into the crypt, and he could hear the shambling horde heading towards them, emboldened by the second attack. Half a dozen men were dead, their throats and stomachs torn out by snapping mandibles and serrated claws. The flies hovered over their kills, waiting for them to show signs of movement, resisting any attempts by the remaining soldiers to drive them away from the bodies.

Suddenly, a thought came to Alfred. As he saw the first signs of the once-men reappearing in the tunnel, he took aim at Moore's body, picked his target and pulled the trigger.

The flamethrower's tank exploded, and Moore's body, the creature that had killed him and the tunnel entrance were aflame. He could hear the screeches and clicks of the shambling horde in response to the sudden bloom of heat and light, while Templeton shouted, "Good man!" The two flies trapped in the crypt by the fire screeched but refused to leave their kills.

"Dynamite!" Templeton bellowed, and one of the remaining soldiers pulled out several sticks of the stuff from a satchel. The man got to his feet, but out of nowhere, one of the flies suddenly leapt into the air, abandoning its kill. It landed atop the soldier. The man dropped the dynamite, just managing to grab the jaws as they were about to shut on his throat.

Alfred Murray reacted instinctively; he'd been a great rugby player at school. He remembered that as he charged, and his shoulder connected with the creature's thorax, knocking it off its prey. It angrily whirled to face the one who'd interrupted it, Alfred raising his gun to shoot, when suddenly a pale white shape leapt onto the monstrous fly's back, stabbing frenziedly with a knife. The creature collapsed, keening frantically, but the figure on its back—a dirty and dishevelled Edmund Dalton—refused to be dislodged.

"Seal the hole!" he shouted as he kept stabbing madly into the dying insect.

It could have just been Alfred's imagination, but Edmund's teeth looked extremely long and sharp…

"Come on!" the soldier who Alfred had saved yelled, snapping him out of his reverie.

As they grabbed the dynamite, Phillips set the last fly and the dead ablaze with a stream of flame. Using the distraction, they lit the fuses and flung them in the direction of the hole leading deeper. The fires from the detonation of Moore's fuel tank had burned down and the horde could be heard advancing, but as they reappeared in the tunnel, the dynamite detonated. Everyone dived for cover as the tunnel ceiling caved in, trapping the monsters lying in wait further down beneath tonnes of rock and earth.

As Alfred picked himself up, a hand grabbed his ankle. He looked round to see one of the soldiers killed in the fight was moving, snapping its teeth as it tried to pull itself towards him. Suddenly, a pair of boots stamped on its back and Alfred recoiled as their owner stomped the living corpse's head to paste.

"You did well." Major Templeton helped Alfred pull himself to his feet.

Behind them, other surviving soldiers smashed the skulls of their dead comrades to ensure they wouldn't rise again and the parasites trying to reanimate them would die with them.

"Edmund, does the tunnel go down to the central nest?"

"Aye, it does," Dalton replied, dusting himself off and recovering his clothes to put on.

Templeton nodded in satisfaction and then snapped his fingers.

"Flood it."

Several soldiers began pouring cans of gasoline into the tunnel, while others rolled grenades down there.

As Alfred watched, he found himself compelled to ask, "What were those things? Did the Nazis create them?"

"No," Templeton replied. "They are something far older, far worse… and they're just one of the many things the Nazis will unleash in their desperate desire to claim this world."

"There are more?" Alfred goggled.

"Hundreds more. Thousands even, and not just like these."

"How do we stop them?"

"I'll tell you again when we make it back to England. For now, we need to get out of here before the Germans come to investigate the explosions."

The major pulled the pin from a grenade and rolled it into the depths. As they made their retreat from the crypt, Alfred heard the roar of flames and explosions, and screams of panic as monsters burned in the depths.

Chapter 11: The Nest

The tunnels of the London Underground were mercifully empty as they continued to follow the spoor Gillian's spell had illuminated. Claire's terror alert had done its job—there was no rattle of approaching trains to disturb the silence. Ever since Halloween, London had been a lot more on edge. The Order had been working overtime to suppress any attempts by survivors to spread photo and video evidence of what had happened in Parliament Square. The government's official line was that a terrorist group had unleashed a nerve gas that caused aggressive behaviour, while claims of demons and monster sightings and the devastation they'd wrought were merely a hallucinogenic side effect, along with a series of bombs that had damaged Big Ben and numerous other public buildings. No criminal charges were pressed against those police officers who had shot members of the public either in self-defence or while under the influence of the nerve gas.

Lucy hadn't expected the public to swallow the lie so readily, but she guessed people would rather accept a comforting lie than a bitter truth if it meant they didn't have to admit the world was crazier and more terrible than they'd first thought.

She remembered a time when she'd have thought the same.

"Well, I don't think we need your spells to figure out where our prey went," Edmund said, pointing at a side door along the tunnel. It had been smashed down, and sickly green slime clung to the frame.

Edmund went first, the two women following in his wake. More slime clung to the electrical cables and piping along the narrow passage.

"Flies like dank, damp environments to breed. Their demonic counterparts are no different," Edmund muttered.

"You sound like you've had experience with this," Lucy remarked.

"The year I first moved to London, there were three cholera outbreaks," he replied. "I grew up in a time before vaccination, when diseases that you've only read about in history books ran rampant through the city. Before I died and rose again, I was well versed in fighting demons that thrive on the spread of disease."

"Have you fought these flies before?"

"Far more than I'd like," Edmund grimaced. "They're extremely dangerous, capable of tearing a man apart with their mandibles, and they're crawling with disease, to say nothing of the adults implanting their young…"

"Implanting?" Lucy winced.

Edmund shuddered in disgust. "Hell-fly mandibles double as ovipositors. When they bite, as well as injecting toxic saliva contaminated with all manner of diseases, they implant a larva into their victim's body. The larva steadily makes its way through the body, weakening the immune system so that the diseases the bite carries can run rampant. As the victim grows sicker, the larva moves its way up into the skull, where it waits for its parent's bite to kill the host…"

"And then?" Lucy prompted, simultaneously enraptured and revolted.

"Once the host is dead, the larva embeds itself in the brain and takes control over its host body's motor functions, along with heightening aggression, compelling the reanimated host to attack suitable victims. The infested host's bite exudes pheromones that mark the victim out to the adult flies as a suitable host for implanting. The larva remains inside its host body until the brain matter becomes too degraded for further use, whereupon the larva will compel its host to collapse in a suitable location, pupate using the corpse as a cocoon, and emerge as an adult hell-fly."

"Well, that's just great," Lucy muttered, her disgust palpable. "The question is, who is breeding such numbers of these bugs and for what—"

There came an almighty grinding of gears, and Lucy let out a scream as the floor gave way beneath her feet.

"Lucy!" she heard Gillian shriek as she slid down a stone chute.

Despite her panic at her sudden loss of footing, Lucy slammed a hand to her belt, setting off a flashlight fastened there. The light reflected off marks in the stone that suggested the chute had been excavated, and by something big and with powerful claws. Lucy hit her belt buckle again, and a blinking red light flickered there.

"You guys better find me quickly!" Lucy raged to herself, hoping the locator would do its job as she saw a sickly green glow fast approaching ahead.

The chute suddenly dumped her out, and Lucy screamed as she landed on her back in a deep morass of melted flesh. She shrieked as she felt chunks of the fleshy sludge cling to her hair and skin, the stink of rot overpowering.

"What the hell is this?!" she spat, brushing chunks of rotting meat off her.

Her skin crawled as she saw bits of skin and hair mixed up with the flesh, to say nothing of fat black flies and long white maggots crawling through the muck.

"Food for the infants. If they are to grow up big and strong, then they need the finest fodder to do so," a gurgling voice said from behind her.

Lucy spun on her heel, drawing the kukri at her hip and taking a good look around the chamber as she did so. She was in a deep, bowl-shaped cavern, the floor a stinking swamp of rotting flesh, the walls lined with more of the giant, pallid cocoons, distorted shapes moving within.

Out of place was a crudely carved stone chair, the figure seated in it with their back to Lucy.

"You are an intruder here, but with an offering of flesh, you may atone for your intrusion into this holy place."

The figure rose from his chair. His face was mostly hidden beneath the hood of his cloak and a moth-eaten scarf draped across his lower face, but the portions she could see had the complexion of a leper. Strands of greasy black hair were plastered to his pallid brow, and his eyes burned with the necrotic green light of one touched by What Lies Beyond.

The figure grabbed something propped against the back of his seat. Lucy's eyes went wide as she saw it was a claymore, as long as she was tall. The blade was orange-brown with rust, but she didn't doubt it would do serious harm if it connected.

Somehow, I don't think the Order's mark will protect me from tetanus.

The figure flung his cloak over one shoulder, revealing the armour of a medieval knight, sickly green in colour, spotted with rust and grime. It strained around the monster's waist, as if trying to contain a swollen gut.

"I am impressed that someone found their way in here. Usually, I have to wait for new deliveries of meat from our patrons. Still, this will give me something to do until then! The children could also do with a feed."

"I think you'll find eating me will give your pets a nasty case of indigestion!" Lucy snarled, baring the mark of the Order on her wrist.

The diseased knight hissed angrily at the sight of the skull and sword. "Argent Blade!" he growled as he raised his sword, spitting a wad of black phlegm at Lucy's feet. "It has been too long since I have slain one of your wretched kind!"

"Well, I'm sorry to disappoint you, but I don't intend on being the one who dies down here!" Lucy shouted back as she charged through the fleshy muck.

The monstrous knight roared and charged her. As he pulled back his sword to swing, Lucy ducked and slid along the floor, suppressing her revulsion as she skidded through the putrid slime and swung out at her enemy's leg. He roared as the blade bit through the greave and into the meat of his ankle. Lucy rolled back to her feet, avoiding a hacking strike at her head that sent chunks of the fleshy floor flying. Uncoiling her whip, she lashed out, and the whip wrapped around the blade. With all her strength, Lucy tugged on the whip, jerking the plague knight forward and sending him stumbling to the ground. She charged in, swinging out at his neck with her kukri.

Whoever this freakshow is, I'm willing to bet he goes down as easily as anyone else when his head's lying two feet from the rest of him!

She brought the blade down, only to hear a clang of metal as the diseased knight raised his right arm in the nick of time. The silver-steel blade easily shattered the rusty metal, biting into the flesh and bone beneath, and stuck there. The monstrous knight's green eyes gleamed maliciously as he rose to his feet, Lucy desperately trying to free her weapon from his arm. Before she could, a gauntleted hand seized her by the throat. She choked as her feet left the ground. The plague knight ripped the kukri out of his arm and tossed it aside, the blade landing point down in the mire.

"Pathetic," he spat mockingly, ignoring the burning pain of the Order's mark as he gripped the skin of Lucy's neck. "I had hoped you might make it more interesting—"

The monster roared as Lucy jabbed a thumb into his right eye. With a hiss, the orb ruptured. Lucy gagged as spots of gelid fluid splattered her cheeks. The monstrous knight howled in pain, lifting her higher into the air. In desperation, Lucy clawed at his masked face with her fingers. The flesh sizzled at her touch. Her fingers caught the edge of the moth-eaten scarf and yanked; Lucy's eyes went wide as she saw what it had been hiding.

Beneath the hood was a rotted once-human face, the nose long-since fallen away, leaving a gaping hole in the centre. The skin and flesh had rotted, leaving yellowed and gnawed bone visible in various places. Lucy grimaced as she saw the jaw muscles twitch when the undead knight grinded his teeth hatefully at her. With a snarl of rage, he hurled Lucy away from him. She landed face first in the muck, spitting out fleshy gobbets as she pushed herself up.

Suddenly, there was an almighty explosion from above. The knight roared in fury as chunks of the cave ceiling came crashing down, Lucy choking as more stinking, meaty slime splattered her face. She looked up, and grinned as she saw her kukri barely a metre away. She scrabbled on her hands and knees and pulled the blade free, delighted to be armed again.

"On your right!" she heard Gillian shout.

She rolled to her left just as the rusty claymore came swinging down, the blade slamming into the ground. She stabbed upwards, her kukri's blade punching through rusted metal and into the diseased meat of her opponent's thigh. All her enemy did was laugh.

"Stick me as much as you like, girl. The god of disease has made my flesh impervious to all wounds! I am beyond you!"

"I'd like to test that theory!" Edmund Dalton snarled from behind.

The knight whirled round to see the vampire had descended silently to the cave floor, his katana drawn.

"I smell death on you, blood-sucker," the plague knight spat. "Why would you fight with those sworn to destroy others like you? You should fight with us."

"My reasons are my own," Edmund snarled, "and I will not have your filth tainting my food supply!"

The vampire charged with a bat-like shriek. Katana and claymore clashed with sparks and screeches of tortured metal. Edmund's sword was the superior weapon, sending chips of rusted iron flying off, but the knight was a skilled combatant, easily holding his own. Fortunately, his back was to Lucy, and she took advantage of that.

The whip cracked again, this time wrapping around her foe's left arm, and she pulled with all her might, twisting the limb away from its grip on his sword. Edmund seized the opening. The katana slashed down, cutting through the weaker armour at the elbow joint and the flesh and bone beneath. A rust-covered arm dropped into the fleshy sludge at their feet, and Edmund bared his fangs in a grin of satisfaction.

The death's head face beneath the hood twisted in fury, and the monster thrust out the stump of its left arm. Edmund's face contorted in confusion, just before a jet of dark blood hit him full in the face.

The vampire's hands flew to his face. Steam rose from both his head and hands, Edmund shrieking in agony, as the knight got back up, laughing cruelly and seemingly unhindered by the loss of his arm.

Suddenly, a fireball descended from above, forcing him to retreat. Lucy looked up and saw Gillian levitating down into the cavern, fire cracking in the palms of her hands.

"Oh, now that is unchivalrous! I shall have to chastise you for that, girl!" the knight growled.

His jaw distended like a serpent's, a low buzzing from deep within his chest growing louder and louder, until a swarm of enormous, fat black flies came shooting out between his teeth. The swarm hit Gillian like a physical blow, smashing her from the air and swarming all over her. With a shrieked word in Gaelic, she thrust out a hand, and her fire exploded into a cyclone that surrounded and shielded her, burning away the flies. The remainder of the swarm retreated to circle Gillian, looking for an opportunity to attack again, and Lucy feared if Gillian tried to cast a spell to help her lover, she'd be overwhelmed.

"Witness me now, my brothers!" the knight cackled, the buzzing of the flies growing louder and louder as he stalked towards Gillian. "Witness me lay low the witch! Her heathen magic shall not stop the great work!"

"Oh, you're not touching my girl!" Lucy snarled as she charged and leapt onto the knight's broad back, stabbing the kukri into the side of his throat.

With a furious bellow, he swung his head back into Lucy's face, stunning and dislodging her. Landing on her arse in the muck, she rolled away as her foe turned and stabbed for her chest with his sword. Lucy stabbed at the monster's swollen belly, only for the claymore to parry and then twist the blade out of her hand. The kukri went flying and buried itself in the wall. Lucy scrambled at her belt, coming up with a throwing knife in her hand. The rust-clad knight gave another gurgling laugh at the sight of the miniscule blade.

"You will need a sharper blade than that toothpick, my girl. Put it down, and I promise your end will be—"

Whatever offer he was about to make was cut off as Lucy flung the knife. It flew end over end and buried itself in his empty eye socket. The knight laughed in derision, oblivious to the winking red light in his skull.

"A worthy effort, but futile," he sneered, his yellowed teeth grinding together. "The gifts my lord has bestowed make me impervious—"

The explosives in the knife's handle detonated. Lucy shielded her face as fragments of skull went flying in all directions. The rusted knight's headless corpse swayed for a second, then fell face-first to the mud, dark blood full of writhing white maggots pouring from the stump.

Lucy retrieved her kukri and spat in disgust on her fallen enemy. Dead in the same instant as their master, the swarm of flies dropped to the ground in a thick black rain, and she shrieked as she dodged aside from the hundreds of insectile husks, before wiping chunks of her foe and the floor—to say nothing of the multitude of dead insects—off her armour and out of her hair.

"Urgh, this stink is never going to come off!" Lucy wailed as she squelched and crunched through rotted flesh and dead flies.

"Oh, I'll help you scrub it off," Gillian said teasingly as she dispelled her fire spell and waded through the mess.

The knight's body was already beginning to dissolve into the meaty slurry, leaving only a medieval suit of armour encrusted with several centuries of rust.

"What the hell was that thing?" Lucy asked.

"I have some ideas, but I'll want to confirm it with Claire before I say one way or another," Gillian remarked. "Right now, I'm more concerned about what he was guarding." She pointed at the cocoons that were beginning to twitch and thrash.

"We should burn this place down," Edmund interjected.

The two women turned to face him and got the fright of their lives. His face looked like it had been bathed in acid, to the point where they could see muscle and even bone exposed.

"Relax," he said with a dismissive wave of his hand as they hastened over to his side. "I've looked far worse in my time. You should have seen me after I finished chasing down an efreet in Chicago in the twenties—what a nightmare that was. But long before your time. Seriously, once we're done here and you've lit this place up, I'll go and find some dinner, and I'll be good as new before you know it!" He gave a wry smirk. "On that note, would you mind, Gillian?"

"Not yet." She turned around and blasted several stalagmites with pale white cocoons clinging to them. "Edmund, be a dear and grab those please? And Lucy, grab that ugly bastard's sword."

Blue sparks began to dance in the palms of her hands, the unmistakeable sign of her about to open a portal.

"What for?" Lucy asked as she waded through the fleshy muck to try and prise the blade out.

"We've never really had a chance to examine and dissect these creatures in depth—and I want that as evidence of what we fought down here. If he belongs to who I think he does, Dad and the others need to see it!" The portal opened with a thunderous crack and the stink of ozone. "Grab those and follow me; I'll go through first. Anne needs to know we've got hazardous materials, so don't leave the armoury until she and I get there!"

Gillian slipped through and left the pair to follow, Lucy dragging a surprisingly heavy lump of metal, Edmund laden down with seven or eight cocoons, each about the size of a watermelon.

"You know when I joined the Order of the Argent Blade, there was no mention of heavy lifting," Lucy griped as they hobbled through the portal with their burdens.

As the portal closed behind them, amidst the slurry of decomposing meat and chitin, something began to move. A skeletal human hand rose out of the muck, grasping a rusty vambrace as diseased skin and flesh began to form around it.

Chapter 12: A Rival Order

"Where are the eggs?" Lucy asked as she sat down in the briefing room, her hair still wet from the shower.

She had showered at least three times, but even with Gillian's help to scrub her clean in two of them, Lucy swore she could still smell the stink of the pit. She unconsciously rubbed her arms, as if the muck and slime from her battle with that disease-ridden knight was still on her.

"Locked in a hermetically sealed casket in the armoury," Lawrence replied. He looked exhausted, no doubt the result of a late-night flight back from Paris, but his eyes were still alert as he studied the plague knight's claymore, sealed in a Perspex box in the centre of the table to contain whatever pathogens might cling to the blade. The Knights were fairly confident demonic diseases couldn't infect them, but there was no sense in taking chances.

"Gillian also put a stasis spell on the insects within. They won't hatch until she dispels it, and that won't happen until Anne takes a look at them. Our Order has never had a chance to examine them carefully. Study might help us find a pathogen to kill the species, or a vaccine to inoculate people against the influence their larvae have in the bloodstream."

Movement at the corner of her eye drew Lucy's attention. Claire was moving around the table, depositing a pair of photographs in front of everyone. One showed a soldier in either Iraq or Afghanistan, his uniform torn to shreds, baring his right arm. The second showed a severed arm in a hospital mortuary, the flesh around the cut blackened with rot and crawling with maggots. The distinctive feature in both was the tattoo of a skull-headed fly in green ink on the bicep. Lucy looked up and saw the same mark engraved on the blade of the rusty sword.

"A cult mark?" she asked.

Claire nodded as she returned to her seat. "One we've not seen for quite some time. It would appear the Knights of Yersinia are back."

"Are they the same as the Blighted Brothers?" Gillian asked. "Wasn't the last confirmed sighting of them back in 1918?"

"Aye, the Spanish Flu pandemic." Lawrence nodded. "We've had whispers of their presence in other disease zones around the world since then. We had reported sightings of them in Syria a few months back, but there wasn't anything concrete, so we let it go."

"Wait, I think I've heard of these," Lucy cut in. "Are they also known as the Missionaries of the Grave?"

"They've gone by many names throughout the centuries, changing it to suit their purpose and evade detection," Claire said. "They formed not long after our own Order, during the worst days of the Black Death. The story goes that a group of knights, on a mission from King Edward, succumbed to the bubonic plague on their travels. It is said that on death's door, their leader renounced God for abandoning them to the ravages of the plague and offered his soul and the souls of his men to any higher power who would spare them. Unfortunately, one was listening. Nergal."

"Nergal?" Lucy asked.

"A minor demon lord in the realms that lie beyond. He's a demon of plague and disease who was once worshipped as a god by the Babylonians. At that time, his power was growing due to the ravages of the Black Death, and he saw the advantage of having human servants in this world to further facilitate his goals. He resurrected the dying knights, imbued them with the power to carry and spread every disease known to man, and made them all but invulnerable to the blades of their enemies. Wherever they walked in his name, they spread his corruption, infecting entire villages, their inhabitants dying and rising again as mindless puppets of Nergal, driven only to spread his diseases across all the world…"

"How were they stopped?" Lucy asked.

Charles rolled his eyes, annoyed at her usual interruptions, but Claire shrugged and carried on.

"We don't know. The records are infuriatingly blank. All we know is that it took all the strength of our newly founded Order to defeat the Blighted Brothers, and that the victory came at an extremely heavy cost."

"Well, the one who wielded this thing was a tough bastard, but he went down eventually, so hopefully the rest will go down as easily," Lucy remarked, tapping the box containing the rusty sword with a big grin on her face. "Who'd have thought that advice from *Shaun of the Dead* would work in real life?"

Her smile fell as she saw no one else was grinning. "I'm not going to like what comes next, am I?" she asked grimly.

Claire shrugged her shoulders and gave a helpless look. "Unfortunately, the Knights of Yersinia are not so easily dispatched. Members of our Order have managed to kill a few—the record is held by Thomas Delaney, a member of the Argent Blade who killed four of those creatures during the Great Plague of 1665—but unfortunately, so long as one of their foul number still lives, the others will regenerate. We believe they are a single entity stretched across six bodies; to permanently destroy them requires killing all six simultaneously."

Lucy pouted and folded her arms. "Well, thank you for stealing my thunder! Anyone else want to completely trash my good mood today?"

"Yeah, you're going back into the sewers tonight," Lawrence replied.

"Excuse me?" Lucy said, eyes wide. "I'm still trying to get the scent of that shit off, and you want me to go rolling around in it again?"

"I'm sorry if you're going to have to take a few more baths tonight," Lawrence replied archly, "but I need to know what else they might be working on. The Knights of Yersinia are followers, not leaders; they work to serve the will of their master. What's more, from what we learned in Paris, something big is going on."

"What do you mean?" Anne spoke for the first time, concerned.

"Our contact told us something big is being planned in Athens. Apparently, our old friend Josef Mengele has been sighted there, and there's rumours on the black market that arms dealers and terrorists are going to have something impressive to buy soon. We know that the Desolated and the Blighted Brothers have worked together before—"

"They have?" Lucy asked.

Claire explained. "Nergal is a powerful creature amongst the hierarchy of What Lies Beyond, but he's not in the same league as the likes of the Pantheon. He desperately wants to have recognition and status amongst the greater demons, so he commands his servants to support the Desolated whenever they come calling, hoping it might convince Typhon and Echidna to toss a few scraps his way."

"And you think that's what's happening now?"

"Hell-flies are creatures Nergal's devotees have long bred," Lawrence explained. "In swarms, they're devastating. The creatures can decimate an entire region in days, and even if they only infect a handful of people with their larvae, it can trigger a disastrous epidemic. We cannot allow those insects or their eggs to be sold on the black market, if that's what's being arranged. I need you to go back into the sewer, check for any signs of transportation or shipping records that might indicate where eggs or live flies have been transported to. If you find anything that suggests movements to Greece, we'll know what the Blighted Brothers are up to. If not, then there may be more going on in this city than we first thought. Charles, you're going down there with Lucy and Gillian."

"Not a problem," Charles said. "After Paris, I could do with clearing my head. A few life or death fights might do just that. I'll be ready." He pushed his chair away and stalked out of the room.

"What happened?" Gillian asked in an aside to her father.

Lawrence shook his head despairingly. "I think he and Liam are just aching for a chance to square off with each other. Hopefully, he can put his pent-up aggression to use on someone I don't need to worry about offending." Lawrence sighed, pinching the bridge of his nose before turning his attention to the Mallory women. "Anne, Claire, I want you to start running tests on the eggs Lucy and Gillian brought back. Why not put our new arrivals to use? The Order's never had a chance to study what a Bane can do up close, and it might help the lad get some sense of what he is, what his purpose might be, if we can convince him to assist us. I only wish Zuberi hadn't had to leave so soon."

"And the girl?" Anne asked.

"Claire's files said she was a nurse. Maybe you can find a way to put that to use. If not, then we'll have her memory erased, move her to a safe location and I'll see if Wyndham has got some promising students who might fancy a bit more experience in a unique field. But I suspect those insects are being used by someone to prepare for something big, and I'd rather we get to the bottom of it before we're taken by surprise again."

Chapter 13: Broken and Mended

"Joshua!" Rosa called out as she roamed the upper levels of the Chapterhouse. "Where are you?"

Her uncle's ward had taken to exploring the house in the absence of anything better to do. The big African man and the priest had departed on what they said were "work-related matters", and the house's other occupants seemed to have forgotten that she and the boy were there, after completely wrecking their lives, not to mention whisking her away from Italy. She dreaded to think what her family might be thinking—by now, they'd have got wind of her uncle's death, and the fact she'd gone missing on the same night would have raised concerns.

In addition, the contents of the house creeped her out: weapons from an array of historical periods, bones and body parts from creatures that defied recognition—such as the monstrous skeleton looming over her from its cabinet, built like a gorilla, but with a dog-like skull and claws that looked like they could disembowel a man. Distracted from her search for the boy, she read the plaque at the bottom and her eyes went wide.

Skeletal remains recovered from Gévaudan, southern France c.1767.

"It can't be," she muttered as she examined the beast's chest, seeing the broken ribs that looked to be the work of bullets…

"It's authentic," a voice said from behind her.

Rosa whirled round in shock. The older woman, Anne was stood behind her, smiling gently.

Anne pointed to the skeleton. "The Beast of Gévaudan was a werewolf; one born in England and with an appetite for killing people. After our predecessors closed in on him, he fled to France and began killing anew, thinking himself safe... but his sins in this country, to say nothing of what he inflicted upon the people of Gévaudan, could not go unpunished. We tracked him down, killed him, disposed of the body and ensured that a local hunter got the credit for killing a rabid wolf, to ensure no one ever knew the truth."

"So that's what you do, is it? Cover up the truth?"

Anne shrugged her shoulders. "For centuries, we've stood on the threshold against the darkness, trying to ensure humanity is kept safe from the predators that watch—"

"You sound like the old man," Rosa said in a pugnacious tone.

Far from being offended, Anne chuckled ruefully. "I suppose he has rubbed off a bit on me, but then we've known each other since our university days."

"You seem like a normal person; how did you get mixed up in all this?"

Anne smiled. "You know, Lucy said something similar when she and I first met. Like you, my entry into all this began in tragedy. My husband, David, was a member of the Order from his youth; he and Lawrence grew up together. When he and I met and started dating at university, I had no idea he was leading a double life... until one night, when he was killed on duty. The police said it was a mugging gone bad, but I learned the truth from Lawrence. It was an ambush in the line of duty."

"So you joined up to avenge your husband's murder?" Rosa asked, sceptical.

"Do I look like a fighter to you?" Anne smirked. "I joined up because I was a single mother with a baby girl and no support. Lawrence convinced the Order to take me and Claire in, and we've been here ever since. There's more to this life than just gunfire and running for your life; I keep them up and running. And if you want to, you could still find a way to put your skills to good use. You're a nurse, right? If you know anything, I'd be grateful for a little help."

"I—I can't," Rosa protested, trying to think of an excuse to get out of it. "I need to find Joshua before—"

"If he wants to be alone, he'll find a way," Anne said blithely. "Believe me, there are plenty of places to hide in this house. Claire, Valerie and Gillian proved that when they were girls trying to get out of trouble for their latest mischief."

"Who's Valerie?" Rosa asked, confused. "I don't think I've met her."

"She was Gillian's twin sister," Anne replied sadly. "She died. Quite recently, in fact."

"I'm sorry."

"I know. I'm sorry about your uncle, too. From what Father Peter told us, he sounded like a good man."

"He was. He really believed in doing good, in serving God by example. I think that was why he helped bring Joshua to Italy. He said it was wrong for the governments of the world to deny people the rights that God gave them, to treat them as lesser beings for whatever reason. Still…" Rosa sighed. "I find it hard to believe in God after what happened to my uncle though."

"This sort of life can have that effect on you. I used to be a good Catholic, before all this made me question everything. The realisation there actually were demons out there, seeking to kill us and tear down our world, was something of a shock, particularly when I discovered that they were what killed my husband.

"As time went on, though, the things I saw and learned about the long centuries the Order of the Argent Blade have spent protecting mankind from such horrors, it gave me hope that, maybe, things weren't so dark as I thought when I stumbled into this madness like you. It's not all blood and death here; members of the Order have reverse-engineered knowledge and abilities from What Lies Beyond to improve the lives of those ignorant of our war. Not to mention, all of our members get significant benefits from being a part of our Order."

"I'm not sure I want to end up a part of all this," Rosa protested. "I mean, I need my parents to know what happened to me. They're probably worried sick about me—"

"Don't worry; they've been taken care of."

"What?!"

Anne winced at her poor choice of words. "I didn't mean it like that! Claire sent them a message via Interpol. They told your parents that your uncle was killed by human traffickers and that you were a witness to the murder, so you're in protective custody until the perpetrators can be arrested."

"What? You lied to my parents!"

"It's for your safety and theirs. If your parents knew what really happened, they would be in danger. Those we fight are determined to silence all evidence of their presence until they are in a position of strength. Their ultimate goal is to prepare their forces for open war, and they will stop at nothing, destroy anything that stands in the way. If you tell your parents that your uncle was murdered by a pack of werewolves, they'll think you're mad or lying, and worse, you'll make them a target for a kill-team to make sure that information doesn't go any further."

"Are you saying I will never see my family again?" Rosa said, her voice choking.

"No," Anne insisted. "I don't know how, but when the immediate threat has died down, we will find a way to transport you back to a safe location, and we can arrange to transport your family there to ensure their safety as well. I know this is difficult for you, but it will not be a permanent situation. Once we have ensured Joshua's safety and that no more assassins will reach him, we will make sure, if you do not wish to join the Order—and you are under no obligation to—that you are free to go without any threats to your life, and—"

Suddenly, Lawrence appeared in the doorway and cleared his throat. "Sorry, Anne, but I need this floor of the house clear tonight. I've got a meeting with a new contact, one who I'd rather keep private."

Anne gave him a suspicious look. "What are you up to, Larry?"

"Setting my affairs in order," Lawrence said simply. "Oh, and by the way, I believe you were looking for him?" he added, ushering in a contrite-looking Joshua. "I found him in my office, about to drink blood from those manti-cores my father killed back in '44."

"Well, maybe you should start locking that stuff up," Anne suggested. "Come on, Joshua; we need your help with something." She smiled warmly.

The boy came out from behind Lawrence, surprising Rosa with how well he responded to Anne.

"Come on, Joshua. We'll be working downstairs for the rest of the night," Anne said.

Rosa was about to stay put, scowling, when she felt a hand tug on her wrist. She looked down and saw Joshua giving her a nervous smile, as if urging her to come on. Despite her annoyance at her circumstances, Rosa couldn't help but return Joshua's smile.

I'm not the only one who's in strange new circumstances.

***

The Chapterhouse, 9 p.m.

"Please, be seated."

Danielle Drake nervously twisted her dyed purple hair around her fingers as she took the seat indicated by Lawrence Templeton, her mother taking the one beside her. The young witch felt trepidation. Before the battle on Samhain and the weeks leading up to it, she'd had little interaction with the Knights of the Order of the Argent Blade. Growing up, her mother and the more senior witches had liked to terrorise the younger girls into behaving with stories of the Knights as boogeymen who'd cut off the heads of misbehaving witches with silver blades. When she'd gotten older, Danielle had learned the Knights were more akin to a police force, helping to maintain the balance that ensured those untouched by the supernatural remained blissfully ignorant of the shadowy conflict being waged all around them since time immemorial.

As Lawrence sat down, Danielle considered him. He was lean and clearly still looked after himself, though as he sank into his chair, he grimaced and winced. *Age must be catching up with him.*

"Are you alright?" Danielle couldn't help but ask.

He shook his head. "Sadly, even your magic or that of your sisters can't do anything about it now," he replied softly, his eyes staring off into the distance, before he returned his attention to the two women. "I had wanted to speak to you alone, Miss Drake, but your mother insisted—"

"Even if she weren't my daughter, I would have insisted on being here," Angela snapped. "As mistress of my coven, it is my business to ensure her safety and make sure she doesn't fall afoul of any who might seek to manipulate her magic for ignoble purposes."

"I am not Nathaniel Danvers," Lawrence replied pointedly. "I am not trying to corrupt your girls away from the coven's teachings, nor to violate the Salem Compact. My desire is to ensure that they can put their magical talents to better use, if they so wish. Danielle Drake"—Lawrence turned his attention to the young woman—"we all saw what you are capable of during the battle on Halloween night. Your spells saved some of my Knights from dying. We have lost brothers and sisters in arms, and their places needed to be filled. Many daughters of covens have risen to prominence, have become legends the Order holds dearly in our storied history, and I don't say this lightly, but I reckon you have the potential to rise high, given what I saw."

Danielle was genuinely surprised, but not displeased. The praise was enough to make her preen a little.

"Thank you for the compliment. I must say, I've always wanted to put my gift to greater use, and given what I saw on Halloween, the hunting and destruction of demons seems like a good way to…"

Danielle fell silent as Lawrence raised a hand to interrupt. "I appreciate your candour, and your talents would be a useful addition to the Order of the Argent Blade, but I didn't solely bring you here for that. There is more that I need to tell you," he added, giving Angela a concerned look.

The elder witch sighed and shrugged her shoulders. "I won't deny a dying man his last wish."

Danielle looked between her mother and Lawrence, completely confused. "Er, if you two want to start making sense anytime soon?"

Lawrence took a deep breath. "A long time ago, I was working a mission in Eastern Europe. One of the coven had gone renegade; she killed a dozen of her sisters along with a number of civilians, then fled to the other side of the Iron Curtain, hoping to evade justice there. A team of witches were assembled, but they needed assistance, and I was one of several Knights who were offered to assist the hunt. During the mission, one of the young women assigned to the hunt and I became close. A combination of the adrenaline, the close calls, saving each other's lives… Well, one thing led to another…"

"Yeah, spare me the gritty details," Danielle said, raising a hand. "Can you just get to the part that's relevant to me?"

"We succeeded in tracking down and killing the rogue witch. My paramour from the covens and I returned to England and went our separate ways, until six months after our return, she contacted me and asked for a meeting. She told me that she'd given birth to a daughter on December second, 1996."

Danielle froze. *It can't be.*

"She insisted that, in keeping with her coven's traditions, she be allowed to raise her daughter without any input from the father. I agreed, rather unthinkingly. I could have refused, insisted I play a bigger part in my child's life, but I took the easy way out and cut myself out of my daughter's life. But now, the time has come to admit my past, and acknowledge who I am. Danielle Drake, I am your father."

"What?" Danielle said, utterly dismayed. She looked to her mother, who simply nodded in confirmation.

"What?" a baleful voice snarled from behind them.

Gillian Templeton was stood in the kitchen doorway, wearing an angry look as sparks crackled in her palms. Charles and Lucy were behind her, agape. All three looked like they'd been in one hell of a battle, but Gillian's expression suggested she was more than ready to start another one.

"Care to explain yourself, Father?"

Chapter 14: The Rotten Depths
3 hours earlier

The sloshing of fuel tanks filled Lucy's ears as they traversed the disused tunnels under Whitechapel. Moira and Edmund's mercenaries were leading the way, some carrying flamethrowers, others lugging canisters of petrol to be ignited when they reached their target.

"You sure about this?" she asked.

The vampires both gave her a cold look.

"Has our information ever been wrong, lassie?" Moira said.

Lucy bit her lip to keep from making a retort. The Daltons had been insistent that one of their agents, an exterminator hired to clear out vermin in the tunnels of the London Underground, had uncovered signs of an insect infestation like nothing he'd seen before. Whatever Edmund and Moira had uncovered when they'd gone to investigate for themselves had worried them enough to call in the Order. When one of their people had turned up at the Chapterhouse, the message delivered had been: "Send everything you can spare. This is big."

"We think we've found another nest, close to the one we raided," Edmund, looking none the worse for wear after his last close encounter with their foe, had explained, when Lucy, Gillian and Charles had arrived at the Daltons' residence to find the house packed to the rafters with armed men. Lucy was surprised that the Daltons had so many men to call upon, but Moira had explained they were a gift.

Probably from Siobhan, Lucy thought. Their adopted daughter, from what Charles had implied, was owed favours by many Othersiders. Clearly among her debtors were private military contractors willing to pay their debts with warm bodies to send into battle.

"We expect to face heavy resistance," Moira had bluntly stated. "The Knights of Yersinia aren't something I've encountered before, but I know their reputation, what they're capable of, so I won't take chances. We get in, we plant the explosives and flammables, and then we burn the place down!"

"Perhaps not everything," Gillian had tried to interject. "Claire and Anne are trying to collect hell-fly larvae and eggs for study."

The vampires had shrugged and conceded the point.

"You want to save something for study, by all means feel free," Edmund had said. "But that nest is getting razed to ash; I won't allow those demonic bugs to infect those we keep watch over. When it's done, you need to find where the knights are based and kill them in one fell swoop, not to mention who's providing them with what they need—I refuse to believe they're doing this on their own initiative."

For a good mile, they'd been following a side tunnel that broke off from the District Line, close to where the Daltons' informant had made his discovery. Gobbets of filthy slime clung to the walls, and the stench of rotting meat was getting stronger the further they went. After their close encounter the previous night, Lucy wasn't looking forward to what they might find, particularly if the Blighted Brothers were waiting ahead.

It was hard enough putting down one of those brutes. If there's more than one at the end of this... Lucy clenched the handle of the kukri at her belt. The only thing that consoled her was the fact they had the advantage of numbers.

"Still so nervous? You're better than you think, so stop worrying!"

Lucy's head jerked up. She could have sworn she heard someone laughing.

"Who's doing that?"

"Doing what?" Edmund instantly went on guard.

"Laughing."

The others looked at her as if she were joking.

"No one's laughing, Lucy," Charles said. "Hearing voices?" he asked, an unmistakable sneer in his voice.

Lucy gave him a baleful look, but before she could retort, Moira interjected.

"Maybe you're getting static over your radio? Anyone else?" she asked the mercenaries, all of whom shook their heads and muttered dismissals.

Lucy tensed again, the laughter ringing in her ears unmistakable. It wasn't a demented cackle or choking gurgle like she might have expected; it was good natured, as if the one laughing was happy to see her. Strangest of all, it sounded familiar.

"Valerie?"

"What was that, love?" Gillian asked, and Lucy hastily shook her head. That was the last thing she needed to say to her lover.

"Nothing. It's most likely just interference," she said with a dismissive shrug.

Gillian didn't look convinced but didn't choose to pursue the issue.

Lucy frowned to herself. While, like the others, she'd mourned for Valerie, it had been as a comrade in arms—she'd not been that close to the elder Templeton sister. *It could be just stress... but if it is something more, why would she come to me?*

"Enough," Edmund snapped. "We've got more important things to do. We need to get as far in as we can before we're discovered. Once the enemy knows we're here, they're going to fight tooth and nail."

The tunnel floor suddenly came to an end at the lip of a gaping hole, descending into the bowels of the earth.

"Down the hole?" Lucy commented. "Anyone remember what happened the last time we did that?"

Charles and Gillian didn't respond to her attempts to lighten the mood, but Edmund shrugged his shoulders.

"You knew what the job entailed. We'll go first. If there's anything down there, we'll let you know."

The two vampires descended into the darkness. The others waited with bated breath, expecting to hear a firefight erupt.

After two minutes that seemed to stretch for eternity, they heard Moira's voice call out. "All clear! Come on down!"

The Knights and the mercenaries began to descend into the hole, though they used ropes and harnesses to safely descend, lacking the benefit of vampiric physiology to cushion the landing. The cavern below was pitch dark, and the strike team quickly ignited torches and flares to illuminate their surroundings, the light casting shadows across rough-hewn walls. Lucy sniffed the air and promptly gagged in disgust, as did the others; the stench of rotten meat was overpowering.

"Helmets on, people," she said. "We've no idea what kind of filth is down here. Who knows what toxic shit we could be breathing in."

The mercenaries hastily complied, as did Gillian and Charles, though she noticed a sullen look on Charles's face before it was covered by his breathing mask. *Does he resent that Lawrence put me in charge?* She knew Charles had once considered himself the de facto leader of the Order in the field, and if he thought he'd been passed over by the leadership…

I'll deal with it later. For now, we've got a mission.

"Moira, Edmund, what way should we go?" she asked.

The two vampires sniffed the air, then pointed to the left.

"Smell seems to be stronger in that direction," Edmund answered.

Lucy nodded and then turned to address the others.

"Safeties off, ladies and gentlemen. From this point on, assume all contacts to be hostile. Shoot to kill."

A flurry of affirmative noises came, and the strike team followed behind the Daltons, the two vampires like hounds on a scent. The tunnel kept on going, and periodically, they could see gobbets of sickly green slime plastered to the walls, as if someone were leaving a trail to follow. After about half an hour, they came to an immense cavern, three paths lying ahead.

"Which way do we go?" Lucy muttered as the strike team waited for orders.

Moira and Edmund sniffed the air, their faces contorting in confusion.

"The scent is coming from all three tunnels, but I can't tell if they all lead to our destination, or if this is a false trail, lassie," Moira said grimly. "Do we split up, try and see which way they go, then reunite further in?"

"I'm leery of splitting up. We have no way of knowing how far these tunnels go, and even with tracking beacons, there's no guarantee we'd be able to link up further in. I'd rather have the advantage of numbers here—"

"Prepare yourself."

The voice came again in Lucy's head.

"We've got incoming," she said, at the same moment Edmund cocked his head and said the same. The vampire gave her a surprised look, but there was no time to dwell on it.

"Form up, take cover!" Lucy snapped, and the mercenaries and her comrades raised their weapons. Lucy kept her Glock raised, eyes darting between each of the three tunnel entrances.

"I think I've got something," a mercenary to Lucy's left said, staring down the scope of his rifle. "Switching to—"

He never finished his sentence. A flurry of bullets erupted from the left tunnel. One punctured the cables of the man's breathing mask and slammed into his throat. He toppled, blood spurting from his torn neck.

"Medic!" Lucy shouted.

Gillian crawled over as Lucy raised her head and shouted a command.

"Fire at will!"

Pandemonium erupted as the strike team returned fire. Lucy flung a flare close to the mouths of the three tunnels, illuminating in harsh red light, human figures in black and green hooded robes charging into battle, firing automatic weapons. She threw an explosive knife at one of the front-runners. He fell forward, the knife buried in his chest, before it detonated, sending chunks of his body flying, buffeting and tripping his comrades. Unlike the Blighted Brothers, these were a familiar sight.

"Desolated!" Charles snarled as he pulled his Glock and started shooting.

Edmund and Moira's mercenaries traded fire with the cultists, but the Desolated, their skull masks instantly recognisable, fought with the ferocity of wasps defending their nest, and there were plenty of them, negating the strike team's numbers.

"Burn!" Gillian screamed, blasting the tunnels with fire from the palms of her hands.

A half dozen black-robed figures collapsed, flailing and shrieking as they burned.

"How can there be so many?" Lucy bellowed as she shot another cultist in the throat. "I thought our Samhain purges should have sent a message—"

Suddenly, she was bowled over, tackled around the waist. Charles loomed over her, his eyes angry, while a fusillade of bullets tore through the air above their heads.

"Less thinking, more killing!" he snarled. "Worry about how they got here when they're beaten!"

Getting off her, Charles pulled the zweihänder off his back and ran his hand along the length of the blade. Pale white flames kindled to life as his blood touched the ancient, sanctified steel.

"Covering fire!" he bellowed.

The mercenaries took his order and let loose a flurry of fire into the enemy.

Suddenly, something round and metal landed at Lucy's feet—a grenade, which suddenly began spewing thick white smoke. Loud thuds told her similar such missiles were landing all around the strike team.

"Gillian, clear this!" she shouted into her helmet.

"On it!"

She heard a sound like a huge intake of breath, but then something came charging out of the mist. Arms wrapped around her waist and tackled her hard to the ground. Boots kicked her, and she hastily covered her head with her arms, when suddenly she heard a shriek and one of the two figures looming over was jerked away. The other froze, and Lucy didn't give them a chance to recover. She slammed her booted foot into the cultist's knee, knocking them down, then drove her kukri through their throat. She pulled her blade free and the cultist pitched backwards, the skull mask falling off to reveal the face of a teenage boy, desperately trying to stem the blood pouring between his fingers.

What lies did they dupe you with to make you their willing servant? Lucy wondered as she watched the young man die, all possibilities he could have had slipping away in a red tide.

Suddenly, there was a roar of air, and the smoke fogging their position was blasted back at the Desolated by Gillian's talents. As the smoke cleared, Lucy saw her saviour— Moira, pulling her teeth from the neck of a dead cultist, her mouth and chin stained with blood.

The Order's forces had not had it all their own way. At least half a dozen mercenaries had been mobbed and killed by the cultists under cover of the smoke, but now the cultists were being enveloped, and the tide was turning. Dancing flashes of white light could only be Charles hacking through enemies with the Champion's Blade, and shrieks accompanied by bestial howls implied Edmund was taking advantage of the situation.

As Gillian continued to manipulate the air to blow the smoke away, Lucy saw Charles in the thick of the fray. His mask had been knocked loose, and his face was set in a snarl. A half dozen cultists surrounded him, but it was as if he couldn't feel their blows. A fist slammed into his jaw; he drove his sword through the cultist's belly. Another slammed the butt of his rifle into the side of Charles's face; he spun on his heel, using the blow's momentum to add force to his next cut, all but bisecting the one responsible. The cultists gave ground before Charles's fury, and the mercenaries seized the opportunity, sniping them down with precise shots.

Having encountered stiffer resistance than they'd expected, the demoralised cultists began to slowly but steadily retreat back to the tunnels.

"Fall back, fall back!" one skull-masked cultist shouted, just before their head parted company with their neck thanks to Edmund's claws.

"Keep shooting!" Lucy bellowed, while the mercenaries flung incendiary grenades at the tunnel entrances, trying to stop the cultists from fleeing and warning their comrades further in.

That was when things went wrong.

As Lucy watched, a hulking figure emerged from each tunnel. They strode through the fire as if it were mist, trampling any luckless cultist who got in their way.

Oh bollocks.

The three of them were every bit as repulsive as the one Lucy had killed. The first obliterated the face of a wailing female cultist with a backswing from his rusted mace, while the second barged his way through cultists, his gut so ponderous and bloated by noxious gases it was astonishing his armour was holding. He wielded a pair of curved swords with notched and rusted blades which dripped black filth that hissed and smoked as it touched the ground.

The third's helmet had split to expose his mutilated lower face, insectile mandibles clicking and snapping. His body was riddled with other such mutations. Cancerous swellings of pallid flesh festooned with buboes had forced their way through his armour, while horny growths of bone had erupted from his spine and shoulders. His right arm was swollen with muscle, clutching a sword as long as a man's arm. The weapon was as pale as sun-bleached bone and looked horrifically organic, like it had been grown rather than forged, its length pockmarked with dozens of miniscule holes that leaked pale green filth.

His left arm was much smaller, held close against the brute's chest, and in place of a hand, it was tipped with a bony, mantis-like claw. Lucy was quickly robbed of any hope that attacking the left side might give an advantage as the smaller limb lashed out, whip-like, and beheaded a fleeing cultist. The creature raised the claw to its mouth, a proboscis darting out to slurp off the blood, and then pointed its sword at the enemy.

"No retreat." Its words reverberated like a fly's buzzing wings. "No mercy. All interlopers will die and feed the nest's growth. Your master commanded your obedience to our brotherhood, now serve! For your masters and ours, kill them all!"

"Take them down!" Lucy yelled, firing at the mutated knight's helmet.

The mercenaries opened up with their rifles. Bullets ricocheted off rusted and stained armour or punctured bloated, rotten flesh with spurts of blood. With a roar and a scream, Charles hurled himself into the fray. White flames danced on the Champion's Blade as he slashed and hacked at anything that got too close, Gillian flinging bolts of flame and lightning into the enemy.

Suddenly, they heard a scream. The plague knight with the mace had reached one of the mercenaries armed with a flamethrower. The man, setting ablaze a pack of cultists trying to flank the strike team, hadn't been able to turn to defend himself before the knight seized his throat and snapped his neck. The wet crunch of bone made Lucy snarl as she took aim and fired at the fuel tanks on the dead man's back.

"Take cover!" Lucy shouted, waiting for her comrades to get clear before she took her shot.

The fuel tanks detonated with an almighty explosion. The Knight of Yersinia staggered back from the blast, drenched in burning fuel that soon had his flesh and skin melting like candle wax. Moira, at the centre of a ring of dead cultists with her husband, saw her opportunity.

"Gillian!" she shouted.

Gillian channelled another gust of wind, putting out the flames coating the Knight so the vampire wouldn't be at risk. Despite his ponderous bulk, the Blighted Brother was still sent staggering, and with a bestial howl, Moira sprinted forward and leapt, wrapping her legs around the monster's neck. Roaring, they toppled to the ground, Moira atop the Blighted Brother. Her fingers seized the base of the plague knight's helmet and pulled. With a horrific sound of metal and flesh tearing, the front of the helmet came away in Moira's hands. The vampire hissed in disgust; in ripping away the helmet, she'd also torn off his face, leaving a mutilated skull drenched in filth and pus-riddled blood, jaundiced eyes rolling in their sockets.

Moira's hesitation cost her. The Knight vomited black filth into her face, and she shrieked. Lucy looked round and recoiled in horror. Moira's face looked horrifically burned, pale white skin sloughing off to reveal dark muscle and bone. Edmund shouted for two mercenaries to pull his wife to safety, seizing the shotgun from the hand of one and shooting Moira's attacker in the face. The Knight roared as his jaw was blasted away, but more from annoyance than pain.

"Fall back! Fall back!" Lucy bellowed, shooting another cultist in the throat.

Charles hacked one in half and cut the legs of another off at the knee.

"No!" Edmund shouted back. "If we retreat now, this nest will keep churning out larvae! We have to destroy it!"

"Lawrence put me in command, Ed!" Lucy shot back, ducking behind a column of rock as bullets cut through the air.

She poked her head from cover and spotted a bloated figure stalking towards her. Lucy fired her Glock, but to no avail. The bullets ricocheted off dull green armour spotted with rust. Lucy ducked instinctively as the serrated, insectile left arm slashed out, cutting through air; had she not moved, it would have torn her throat out.

"Know your death comes at the hands of Brother Trypanos, honoured brother and servant to—"

The plague knight's pompous boasting abruptly came to an end as a pale white blade punched through his left shoulder. He roared in fury as the flames wreathing the zweihänder burned him, but he managed to focus through the pain.

"Not very chivalrous, boy!" the Blighted Brother snarled as he swung over his shoulder with his unholy sword.

Charles darted back, pulling his sword free, but Trypanos spun around and Charles cried out in pain as the bony blade sliced across his triceps. Lucy grimaced as she saw blood running down his arm, his guard a little lower.

I just hope our mark protects him from whatever diseased filth is on that thing!

"Let me teach this boy true chivalry, worthy of a knight," a burbling voice called out—the Blighted Brother with the twin swords.

"Nay, Brother Ebolae." The third, wielding the rusted mace. "Such a craven foe does not deserve a worthy end! We tear him apart together!"

"Agreed," Trypanos snarled, his voice tainted by insectile buzzing.

Charles raised his zweihänder. "Lucy, do what needs to be done! I'll keep these ugly bastards busy!"

"Charles, no!" Lucy tried to protest. "I don't need a hero—"

"Go!" Charles snapped as he kept his gaze on Trypanos.

Lucy watched Ebolae and the third, unnamed knight stalking up on him from behind.

"Charles, I'm in charge! You have to—"

Whatever order she was about to speak never came. With a roar, Ebolae lifted his visor and spat a globule of black slime at her. Lucy ducked and shot him in the face before he could close his visor. Ebolae staggered back, spitting black filth.

The mace-wielding knight turned to face her, and Lucy's hand went to her waist. Quick as lightning, her silver, barbed whip lashed out, ripping through the rusted metal of the helm. Charles seized his moment and flung himself at Trypanos, but the bony blade rose to parry the zweihänder with a crack. Loath as she was to leave Charles to it, Lucy forced herself to analyse the situation.

The Knights of Yersinia had emboldened the cultists, and more were pouring out of the tunnels with every moment. Fewer than half a dozen mercenaries remained, and they were embattled. Gillian had been forced into the fray, back to back with Edmund. Standing over the badly hurt Moira, he struck out with his claws and bit out the throat of any who got into reach. At close quarters, Gillian's spear was practically useless, and she cast it aside, her palms glowing orange as her fingers curled into claws. With a keening howl, she thrust out her hands and shouted in Gaelic. Serpentine torrents of flame speared into the charging cultists, coiling around them and igniting their clothing. Others died as Gillian's fires darted out, cobra-quick, to lash ammunition and grenades at their belts and blow them to bits. Some of the cultists tried to charge, thinking Gillian might be an easy target, but to their shock, she clapped her hands together and the flames lengthened into spectral blades of dancing fire.

With a shriek, Gillian flung herself into the fray, slashing and hacking with abandon, her face contorted into a snarl of rage. Any who got in the way of the fiery swords never had a chance. One woman fell to her knees screaming as Gillian sliced off both her arms at the elbows, the wounds cauterised in the same blow. Gillian didn't even bother to finish her off, striding forward to slice through the rifle of another cultist and carve a fiery X into his chest, before pivoting on her heel and decapitating another cultist.

"We won't make it to the nest!" Lucy shouted as she fought her way over to their diminishing forces. "Edmund, how good is your throwing arm?"

"Been a while since I played cricket! Why?"

"Reckon you can fling this over all their heads to there?" Holding up a satchel packed with explosives, she pointed at the mouth of the central tunnel, held up by two rock pillars.

"Only one way to find out!" Edmund said with a shrug. He motioned for the satchel, while Lucy turned to Gillian.

"The second it hits the ground, you blow it up!" Lucy ordered as she pulled her burning blades out of the belly of another cultist.

Gillian nodded, one of her blades contorting into an orb of flame, when suddenly a scream of pain caught their attention. It was Charles, and he was in really bad shape. The Knights of Yersinia were *toying* with him. Every time he flung himself at one of them, the foe in front of him held him in place while the others pricked and sliced at him with their weapons. None of their strikes were fatal, but Charles was clearly weakening, his guard sinking a little more after every failed attack, his parries and attacks a little slower.

He's still alive only because they're enjoying their sport, Lucy knew. *As soon as they get bored...*

"Back off!" Gillian shrieked, flinging fireballs at the Knights of Yersinia. It didn't seem to have any effect, save distracting her.

"Gillian, on your left!" Edmund shouted.

She turned just in time to take a rifle butt to the face. As she toppled and Lucy shrieked her name, Edmund leapt over her, seized her attacker by the throat and pulled. The man collapsed, leaving his windpipe in Edmund's grasp. Brother Ebolae and the mace-wielder were distracted, trying to pat out the minor fires Gillian had started on their oily skin, and Charles flung himself at Brother Trypanos with all his strength. With a roar of fury and a spurt of black blood, Trypanos's insectile claw of a left arm fell to the cave floor.

Charles gave a cry of satisfaction, only to retreat as Trypanos's sword sliced at his throat. The blade's tip missed his neck by inches as a stentorian voice bellowed from behind him.

"Witness me now, brothers!"

Charles turned in the nick of time as Ebolae brought both of his blades slicing down. Holding the Champion's Blade in both hands, he parried the strike, but Ebolae's strength was incredible and the zweihänder clattered to the floor as Charles lost his grip. He rolled under a cut of the blades aimed at his head, recovered the Champion's Blade and lunged. The burning white metal punched his swollen foe's belly and emerged from his back.

To Charles's astonishment and horror, the Blighted Brother showed no discomfort at the fact that a metre of blazing steel was burning his intestines from the inside out. Instead, the knight growled and started choking. Charles gagged as stinking green vomit oozed from the knight's visor, dripping onto the Champion's Blade.

"On your right!" Lucy shouted, and Charles turned as Trypanos projectile-vomited at him, another stream of tainted filth almost drowning out the flames of his sword.

It could just have been Lucy's imagination, but she swore she could see glowing cracks appearing down the blade of the zweihänder…

"First we break your weapons, and then we break *you*!" the mace-wielding knight bellowed as he brought his weapon crashing down.

Charles was sent staggering back, clutching an ornately detailed hilt and a broken, six-inch long spike of metal as, with a clang like the toll of a bell, the Champion's Blade was shattered. He watched in horror as the ravaged visage of his foe twisted into a monstrous smile, before the mace smashed into his chest, knocking him off his feet. The brute pounded his chest with a fist and raised his mace above his head, ready to bring it smashing down—

"Oi, bastards!"

One of Lucy's explosive knives hit the knight in the chest, and Charles hastily covered himself as it detonated. The force of the blast sent the trio of diseased knights staggering back, and Lucy nodded to Edmund, who flung the cache of explosives.

"Charles!" she shouted.

This time, he obeyed her, drawing his pistol and shooting. The satchel detonated, and with a thunderous cacophony, the pillars supporting the tunnel entrances began to crack and collapse.

"Back to the nest!" Trypanos bellowed, he and his diseased brethren hobbling away, clearly not caring if the cultists got clear or not.

The force of the explosion sent chunks of the cavern roof falling, crushing anyone below. Even worse, the cave floor seemed to be more fragile than they'd first thought. As the ceiling collapsed, the falling pieces smashed gaping holes to swallow more panicking cultists.

"Fall back!" Lucy shouted to the survivors of the raid.

Edmund hauled his wife onto his shoulder while one of the mercenaries helped the dazed Gillian up. As Lucy turned, Charles scooped up the wreckage of the Champion's Blade and shouldered his way through the panicking cultists. She heard an ominous crack from above.

"Charles, look out!"

Charles managed to dive clear as the falling boulder hit where he'd been a second earlier, but as he got back up, the ground gave way beneath his feet, a gargantuan crevasse opening as more and more of the collapsing ceiling smashed the floor below. Lucy lashed out with her whip, wrapping around Charles's left arm as he desperately tried to cling on.

"Hang on, I've got you!" she insisted, straining to pull him back from the void, when she heard a crack from above and looked up.

"Oh shit."

An enormous stalactite broke from the ceiling and fell towards her like a spear. Lucy flung herself out of the way, cursing as she realised what she'd done and heard Charles scream as he went plummeting into the void, but then the ground caved in beneath her, and she was screaming as well as she too plunged into the abyss.

Chapter 15: Unexpected Help

"Lucy, come on! Get up!"

The sound of Charles's voice, combined with a slap to her face, brought her around. She shook her head groggily, wincing as the pain of a dozen scrapes and bruises hit her all at once.

"Well, if you're here, I know this isn't heaven," Lucy opined with a raised eyebrow. "And since there's not enough flames for this to be hell, I'm going to assume we're still in the land of the living."

"Oh ha, ha." Charles flipped Lucy off as she pulled herself to her feet.

He winced as she slammed her fist into his shoulder.

"What the hell was that for?"

"You trying to get yourself killed?!" she snapped, furious. "I gave you a damn order not to engage them all by yourself, but what do you do? You go charging in like Rambo, trying to be the glorious hero, and nearly get yourself hacked to bits! You're lucky we were able to salvage this!"

"Salvage this?" Charles scoffed, his expression disdainful. "Yeah, you *really* salvaged this! Half our team lost before we even got close to our objective, not to mention you've now alerted those defending the main site to the fact we know they're here, which probably means by the time we've regrouped, they'll have moved their facilities and we won't have the first fucking clue where! Bravo, Lucy, bravo! I really can't wait to hear you explain this to Lawrence!"

"Are you implying I'm not fit to lead?" Lucy snarled.

"Not implying. Outright saying."

Lucy rose to her full height and shoved Charles back with all her strength.

"Well maybe if you stopped trying to drink yourself into an early grave and moping around the Chapterhouse feeling sorry for yourself, Lawrence wouldn't have to turn to me!" Lucy shot back. "You're not the only one missing Valerie!"

"Don't," Charles snapped, pointing a finger. "Don't—"

"Or what? What are you going to do?"

"Yes," a reverberating voice whispered from behind them. "I would like to see that too."

They both whirled round. It was Brother Trypanos. He hadn't survived the cave-in unscathed; his pallid skin was torn and bloodied, weeping dark blood and pus from multiple wounds. He was limping, his head bent at an awkward angle and his armour crushed and rent in places while the maimed stump of his left arm bled stinking ichor, but he was still shambling towards them, his bony sword drawn.

"Why aren't you dead?" Lucy demanded, pointing at the Blighted Brother with her kukri.

She heard a rasp as Charles drew his, their brief animosity put aside in the face of the new threat. Lucy found it strange to see him without the Champion's Blade in hand. *What will we do now? Something powerful enough to destroy so sacred an artefact... What can we do to oppose that?*

Trypanos laughed gutturally. "Your predecessors couldn't kill me and my brethren when they brought an entire castle crashing down on our heads. Did you really think you would have a chance with a few little bombs?"

"Fine," Lucy snarled. "Let me cut your head off, see if that works!"

Trypanos laughed again, the hideous sound grating on their nerves. "I'm not so big a fool as Brother Paramyx. And even in your weakened condition, I can't really afford the delay if you somehow succeed, so…"

The Knight of Yersinia began to heave and choke. Black filth spilled out through the grill of his helmet, and they wrinkled their noses at the stench of rotted meat. Worse, small white shapes squirmed and writhed amidst the spreading pool of black sludge—pallid maggots crawling towards the other dead bodies in the chamber. From the passage behind Trypanos, insectile buzzing and clicking grew louder and louder. Dozens of glowing yellow eyes materialised from the dark behind Trypanos as the Blighted Brother spread his arms, summoning them to his side.

One of the Daltons' mercenaries lay dead amongst the dozens of bodies that littered the chamber. Lucy grabbed a flare from the corpse's belt, ignited it and flung it at Trypanos's feet, illuminating the chamber with flickering red light. Lucy and Charles grimaced as they saw the creatures at his flanks.

Adult hell-flies. Each one was the size of a lion, covered in bristling spines. Clicking mandibles dripped poisonous slime, staring yellow eyes sighted fresh prey. Trypanos snapped his fingers at the heaps of corpses from the battle above and let out a series of clicks and snarls. The flies stalked towards them, the closest one sinking its mandibles into the chest of one of the corpses… and then, to Lucy's horror, the body started twitching.

"Okay, fuck this!" she snarled.

Checking her waist, she saw she had two of the explosive knives left. She flung one at the fly on top of the heap; it hit the creature's thorax and detonated. Trypanos roared in fury and stalked towards them, while the other flies screeched and sank their jaws into the corpses. With a flurry of buzzing, more poured into the chamber.

"Lucy, run!" Charles bellowed, trying to push her behind him as Trypanos advanced, sword raised.

Lucy pulled him back as he tried to charge. "Stop trying to be a fucking hero! It really doesn't suit you," she hissed, lashing out with her whip.

The barbed whip slashed across the exposed flesh of Trypanos's arm, leaving a deep red gouge mark.

"You think that's going to stop me, girl?" the monstrous brute sneered.

He growled again, and Lucy saw movement in the corner of her eye. She barely managed to turn before one of the monstrous bugs was on her, crushing her; Lucy just got her hands up in time to stop the snapping mandibles from slicing open her throat. She could hear the clash of blades and guessed Charles was too busy throwing himself at Trypanos to give her any help. The demonic insect's snapping jaws were getting closer and closer...

"Get back!"

The familiar voice shouted again, accompanied by a blinding flash of light. The hell-fly screeched, disorientated by the sudden burst of illumination, and Lucy heard a cry from Trypanos, then a wet thud of something cutting into meat. The demonic insect reared off her, shaking its head in confusion, and Lucy seized her opening. She slashed up with her kukri. The monstrous fly's buzzing reached a crescendo as her blade connected with the right side of its head, bursting its eyes like pustules. Lucy gagged as she got a face full of stinking ichor.

"Oh that is fucking disgusting!" she cursed, only for her eyes to go wide as the creature flung itself at her with a shriek of fury.

Lucy rolled away and its mandibles snapped shut on air. She scrambled to her feet, trying to drive it back with her blade—

Suddenly, a cacophony of shots rang out and the hell-fly reared up, keening in pain. Charles had emptied a full clip of bullets into the insect's back. Chancing a look, Lucy saw Trypanos was shoving his entrails back into a gaping wound across his belly. She doubted it would slow him down for long, but it would give them an opening. Charles's gun clicked empty, and Lucy's blood ran cold.

The other hell-flies were working their way through the corpses around the cavern, biting with their mandibles and then moving on. The reason why quickly became apparent. More and more dead cultists—and to their horror, some of Moira and Edmund's men—were dragging themselves back to their feet and stalking after the two Knights. Their movements were slow and herky-jerk, but they already outnumbered the pair and more were getting up, and Lucy didn't want to think about what diseases they were carrying. One of the cultists ripped back his hood, and Lucy's gorge rose as insectile mandibles pushed their way out of his mouth and a long, barbed tongue whipped the air.

The Knight of Yersinia staggered back to his feet and, pointing a finger that was mostly exposed bone and meat at the pair, growled to his new troops, "Kill them."

"Run," Lucy hissed.

Charles didn't have to be told twice. Having quickly reloaded his gun, he fired, sending one of the insectile zombies staggering back. Its flailing arms knocked down a number of its brood, buying the pair a few seconds. They ran, Charles firing over his shoulder every time a mutated head came into view.

"Unless you can magically replenish your ammo, you're just wasting bullets!" Lucy yelled. "We need to find a way to turn the odds in our favour and—oh shit!"

She threw out her hands just in time to shove away another diseased zombie charging at her from a side tunnel. She slashed out with her kukri, but the mutant darted back and slapped the blade away, sending it clattering to the floor. Its clawed fingers went for Lucy's throat, slamming her back into the wall, hard. The moaning and groaning of the horde was getting closer.

Suddenly, blood stinking with corruption hit her in the face. The zombie's grip loosened around her neck, and Lucy saw it had been one of the Daltons' mercenaries, a belt of grenades wrapped around his chest and Charles's kukri buried to the handle in its brain.

"I'll be borrowing this." She pulled the blade out of the dead monster's skull, slashed through the belt and ran with it as the monster fell forward.

Two more of its ilk came shambling after them. Charles put a bullet apiece in their heads and kept sprinting through tunnels that looked to have been carved more than excavated. Rumbling footsteps got closer and closer, as if more and more were joining the pursuit.

How many are down here?

Suddenly, Charles stopped running, snatching his kukri back from Lucy and going en garde.

"Keep following the tunnel, I'll hold them here, maybe buy you some time to get back to the surface."

"It's fucking suicide!" Lucy protested. "I'm not going to let you throw your life away—"

"You don't get a say!" Charles snapped back, but Lucy gave him a baleful glare.

"I'm in command here, Charles Pryce, and I am *ordering* you to fall back!"

"Fuck off!" Charles snarled, throwing Lucy's hand off his shoulder as she tried to pull him away.

The pair of them rounded on each other like snarling dogs, oblivious to all but each other, the moaning of the horde a sidenote even as it got closer. Lucy's fingers curled into a fist, wondering if she could knock him out with a single blow...

"Enough! This behaviour does not behove Knights of our Order! You bicker like children in the face of the enemy and forget your greater duty, that we fight not for personal glory, but the safety of mankind against the demonic scourge! Would you let your pride and arrogance let your brethren go into battle undermanned and unprepared?!"

Their anger and frustration bled away in an instant. They'd both heard the same voice bellowing in their ears as if the speaker were stood right beside them, and it was one they recognised.

"Did you...?" Charles asked, his tone incredulous, eyes wide in disbelief.

"Look out!" Lucy shouted, shooting over his shoulder, and the head of another insectile zombie snapped back in a spray of black filth. "Maybe discuss this later?"

His earlier anger forgotten, Charles nodded and they ran on.

The pair kept running until they came to a large chamber with a single pillar supporting the roof. The horde was getting closer. Thinking quickly, Lucy tossed the belt of grenades at the foot of the pillar as the frontrunners of the horde entered the chamber.

"Move it!" Lucy shouted at Charles who, for once, obeyed and kept sprinting down the passage.

As Lucy caught sight of the Blighted Brother lumbering after them, barging his way through the crowd, she depressed the arming stud on her last throwing knife and flung it. The blade embedded itself in the rock just above the grenades. Lucy gave Trypanos a grin and a raised middle finger, then dived out of the chamber just as the explosive knife detonated. She landed in Charles's outstretched arms, and he spun her around, shielding her from the blast as, with an almighty grinding, the chamber ceiling caved in, the monsters shrieking as they were crushed beneath chunks of stone and earth.

Once the bedlam had come to a stop, Lucy looked up over Charles's shoulder. The chamber they'd fled from was completely sealed. It would take the enemy a long time to dig through, and Charles and Lucy would be gone by then.

I hope.

"Nice work." Charles slapped her on the shoulder.

Lucy gave him a cold look. "Are you actually complimenting me on a job well done, after nothing but shit all the way through this?"

Charles's smile, caught up in the heat of the moment, became a scowl. "Don't get used to it." He promptly became more practical. "Still, that should buy us some time to get out of here."

"Any ideas how?" Lucy asked. "We are a good few miles underground, and I doubt that will hold them forever. For all we know, they've excavated tunnels all under this city. They could bore into the Underground, move through the lines and spread whatever kind of disease in half the boroughs of London before we'd even have a chance of containment!"

"*Lucy...*" a soft voice whispered.

Lucy whirled on her heel, but there was nothing there.

"*Lucy...*"

Lucy spun again, blade raised.

"Valerie?! Is that you?" Lucy called out, but there was no answer.

Instead, she saw a sudden gleam of light to her right, down the end of the tunnel.

"Come on, this way!" she shouted to Charles.

Both of them followed the corridor. At its end was a corroded iron door, covered in slime but otherwise untouched. The light came from sparking electrical cables that probably hadn't been touched in decades.

"Well, let's see what's behind door number one." Charles kicked the door open, revealing an old, but still intact, iron spiral staircase. "Looks Victorian. Wonder how many years this has been locked up."

"Where do you think it leads?" Lucy wondered, looking up the stairs.

"Well, it can't be any worse than down here," he said. "Ladies first."

Lucy gave him a frosty look as she pushed past and began to ascend the stairs.

***

"Fall back," Brother Trypanos growled to the horde, motioning for them to withdraw to the main nest.

The infested growled and buzzed in frustration but did as they were bid, as did the hell-flies, the immediate threat to the hive neutralised for now. Despite his irritation, the Blighted Brother was confident.

"That collapse might have bought them an escape, but it will buy us time. As the Emissary insisted, London is only a temporary measure, and now we have plenty more resources to transport to the primary hive, which they are still to locate…"

The Knight of Yersinia's musing was interrupted by a sound he was familiar with: the gasping of a human trying to breathe with a punctured lung. Looking round the chamber, he saw a figure weakly trying to drag themselves off the heap of bodies. Two of the hell-flies saw potential prey and started stalking forward, but Trypanos drew his sword and stepped in their way. The demonic insects backed down in the face of a superior threat. Sheathing his blade, Trypanos lifted the dying cultist by the throat, grinning beneath his helmet.

"Fear not, human. This is not the end for you. You will be given new purpose."

Handing the wounded cultist over to the once-men, the Blighted Brother snapped, "Take him back to the main nest," as he bent down beside one of the hell-flies the girl had slain and pulled free something caught on the insect's mandibles.

Strands of raven black hair.

***

The staircase finally came to a sealed and padlocked door. Charles rammed his shoulder against it, to no avail.

"Oh bravo," Lucy said, clapping sarcastically, before motioning for him to stand aside.

She pulled out a pouch from her belt and fiddled with a number of lock picks. Charles, for once, maintained a sullen silence, but as Lucy continued trying to open the door, he finally spoke, broaching something both of them both suspected and yet feared to say.

"The voice…"

"Sure I'm not just hearing things?" Lucy replied testily.

Charles ignored the sarcasm and pressed on. "We both heard it. It was *her*."

Lucy turned away from her work to look him in the eye. "Yeah, I'd believe it too, if I wasn't sure it wasn't her. I mean, how do we know for certain it was? I know we deal with all manner of horrible shit in this world, but I've never seen anything like ghosts. Have you?"

Charles shrugged. "I don't know anything concrete, but there are rumours that, in the past, Knights have communed with the spirits of their fallen brethren, or that they've received inspiration or advice from a long deceased member of the Order. We'd have to look it up; Claire can probably find the suitable records…"

Lucy heard a hopeful note in Charles's voice and knew what he was thinking. She wanted to believe it too, but something made her speak her concerns.

"But it could be something else. A demonic entity, toying with us? For its own amusement, out of rivalry with the Blighted Brothers, to humiliate them?"

Charles scowled but nodded. "Possibly, but if it is Valerie, do you realise what it means?"

"I do. And frankly I'd rather it be a demon toying with us…"

"Why?" Charles demanded. His anger faded a little as he saw the sadness in Lucy's gaze.

"Because the alternative, that Valerie is still here, trapped on this earth, unable to move on, is something I don't want to imagine."

Fortunately, at that moment, the lock clicked and she gave a cry of satisfaction, her sadness put aside. "Open sesa—"

"FIRING LINE!"

"Get down!" Charles roared, pushing Lucy down as a fusillade of gunfire opened up.

"Hold your fire! Hold your fire, it's us!" he said, shouting to be heard.

The gunfire steadily died away, and they heard Gillian bellowing at the shooters as they lowered their weapons.

"Fucking idiots! I told you to hold your fire, let me deal with it!"

"I had to be sure!" someone shouted back. "We might have been tracking their life signs, but who's to say it wasn't someone using their corpses to lure us into a trap?"

Lucy and Charles heard running feet, and then Gillian hit them like a charging bull, wrapping her arms around their necks. Heat rose to Lucy's cheeks as Gillian kissed her repeatedly on the brow, nose, cheeks and lips.

"Please don't," she protested as Gillian pressed her mouth to both her cheeks. "You don't know where we've been!"

She rolled her eyes as Gillian grimaced at the muck on her lips.

"Told you."

"Don't I get a kiss?" Charles said.

Gillian stuck out her tongue and then pecked him on the cheek.

"I knew you were alive. I said it would take more to put these two down!" she shouted over her shoulder, and Edmund gave her a withering look. Beside him, Moira was seated on the floor, her burned face hidden behind a cloth.

"Fine, I was wrong." Edmund scowled. "What did you find down there?"

"Hell-flies, and their walking cocoons," Lucy replied bluntly. "We managed to seal the tunnel. There wasn't much else we could do—trying to fight our way to the nest was suicide. I'd recommend we blow this stairway up. It'll take them some time to punch their way through the rubble, assuming they don't cut their losses and evacuate their lair down there—but if they do decide to make their way up, I'd rather they not have a direct path to the surface."

"Allow me." Gillian pushed Charles and Lucy aside, her palms glowing orange as she prepared to cast a spell.

Edmund cleared his throat. "Perhaps sit this one out and let the professionals do the demo job?"

Gillian rounded on the vampire, her eyes smouldering. Lucy noticed with concern that Gillian's irises were the same orange as her palms, which were starting to smoke…

"Are you implying I'm not up to the job, Edmund?"

The vampire showed no signs of fear, but the surviving mercenaries were backing away, as if fearing getting caught up if the talking spilled into violence…

"Gillian, you kept blacking out all the way through the retreat. It will be a wonder if you don't have a concussion. Besides, we have explosives left over, and I'd rather you save your power for getting us all out of here."

Gillian didn't look appeased, but Lucy took and gently squeezed her hand, and she finally let out a sigh and nodded. "Fine, let your daughter's toy soldiers do their work," she snapped, motioning for the mercenaries to head down the stairway to attach what little Semtex they had left to the supports of the staircase.

"Who built this place? And why?" Lucy wondered.

Edmund shrugged. "This city's got a lot of history, and not just that of humans. This might have been access to any manner of facilities for Othersiders like us," he said, motioning to Moira and himself.

"She going to be alright?" Charles nodded to the motionless female vampire.

"I'll get fresh blood into her when we're home, but I think she might be out of action for a time," Edmund said, as the mercenaries returned.

"Ready when you are, boss," said one, bald and scarred.

Edmund looked to Lucy, who gave the nod. "Do it."

"Fire in the hole!" the mercenary shouted, depressing a button on a handle.

They were buffeted by the explosion, which was followed by the clatter of metal falling and smashing to pieces as the wreckage fell down the shaft.

"Best seal that up," the mercenary added. "No way up for normal troops, but if they've got any more of those bugs, they'll scurry up the shaft no problem. Anyone bring any welding gear?"

A few of the survivors murmured before Gillian sighed, "Leave it to me."

The door slammed shut as she raised her glowing palms, then clenched them into fists. Orange light lanced from her hands to the edges of the door. The metal glowed as she moved her hands up and down, causing the door and its frame to melt. After a few moments, she cut off the spell, confident no one would be opening that door any time soon.

"Let it never be said I'm not up to the job," Gillian said with a pointed look at Edmund.

The vampire chose not to press the matter, but Lucy knew he saw the hairs that came free when Gillian swept her locks from her face, same as she did.

"Now, let's get out of here," Gillian snapped, clapping her hands, which glowed blue as she summoned up more energy for a portal spell. "I'll send you lot back to your lair first, then we need to report back to my dad. I dread to think how this is going to go over with him."

A thunderclap sounded as the familiar orb of blue-energy ignited to life. The mercenaries gratefully headed through, followed by the Daltons. As soon as they'd departed, Gillian clenched her fingers into a fist, sealing the first portal and then opening a new one to the vestibule at the Chapterhouse.

"Come on, let's get out of here!" Gillian said as she stepped forward, Lucy noticing more hairs falling out as her girlfriend walked into the portal.

Lucy and Charles followed suit, hearing muted voices speaking. It sounded like Lawrence…

"I agreed, rather unthinkingly. I could have refused, insisted I play a bigger part in my child's life, but I took the easy way out and cut myself out of my daughter's life. But now, the time has come to admit my past, and acknowledge who I am. Danielle Drake, I am your father."

"What?" a young woman asked.

"What?" Gillian snarled, stalking into the kitchen to find her father, Angela Drake and a young witch Lucy vaguely recognised from both Halloween and the hair salon where the Camden coven made their lair. Lucy could only imagine the state they must have looked to those sat at the table, but Gillian was focused on only one thing.

"Care to explain yourself, Father?"

Chapter 16: The Truth Will Out

Lucy vaguely heard Charles mutter something about having left something on in his room and the sound of his footsteps as he fled upstairs. *Heart of a lion, Charles. So brave!*

"How long have you been hiding this one away?" Gillian snarled, her eyes smouldering. "When was she born?"

"Gillian, please—" Lawrence tried to say, his voice shaking, but Gillian wasn't going to be fobbed off.

"*When*?!" she repeated.

Lawrence kept his mouth shut, and Lucy heard someone take a deep breath. Gillian's head turned to Angela, as the older witch replied, "Nineteen ninety-six."

Gillian's brow furrowed as she joined the dots, and then her confusion melted into fury, her teeth bared in a feral rage.

"Oh, you have *got* to be fucking kidding me!" she shrieked, storming in.

Angela and Danielle Drake scrambled to their feet, unnerved by the spellweaver's rage. Fortunately for them, she turned it on someone else.

"Mum was in the ground barely a month and you were already chasing some new piece of skirt?" Gillian snarled at her father. "Valerie and I were six, our mum had just died, we needed you, and instead you dumped us on Anne so you could jet off playing the hero and screw some coven slut on the side?!"

"Don't you dare talk about my mother like that!" Danielle snapped, only for her anger to wilt as Gillian turned her furious gaze on her. She looked nervously at the sparks flickering in Gillian's palms.

"I'll get to *you* in a minute!" Gillian spat, before turning back to her father. "What the bloody hell is she doing here? Why are you trying to reconnect with a girl you didn't even acknowledge existed before Samhain?!"

"There are things that need to be set in order—"

At that, Gillian gave a humourless laugh. "Oh, now I see! Valerie's gone, and my tastes don't exactly conform to your plans, so what did you plan to do? Find the bastard you had, reconnect so as to get her on your side, legitimise her and then what? Fob her off on Charles so maybe, just maybe, you can get that grandson you always wanted to carry on the family line, preserve the precious Templeton family legacy you clearly love so much—certainly more than your wife and daughters!"

Danielle's head was bobbing back and forth between the two Templetons, looking offended at Gillian's implications, but it was Lawrence who stormed to his feet, his face red with anger.

"You don't know what the bloody hell you're talking about!"

Gillian pulled back her right hand, her palm glowing again, but Lucy quickly darted forward and dragged her back.

"Don't, love. You'll only regret it later."

While Gillian glared daggers at her father, Lucy hastily turned her attention to Angela and Danielle and nodded at the door, urging them to leave before it was too late.

"You want to play happy families with these two," Gillian spat, nodding dismissively after the fleeing witches, "be my guest. But get one thing into your head, *Lawrence*. She is not my sister. I had a sister, and in case you've forgotten in your haste to get an heir with a Y chromosome, she's ashes on the breeze, much like Mum... if you even remember them."

Lawrence's expression became one of molten rage. "I remember your mother and sister! I will *never* forget them."

"Alright, you two, let's calm this down before something gets said that we all regret!" Lucy shouted as she held the struggling Gillian back, who now was snarling in fury, looking like she wanted to hit her father.

"Yeah?! You've got a funny way of showing it!" Gillian spat in disgust at her father's feet, before turning on her heel and storming out.

Lawrence made to chase after her, his rage melting into regret, but before he took two steps, Lucy placed a hand on his chest, stopping him in his tracks.

"No. Larry, you're the last person she's going to want to talk to right now. I'll go after her. You need to talk to Charles; things went horribly wrong tonight on the mission. We'd best brace ourselves for a backlash."

Lucy quickly shrugged on a coat and made for the front door. It was raining outside and there was no sign of Gillian. A few faint sparks of blue light were guttering out of existence on the pavement. A portal spell.

"Do you want me to divine where she went?" a voice asked.

Lucy turned to face Danielle, stood guiltily in the Chapterhouse doorway. The young witch raised her hand, a faint blue sheen gleaming in her palm. "I'm getting traces that point in the vicinity of London Bridge, but I can't be more specific than that."

"That's enough," Lucy replied brusquely. "She has places she likes to go; I'll go through all of them until I find her."

As she made to leave, Danielle cleared her throat.

"I didn't mean… It wasn't my intention to cause trouble. I had no idea about what he and I were before tonight, or what Lawrence intended when he invited me here," the girl insisted.

Lucy allowed her expression to soften a little. "I know, but I don't think it's wise for you or your mother to be here when I get back… at least until she and her father calm down a bit. Call it paying back the favour for saving my arse on Halloween."

***

In a disused chamber beneath the London Underground, cultists chanted as Nathaniel Danvers approached the bed, salvaged from a condemned hospital, a ceremonial dagger clutched in his hands. Lying on the bed was a mortally wounded cultist, injured fighting off the Order's aborted attack on the breeding facility. The facility they were in was one of the few tied to the Phoenix Initiative that the cult had managed to hide from investigators, the result of the British government cracking down on them at the Order's behest in the wake of Halloween. The man was too weak to try and spawn an Einherjar from his body, but that wasn't what Nathaniel, nor the creature within him, had in mind.

The growls to his right got Nathaniel's attention; Brothers Trypanos, Necrosai and Falciparum watching from the side-lines. It was at their insistence that he was going through with this rite, to summon an extremely powerful demon that would strike back for the insult the Blighted Brothers felt had been done to them. In rusted gauntlets, Falciparum held strands of red and black hair, collected after the battle in the tunnels.

"Let us begin," Nathaniel said simply, and slit the man's throat.

As blood spilled onto the pillows and sheets, the cultists' chanting grew louder and louder and the blood began to slow, the processes of death reduced to a crawl. Nathaniel nodded to the Knights, who promptly placed the hairs into the blood. All those present heard the sounds of something sniffing, getting the scent of the hair, and growling lowly.

Blood dripped off the bed onto the floor in a spreading red puddle. When it was a metre across, a large bubble began to form in the blood. Nathaniel grinned as it grew ever larger, a human-shaped figure at its centre. The bubble of blood finally burst, spattering those around with a fine mist of gore, but before the creature could fully rise from within, Nathaniel drew a revolver and shot the newborn demon in the head.

The Blighted Brothers watched suspiciously, but then two more drops of blood fell from the bed, and the same process of growth and birth began again as two bubbles grew, each containing a humanoid shape. Long, bony talons punched through the filmy surface as the creatures within freed themselves. Nathaniel raised his gun and fired at both of the demons, but this time, the creatures dodged the shots.

Snarling angrily, they made to charge, only for Nathaniel to raise a hand and growl at them, baring his teeth. The two demons reluctantly backed down, cowed by a superior predator. Satisfied that they knew their place, Nathaniel looked from one demon to the other, impressing upon them his will.

"For each one of you that falls, I guarantee two more will arise. Every time you are slain, you will come back stronger, faster, swifter to adapt. You will return again and again until your hunt is complete. You have the scent of your quarry. You will hunt and die and rise again until you bring me the heads of Lucy Murray and Gillian Templeton. Their interference will no longer be tolerated, and with them gone, the Order of the Argent Blade will suffer a grievous blow. Bring back their heads and ensure that their bodies are never found. Now go," Nathaniel snapped, pointing to a side tunnel that would lead up to the surface.

Chapter 17: Recriminations
The World's End tavern, Camden, London

Lucy had a strong suspicion where her girlfriend had gone. Sure enough, after waving her ID at the doorman, she descended down the stairs to one of the lower seating areas and found Gillian nursing a glass of whiskey, her eyes red and somewhat glassy.

I don't think that's her first, Lucy mused as she sank down at the table, sitting opposite Gillian.

She could tell Gillian had used her magic to clean herself up, while Lucy had had to change clothes and use deodorant to cover up the reek of the battle before heading out to find her.

"Come to join me as I get wasted?" Gillian muttered, rattling the ice cubes in her glass. She took another swig and slammed down the empty glass.

Lucy gave a reproving look as she gently took Gillian's hand and pried it off the glass.

"I'm taking you home. Sweetheart, this is the last thing you need—"

"Is my father's whore and his bastard still there?" Gillian seethed. Lucy couldn't help but notice sparks crackling in her palm. "Or has my father decided to completely erase all memory of his actual daughter in favour of replacing her?"

"No one will replace Valerie," Lucy tried to insist.

Gillian slammed a fist on the table. "Well my father seems determined to!" she shrieked, only for her furious expression to crumble, and she broke down sobbing into Lucy's chest.

A number of pub staff came over, concerned about the racket, but hastily retreated when they saw Gillian bawling her eyes out.

"It wouldn't be so bad if I could just talk to him about her," Gillian said in between outbursts of wailing, "but he refuses to even speak her name!"

"Maybe it's too painful for him?" Lucy suggested. "I'm just playing devil's advocate," she added hastily as Gillian looked up at her with eyes blazing. They tended to shift from green to blue and back when she'd been drinking. "But you don't know how he's dealing with his grief. When my parents died, I became an absolute hellion to my grandparents for a while. We all deal with the loss of loved ones in different ways, my darling."

"So why did he invite that little bitch into my home, after barely having any interaction with the girl for so many years?"

Lucy shrugged her shoulders helplessly. "Only Lawrence knows the answer to that question. Maybe ask him about it when you get home?"

Gillian seemed determined to dig her heels in. "No. I really, really don't want to go back to the house tonight. I don't want the reminders…"

Another wave of sobbing overcame her, and Lucy just sat there, hugging her.

"I know—I know how hard it is," Lucy tried to console her girlfriend. "I didn't know Valerie as well as I'd have liked, but I know how close you were. Sometimes, when you try to hold it in, it ends up just exploding out of you. Frankly, I think you and your father need to talk through your feelings about Valerie—as does Charles, because if he carries on the way he's going, he's going to put himself in an early grave. I know her death was a shock to you all, but she wouldn't want you to give in to despair."

For a brief moment, she contemplated telling Gillian what she suspected—that her sister might not be as gone as they once thought—but held her silence for now.

She's got enough on her plate without me rattling off conspiracy theories that Valerie's still trapped wandering this earth.

"Can we not go back to the Chapterhouse tonight, please?" Gillian pleaded, when she managed to get her crying under control. "I just, I just can't face it tonight. Let's just find a hotel, I'll pay... I just want to be alone with you tonight," she murmured, nuzzling against Lucy.

"Of course," Lucy said, trying not to get distracted as Gillian's hands and lips started wandering.

Satisfied, her girlfriend let her go, and Lucy watched as Gillian downed the last of her whiskey, her eyes turning an icy blue.

"Why do your eyes do that?" she asked. "I've noticed it before but I never remarked on it..."

"I like to use a few cosmetic spells to help lessen the chance of me being noticed in public." Gillian's speech was a little slurred. "But my unique abilities and the concentration needed to maintain them don't work so well with alcohol—"

"Was it really a wise idea to go out drinking then?" Lucy asked, her tone somewhat chiding.

Gillian shrugged her shoulders as she put her coat back on. "Probably not, but the mood I'm in, I really didn't care!"

Lucy had to help her girlfriend out of *The World's End*. The doorman chuckled softly to himself as he watched them go, one clearly staggering, the other keeping an eye on her. They wended their way across the road to Camden Town Underground station.

A number of beggars sat outside, haranguing those entering the station for any coin. As they made their way up the stairs, Gillian stumbled. Lucy looked round to see a beggar's hand had snagged the hem of her coat.

"Excuse me, miss, spare some change?" a soft voice asked.

"Oh piss off," Gillian snapped waspishly, turning to face the speaker... and then Lucy heard the rasp of a sharp blade being drawn. She reacted in the nick of time.

"Get away!" Lucy shoved Gillian out of harm's way as a blade protruding from the attacker's coat sleeve stabbed towards her stomach. Gillian hit the pavement, winded but still alive.

With a roar, Lucy's kukri was out, parrying a slash to her face. She swung high. Her enemy ducked under a cut that would have split its head open. Roaring, the creature shrugged off its tattered beggar's guise, revealing a lean, wiry body with coal-dark skin, gleaming yellow eyes sizing up its prey, and long talons of serrated, razor-sharp bone jutting from its wrists. It was unlike any demon Lucy had seen before.

This is going to be a challenge, she thought, even as she brandished her kukri. "Come on, you ugly bastard! No one touches my girl and gets away with it."

The shrieking demon charged straight at Lucy. Her blade stabbed into its chest as its arms wrapped around her, smashing them both through the ticket barrier. Lucy went down hard and twisted away as one of the bone claws stabbed into the concrete, missing her forehead by inches.

"Oi, oi!" she heard one of the station staff bellow.

Two men in orange high-vis jackets ran over, seeing the fracas. Several party-goers heading up from the platform caught sight of what was going on and started pulling out their phones to record. Lucy was about to bellow at them to run, but what happened next made it irrelevant.

"Alright, mate, that's enough!" One of the station staff, a burly man in his fifties, grabbed the demon by the shoulder, thinking it some London reveller who'd had too much to drink and gotten into a fight with his missus, when the demon spun round and drove its right talon through the man's thick neck.

His colleague, a young Asian man, barely had time to process the sight of his co-worker on his knees, trying to stop the blood pouring from his throat, before the demon's claws swept out and his head went flying towards the onlookers crowding by the escalator.

For a moment, there was just stunned silence. Then one woman screamed, and pandemonium erupted. The demon roared, spreading its blood-smeared claws wide, baring shark-like teeth at the panicking crowd, revelling in their terror, and then it shrieked as Lucy drove her kukri through the back of its right leg. Howling in pain, it lashed out with a clenched fist, hitting Lucy full in the mouth. She landed hard on her back. Shaking her head to clear it, she spat out a mouthful of blood and glared at her attacker.

"YOU'LL BURN FOR THAT, MONSTER!"

The demon turned to face the speaker, and a torrent of fire hit it full in the face. Fuelled by the alcohol in her blood, the heat of Gillian's inferno spell was incredible. Lucy felt it on her face even as she crawled away. The monster screeched, clawed hands clutching at its face as meat and skin ran like candle wax, baring the bone beneath. Gillian's eyes glowed an icy blue as she poured more and more of her fury into their attacker. To Lucy's shock, long threads of white were appearing in Gillian's mane of red hair, growing more and more prominent as Gillian pressed her attack…

"Die, die, FUCKING DIE!" Gillian bellowed, advancing on the demon.

The creature tried to get back to its feet, pulling back its bladed arm to stab at her belly. Lucy shouted a warning, and Gillian thrust out her other hand to strike the demon with a blast of telekinetic energy. The force sent the creature flying down the escalator. Lucy and Gillian raced down after it, weapons raised as the creature staggered up and stumbled in the direction of the train platforms. Lucy flung one of her toxin-loaded knives into the back of its thigh. The demon yowled, bending down to pull the blade free, only to collapse as the poison flooded its veins.

Before it could try to overcome the toxin, Gillian stretched out her hand, and another telekinetic burst smashed the demon into the tunnel wall. Her fingers clenched into a fist, and the monster was jerked back like a fish on a hook, landing in a crumpled heap at their feet. Lucy kicked it hard, knocking it onto its back.

"Who are you?!" Gillian demanded of the creature, her fists wreathed in fire.

"My name is Legion, for we are many," the creature spat.

Gillian recoiled from those words, and that was all the opening the creature needed. It flipped from its back onto its feet once more, the talons protruding from its wrists slashing at Gillian's face.

The thunderous crack of a gunshot rang out, and suddenly the gaunt demon was falling, its arms wind-milling, dark ichor pouring from the bullet hole the smoking gun in Lucy's hand had blown through its throat. The creature staggered towards the platform edge, and Lucy didn't give it a chance to recover before putting two more silver rounds into its skull. The demon toppled over the edge, straight into the path of an oncoming train. Lucy choked in disgust as black blood splattered her face. Spitting, she wiped bits of demon carcass from her face and clothing. Chunks of pulverised meat lying on the platform or sliding down the walls were already dissolving into stinking slime.

Lucy lowered her gun, breathing a sigh of relief, and then something leapt from the top of the train and tackled her about the waist. Lucy went flying with a yelp. As she hit the ground, the Glock clattered out of her hand and slid over the edge of the platform. Lucy rolled onto her back, and then she was choking as a clawed hand hauled her up by the throat. Gasping for breath, Lucy found herself staring into another pair of malevolent yellow eyes, her attacker identical to the one she'd just dispatched. *Two of them.*

The passengers about to disembark the train got one look at the monster and promptly pressed themselves back inside the train carriage, screaming as it turned and roared at them. Gillian reacted instantly. A translucent dart flew from her fingertips and hit the driver's carriage, causing the driver to feel a sudden impulse to get the train moving again.

Feeling the claws tighten around her throat, Lucy's eyes went wide as a dagger-sharp spur of bone began to extend from its left wrist. She instinctively pressed the palm of her right hand into its forehead, and the demon recoiled, dropping her and shrieking in pain as her mark hurt it, an ugly red handprint burnt into its dark skin.

It slashed out at head height, but Lucy ducked below its strike, her kukri darting out. The demon howled as the silver blade sank into its belly. For a human, it would have been a gutting wound. Even for a creature like this, it clearly caused pain, but as Lucy made to press her attack, the demon recovered. It spun on its heel, its clawed foot catching Lucy under the jaw. Stunned, she went flying and hit the ground hard, her kukri flying from her hand. The creature loomed over her, pulling back its arms to bring its wrist claws stabbing down—

And then stinking black ichor spattered her face again, accompanied by a keening shriek. Blinking to clear her vision, Lucy saw the kukri buried halfway to the hilt beside the demon's left eye, the blade glowing as if red hot. She could smell ozone and guessed Gillian had used her magic to fling the dropped knife into the demon's head.

"Lucy, catch!"

Catching Gillian's own kukri as her lover threw the knife, Lucy charged and, with a leonine roar, brought the blade down onto the crown of the demon's skull as its hands clutched at the one buried in its eye. Shrieking in agony, the demon collapsed, its knees hitting the ground. Without a moment's pause, Lucy pulled both blades free of the demon's skull and slashed them through its neck.

The demon's head remained balanced on its neck for a moment, then rolled free. Lucy kicked the decapitated corpse to the floor. Its limbs twitched frantically for a few moments and then fell still. Without thinking, Lucy spat on the demon's slack features in fury and stepped back as the head and body began to crumble into ash.

"We need to get out of here," Gillian insisted. "There's no way the police aren't going to come running for this.

Two dead TFL staff and bloody fighting in the Northern line—we don't want to be here when they show up!"

"Wait." Lucy seized the demon's limp arm before it could crumble away and hefted her blade. "I want to know what the hell this was."

With a wet crack of flesh and bone, the demon's forearm came away, severed at the elbow. Gillian snapped her fingers and a haze shimmered over the severed limb. "That'll stop it from disintegrating long enough for Anne to do an analysis."

"You got any ideas what this is?"

"Some, but I want it confirmed before I start jumping to conclusions."

Gillian's hands began moving again, blue light kindling to life in her palms. Lucy recognised the signatures of a portal about to open.

"I'll let Claire and Anne fill you in," Gillian said, the severity of the foe they'd just faced completely overriding her aversion to returning to her father's home.

Chapter 18: Welcome Home

"Gillian? Are you alright?" Anne asked as they came up-stairs from the armoury. "We've been worried sick about— Jesus Christ, what's happened to you two?" she gasped, goggling at the spatters of black blood on their clothing and faces. "What did this?"

By way of an answer, Lucy held up the severed arm. Anne wrinkled her nose at the stench.

"Get everyone in the briefing room," Gillian said simply. "Someone's put a hit on us; we need to respond."

"I'll get Claire," Anne said, gingerly taking the severed limb from Lucy.

"I'll find Charles. And where is he and his… *guests*?" Gillian asked, the pursing of her lips and the tone of her voice indicating that she had a vastly different word in mind to describe Angela and Danielle Drake.

Anne gave Gillian a very disapproving look, but replied reasonably. "They've gone home. He took to his study in a bit of a state after you stormed off—"

"I'll get him," Lucy said, trying to be the peacemaker before Gillian's temper flared and she got into another argument.

Heading upstairs to the first floor, she turned right and gently rapped on the door at the end of the corridor.

"Lawrence, you in there?"

There was no answer, and she gently pushed open the door. The smell of whiskey hit her as she stepped into Lawrence's study.

"Like father, like daughter…"

Lawrence was asleep at his desk, his left hand clutched around a bottle of Glenfiddich

4, his right outstretched towards an empty shot-glass lying on its side inches from his fingers. Shaking her head, Lucy gently pulled the bottle from his limp grasp, only for him to jerk awake.

"You two are more alike than your daughter wants to admit," Lucy noted as Lawrence rubbed sleep from his eyes and angrily motioned for her to hand him the bottle. "You and her, both indulging in whiskey to hide your problems."

"Yeah, and on that note…" Lawrence snapped, tapping the top of his desk with the empty glass.

"I'd say you've had enough, Larry," Lucy insisted, but Lawrence shook his head as he rooted around in his desk and pulled out a box.

"No. I'm on some heavy-duty pain meds at the moment. That helps wash it down, otherwise I feel like I've been kicked in the head by a horse."

"Of course you do," Lucy sighed, shaking her head disdainfully.

"It's for the cancer."

Lucy took a step back, utterly stunned. Lawrence's expression was grim.

"Leukaemia. The doctor gave me a year at the outside; that's who I've spent so much time on the phone to lately. Some days I feel fine, strong as I've ever been. Other times, I feel so weak it's a miracle I can muster the strength to get out of bed."

"Does Gillian—"

"No, and you are not to tell her," Lawrence snapped.

Lucy shook her head in disbelief. "She has a right to know!"

"What am I supposed to tell her? That in less than a year, she'll be the last of the Templetons?" Lawrence sank into his chair with a heavy sigh and shook his head. "I have a hard time believing it myself sometimes."

"Is that why you were reaching out to Angela and Danielle?" Lucy asked, sympathetic even though she was supposed to be on Gillian's side.

"I stayed away at Angela's insistence. The witch covens prefer to raise their daughters alone, with no interference or assistance from the girls' fathers. Witches like teaching their girls to be self-sufficient, to not have to rely on men, but at the end of the day, she is my flesh and blood, and I'd be remiss if I didn't at least try to offer her some support as I put my affairs in order."

"And inviting her to join the Order?" Lucy asked with a raised eyebrow.

Lawrence shrugged, fighting down a coughing fit, before continuing on. "I'm a Knight of the Argent Blade first and foremost; it's my job to look for promising new recruits. Danielle showed a lot of promise back on Halloween, but the decision on whether or not to recruit her will probably fall to you…"

"Why me?" Lucy asked, utterly bemused.

"Well, I thought, when my time comes, of passing the mantle of Grand Master over to you," Lawrence said earnestly.

In that moment, Lucy couldn't have said what surprised her more: the fact that Lawrence was offering the position to her, or that he was passing over others more experienced.

"Why me? Why not Anne, or Charles, or Claire, or anyone who's been in the Order far longer than me?"

"Others who've been in the Order for far less time than you have taken command in our history. Once, I might have considered Charles for the position, but he took Valerie's death so hard. It's changed him. He's too aggressive, too headstrong and eager to throw himself into the thick of the fight. Someone who thinks so irrationally would lead to disaster in command, so unless Charles changes, I have to discount him. Anne and Claire are subordinates, not leaders; they're better suited to being off the front lines, and though in recent times, I've taken a more 'commanding from the rear' approach, at times you have to take the field… and in addition to your natural talent on the battlefield, I've seen you can adapt, think for yourself—all invaluable in our line of work."

"Well, that's true, and it came in handy about an hour ago," Lucy muttered, remembering how they'd had to improvise to deal with the demonic assassin.

"What do you mean?" Lawrence asked, confused, as he pushed himself up from behind his desk.

"There was an incident in Camden when I found Gillian. Something was sent after us, and it knew where to look. I think, before you put too much effort into connecting with your long-lost daughter, you should try and work towards keeping the one you still have alive."

Slightly unsteadily, Lawrence followed Lucy out of his study. As he closed the door behind him, Gillian and Charles appeared on the landing. Father and daughter tensed at the sight of each other.

"Gillian…" Lawrence started to say, but Gillian just held her hand up to silence him.

"Save it for later," she snapped.

Charles and Lucy exchanged wary looks and Lawrence watched sadly as she walked away without a backward glance.

***

"What was this thing?" Lucy asked as she pointed at the severed arm lying on the table, the talon still protruding from above the wrist.

Anne and Claire stared in silence, both looking repulsed. Charles pulled the arm towards him, studying it from a professional capacity. He winced as he ran his thumb along the edge of the bony talon jutting from the wrist and pulled it back bleeding. The destruction of the Champion's Blade, its pieces secured in the armoury until they could decide what to do, seemed to have sobered him; he looked more alert and professional than he had in a long time.

He's been humbled, reminded he's not invincible. Perhaps it'll motivate him to do better, Lucy thought hopefully. Lawrence and Gillian were not the only ones struggling to come to terms with their grief.

"They can't have…" Claire muttered.

"My name is Legion, for we are many," Anne quoted and Lucy rolled her eyes.

"Yes, thank you, I heard it the first time. I'm more interested in why the thing I took that arm off was quoting the text of a faith that's anathema to it."

"Because that's how it identifies itself," Claire explained. "That passage from the Gospel of Mark is one of the few documented instances of our shadow war. Legion is a demon we have faced many times; it is the finest, most single-minded hunter that those who serve What Lies Beyond can call upon. Give it a name, a scent, and it will never stop coming, never stop trying to kill its prey… but that is not what makes it so dangerous. No, what makes Legion dangerous is the fact that every time it is killed, it returns. Slay it once, two will return. Slay the two that have been born, four will rise in their stead, and on and on it will go. Worse still, each time it is reborn, it will retain the memories of its previous incarnations. It will learn from its mistakes and correct them, becoming a faster, stronger, deadlier hunter each time you cut it down."

"How do we put it down for good?" Lucy asked. "I've never heard of this monster—what?" she said defensively as Anne and Claire gave her a surprised look. "There's only so much research I could do in one go. At any rate, that's beside the point—you can chastise me for my lack of reading later! How do we destroy this foe? If it's truly as dangerous as you say, and since we have no idea who its target is—though I think we can guess," she added with a look at Joshua, sat in the corner, obliviously listening to music through headphones, "we need to get rid of this threat before this demon gets a shot at him. I saw what it was capable of, and next time it will be even more dangerous, if what you say is true."

"Legion is summoned into a living body, kept immobile at the very cusp of death, and as long as life remains in that body, Legion will always return to the hunt, reborn from the cells of that body. Only if that body is destroyed can Legion be banished… and whoever summoned it will doubtless be keeping that body somewhere very safe."

"So what do you suggest? I take it we'd gain nothing from taking one of them alive and trying to interrogate it?"

The pitying looks she got from the others were answer enough.

"It may be a formidable fighter, tracker and killer, but at its core, Legion is little more than an animal," Claire explained. "Trying to interrogate it would be like trying to get information from a dog. When it's been set against us before, our previous attempts to capture one all ended in failure; Legion will always kill itself so it can create the next generation. Our only hope is to find out who summoned it, track them down and kill them and Legion's host body before it's too powerful to stop."

"Our best cure is prevention, and to that end, we have a solution." Anne held up two vials of blood. "As attested by the Gospel of Mark, Legion cannot withstand the presence of a Bane, and while the original demon did not, in truth, beg Jesus to let it destroy itself inside a herd of pigs, we can at least infer from the Bible that a Bane's abilities can harm it. I don't know what the best solution will be, whether you should smear it on yourselves or try to douse the demon in it the next time you see it, but I definitely advise keeping it on you two at all times."

She passed the vials over to Lucy and Gillian.

"How much of this do you have?" Lucy asked. "I can't imagine Rosa's pleased."

"The wishes of a civilian are of little interest to me," Lawrence groused, his speech slurring a little. "I will not— not—lose two of my best over a little discomfort—"

"All the same, it's better to keep her on side," Anne cut across Lawrence, patient but firm. "She may not be his guardian, but she does seem to have developed a sense of responsibility for him. Plus, she's got training as a nurse, and there's only so much Claire and I can do. If we keep her on side, treat the boy well, involve her in the tests we're running, we may gain some useful help."

Lawrence rolled his eyes, but finally nodded. "Fine, fine, if it makes her more useful, keep her in the loop. But I need to know if the boy can help us. If Legion has been summoned and sent after two of our people, there's a hand behind it, and certainly not the Knights of Yersinia. Such a militant action is far out of character for them—they prefer to do their work in out-of-the-way areas where they won't be easily located. The Desolated are behind this, and I will not lose anything more to those bastards. No more," he muttered, his anger seeping away into melancholy.

Lucy chanced a look at Gillian, but her girlfriend's expression had turned icy. She rose from her chair and left the briefing room without a backward glance at her father. As she walked away, Lawrence's brow furrowed in confusion. He turned to look at Lucy, who nodded, both of them concerned by the increasing streaks of white hair on Gillian's head.

***

Thirty miles off the coast of Greece

Ahmed woke up again in hell. Time had ceased to have any meaning, and he'd long since got used to the stink of rotten meat and faecal waste that pervaded this prison. He and a handful of men were all that was left of those who'd been pulled from the sea when the promised ship had arrived. The men, women and children had been separated at gunpoint and led into the ship's hold. Judging from the screams Ahmed had heard over the days that followed, the women and children had not lasted long. Every so often, he heard the sound of massed footsteps, whimpering, screaming, pleading and shouting—audible even if deadened by the heavy metal door sealing his cell.

The guards prowling outside the cells didn't interact with the prisoners; that role was saved solely for the Green Knight. That was the title Ahmed and the others in his cell, now long gone to whatever fate waited beyond the cell door, had given to the hulking figure in armour they'd see when, every few days, he commanded the guards open the cells in turn, clearly examining the prisoners for something only he could determine. Ahmed had been spared so far, but he'd seen Mohammed and heard others be taken from their cells, screaming and shouting as they were dragged away to who knew what fate.

At first, he had prayed for deliverance from this evil place. When that had failed to come, he'd pleaded for death, that he might be spared whatever torment awaited when they took him like all the others.

As he heard footsteps approach and come to a stop outside his cell, Ahmed gave a humourless laugh. Allah had ignored yet another of his prayers.

A key turned in the lock, and Ahmed tensed at the creaking of the rusted hinges. As the door swung open, he expected to see the doctors, the men in white coats who took his blood and jabbed him with needles, but instead it was far worse.

The Green Knight stood in the doorway.

The brute stalked into the cell and seized Ahmed by the throat. He tried to resist, but the ravages of illness and the experimentation he had endured had left him weak as a child. The Green Knight slammed the back of his head into the wall, stunning him, then let him drop to the floor. As he rolled on the ground, a hand seized him by the back of the neck and dragged him from the cell. Looking up weakly, Ahmed saw two guards with rifles ready standing beside five more weak men, chained together at the neck. The

Green Knight drove his fist into Ahmed's belly, forcing the wind from him. As he desperately sucked down air, he felt a collar placed around his neck and sealed with a click. He was abruptly hauled to his feet, the chain attached to the collar and binding him to the other prisoners pulled taut.

"Move," the Green Knight growled in a guttural, rasping voice.

The guards shoved the rearmost prisoners with their rifle butts, and the coffle began to descend into the bowels of the ship. The stench of rotting meat and decay and the sound of buzzing flies grew louder and stronger the deeper they went. Ahmed felt several of the black-bodied insects land on his shoulder and started in shock—each was as long as his thumb. He cried out and tried to shrug them off, but as they took wing, one of the guards smacked Ahmed in the head with his rifle butt. He fell to his knees, coughing and spitting up blood and at least two teeth.

"Do not think to harm them. They are worth more than you," the Green Knight snarled as they reached the bottom of the metal staircase and entered the hold.

Ahmed felt his gorge rise as his feet sank into a slushy red mire that reeked to high heaven. His fellow prisoners made similar noises of disgust and revulsion, but then the Green Knight rapped his rusted gauntlets against his breastplate, creating an almighty cacophony.

"I bring you fresh meat, children. More meaty parcels for your eggs to be warm and safe while they grow!"

The guards forced the prisoners to their knees. As the echo of the knight's croaking voice faded away, a deafening buzzing erupted around them. Fleshy structures all around the ship's hold burst like blisters, and long, clawed limbs tore their occupants free. Ahmed and the other prisoners, chained together, could do no more than scream as a pack of monstrous insects—grey-skinned, red-eyed, each the size of a lion—stalked towards their helpless prey, mandibles clicking hungrily.

Chapter 19: Sisters?

"Why didn't you tell me about this sooner?" Danielle demanded.

Angela sighed and shrugged off her coat. They shared their flat above Hecate's, a hairdresser's in Camden, with several other women of the coven, and as expected, the walls were festooned with magical iconography and secretive acknowledgement of Angela's position as head of the Camden coven.

"It wasn't relevant. It's not our custom for your father, whoever he might have been, to have any involvement in your life. It was only because Lawrence insisted on potentially inducting you into the Order of the Argent Blade that it became an issue; I was suspicious he might have had ulterior motives for trying to recruit you."

"Is it true he just wants me as a replacement for his dead daughter?"

Angela shrugged her shoulders, uncertain. "I don't know. Even years on, that man is an utter mystery to me. I learned fairly early on in our liaison what he and I had was just physical, the outpouring of pent-up emotions and stress after fighting for our lives, needing to reaffirm—"

"Yes, thank you, Mother! I don't need all the details!" Danielle said with a grimace, hastily screwing up her eyes and putting her fingers in her ears: *I don't need mental images!*

After a few moments, she opened her eyes to see her mother had adopted the stern look she'd always used when Danielle had been a little girl who'd done something wrong. Danielle stuck out her tongue teasingly, and the two women laughed. Their relationship had always been one based on levity and sarcasm.

The good humour quickly dissipated, and the mood became serious again.

Danielle rubbed her temples and said, "So, what do you think? Should I join? I mean, what is the coven's position on the matter?"

Angela sighed. "Ultimately, the coven cannot make the decision for you. The Salem Compact requires us to support the Order of the Argent Blade in times of need, but we're not obligated to hand our girls over to them whenever they experience a dip in manpower. Witches from an array of covens have become Knights of The Argent Blade, but the girls in question always made the choice themselves. It is a major responsibility, and one that I would advise you to think about in great detail, sweetheart. As my own mother used to say: once you let the magic go, there's no way to bring it back. Don't go rushing into this, darling. Do some research, think it over, consider your options... and only then, give Lawrence Templeton your answer."

"And what about the... other matter?" Danielle asked "I know the coven's position on male involvement in our lives—that it causes trouble—but I'm curious about finding out for myself."

Her mother gave her an ambivalent look. "You've lived without a father in your life for almost twenty years. It's up to you if you want that to change. Just don't be surprised if you find the rest of his family aren't as welcoming..."

**

"That old bastard! How dare he, how fucking dare he?! My mother was barely in the ground and he was cavorting with some coven whore! And now, barely weeks after my sister has been laid to rest, he brings his bastard by-blow into my home and tries to play the good father after years of pretending she didn't exist? I am never going to forgive him for this!"

As Gillian raged, Lucy looked up at her from the bed, biting the inside of her mouth. Part of her wanted to tell her what Lawrence had said, but she kept her silence.

He has a right to his privacy, and if he wants to wait for the right time to tell her... But Lucy wasn't good at keeping secrets, and it was hard watching their family tear itself apart when she knew something that might be able to mend it.

"Maybe he has a good reason..." she muttered to herself, only to have Gillian whirl around, eyes blazing.

"Are you defending him?!" she snarled.

Lucy hastily raised her hands. "I'm just playing devil's advocate, darling."

Gillian inhaled sharply, as if she was about to start breathing fire.

"I know you're angry, and your father was tactless to do this so soon, but maybe the fact she's related to you is incidental. You heard him say he wanted to offer her a position in the Order; perhaps it's nothing more than that."

"Are you completely stupid?! Why aren't you angry about this? He's insulting you too! The only reason he's invited that little bimbo in is because his desire to ensure the family line continues doesn't work with me and you—"

"I really think you're being unfair to the both of them," Lucy snapped, letting anger colour her voice. "I know you're angry and upset, but don't take your foul mood out on me. The girl had her uses on Samhain; maybe your father wants to capitalise on that. I thought you'd be more supportive of another magic user joining our ranks—surely that would give you some common ground—"

Gillian gave a snort. "Please! Comparing that amateur to me is like comparing a lion to a housecat."

"You're becoming rather elitist, you know? You don't have to like the girl, but if she does decide to join our ranks, you may have to work with her. And believe me, I know you're angry with your father, but please, talk to him. I know what it's like to leave things unsaid and then lose the chance to get closure. By all means, take as long as you want, but don't leave it too long. Given how short our life expectancy is, you may not have another chance."

Chapter 20: Testing the Waters
The Chapterhouse, a week later

Lucy rolled under another fireball flung at her head, the red witch shrieking angrily as she missed again. Lucy pulled two knives from her belt and flung them one after another. The witch staggered as the first hit her full in the chest, then collapsed as the second struck her in the brow.

Lucy laughed, then a roar came from her right as a bulky figure swung an axe at her head. Lucy rolled under it and kicked out at her enemy's knee. He fell back with a grunt and Lucy retreated, putting distance between them. She flung another knife, but the axeman twisted away, the blade hitting him in the upper arm instead of his chest.

Lucy braced for another swing of the axe, but instead, her foe rushed her like a bull, bearing her to the ground. Lucy wasn't done, however; as they went down, she managed to position a leg under her attacker and kicked him off her hard, following up with a kick to the groin. With a bellow of thwarted rage, he brought the axe down towards her head. Lucy rolled away, the blade cracking stone occupied by her skull an instant earlier, and the short sword in her right hand chopped into the back of the axeman's legs. With a cry of shock, he fell backwards, and Lucy was on him like a lioness, stabbing for his throat…

"CEASE!" a female voice interjected.

Lucy got back to her feet, holding out a hand to Charles while Gillian sat up, rubbing a lump between her eyes.

"That hurt, you know." She pouted as she got back to her feet.

"I'll make it up to you later," Lucy replied with a wink, before turning to Claire, who'd been watching from the side-lines, stopwatch in hand. "How long did I take?"

"Three minutes, forty seconds. It's an improvement over last time."

"Still too long." Lucy grimaced as she sheathed her sword—she had taken to using a longer blade in training. "We need to be making our kills faster, dropping enemies more quickly and moving on. If the Blighted Brothers come for us again, they'll likely come in force, and since they're going to be the toughest to bring down, we need to make sure any minions are down and out for the count, so we can focus all our attention on those bloated—"

"Well, if we're doing that again, I insist on some time off and some frozen peas down there until I stop throbbing," Charles griped, while Gillian left to find a mirror and see how badly battered she was.

The bruises she and Lucy had gotten from their clash with Legion had started to fade. The official story for what had happened at Camden Town station was a drunken fight that had gotten out of hand and ended in murder. The police had made some noise about dealing with violent crime, but thankfully, Claire was reporting no signs of pictures of Legion turning up on the Internet to counter the story she'd put out.

"Right, come along," Claire said as she and Lucy entered the armoury. "If we've got time to spare, I've got a few new toys for you to test out."

First, she handed Lucy what looked like a pair of non-descript steel-toed boots. Lucy quickly put them on, then gave Claire an expectant look.

"What now?"

"Stamp your right foot."

Lucy did so and gasped as a six-inch-long spike protruded from the toe of the boot.

"Coated in tetrodotoxin, one of the most powerful neurotoxins in the natural world, cultivated from the salivary gland of the blue-ringed octopus," Claire explained. "Causes death through paralysis of the respiratory and nervous system. I know you're quite fond of kicks to put your enemies off balance, so this will give you even more of an edge. To retract the blade, simply drag your heel across the ground—and try not to cut yourself if cleaning your boots. You'll be dead before you know you've had an accident."

Lucy grinned as she followed the instructions, imagining how she might put this new toy to use. With her natural tendency to use her kickboxing skills, she was already thinking of all the places on an enemy's body to target.

Next, Claire pulled out a wooden box. Inside, a pair of matched kukris lay on a bed of red velvet, a bead of red glass set in their pommels. Lucy picked one up, spinning the blade in her grasp.

"Upgraded version of the throwing knives you love so much," Claire explained. "Six-second fuse once the pommel stud is depressed. Make sure you jam it in deep and then get clear. I'd recommend you save these for something big; we could only make six in total."

"We?"

"I know a guy," Claire replied with a shrug. "He's quite talented at this sort of thing."

"Do I get to meet him?"

Claire shook her head. "Not at present. He's currently working on a commission we put in a while ago. We're trying to see if we can get the Champion's Blade reforged—"

"Can you do that?" Lucy asked, genuinely surprised.

"The sword's been broken and reforged many times, dependent on the whims of who wields it. Sigismund Wildegraf first used it as a broadsword; one of our men killed the Emissary with it at the Battle of Waterloo in the form of a cavalry sabre. It was the Champion before Charles who had it forged into a zweihänder; he adapted his fighting style to it, but it may be time for something different. I'm not sure what Charles specified—he did it all by Skype— but I'm sure it'll be impressive. Still, while we're on the subject of blades, I've got something else you'll really love,

Lucy." Claire grinned. "I mean, technically everyone could make use of them, but I know these are your favourites…"

Claire walked over to the table and unfolded a cloth bundle. Lucy's eyebrows rose at the sight of a half dozen throwing knives. They looked identical to the poisoned blades she'd used before, with a small glass ampoule to be crushed before throwing, ensuring the toxin would go straight into the target on impact, but the glass contained red fluid instead of green.

"Joshua's blood?"

Claire nodded with a smile. "Five ccs in each. Judging by the tests we've run, demonic destruction will occur in under a minute. We're running more tests to see if we can get a specific time to complete destruction once injected into the enemy."

"How many more of the eggs have you got to work through?" Lucy asked. She knew that Claire and Anne, with Gillian's help, had been hatching the hell-fly eggs to test Joshua's abilities and the effects of his blood first-hand.

"Enough," Claire said with a wave of her hand. "Mum's press-ganged Rosa into assisting her. Once I'm done with you, I'll go back to overseeing their experiments."

"How soon before you guys have something to counter those bugs?" Lucy asked.

Claire shrugged her shoulders. "I'm not a biologist, so I can't comment, but the initial tests with Joshua's blood show promise. Now, if we can find a way to get the ratio correct so the properties in the blood of a Bane only affect the demonic taint without harming or killing the host… So far, we've been running tests with corpse flesh, but while they completely purify the demonic taint, it also causes severe cellular damage. Last thing we want to do is create a cure worse than the disease."

"Now, we seem to be missing someone important for what I need to do next. Whereabouts is he?"

Up in the main body of the Chapterhouse, they found Joshua sat silently in the main room, staring intently at the television. It looked like he was watching BBC News, Huw Edwards talking about something or other. Lucy barely paid it any heed until she heard two words that always put her on edge.

"The hospital ship, a new initiative spearheaded by the international health conglomerate, Ouroboros Industries, has managed to rescue another ship close to sinking in the Mediterranean. The vessel was filled with sixty people, largely a mixture of Libyan and Sudanese refugees, seeking to reach and claim asylum in Italy. The *Siren* will now convey them to the Moria camp on the island of Lesbos before continuing to patrol the Mediterranean to try and prevent more tragic drownings as were seen over the summer. A representative for Ouroboros insisted this was—"

"That's quite enough of that, thank you very much," Lucy snapped, pressing mute on the remote.

Joshua looked at her askance, and Lucy shrugged her shoulders defensively.

"Trust me, you don't want to believe even half of what you hear on that thing," she said.

Claire held out her hand, motioning for Joshua to follow her.

"Come on, we need your help, Josh," she said with an encouraging smile, and the boy pushed himself up from his seat with a huff.

As Claire held the door down to the basement open for him, the doorbell rang. Lucy made to answer it, only for Charles to get there first. To Lucy's surprise, it was Liam. The werewolf had a long wooden box under his arm and a big grin on his face.

"Well, it took a bit longer than anticipated, but I can't complain about a week-long trip to Wicklow on the company account," he remarked, holding out the box to Charles. "Cerdcha Ghaibhnenn don't usually make weapons in this style, but you were rather specific and he's well paid, so…"

"Can we offer you a coffee, Liam?" Lucy offered, but the werewolf shook his head.

"Nah, I've got places to be. Just stopped here to drop that off," Liam said, before turning on his heel and heading off.

As Lucy closed the door behind him, Charles placed the box on the table and unlocked it. He opened it with Lucy and Gillian looking over his shoulders. They gasped as they saw its contents. Lying on a bed of red velvet was a curved sword, a type of blade Lucy recognised from her history textbooks as a falx, its silver-white blade gleaming in the late morning light. A long wooden handle designed for two hands and engraved with the Order's horned skull and sword sigil took the place of the hilt the Champion's Blade had once possessed.

"What made you decide to have it reforged like this?" Lucy asked.

Charles shrugged. "My fighting style favours a two-handed grip, but since not enough of the metal from the zweihänder was salvageable, I decided to go with something like this. These swords were said be extremely effective, with incredible cutting power, and given what we've been fighting over the last few weeks, I thought something that could cleave through tough hide might be of use…"

"Well, let's just hope you don't have to use it too soon. After everything in the last few weeks, I could do with a bit of time to get our house in order, try and make sense of everything that's going on before we have to head back into the fray…"

***

Secret compound beneath the Piccadilly Line, London

"Please, kill me… "

"Kill me… "

"Pity, please… Let me die…"

"Oh stop your moaning," Nathaniel groused at the moaning wretches in their cages.

The red witch beside him clapped her hands, sealing the portal through which they'd arrived from the *Siren's* current mooring. The facility they were in had originally been abandoned before the events of Halloween, one of several they'd used to transport experimental subjects for the Einherjar birthings before moving them to the main facility ahead of the strike on Westminster. It was merely a temporary stop-gap, but it was the best location he knew of for what he intended.

He turned to the red witch, one of the few the Desolated had left in their service. She bared her distorted teeth in a feral smile and raked claw-like nails along a pale arm, drawing blood from three long cuts. She began to chant in a guttural, half-forgotten tongue as blood continued to fall from her arm into a steadily spreading puddle. Nathaniel stepped back to avoid it splattering his finely made shoes. Half-formed figures began to rise amidst the crimson muck.

"Captain, you are in position?" he asked.

One of the humanoid shapes nodded, its voice distorted by rippling echoes.

"Ready to strike as soon as the word is given."

The man on the other end was head of a private security company Ouroboros Industries had used in clandestine operations across the world. Their men were brutal, professional enough not to leave tracks and utterly devoted to the cult's cause of purifying the world.

Unsurprising, given the atrocities they've seen and committed. Enough to make anyone think humanity not worth saving.

"Your orders are simple: kill everyone inside the Chapterhouse. The Order will not be expecting a strike so soon after Samhain, and I will not tolerate further interference from them. Once you've made a breach, additional support will be made available to you. And remember, captain, you must follow specific orders to deal with the boy. Kill him at range. The fact you're human should give you some degree of protection from his abilities, but do not take chances.

Once you have killed him, exsanguinate the body and ensure it is destroyed; I will not risk a Bane's blood getting into general circulation or onto the black market. Even if the Order is destroyed, there are too many who'd seek to use it, and when the Pantheon is established, there can be nothing left to threaten them. Destroy the Chapterhouse and proceed to the established extraction point."

"Understood, sir. Can you anticipate what level of resistance we might expect?" the fleshy simulacra of his underling asked.

"I have one last thing to put in place. Once that is dealt with, the main sources of resistance will be drawn away; all that should be left within the Chapterhouse when you arrive will be non-combatants. They may affect some token resistance, but nothing you can't handle."

"Understood, my lord."

With a nod from Nathaniel, the witch severed the spell, and the red figure collapsed into clotted gore. Nathaniel stepped back as it seeped into the ground.

His eyes glowed yellow as the Emissary reached out to others of his kind, already in the depths below the city, giving them their orders.

"Lakshmi, Brother Falciparum, Brother Ebolae, the strike team is moving into position. Be sure you are ready when your aid is requested."

His answers were a snake-like rasping hiss and two death-rattle whispers of "Affirmative".

Nathaniel bared his teeth in satisfaction, then both he and the Emissary spoke simultaneously.

"Move those into position, and then turn them loose." He nodded towards three of the moaning figures on the gurneys.

Cultists began to push the gurneys down into a tunnel, and the red witch idly picked up a soft, spongy sphere from a corner table, grinning and crooning softly as mandibles tore through the surface of the demonic egg.

Chapter 21: Uncertainties

"What's wrong?"

"Noth—"

"Don't say nothing!" Claudia snapped as she joined Danielle and Lydia on their break, leaning against the wall outside the hairdresser's. "You've been out of sorts for weeks on end—it's not just me who's getting worried about you! What's eating you? It has to be something big."

Danielle looked at her coven sister, before reaching into her coat pocket and pulling out a packet of cigarettes. Claudia gave her a raised eyebrow.

"Don't let your mother see you puffing on those."

"Oh don't start! I just need something to take my mind off things." Danielle covered the tip of her cigarette with her hand, casually lighting up with a spark from her fingertip.

Lydia cadged a cigarette out of the packet and lit up herself, but Claudia shook her head when offered.

"So what's gotten into you?" she asked.

Danielle took a deep breath and spoke seriously. "Did you ever know your father?" she asked.

Claudia gave a snort. "No, and I never felt any desire to. From what my mother told me, all he was good for was one thing, and after she got me, there was no reason to linger around, so she got out of dodge," she said. "Come on, you know the drill; the coven's always been a girl's only group. Men are only useful when it's time to bump up the numbers."

"Same," Lydia agreed. "My mum picked up a bloke at a nightclub solely for the purpose of having me. Once she got what she wanted, she made sure there was no way he could find her to interfere. Why is this bugging you all of a sudden? You never made a fuss about it before."

Danielle sighed, and chose her words carefully. She cared about her sisters in the coven and knew they, like her mother, wanted the best for her, but…

"A couple of weeks ago, my mother introduced me to my father. It turns out she had an illicit affair years ago, with the leader of the Order of the Argent Blade. For reasons best known to himself, now he's decided to try and establish a connection with me… along with offering me a position amongst the Order."

Claudia raised an eyebrow. "Yeah, that would turn anyone to smoking!"

She and Lydia snickered, only to stop when they realised Danielle wasn't laughing. Looking more contrite, Claudia put a hand on her friend's shoulder and squeezed, asking, "So, you've had a different job offer. What's your mother got to say for herself?"

Danielle shrugged. "She says it has to be my decision, that the coven doesn't have any say in the matter. I must admit, it's a bit of a temptation, but I'm not sure. The job doesn't come with a retirement plan, not to mention I'm quite sure there's some who won't want me in the Order…"

"Anyone in particular?" Claudia asked.

"His daughter by the woman he married."

Claudia winced. "Yeah, I can imagine that would be a bit of an awkward situation. Didn't he have two?"

"Yeah. Unfortunately, one of them died at Samhain and the other is convinced her father just wants me as a replacement."

"Do you believe that?" Claudia asked.

"I don't know. I don't know what I want…"

At that, Lydia stamped out her cigarette and took charge. "Right, you two, grab your coats! We're due a lunch break, and I think we could do with some time away from this place. Come on, let's get something to eat and take our minds off things!"

Danielle hastily stubbed out her cigarette and headed back into the hairdresser's with Claudia, but as she grabbed her coat, Danielle saw her mother on the phone, her expression somewhat grim. Danielle shook her by the shoulder and gently whispered, "Me, Claudia and Lydia are taking our lunch break. You want us to bring you back anything?"

Angela turned to face her daughter, and Danielle was shocked to see her mother's eyes were wide. Whatever the person on the other line was saying, it wasn't good.

"You cannot be serious, Larry. This soon?"

Angela winced as Lawrence yelled something back at her. She hung up, and turned her attention to the watching young women.

"Danielle, Claudia, Lydia, Sara, you need to get over to Bloomsbury right now. Lawrence Templeton apparently thinks something is happening there, and he's insisting he needs magical help…"

***

Lucy and Gillian were trying to distract themselves by playing table tennis for want of anything better to do. Charles was still running a few practice drills with the new Champion's Blade, getting himself used to the feel of it. Claire and Anne were down in the basement, busy with their experiments on Joshua's blood, and Lawrence was still sealed in his office.

The Daltons had sent men back into the sewers, but the Blighted Brothers and their creatures had vanished without trace. Intelligence recovered from the raid indicated they'd scrapped their operation and retreated back to Europe, and Edmund had insisted Siobhan and her contacts on the continent try and pin down their current location. The Order of the Argent Blade were taking the time to enjoy a rare moment of peace.

That peace was shattered as a blaring alarm rang through the whole Chapterhouse.

Lucy and Gillian dropped their bats and raced for the armoury. As they burst through the door and down the stairs, they saw Claire was already at her computer.

"Incursion," was all she said.

"Another one in daylight?" Lucy groaned, remembering the events at Piccadilly Circus all too well. "Where is it this time?"

"Bloomsbury. Looks like the Brunswick Centre." Claire brought up a map, a blinking red icon marking the point where signs of demonic activity had been detected.

"In other words, another demonic outbreak in a public place that is likely to be teeming with people, ensuring a potentially high rate of civilian casualties." Lucy stormed over and began arming herself for battle.

Claire nodded in agreement. "Couldn't have put it better myself. You'd best get over there."

"I'll take Gillian and Charles with me." Lucy picked up a Glock from a nearby gun rack, slammed a fresh clip into the gun and holstered it at her hip.

Anne, looking up, gave her a warning look.

"Go in civilian clothes and try not to tool up too much; we'd best not start a panic."

Lucy nodded, but her thoughts were already elsewhere.

"If Danvers and his crew are behind it, I'm fairly sure they won't use the same trick twice. Whatever they've sent, it'll be more subtle than a pack of Surtr!"

Gillian extended her hands, her palms glowing as she began to prepare a portal spell. Much to Lucy's concern, the red of her lover's hair began to fade, white streaks appearing again at her temples as she channelled her magic.

Chapter 22: Distraction

The portal spell deposited the trio in a small park. After a quick scout around to make sure they hadn't been noticed, the three raced towards the shopping centre in the middle of the plaza.

"Right, look for anything suspicious!" Lucy commanded. "We have no idea what we're dealing with, so—"

She was abruptly cut off as she collided with a burly man. She staggered and Charles caught her before she fell on her backside, but the three of them rapidly saw this was not just the lunchtime queue for Starbucks. A horseshoe-shaped crowd had formed around something in the plaza. Police and paramedics surrounded a supine figure on the ground.

"Everybody stand back, stay back!" a policeman yelled at the crowd.

Without being asked, Charles pushed his way through the crowd, Lucy and Gillian following in his wake. When they reached the front, Charles stopped as a police officer's hand pressed against his chest.

"Please, sir, step back! This may be a public health issue—"

"That's why we're here," Gillian interjected. Her palm glowed blue as she held it up to the officer's face, and his expression became somewhat neutral, his eyes glassy. "We're from the Hospital for Tropical Diseases; we've reason to believe this is an outbreak of a rare pathogen. It's imperative we're allowed to perform examinations."

The policeman nodded blankly and stepped back. "Of course. Right this way, doctor."

Waved through, they raced over to a trio of paramedics on their knees, desperately trying to help an African-looking man thrashing on the pavement as if suffering a seizure. Looking round, Lucy saw two more clusters of paramedics trying to treat another pair of sickly-looking men close by.

"We're going to have to sedate him!" shouted a female paramedic with red hair tied behind her head. "We can't risk another convulsion like that!"

"Oh gods, what is this stuff?!" another paramedic, a shaven-headed man, cursed as the patient rolled onto his side and vomited pus and blood so dark it was almost black.

Charles pulled a tablet from the bag slung over his shoulder and handed it over to Gillian. She tapped it with glowing fingers and Anne's face appeared on the screen.

"Talk to me, Gillian. What are we looking at?"

By way of an answer, Gillian knelt down beside the paramedics as they tore open the man's shirt. All present covered their faces in disgust as the stink of rotted flesh assailed their nostrils.

"What the bloody hell is that?!" the female paramedic cursed.

The man's chest was a cross-stich of surgical scars and sutures. Boils and pustules festooned his chest and arms, most seeping blood or worse; judging by the stink of decay and the clear patches of gangrene on the man's limbs, they were badly infected. Lucy gagged at the sight of fat white maggots crawling and writhing amidst the rotting flesh.

"Jesus Christ, if I didn't know any better, I'd call this a case of bubonic plague," Anne muttered over the Skype link, "but this is far too swift. You need to get this patient isolated immediately!"

"Did I just hear you right, doctor?" the male paramedic yelped, looking at Anne's face on the tablet in utter disbelief. "Did you just say bubonic plague? Like the Black Death?!"

"You need to isolate this man immediately," Anne repeated with a nod. "He poses a severe public health hazard. Inform the police they need to lock the entire area down, and ensure you get disinfected as soon as you get back—"

"Anne, something's happening!" Charles cried, and Lucy looked round to see that 'something' did not begin to cover it.

The sick man thrashed and writhed on the ground, his convulsions so violent that Lucy could hear the snapping of bone. Ugly nodules and spines of bone began to punch through the skin, spitting out gouts of pus and blood as they broke through. The paramedics recoiled in disgust.

"What the bloody hell is this?!" the female paramedic shouted.

The eruptions ceased along with the man's convulsions, and he clutched at his chest, gasping for breath.

"Oh shit! He's going into cardiac arrest," the male paramedic shouted.

Gillian and Charles tried to hold them back, but they forced their way through, pulling on rubber gloves and trying to perform CPR on the stricken man. All of a sudden, the man started trying to speak in broken English. Lucy could just about make out the words.

"Kill... me..."

It was all he managed before his breathing petered out in a weak rasp and he fell back against the pavement, motionless.

"There's no pulse!" the male paramedic cried out, desperately pounding against the victim's chest.

"Sir, you need to step back," Charles insisted, the paramedic looking up from his efforts to restart the sick man's heart. "This is now our matter to resolve."

"What are you talking about?" the paramedic demanded, freezing as he noticed Charles's hand was resting on the pistol holstered at his hip.

Lucy tried to make a move to tell Charles not to be so stupid, particularly as one of the police officers trying to hold the crowd back caught sight of the gun and shouted, his colleagues moving to try and seize Charles...

And then the female paramedic screamed, "Oh shit!"

All eyes looked down. The sick man was still lying motionless, but his eyes were wide open, the irises red from burst blood vessels. He opened his mouth, baring his teeth, and Lucy saw that in place of many missing teeth, jagged fangs had pushed their way through his gums.

Before anyone could react, the dead man lunged with impossible speed, wrapping his arms around the bald paramedic as if to embrace the man trying to save him... and sank those unnatural fangs into his neck. Blood spurted as the dead man tore out the paramedic's throat.

Screams of terror erupted from the panicking crowd. Charles reacted first, shooting the attacker in the head. The monster's head snapped back. Missing half of its upper skull, it snarled. Lucy felt her gorge rise as she saw the swollen, pulsating white mass inside the dead man's ruptured cranium, fibrous tendrils waving in the air, trying to find purchase on something.

Suddenly, two police officers grabbed Charles, trying to disarm him. Charles slammed his right elbow into the face of one and then swung his head into the nose of the other, dislodging both officers. Before they could recover, a new problem arose: one of the police officers slammed into a figure behind him. He turned, and the bald paramedic, back on his feet despite missing half his throat, attacked.

Screams turned Lucy's attention. As expected, the other two diseased individuals the paramedics had been trying to treat were standing. The paramedics who'd been trying to treat them had had the sense to run when they'd realised something was wrong, but the female paramedic who'd been with the first victim was screaming as one of the new attackers sank jagged teeth into her forearm.

Lucy pulled out her own gun and shot the undead monster in the head. Unlike Charles's shot, it went clean through the centre of the head. The dead man collapsed, the parasite animating the corpse killed along with its host. Clutching the bleeding bite wound on her arm, the paramedic tried to crawl away.

"Get the civilians out of here!" Lucy shouted at the police officers, who didn't need telling twice, though the crowd was already trying to flee in multiple directions, screaming and running.

Or at least most of them, Lucy thought in disgust as she saw a few civilians using their phones to record the chaos.

A Chinese tourist was so busy recording Charles slicing off the arm of one of the plague zombies with his new blade, he didn't see the first creature, the one whose head had been half-destroyed, until it collided with him. Both went down. The zombie sank its teeth into the man's cheek.

"Claire, we have a major emergency!" Lucy screamed into her earpiece as she ran over and pulled the dead man off its victim. "We need you to lock down the Brunswick Centre. Some sort of biological attack has been unleashed, and we've got zombies! We need a full evacuation and a medical cordon. We need magical healers to counter whatever this is!"

To her horror, there was no reply from Claire, only static. She tried contacting Anne and Lawrence, but nothing. As the man clawed at his wounds, a dart of blue energy struck him full in the face and he fell back, unconscious but still alive. Lucy turned and saw Gillian lower her hand. To her concern, her lover's hair was liberally streaked with white.

"Lucy, watch out!" Gillian shouted.

Lucy turned in the nick of time as one of the dead men came charging at her. Her gun went flying from her hand as the undead man collided with her. Jaws snapped inches from her nose as she desperately held it at bay. Smoke rose from its flesh as her mark burned it, but the creature was too crazed to care.

"There is no stopping this..." a rasping voice declared.

Lucy's stomach twisted. The dead man was continuing to try and bite her, but she couldn't see any sign of the speaker...

Ropes of stinking saliva brought her back to the present. Out of desperation, Lucy swung her forehead into the undead man's face. As it recoiled, snarling and snapping, Lucy ripped her kukri free of its sheath on her thigh. The zombie lunged at her again, and she buried the knife into its throat, pushing it all the way in until she felt it catch on vertebrae. She twisted the blade, and the creature went limp as its spinal cord was severed, denying the parasite moving the carcass any control.

Suddenly, the dead body began heaving and retching, as if it were trying to expel something. Lucy threw the body off her in disgust. As something long and white began to protrude from between the corpse's teeth, she slashed out. Two halves of the demonic maggot hit the floor, thrashing weakly before finally lying still. Lucy squished both for good measure.

"Not fast enough," she sneered.

I'm glad they die just as easily as the usual kind, she thought as she watched Gillian and Charles put down the last of the zombies. Charles's falx sliced low, severing the undead cop's legs at the knees. As the creature pitched forward to the ground, his blade swept down, severing the zombie's head from its neck, and then the blade fell again, splitting the severed head in two and spearing the parasitic maggot. The last one wrapped its hands around Gillian's throat, but she grabbed the zombie's wrists. Her hands glowed, and the smell of burning flesh grew stronger. The undead monster tried to break away from Gillian, but she held it fast, until—to all their surprise—she tore off the creature's hands at the wrists. It staggered back, suddenly free, and Gillian snapped her fingers. The creature's hissing turned into shrill screams as its head and shoulders burst into flames. Gillian let it stumble away for a moment, then promptly shot it through the head.

Lucy let out a breath she hadn't realised she'd been holding. *That seemed surprisingly easy.*

Charles cleaned any vestiges of demonic blood off the sword and returned it to the sheath on his back.

"This is a really strange plan of attack for the Desolated, if it was them," he admitted. "Only a handful of zombies, easily contained, barring a few civilian casualties. This seems like a really poorly thought-out way to hit back at us, or to make an impact. They could have released a dozen of these things in a major train station or a hospital to have greater effect... This whole thing stinks of wrong."

The same thought had occurred to Lucy. After their previous encounters with their newest enemy, she would have expected them to have released dozens of hell-flies in all directions, more than the Order had the resources to stop from escaping, and then leave them scrambling to track the demonic insects down before they could establish a hive somewhere in the city to spread their contagions. This behaviour was unlike anything she'd seen before.

"Lawrence, it's Lucy. Situation at the Brunswick Centre is under control," she said over her earpiece.

Once again, all she got was a buzzing in her ear.

"Still nothing but static," she muttered. "What the bloody hell is Larry playing at?"

"Over here, we need help!" a weak voice called out.

Lucy turned. It was the female paramedic, somehow lost in the confusion, who'd crawled over to the unconscious tourist.

"What's wrong with him?" she asked in a panicked voice, pointing at a swollen bulge in the man's right eye that was slowly moving upwards.

"Not just him," interjected Gillian, slumped against a bench, completely exhausted. Her hair was heavily threaded with white, and there were deep bags under her eyes.

Lucy's eyes went wide with horror. "What's happening to you?" she asked, concern in her voice.

Gillian waved her concerns aside and turned her attention to the female paramedic, who was looking at her in utter confusion.

"Gillian, talk to me. This keeps happening every time you try to—"

"Not now," Gillian snapped in a hoarse voice.

She ripped up the sleeve of the woman's coat near where she'd been bitten. The woman's eyes went wide with horror as she saw the bulging lump slowly slithering its way up her arm.

"What is that?" she yelled in terror.

Lucy placed a hand on her shoulder, trying to keep her from panicking.

Containment is the name of the game now.

"Your only hope is to get the parasite that thing implanted in you surgically removed before it reaches the brain," Lucy explained in a calm, even tone. "Don't worry, we've got a top-notch medical facility to deal with this kind of thing; you and he are both going to be—"

"Look out!" Charles shouted.

Lucy looked up in time to hear a keening screech, and rolled to her side as a serrated bone blade sliced through the space where her throat had been. The paramedic wasn't so lucky. Her hands flew to her throat as Legion's talons ripped through her neck. She fell onto her back, spasming as she bled out. Her killer stepped over the dying woman's body without a care.

With a roar of fury, Lucy started shooting, but to no avail; Legion dodged every bullet. The demonic assassin snarled angrily, pointing with its bloody talons at Lucy. Its toothy jaws contorted into a mocking smile as her Glock clicked empty.

"My name is Legion, for we are—"

"Yeah, yeah, I've heard it all before." Lucy scowled dismissively. "So where's the rest of you?" she demanded, remembering the warnings from the briefing. There had been two the last time they'd fought, which meant they could expect four this time.

Gillian staggered back to her feet, overcoming her fatigue, sparks crackling in the palms of her hand, when suddenly, something small and dark flew at her head. Reactions dulled by tiredness, she failed to dodge in time, and a rock fragment hit her in the side of the head, leaving her in a motionless, crumpled heap. Hearing another keening screech, Lucy looked up to see another dark figure leaping from the shop roofs at the supine Gillian.

Not on your life, ugly!

Her whip lashed out with a crack, and the Legionary yelped as the barbed silver lash wrapped around its neck and jerked it down hard. The creature landed on its back with a dazed hiss, but before Lucy could press her advantage, the first one attacked, its talons stabbing for her chest. She gave ground as it swiped at her again and again, then spun on her heel and kicked out. Her foot caught Legion full in the jaw, knocking the demon onto its back.

"Look out!" Charles pulled out his gun and aimed at Gillian.

Lucy heard a shriek. The Legionary she'd brought down had seemingly recovered enough to try and kill Gillian. Charles's shot had hit it full in the face, and the demon was staggering away, one eye reduced to a crater weeping dark blood. Charles followed it up with two more shots to the head, and the monster pitched backwards, its skull split apart.

"Nice shot—Charles, behind you!" Lucy shouted.

A pair of dark shapes leapt down from the roofs. One landed right in front of Charles and leapt up, dropkicking him in the chest with both feet. As he tried to get up, the other slashed him across the chest. Blood spurted as Charles toppled with a cry of pain. Surprisingly, the demons didn't try to kill him once they were done, just stepped over his body and charged towards Lucy.

At least their compulsion to kill me and Gillian will make them overlook other potential victims so long as they don't try to interfere in Legion's mission, Lucy thought.

The Legionary she was already up against stabbed low, this time at her belly. She spun away from the attack, only to cry out as a claw raked through the weaker armour on her right leg. Lucy stumbled and fell onto her back, the talons that had been slicing towards her throat passing over her head.

"Fuck off!" she shouted, kicking out.

Her booted foot connected with the Legionary's knee and knocked it down. Lucy slashed for the demon's face with her kukri, but to her shock, Legion parried the blow, trapping her blade between its wrist talons. With a roar, the monster swung its head forward, its bony brow connecting with her face. Blood streamed from her nose. Before she could recover, the Legionary's clawed hands seized her by the throat and bodily smashed her to the concrete.

The breath was driven out of Lucy as she hit the ground hard. *Oh, I've definitely broken something*, she thought, just before a clawed foot stamped down on her chest. She cried out in pain as the Legionary bent down and seized her head in its grasp, forcing her to look to the side. The demon groaned in pain as it came into contact with her marked skin, but just gritted its teeth. *Perhaps the newest iteration is better evolved to resist that.*

Such hypothesising went out the window as Legion snapped a command and cold hands wrapped around her throat. Frantically looking round, she saw the dead para-medic was the one restraining her, slack-jawed and glassy eyed as the insectile demon puppeteered her corpse, but that was nothing compared to what else she saw.

The two Legionaries that had taken out Charles, who she could hear choking and coughing as he tried to overcome his pain, had turned their attention to Gillian. One was holding her arms down; the Chinese tourist, now a larval puppet, was holding her legs; and the third Legionary squatted over her chest, its head twisting from side to side as if debating whether to stab her through the heart or slit her throat.

"Get off her!" Lucy shouted, but as she tried to struggle free, the plague zombie seized her left hand, while the

Legionary threatening her stomped on her right wrist for good measure.

It nodded to its ilk hovering over Gillian. The demonic assassin pulled back its arm, ready to slash…

Suddenly, the Legionary let out a roar of frustration. Its arm was held frozen in mid-air. It tried to struggle free, but to no avail; a band of glowing golden light wrapped around the demon's wrist like a manacle. The Legionary was jerked up into the air, off of Gillian, as a woman's voice shouted words in Gaelic. The creature shrieked and thrashed in mid-air, but whoever was holding it suddenly flung it through the front of a deserted Starbucks with a shriek of fury. At the same time, the demon and the plague zombie holding Gillian's arms and legs suddenly ignited. As they desperately tried to pat out the flames chewing them, they were jerked away by the same telekinetic force that had smashed aside their compatriot. The zombie hit a concrete wall with enough force to reduce its skull to splinters, while the Legionary smashed through the front of an Ann Summers, sending broken glass everywhere.

Lucy, taking advantage of the distraction, stamped her foot; the blade in her boot slid out. Twisting her body, she kicked upwards, and the Legionary shrieked as she caught it in the side. The poison couldn't kill it, but the silver blade made the demon recoil. With her right hand free, Lucy seized her fallen kukri and drove it through the head of the plague zombie trying to keep her pinned. She rolled to the left as the Legionary, recovering from the unexpected attack, stabbed down. The blade pierced the concrete, and Lucy slashed out. The Legionary screamed as her serrated blade bit into its elbow joint, half severing the arm.

"Here!" Charles shouted from behind her foe.

The Legionary's fanged mouth contorted in confusion before a curved blade dancing with white flames erupted from its chest in an explosion of dark blood. The Champion's Blade jerked free and then Charles swung low, cutting through its waist. The demon's body collapsed into pieces that swiftly dissolved into black sludge.

Lucy looked round and saw a sight she would never have guessed would be her salvation: Danielle and three other young women that Lucy recognised as members of the Camden coven.

I have no idea what they're doing here, but beggars can't be choosers! Lucy thought, before she heard a crunch of glass; the last Legionary was back on its feet.

Realising it was outnumbered, the demon turned and ran, ducking its head as the witches flung fireballs and Lucy shot her last bullets at its back.

"Help Charles and Gillian!" Lucy shouted as she scooped up her whip and gave pursuit.

The demon had a head-start, but Lucy felt something like a physical blow hit her in the small of the back and fling her forward. She collided with the Legionary, and the pair of them hurtled through the window of a nearby restaurant. Lucy covered her face as it shattered around her. With the crash of wood, broken glass and crockery crunching underneath them, they collided with abandoned tables.

Legion got back to its feet first and backflipped, sending Lucy staggering back as its clawed feet connected with her jaw. With that advantage, it fled in the direction of the restaurant's kitchen, narrowly avoiding Lucy slashing at its head with her whip.

Lucy gave pursuit, ducking as a bony claw swung out at her head, sending pots and pans clattering from their hooks. She fell to her hands and knees, only for a clawed foot to stamp down on her right hand. Without hesitation, she darted forward and sank her teeth into the demon's ankle. It tasted like rotten fish, and she instantly spat in disgust, but it had the desired effect; the demon recoiled with a keening screech, and Lucy's kukri went stabbing up into her foe's groin. Black blood spurted into her face, temporarily blinding her, and a foot slammed into her chest. Lucy went flying and crashed into an oven. She thrust out an arm to arrest her fall, and all of a sudden she felt heat and pain run down her right arm. She wiped her eyes clean of the filth and saw to her horror that her arm was on fire, having knocked off a frying pan that had been left on the gas when the chef had fled for their life. Legion was advancing on her, snapping its jaws hatefully, when she heard a grunt of exertion and a glass bottle shattered against the back of the demon's head, drenching it in something sticky.

"Lucy, now!" Charles bellowed.

Despite the pain and the heat, Lucy backhanded Legion, the flames licking the back of her right arm igniting the cooking oil Charles had drenched the creature in. It screamed as fire spread across its head and shoulders, and Lucy winced as spontaneously, ice crystals began to form over her right arm, smothering the flames. She looked round and saw Danielle. The coven witch followed up with another spell, a dart of pale white light that struck Lucy's burnt arm. Lucy let out a sigh of relief as the spell alleviated the pain.

She grinned at her fellow Knight and the young witch, before turning her attention to her burning foe. Without hesitation, she charged at Legion, tackling the demon around the waist. The pair of them went straight through an open doorway and, with a shriek from both, toppled down a flight of stairs, landing with a thud outside the customer toilets. As Lucy lay dazed, she heard Charles and Gillian call out to her.

"Lucy, you down there?"

"I'm alright—"

"Not for long!" Legion snarled.

Clawed hands grabbed her around the waist and flung her through the door into the men's toilets. She hit the tiled floor hard, and a clawed foot stamped on her back. She cried out, only for Legion to seize her by the back of the head and slam her face into one of the urinals. Chunks of porcelain clattered to the floor as Legion slammed her face against it again and again. Dazed and bleeding, Lucy felt the clawed hands close around her neck to choke the life from her.

Legion lifted her up off the ground, and Lucy's feet thrashed as the grip around her throat tightened. Whatever dark sorcery had been poured into this creature, it was enough to make it able to ignore the pain of touching one marked with the Order's sigil, to say nothing of the burns it bore from the fire, all but burnt out now. She kicked out with the blade protruding from her boot, but Legion didn't even flinch.

As dark spots darted in front of her eyes and breathing became more difficult, Lucy vaguely saw Legion pulling back one of its bone blades for a killing blow. Suddenly, a flash of white and the smell of ozone filled Lucy's nostrils and vision. Legion dropped her, screaming in pain, Lucy gagging in disgust as inky black blood splattered her face. Wiping it away, she saw that Charles had sliced its right arm off at the elbow with his falx.

Perfect timing as always, Charlie!

Not slow to take an advantage, Lucy drove her kukri into the back of the demon's neck. On a human, the silver blade would have severed the spinal cord at the c4 vertebrae, severing autonomic functions like breathing. On a demon, it was a partial decapitation. As the Legionary gave a weak groan and slid to the floor, Charles beheaded it and spat on the corpse for good measure.

"Thanks," Lucy gasped, breathing in hastily.

"Hey, you kept it busy long enough for me to get here. Claire set you up good," he said with a grin, pointing at the blade protruding from the tip of her boot. Dark blood clung to its tip.

"I thought you were hurt bad?" Lucy asked. Though his clothing was ripped and she could see his bare chest where the Legionary had hit him, there was no sign of an open wound.

"Angela's witches know their stuff. They even managed to get Gillian back on her feet—not that you'll ever hear her say thank you for it."

"Oh, I'm sure you can make up for her lack of gratitude," Lucy said with a raised eyebrow and wry smirk.

"Guys, you two down there?" Gillian's voice interrupted. "What's happening?"

"The Legionaries are dealt with; we'll need you down here to help us destroy the evidence—"

"I think we have a bigger problem," Gillian cut across Lucy's response. "I still can't reach Claire or the Chapterhouse. Even if we had a communication problem, she'd set up a secondary channel so we weren't completely out of contact. Something's not right…"

Suddenly, all three of them clutched their heads as the static on the radio channel was broken by a blood-curdling scream and the sound of gunfire. Without a word, Lucy and Charles ran back up the stairs to street level.

"Gillian, we need a portal. We have to get back *now*!"

Chapter 23: Deceived

"What are you working on?" Rosa asked over the intercom, looking into the sealed examination room.

Both Anne Mallory and her daughter were wearing rubber gloves and looking at a hermetically sealed box that contained a newly pupated hell-fly. The creature was about the size of a border collie, buzzing frantically as it tried to claw its way out of the box.

They'd been keeping the demonic insect contained in a purpose-built lab they'd hastily erected in the basement amidst racks of gleaming guns and other weapons that had really impressed Rosa; she suspected a lot of army barracks weren't so well stocked. A specially prepared cadaver had been used as a cocoon for the maggot that had hatched from one of the confiscated eggs. When it had finally pupated a few days ago, Rosa had watched Charles and Lucy seize the monstrous bug as it emerged from its fleshy cocoon. Anne and Claire swiftly amputated its wings, ignoring its frantic efforts to get free of their grasp. Once it was done, the demonic fly had been tossed into its current confines and locked in, ensuring there was no chance of escape.

"We're going to be running more tests of the effects of smaller doses of Joshua's blood," Claire said, sounding really enthused. "Pure blood from a Bane causes near-instant dissolution of demonic cells, but we want to see if diluting the concentration will have the same effect. If we can confirm smaller concentrations have the same effect within a suitable timeframe, it offers up so many opportunities; we can aerosolise it, sneak it into water systems or sprinklers. If diluting his blood doesn't damage its effectiveness then we can use it to strike surreptitiously at demon enclaves around the world: a poison that will be of little concern to humans but lethal to anything from What Lies Beyond! This could truly tip the scales in our favour!"

"Can I help?" Rosa offered, both to change the subject, feeling a little unsettled by Claire's fervour, and wanting to show she wasn't just taking advantage of the Order's hospitality. "I'm trained as a nurse; I might be able to—"

"I appreciate the offer, dear girl, but the contents of this room are extremely biohazardous, deadly to anyone without proper protection," Anne said.

"You've not got biohazard gear?" Rosa asked, surprised.

"We do, but we're dealing with highly dangerous creatures that carry all manner of infectious diseases, and while we have a degree of protection from the contagions they can spread because of what we've gone through, and Joshua there is safe because of what he is"—Anne added with a wave to the boy stood beside Rosa—"you're still just a civilian, and our remit is to protect you from the dangers What Lies Beyond poses."

Claire cleared her throat and tapped a syringe filled with pinkish fluid. "If you're ready, Mum?"

Anne turned to face her daughter and nodded, before looking over her shoulder at Rosa. "We'll pick this up in a moment."

Anne seized the monstrous bug from its cage and slammed it onto the table as the demonic fly tried to break free of her grasp. With a snarl, Anne swiftly secured it to the examination table with pins through its joints. The hell-fly buzzed the stumps of its wings and snapped its mandibles angrily, about the most violence it could manage, as Claire advanced on it with the syringe.

"Injecting a solution of holy water and Bane blood, seventy to thirty percent ratio," Claire said into a Dictaphone resting on the examination table. "In three, two, one."

She jabbed the syringe into the hell-fly's thorax. Anne started timing with a stopwatch. All four observers watched as the demonic insect tried to free itself, shrieking angrily...

until suddenly its trashing became even more frantic. Ugly red lesions that exuded smoke appeared all over its thorax and abdomen. Rosa made a noise of disgust, and both Anne and Claire recoiled as the hell-fly suddenly vomited black filth from between its hooked mandibles. Small white maggots writhed weakly amongst it.

As they watched, the demonic insect gave one last keening screech of defeat and slumped dead. The carcass looked as if they'd injected acid into the insect's body, swiftly dissolving into black sludge.

Mother of God, it actually works! Rosa goggled in astonishment, and Joshua looked on. Claire looked at her mother, who examined the stopwatch.

"Time to death: three minutes, four seconds."

"Impressive," Claire commented. She and her mother exited the lab after a swift decontamination, leaving their biohazard gear behind. "Well, it's good to know that we have a solid foundation. Unfortunately, diluting the blood runs the risk that any afflicted foes would still have sufficient strength to injure or kill civilians before the blood debilitates them completely."

"Shame," Anne agreed. "Maybe if we increase the concentration of holy water, have several priests bless it at once to increase its effectiveness, that might hopefully counter the effects of diluting the blood—"

And that was when, with a mighty explosion, the floor of the armoury caved in. Joshua and Rosa threw themselves away from the source of the blast as chunks of debris went flying in all directions. An enormous hole had been blown in the centre of the floor, and as the dust settled, they could hear the sound of running footsteps fast approaching from the depths below.

Anne bellowed a battle cry as she and Claire pulled guns from the closest rack and shot a hulking figure clambering out of the hole. Rosa's gorge rose; the smell of rot and decay it exuded was worse than an open sewer. She saw rusted armour and bloated flesh, a pair of corroded swords clutched in its meaty fists, heard the distorted voice through the visor of its fully enclosed helm roaring mocking death threats. Claire and Anne emptied their guns into the swollen monster's belly, to no avail. Their guns clicked empty, and the brute laughed. The Blighted Brother looked over his shoulder and down into the hole, utterly unconcerned as the two women reloaded their guns.

"We are in the enemy's stronghold, Falciparum! No mercy!" the bloated figure roared.

Another swollen monstrosity clambered from the hole, clutching a notched and rusted sword, face hidden behind a cloth veil under a coif of rusted chainmail. Claire and Anne started shooting again, but the newcomer raised a kite-shaped shield. The bullets ricocheted off. Suddenly, a trio of grenades flew over the heads of the deformed knights, landing close to Rosa and Joshua.

"Everyone out! Move!" Anne shouted.

She seized Joshua as Claire pulled Rosa to her feet. They bolted for the door to the upper levels of the house as the grenades detonated behind them and Rosa heard a growling voice bellow, "After them! No survivors!"

Once they were out of the armoury, Claire slammed the door behind her, locked it, then placed a couple of steel bars in front to barricade it.

"Will that hold them?" Rosa asked.

Claire gave her an incredulous look. "Only for a few minutes. We never thought this place would come under attack, certainly not during daylight hours. This is a house, not a fortress," she replied as they raced up into the atrium.

"Lawrence, get down here! We need to evacuate!" Anne shouted up the stairs.

Another thunderous explosion blasted the front door off its hinges. Anne put herself in front of Joshua and Rosa, taking the brunt of the impact as spars of broken wood flew in and clubbed her to the ground.

"Help me with her," Claire urged, grabbing her mother under one arm.

Rosa did likewise. As they began to head up the stairs, they heard shouts from behind.

"Get to the briefing room!" Claire snapped as she reached behind a stand of books halfway up the stairs, pulling out a Glock pistol. She pulled back the hammer just as a shadowy figure appeared in the doorway, unidentifiable through the dust but clearly human.

Claire didn't waste time asking; she just aimed and fired. The figure in the door collapsed like a puppet with its strings cut, and then bullets tore the furnishings of the landing apart as his comrades returned fire, Claire and the others fleeing upstairs.

***

The sounds of gunshots immediately jerked Lawrence awake. A glass fell from his hands as he tried to shake the whiskey from his system. He groggily shook his head, recognising the sound of Heckler and Koch automatic weaponry.

"Someone's come for the boy," he muttered, grabbing his own kukri and sword cane from their resting places in his study before heading over to the wardrobe.

Behind the clothing, he found the hidden latch and opened it: a secret passage that would allow him to slip from one room to another. One of his ancestors, Marcus Templeton, had installed them in every room, a means of escape or getting the jump on an enemy that was brave or stupid enough to directly attack the Order's headquarters. He'd never had to use them before.

"Let's hope Great-great-grandpa Marcus knew what he was doing…"

Lawrence drew his kukri and slipped through into the next room, looking for the hidden passage that would let him circle around his foe.

***

Lakshmi Varsani stalked through the door and into the entry hall of her faction's greatest enemy, amused at the blasphemy of treading in such a place. Behind her, black-clad gunmen stalked into the house with only one order: kill the blessed mutant and any of the Order who tried to defend him. They were a squad of the Desolated's finest—or at least the best of those who'd survived Samhain.

Evidently not good enough though, Lakshmi mused as she saw one of her men lying on his back, bullet holes blasted in his skull.

She nodded to her second-in-command. She hadn't bothered to learn his name, and he was certainly no equal to Cyrus Zeller, but he was brutal and efficient, a former American soldier discharged after one too many savage beatings of prisoners at Bagram for his own amusement. He quickly began shouting orders.

"Spread out, scour the house room by room. Orders are shoot to kill, assume all occupants are hostile—"

The soldier's command was cut short as his throat exploded. He toppled, clutching at the ruin of his neck. The rest of the squad took cover as Claire Mallory emerged from her hiding place behind a doorframe to shoot at the interlopers. Lakshmi shrieked, baring her teeth as she pulled a Desert Eagle from her belt and returned fire. Claire ducked out of sight, shouting, "Fall back! Fall back!"

Lakshmi motioned for the mercenaries to press the attack on the upper floors. They had a limited window of opportunity; the rest of the Order would soon realise they'd been sent on a fool's errand to Bloomsbury and when they did…

This is no time for subtlety. Lakshmi shrugged off her jacket and body armour, letting the demon within her take full control. Her hair retracted and her dark skin became scaly. The Order had left only weaklings and desk jockeys to protect its fortress. This would be no challenge.

***

Claire kept her gun aimed at the door. Outside, they could hear something moving swiftly, the stairs thudding as it crawled up them. The door rattled on its hinges as something hit it hard at speed.

"Help me move this," she urged Rosa, who ran over to help her shift chairs and the long table to barricade the door, while Joshua kept an eye on the unconscious Anne.

The door rattled again but the makeshift barricade held. Claire quickly pulled out her mobile phone and began dialling.

"Who are you calling?" Rosa asked.

Claire didn't look up from her phone. "Someone, anyone, who can help us now." As soon as it connected, she blurted out, "If you're still in the area, I need help, Liam! The Chapterhouse is under attack!"

The attacker hit the barricaded door again. The door held, just barely, and whatever was on the other side shrieked in frustration, a sound born of nightmares. Claire raised the gun in her right hand as her left ushered Rosa and Joshua back.

With another keening shriek, the door was smashed free of its hinges, revealing a tall, serpentine figure. Claire threw herself flat as the door sailed over her head, then scrambled back to her feet, shooting at the intruder. The creature in the doorway was not human; to Rosa's shock, it looked like a cobra as tall as a man, but with clawed arms and a humanoid torso rippling with lean muscle.

The cobra creature hissed angrily as Claire shot it twice in the upper chest, but still it slithered into the room, lashing out with its muscular, scarred tail. Claire tried to dive out the way, but the tail clipped her across the chest. She went flying, her gun slipping from her hands as she crashed heavily into a nearby bookcase. Amidst broken wood and torn paper and leather, she hit the ground in a dazed heap.

Rosa had no idea what she was thinking, but she shoved Joshua under a table and dived for Claire's fallen gun. The cobra monster shrieked, and Rosa barely avoided a spray of oily green phlegm it spat at her. The spittle hit the floor, and the carpet began to smoke and smoulder as if touched by acid. Rosa, her hand closing around the gun, gaped in shock, before she raised it in a shaking hand and fired.

Both of her shots went wide, and then the gun clicked empty.

The snake creature let out a strange, rattling hiss. It took Rosa a minute to realise the creature was laughing as it rose to its full height above her. Rosa stood frozen in fear, before a scaly fist connected with her chest, smashing her off her feet into the wall.

Dazed, gasping for breath, Rosa raised her head to hear Joshua whimpering in fear as the monster overturned the desk he'd been hiding under with a loud bang. The creature's clawed hands reached out for his neck, but inches from seizing him, the serpent recoiled, as if repulsed by the idea of laying hands on the boy. Snarling, the snake monster opened its fanged mouth, ready to spit its venom again...

Behind them came a shout. "OI, BITCH! Over here!"

The snake spun round in time to catch the small glass figurine of a woman Lawrence had thrown at it. The monster let out that hissing that passed for laughter, crushed the figure into fragments in its fist... and then screamed in agony as clear fluid ran between its fingers, the scaly skin and flesh smoking and bleeding.

The monster thrashed and howled when another figurine smashed against its scaly brow. Its screeching reached a crescendo as runnels of blood ran down its face, dripping onto its chest and neck. It tried to wipe off what looked to Rosa like water, but that only made its blistered, bleeding hands worse.

"You know what that contained?" Lawrence sneered at the screaming reptilian monster. "Fifty millilitres of blessed water from the shrine of St Bernadette of Lourdes. Harmless to me... to you, like showering in sulphuric acid. Compliments of my daughter, a little souvenir she brought back from a school trip years ago." Lawrence smiled viciously. "When you get back to whatever hell you crawled out of, Lakshmi, tell Cyrus Zeller the Templetons send their regards!"

With a shriek, Lakshmi struck at Lawrence with her tail, smashing him aside, and slithered out of the room, screaming and clawing at her bleeding face. Lawrence snarled as he pulled a revolver from a holster at his belt, intent on finishing what he had started back on Halloween, and shot into Lakshmi's retreating back. She shrieked as the bullets perforated her spine, but then Lawrence had to dive for cover as the mercenaries came charging up to support their mistress. Bullets filled the air, Lawrence returning fire and dropping two men with well-placed shots before a guttural roar caught everyone's attention.

Two hulking figures stormed into the room. Brothers Ebolae and Falciparum glowered down at the mercenaries as they shouldered their way through.

"Keep the authorities at bay when they respond to this. They cannot harm us but they will prove a nuisance," Falciparum growled, raising his sword. "These wretches are ours!"

Ebolae gave a rattling chuckle in agreement, clashing his rusted swords together. Lawrence struggled to his feet, raising his pistol and aiming it at Falciparum's head. He let the sword cane fall to the ground, and the two disease-riddled knights erupted into laughter.

"How the mighty Order of the Argent Blade has fallen!" Falciparum laughed. "I remember when knights of legend, warriors of countless battles filled your ranks, broke the backs of armies and destroyed demons of incalculable power. Now look at you, sickly old men and frightened women cowering before the blade!"

The two knights breathed deep, and gave a sigh of satisfaction.

"The great one's touch is already in you. The gift is spreading through your veins, turning your innards to rot... but it need not be that way. We can give you all the gift, purify the false and failing blessing of your weakling god from you, initiate you into the true path. Disease, decay, putrefaction—all are the fate of this world. Why fight it when you can use it, become empowered by it?"

Lawrence hawked and spat at Falciparum's feet. "Yes, well, you see, I am currently a servant of a much greater power than Nergal…"

"And what is that?" Falciparum sneered, while Ebolae growled angrily at the perceived blasphemy.

"High-proof alcohol."

He slid open a desk drawer and grinned when he saw what was in it. *I thought Anne hid you from me.* A bottle of brandy that had been given to his father as a gift of thanks for loyal service by Winston Churchill.

Lawrence grimaced at the thought of what he was about to do. "Sorry, Dad."

Falciparum looked at him askance. "A final drink for the condemned man?" the Knight of Yersinia sneered as Ebolae growled.

"Not exactly." Lawrence hefted the bottle of liquor and threw it.

As it shattered on Falciparum's chest, drenching him in brandy and broken glass, Lawrence nodded. Claire pulled the trigger of her gun.

Falciparum roared in horror as the incendiary rounds she had hastily loaded ignited the alcohol. With a bellow of outrage, Ebolae seized a chair and flung it at Claire. It hit her full in the head and shattered to pieces, leaving her in a crumpled heap with Joshua and Rosa trying to revive her and Anne. Ebolae charged forward, but Lawrence scooped up his cane sword and lunged, blocking the Knight of Yersinia's rusted swords as they cleaved for Claire's head.

"That was a mistake, old man," Ebolae growled.

"No, thinking an old man and women are harmless was yours." With his free hand, Lawrence drove his silver kukri through the rusted visor of Ebolae's helm.

The diseased knight roared as the sanctified blade punched into his face, then hefted his swords and swung for Lawrence's head. Lawrence ducked and slashed out with his sword cane, slicing chunks of flabby flesh from Ebolae's exposed chest. Snarling, Ebolae lumbered at him as Lawrence gave ground. The warrior hacked at Lawrence with a frenzied intensity. The sword smashed through an overturned desk, and Lawrence threw his arm up to protect his eyes from wood splinters. His sword cane darted out again, only infuriating his opponent more.

"I thought you were supposed to be powerful, but this is easier than slicing up a Christmas turkey!" Lawrence taunted as he ducked under an attack that would have taken his head off.

Suddenly, something seized his ankle. Lawrence looked down for half a moment—one of the dying cultists had grabbed him. He kicked the wretch off him, but the distraction was all his enemy needed.

The sword in the Blighted Brother's left hand sliced Lawrence's thigh as he pulled free of the stricken cultist's grip. Lawrence was doubled over in pain in an instant—while the mark upon his arm protected him from demonic taint and possession, it couldn't protect him from natural illnesses. The Knights of Yersinia couldn't afflict the Order with the plagues and toxins they bore with them from What Lies Beyond, but they had other means of weaponising disease to their advantage.

The pain of the cancer in his blood was like being doused in flaming petrol, overwhelming the painkillers he'd been given to try and alleviate it, but even through that, Lawrence tried to keep his enemy's attention on him as the Blighted Brother sought other prey to infect now Lawrence was incapacitated.

"A pity I can't watch you suffer, but there is more work to be done," the monster sneered through its visor, but Lawrence wasn't down. As soon as the brute's back was turned, he used the wall to pull himself to his feet and, lifting the cane sword, lunged.

The blade went through the Blighted Brother's neck, scraping against vertebrae. It took all his strength to push the sword cane through to the hilt. Without warning, an elbow as hard as a concrete block slammed into his gut, and any strength he had left went out of him along with his breath.

Lawrence fell to the floor, desperately sucking down air as a shadow fell over him and burbling laughter filled his ears. The Blighted Brother turned to face him, light glinting on the tip of the sword cane's blade jutting from its neck, and Lawrence knew what was coming next.

He was surprised to find out he was wrong. Ebolae drove a gauntleted fist into his gut, then seized him by the throat and flung him across the room. Lawrence hit something hard and landed awkwardly, the impact jarring him. Pain ran through him like lightning, and he could feel what felt like multiple fractures. Suddenly, a flabby, teratoma-covered arm shot out with surprising speed, seizing him by the back of the throat and lifting him off the ground.

To his surprise, the brute didn't bother with any boasts or mockery as it held him aloft. There was an explosion of pain in his back, pushing its way through until the notched tip of a sword emerged from his chest. Lawrence tasted blood on his tongue, hearing Falciparum laughing in his ear. He chanced a look to his left and saw the burned, diseased flesh of his killer's hand holding him fast.

"Just one more, and then our wretched bloodline ends as it should have done, with the maggots supping from our flesh. The difference is I will live on, whereas you and all the rest will be forgotten," Falciparum sneered, before Lawrence felt the blade torn from him. Things within him shifted by its absence.

I let the Desolated strike twice: first in the city I was sworn to protect, and now in my own home. I lost all of my daughters because of my decision and shamed the legacy of my family. I fear what comes next will not be kind to me.

As things began to fade, Lawrence smelt ozone and heard a familiar rushing sound. He tried to raise his hand, reaching out as blue light erupted in the centre of the room. He could see silhouettes set against it, but his strength failed him.

The last thing Lawrence heard before the darkness was the sound of his daughter screaming for him.

Chapter 24: Counterattack

With a shriek, Gillian thrust out her hands, her full attention on Brother Falciparum. The Knight of Yersinia crouched behind his shield as the flames bursting forth from Gillian's palms washed over him.

"Pitiful!" Falciparum sneered, advancing through the flames, his gaze fixed on Gillian. His rusted sword dripped with Lawrence's blood. "For too long have I waited to exterminate the tainted bloodline of the Templetons, and at long last, I will complete—"

Falciparum's words were abruptly cut short as, with a yell, Gillian severed her flames and Charles lashed out with his new falx. The Champion's Blade, its new form dancing with white flames, smashed into the burning wood of the plague knight's shield. It shattered, but the blade carried on into Falciparum's chest. The monstrous knight howled, his flesh blackening and burning, before Charles pulled the Blade free and ducked under the retaliatory swing of Falciparum's sword.

"Who dares?" Falciparum roared.

Charles grinned savagely. "I think I do!"

He swung low, and the burning white falx bit into Falciparum's right knee. Despite the blubber, the blade cleaved into the knee joint, catching on bone and sticking fast.

"Ah, the arrogance of youth," Falciparum mocked, as Charles tried to free his sword. "I remember that once—"

This time, Lucy cut the plague knight short, with a shot in the face as he pulled his blade back for a decapitating swing. Silver bullets tore into his skull.

"Thanks a lot, Lucy!" Charles snapped as Falciparum staggered back, yanking the haft of the falx, still buried in the plague knight's knee, out of his grasp.

It was Gillian's turn to intervene. Her palms glowed blue, and Falciparum's feet left the ground as bands of pale blue energy wrapped around his torso, pinioning his arms, before with a roar, Gillian flung him through the closest wall. Lucy winced as Falciparum was sent tumbling down the Chapterhouse stairs with a thunderous crash. The Champion's Blade snagged on the doorframe and tore free from Falciparum's knee with a spray of maggot-infested black blood that smeared the wall and floor. Flames burned amongst the black slimy morass.

"You're alive, aren't you?!" Lucy shot back at Charles.

"Don't count on it!" another gurgling voice roared.

Charles's eyes went wide and he rolled aside as both of Ebolae's swords came chopping down, sending chips of wood and carpet flying. Charles scrambled to his feet, seizing the discarded cane sword. He dodged back as Ebolae tried to cut him in half, and aimed precisely at the plague knight's face. The thin blade stabbed into the slits of his visor, and Ebolae howled, dropping one of his swords to try and pull the sword cane from his skull.

"Charles!" Lucy grabbed the Champion's Blade from where it had landed and flung it across the room.

He caught it in mid-air. The flames on the curved blade crackled as Charles spun on his heel and swung. Ebolae roared in fury, until the Champion's Blade connected with his neck. With the holy enchantments, the heat of the steel and the force Charles put into the blow, Ebolae's head was cleaved from his shoulders. The diseased, swollen body pitched forward, maggots and black blood spilling from the stump of the neck. Without pause, Gillian made to stretch her hands out, but Lucy grabbed her wrist.

"What?" Gillian demanded.

By way of an answer, Lucy pointed to her hair.

"God, what's happening?" Danielle whispered, shocked. Charles also looked stunned.

Save for a few strands of red and her eyebrows, Gillian's hair had turned near completely white.

"Reinforcements! I need reinforcements!"

Falciparum was back on his feet, shouting and pointing at the upper levels. Black-clad figures were forming up around the Blighted Brother as he gestured up the stairs with his sword.

"Kill them all!"

Suddenly, the window behind them shattered, and Liam, fully transformed, bounded through the room and flung himself down the stairs as the first of the mercenaries began charging up. He swung out with both hands, and the roars of the charging men became screams as heads and limbs went flying in sprays of blood.

"You two, stay here with them, try and help Lawrence!" Lucy commanded. "Charles, come on!"

She raised her kukri as they charged out, and ducked as Liam flung a body in black body armour up the stairs. The luckless mercenary hit the wall hard, slumping close to where Claire lay dazed beside her mother, Rosa and Joshua crouched behind her in fear. Lucy stabbed the body for good measure.

Charles swung out with his falx, bisecting a mercenary who was trying to circle around Liam for a clean shot. The werewolf whirled and roared as a firing line of a half-dozen mercenaries formed up inside the atrium. Charles and Lucy ducked for cover, and the mercenaries opened fire. Liam roared in frustration, but despite the blood spurting from his multiple wounds, he didn't fall.

"No silver, you idiots!" Charles shouted as he and Lucy re-emerged and retaliated.

Suddenly, a series of gunshots came from the upper floors, followed by a scream for help.

Lucy's head turned as Falciparum gave a snarl of satisfaction, then bellowed at the mercenaries, "Cover my retreat, then withdraw to your escape points. Your work is done!"

With a roar, Liam and Charles charged forward, claws and blade swinging, but the mercenaries charged to meet them. It didn't matter that they died in droves, they didn't stop trying to pin the arms and weapons of their foes. Some threw themselves on the Champion's Blade, letting it catch in their bones and guts to allow their compatriots a chance to strike a blow. Lucy emptied her gun trying to shoot down Falciparum, but her bullets ricocheted off his armour or didn't even make him flinch as they hit his flesh. The hooded head turned to face her, and Lucy felt sure he was grinning as he retreated to the lower levels of the house, back the way he'd come, with a wall of flesh to ensure his escape.

***

Gillian crawled over to her father. He was still breathing, but weakly.

"Dad, wake up! Wake up!"

She tried to shake him awake, but Lawrence remained unresponsive.

"Daddy, please wake up!" Gillian pleaded, her voice starting to break. "I'm sorry, I'm sorry, just please wake up!"

Danielle scrambled beside her, palms glowing as she channelled magic into Lawrence's gaping wound. The bleeding began to slow, but it didn't stop, and the wound refused to close.

"DO SOMETHING!" Gillian shrieked at her half-sister. "Do something useful and help him!"

"I, I can't," Danielle stammered. "This is too much, even for me. I only know basic healing magic—"

A gasp from the man lying between them drew their attention. Lawrence had opened his eyes, and was trying to reach up with a blood-soaked hand for Gillian's cheek. She grabbed it and pressed it to her face, heedless of the blood.

"Daddy…"

"My little girl… what have I done to you?" Lawrence whispered, his eyes sad as he looked at her pale hair, stripped of life and colour by her power… and then something went out of his eyes, and a rasp, soft as a whisper, escaped between his lips.

"No, no, please! Please, don't go! Don't leave me!" Gillian pleaded, her face crumbling. "Help him! You, or Anne! Where's Anne?!" she cast about desperately.

At that moment, Anne appeared, leaning on Claire, both looking beaten and battered, with Rosa and Joshua, shocked and afraid but otherwise unhurt, bringing up the rear.

Suddenly, the thunderous bang of a gunshot rang out. All eyes turned and saw Joshua stagger, a bright red spot appearing in the centre of his chest. Two more shots followed, and the boy toppled.

"No!" Anne shouted, and she ran over to try to stem the bleeding.

Claire turned and saw a mercenary, trapped under the heap of rubble where Liam had flung him, lower the pistol in his hand, a content look on his face.

"My work is done." The man sighed.

Claire snarled and reloaded her pistol, stalking over to him. As the barrel stared him in the face, the mercenary looked unafraid, so proud of himself for gunning down a child.

"The Bane is lost. Nothing will stop the glorious future that is to come!"

"Whatever comes next, you're not going to be here to see it," Claire spat, and pulled the trigger.

The shot blew blood, bone and brain matter from the cultist's head over the carpet. Claire tossed the gun aside and ran to where her mother was kneeling by Joshua. Her hands were clutching a bleeding wound in Joshua's neck, her fingers stained bright red.

"No, no, just stay with me, Joshua!"

But his eyes were flickering, his movements steadily becoming weaker as he bled out.

"I need a healer or he's not going to make it!" Anne bellowed, her voice frantic.

Claire looked down at the small form in her mother's arms and shook her head. "Mum…"

"No, I won't lose him!"

Desperately trying CPR, Anne thumped on Joshua's chest, her expression frenzied. A hand appeared on her shoulder, dark fur retracting into pale skin and claws turning into nails as Liam loomed over the pair, his expression solemn.

"Anne, it's too late."

"No!" Anne raged, but Claire pried her mother's fingers from the body and made Anne look her in the face.

"Mum… Mum, he's gone."

Chapter 25: Laid to Rest
Highgate Cemetery, London
Eight days later

Heavy rain fell as a small party of figures stood around a fresh grave to bid farewell to one of their number. It felt strange for Lucy to be back here, the place where her life had irrevocably changed. She'd walked past the place where her one-time friends had revealed their true allegiance and tried to kill her, the spot where Charles and Gillian had fought to protect her, and now she was here again, to say goodbye to the man who had opened her eyes.

Unlike Valerie, Lawrence had stipulated he wished to be buried alongside his parents. Beside two weathered tombstones bearing the names Dominic and Anya Templeton stood a fresh one of black marble bearing Lawrence's name.

As Father Peter intoned the ceremony, all of the Order, accompanied by Rosa, Moira, Edmund and Liam, stood with heads bowed, all of them clearly thinking the same.

Where do we go from here?

Lawrence had been such a towering figure in the Order, the man who had taken them all in, given them a purpose, made them a part of something greater than themselves. This wasn't how they'd expected to live their lives, but Lawrence had given them a home, a family, in his own way.

Anne and Claire were particularly distraught. With Lawrence's death, Anne had lost not only an old, dear friend, but one of the last links she had to her late husband, and Claire had lost the only father figure she had ever known.

Their grief, however, was nothing compared to Gillian's, who was inconsolable. Her misery at the hateful, bitter words she'd said to her father, and that she'd never be able to reconcile with him, was clearly eating at her as much as Valerie's death had at Charles. She'd barely reacted when Danielle had placed a sympathetic hand on her shoulder, when previously she'd angrily have shrugged it off and more than likely taken a swing at the young witch's face.

Angela Drake and some other members of the Camden coven were standing at the funeral's peripheries, allowing those closest to Lawrence to pay their respects. Lucy gave a friendly nod to Danielle. She felt sorry that the young woman—who, by Lucy's understanding, had never had a father figure in her life—would now never have the chance to know if that was something she wanted.

So many young women in our world have lost their fathers: me, Claire, Gillian, Valerie, and now Danielle. In some way, Lawrence gave us that; he was stern, but supportive. He never stepped in to do things for us, but ensured we had the tools we needed to do what we had to.

As Father Peter closed his Bible, and Charles and Liam began to lower Lawrence's body into the grave, Rosa broke ranks from the group, a small urn clutched in her hands. Moira and Edmund, their faces and hands completely covered even though the sun had yet to break through the thick grey clouds overhead, made to follow, along with Father Peter. The irony of a priest walking side by side with vampires brought a smile to Lucy's lips despite the sombre situation.

It faded as she remembered where they were going: to find a suitable place to lay Joshua to rest. She dipped her head, feeling the same sense of regret that she always did when she thought of that boy.

We promised to keep him safe. We failed. The best we can do is ensure he rests in peace.

They'd chosen to cremate Joshua, lest others find his body and exhume it, thinking to achieve some benefit. Claire had mentioned certain cultists might seek to offer his organs or scrimshawed bones up to the Pantheon as a token of devotion. After his short life and the violence of his death, the boy deserved better than that.

Rest in peace, Joshua. May what lies beyond the veil treat you better than this world did.

As the funeral party began to break up, Anne cleared her throat, pulling a letter from within her dark coat. "As you know, when a Grand Master of the Order of the Argent Blade is slain, it is tradition for him or her to name their successor ahead of time, so that the successor may be confirmed at the graveside of their fallen predecessor, a passing in spirit of the burden of duty from one to the other…"

"Is this really necessary?" Gillian protested, but Claire silenced her with a raised hand.

Anne gave her a sympathetic but firm look. "It's the tradition. You of all people know how important that was to your father."

Gillian reluctantly nodded and went back to toying with her hair. The red was coming back into it, save for a few white streaks that stubbornly refused to fade. Lucy had tried to tease her lover about how it suited her, in a bid to rouse her spirits in the days after the attack on the Chapterhouse, but it had not lightened Gillian's concerns.

"It's been getting more frequent. Ever since Echidna, every time I cast a spell, the white creeps in, and every time it takes longer for the red to come back," she had said fearfully.

"What does it mean?"

"I don't know. I have theories, that's all," Gillian had replied. "I fear that, somehow, using my powers is accelerating the negative effects of being a spellweaver, speeding up the aging process, weakening my immune system… I don't know if it's a natural process, if Echidna cast some curse on me with her last breath, or if it's because of the scale of the power I used to destroy her."

"Can you do anything about it?"

"I don't know." Gillian had sighed. "When this is over, I need to go back to Cornwall, consult with the coven who helped tutor me, see what they can help me find out…"

Anne cleared her throat to get silence and opened the envelope, sealed with a wax stamp marked with the Order's sword and horned skull emblem.

"In the event of my death, I, Lawrence Templeton, Grand Master of the Knights of the Order of the Argent Blade, transfer my rights, duties and privileges of the rank of Grand Master to Miss Lucy Rose Murray. May all loyal Knights accept my decision, and may the Othersider conclaves understand that she is to be afforded the due respect our Order's position requests."

Charles made a noise of frustration and looked away, trying to hide his scowl. No doubt he'd still hoped Lawrence might overlook his shortcomings since Samhain and bestow the title on him. It was something that was going to have to bear watching; Lucy would either have to get him back on side or have him reassigned somewhere away from London. *He's a valuable asset to our cause, but I can't have jealousy on his part putting our work in jeopardy.*

Claire, Anne and Gillian bowed their heads in acknowledgement of Lucy's new status.

"What are your orders?" Anne asked.

Lucy had no answer to give her.

Chapter 26: A Glimmer of Hope

"Well, as Ethan used to say, this is well and truly FUBAR," Lucy muttered as she took in the task ahead of her.

It had been almost a fortnight since the attack, and the deaths of Joshua and Lawrence, and a sense of defeat and futility hung over the Chapterhouse.

"We were played for fools," Lucy said bitterly. "We went haring off, and the Desolated kept us busy with their plague zombies and Legion lying in wait. If they'd killed us there, it would have been a bonus, but it wasn't what they wanted. They killed our leadership and what might have been one of our greatest assets in the shadow war... and I have no idea what to do now." She sighed, rubbing the healing cut on the back of her neck, the latest souvenir of the demon assassin.

"Strike back now. Blood for blood," Gillian insisted.

"There's no point. Moira and Edmund tracked the origin point of those undead to an abandoned Phoenix Initiative laboratory. It had been cleaned out. The Desolated used it and then fled. There's nothing left," Lucy replied. "This wasn't them setting out their stall. This was a hit and run; they just wanted to hurt us and then slip away. They succeeded... and now we have no idea how to retaliate."

"Not to mention we fucked up. We promised to keep that boy safe, and we failed him," Claire said sadly.

She was walking with a limp and frequently clutched her sides. Lakshmi had broken several of her ribs, and she still had several healing bruises and a swollen, split lip. She sank into a chair with a hiss of pain.

"Then we find a way to make sure he didn't die for nothing." All eyes turned to Rosa, standing in the doorway.

"They wanted him dead, the whole purpose of this attack was to kill him; I heard the mercenaries say multiple times that their target was the Bane. No doubt, they'll be complacent now, confident that they've dealt you a crippling blow. You can take that and prove them wrong, smash their arrogance at a stroke."

"And how do you propose we do that?" Charles muttered sullenly.

Rosa gave him a cold look. "Humour me. What was Joshua's blood type?"

Anne got to her feet and began sifting through her notes from the tests she'd been running. "O negative."

"How much of his blood did you manage to take from him before he died?" Rosa asked.

Anne gave the young woman a confused look but said, "Between about five to eight litres. We were doing regular blood draws for the last few weeks."

"Then you have the medical equipment to perform a blood transfusion," Rosa said confidently. "Come on."

"What are you talking about, you little idiot?" Charles snapped. "Even if you put that boy's blood into yourself, there's no guarantee you'll become a Bane!"

"Has anyone ever tried?" Rosa replied with a pointed look.

None of the gathered Knights could answer her.

"I think this was why my uncle invited me to stay with him at the same time he was fostering Joshua. He must have feared an attack was imminent, hence why he called you in. I guess he knew we share the same blood type and wanted to make sure he had a back-up plan."

"Sounds rather cold," Danielle remarked.

Gillian shrugged. "For those of us who fight the encroachment of the darkness into this world, sometimes hard choices are made. My father understood that... and he always said that a desperate solution is better than doing nothing."

She got to her feet to address Rosa. "Of course, the decision has to be yours. We're not like the Desolated; we don't force people to die for us. You do realise that if we do this and it works, you're going to have a target painted on you. We will do all in our power to protect you, but you need to know, you don't have to do this. If you still want to walk away—"

"No," Rosa insisted. "I won't let Joshua die for nothing if there's a chance it could work."

"It's worth a shot," Anne said. "Let me get things ready."

***

Two days later

Rosa shook her head as she stepped into the sealed lab. At the far end of the room, a pulsating egg the size of a human head sat on a table.

"I'm going to be right here," Lucy said, holding her silver kukri ready.

She gave Rosa an encouraging squeeze on the shoulder, and followed as she took a step towards the bulging egg. As they watched, the egg split apart. A long, white maggot tore its way free with snapping mandibles, and slithered out. Lucy raised her blade as Rosa extended her hand towards the wriggling demonic larva. The maggot suddenly tensed, sensing a potential host to implant itself into, its mandibles clicking eagerly.

The moment of truth, Lucy thought.

The rest of the Order—along with Danielle, who seemed to have become a permanent houseguest since Lawrence's death—watched with bated breath.

The maggot lunged from the tabletop and landed on Rosa's arm. Rosa screamed as it bit into her skin, drawing blood. Blood trickled from the wound as the creature squirmed from left to right, trying to get purchase to burrow into her flesh. Rosa's screams of pain were getting more intense—

"Lucy, get it off—!" Charles bellowed.

Anne cut him off. "Lucy, wait! Look!"

Lucy's gaze fell to Rosa's arm. The maggot was covered in Rosa's blood, but the demonic larva was reacting like it had been soaked in acid. It lost its purchase on Rosa's arm, and Lucy angrily swept it off. It writhed and squirmed on the floor, screeching shrilly. Smoke rose from its body, which seemed to be collapsing in on itself.

"What's happening?" Rosa asked.

"It's dying," Lucy said simply.

The maggot dissolved into pale white filth at the centre of a puddle of blood. All eyes went wide at the complete dissolution of the demonic creature.

"Well, that seems promising," Lucy said to the others behind the glass.

Charles's eyes were gleaming with something Lucy hadn't seen in them for a while: optimism. Gillian also looked intrigued, but Anne and Claire remained impartial.

"I never accept the evidence of a single experiment." Anne turned her attention to Gillian. "Be a dear and bring up another batch. Three this time."

Gillian nodded, and through the glass, Lucy saw her lover's palms glow. With a flash of bright red light, three more hell-fly eggs landed on the table where the last one still festered. They began to twitch and ripple as the maggots within came alive at the prospect of a host.

"Now, Rosa, let an equal amount of your blood land on each of them—let's say three drops," Anne requested. "Use one of the pipettes. Lucy, keep watch."

Rosa did as she was bidden, filling a pipette with her blood and walking over towards the pulsating eggs. As one of the eggs split apart, Rosa squeezed three drops of blood into the fleshy fissure, and almost immediately, smoke began to rise. She quickly did the same with the other two eggs. Again, smoke rose, the eggs collapsing in on themselves as if acid had dropped on them. A horrific screeching filled the lab. The occupant of the first egg emerged, drenched in Rosa's blood and screaming as it dissolved into pale mush. The other two eggs resembled deflated footballs, the maggots shrieking as they slowly dissolved, trapped inside.

A stunned silence fell.

"Ladies and gentlemen, today we have witnessed history," Anne said, a tremor in her voice that could only be described as disbelieving awe. "We have confirmed that the unique properties of a Bane's blood can be passed from one person to another by way of a blood transfusion. We have an opportunity to circumvent the rarity of that ability, and that cannot be overstated."

Lucy looked to Claire. The younger Mallory had a look on her face that Lucy imagined Newton, Darwin and Jenner would have worn upon making the discoveries that put them in the history books.

"Let's not get ahead of ourselves," Claire said, taking it upon herself to be the voice of reason. "We still don't have all the pieces to make a comprehensive plan—"

"No, but we've got a first step, and from there, we can start planning," Lucy said over the intercom. "We cannot defeat this threat by ourselves. We need allies this time, and more than we did at Samhain. It's time to cast a wide net. The Desolated are building an army. We need to make one of our own."

Chapter 27: Business Meeting
Paris, France

"Well, I must say, I wasn't expecting to be updating one of my most prestigious contacts so soon," the figure on the other side of the desk said in a sepulchral voice.

Lucy, as advised, suppressed the urge to curl her lip at his withered countenance. Charles had briefed her on the Russian arms dealer Konstantin.

"I was sorry to hear of the death of Lawrence Templeton—a most diligent man and one who, like me, suffered great loss in the line of his duty. I regret I did not have the opportunity to do much in the way of business with him, but perhaps with you, my dear, we can open a far lengthier partnership." The revenant gave Lucy a toothy smile.

She determinedly kept her face neutral. "You said you had valuable information for me."

The decrepit visage smiled at her, before he snapped bony fingers.

"What is this?" Lucy asked as Siobhan stepped forward and handed over a manila file.

She opened it; inside were printouts of bank statements and invoices.

"Payments from a shipping company based in Athens to a bank account in London. What's funny is that the shipping company and the bank account are both licensed to subsidiaries of Ouroboros Industries. I understand you know where their ties lie, yes?"

Lucy nodded tersely as Konstantin went on. "The bank account is registered to a Mr Nicholas Webb—don't bother looking into it; it's a pseudonym for our mutual acquaintance Nathaniel Danvers that he's used to cultivate ties to numerous organised crime and private security groups. That's how those cultists got the weapons they used to attack your home, kill your former leader, and that rather valuable asset you were hiding," Konstantin finished with a ghoulish smile.

Lucy returned a scowl, inwardly relieved that thus far, the underworld hadn't heard of their little experiment.

Good. We'll keep that card as close to our chest as we can, until revealing it gives a distinct advantage, Lucy thought, only to catch herself as she realised she was sounding like Lawrence.

Is that a good or bad thing? Am I thinking like a leader at the cost of losing my soul?

Konstantin and Siobhan were staring at her, and Lucy composed herself, clearing her throat and nodding. "Well, thank you for that information. I think…"

She fell silent as Konstantin raised a bony finger.

"You might want to wait a moment." The revenant motioned for the vampire to hand over another folder.

Lucy opened it and a number of photos fell out. As she sifted through them, her expression grew darker and darker in fury.

"Where did you get these?"

"Drones, spies and various contacts I have in the Mediterranean. Something big is being plotted. While you've been chasing your tails on vaccines and playing with insects, the Desolated have been preying on the sea, looking for victims no one will miss to prepare their latest strike against the world of men…"

"I'm surprised you care about such a thing, given you're not a part of it."

Charles winced at her brusqueness, but Konstantin merely laughed.

"Demons may not be interested in me, but if any of those bone-headed dolts you oppose succeed in unleashing something major from What Lies Beyond, while I'd see an initial upsurge in my business as the humans try to contain it, ultimately my losses would outstrip my gains; demons don't use the kind of munitions and wares I sell. So I'd rather you folks keep on top of things—apocalypses are somewhat bad for business!"

"Any suggestions?" Lucy asked Charles as she passed him the photos to examine.

Konstantin cleared his throat. "Far be it from me to advise you, but I'd suggest dusting off some of your predecessor's contacts in the British military. The Desolated have a very fortified location, as close to a fortress as they could create without being detected. I'd advise you to make sure you have the best on hand for this…"

***

The Mediterranean,
one hundred miles from the Greek coast

The hold of the ship had been converted into a makeshift temple. Dozens of fleshy cocoons, fastened to the wall by natural resin, pulsated and throbbed as the gestating life forms within them grew ever larger. As dozens of guttural voices chanted in Latin, two figures in rusted green armour stalked towards a makeshift altar at the chamber's centre, carrying one of the bulging cocoons between them. Behind them shuffled a man in a lab coat, his hair bleached white, his face lined with age and marked by a burn scar the shape of a handprint.

The knights placed their fleshy burden on the altar, and the man in the lab coat approached, studying it for something only he could see. Finally, he stepped back, his face contorted into a ghoulish smile, and he nodded to the figures looming over him.

"Vitals seem strong. What's inside that cocoon is developing at a healthy rate… which should make it an ideal host for what you want."

"Good," Brother Falciparum growled, waving a dismissive hand, and Josef Mengele retreated with a servile bow.

Through the ranks of cultists in dirty green and black robes stood in three concentric circles around the altar, Mengele moved to stand beside a woman in black body armour, her face hidden beneath a hood, and a tall, dark-haired man dressed in an expertly tailored suit, both watching the proceedings with a supreme look of disinterest.

"Come, Josef. Lakshmi," Nathaniel Danvers said. "What comes next is not for us to see. We must respect our allies and their 'martial traditions', quaint as they are," he added with a bit of a sneer, only for a booming voice to bellow from within the depths of an enclosed helmet.

"Be gone. Leave us to our work, and pray we do not inform our lord of your disrespect!"

"Apologies, good knight." Danvers clasped his hands and bowed his head respectfully. "I assure you, no disrespect was intended, nor insult to your rituals."

The trio ascended a metal staircase, their footsteps clanging loudly as they departed.

For a few moments, there was nothing but the trickle of noxious fluids and the buzz of darting flies, but then came heavy footsteps, accompanied by wet, sucking sounds as something was trudging its way through whatever slushy substances made up the floor… and then they came into view, illuminated by the torches clutched in the hands of numerous cultists.

There were four of them: huge, heavyset figures moving to stand beside their brethren. They were clad in medieval suits of armour, red-brown with centuries of rust, buckled and bent both from the blows of men who'd tried and failed to kill them throughout history, and where their swollen, maggot-white flesh had pushed its way through as they had bloated from the countless diseases that flowed through their veins. The stink of open wounds and sores, pus-filled boils and blisters that periodically burst and patches of necrotic flesh added to the charnel reek of the pit the ship's hold had become.

Brother Falciparum addressed his brothers-in-arms, his voice harsh and rasping, his mouth twisting into a ghoulish smile. "Let us begin, my brothers!"

One by one, the rust-clad knights genuflected to the squirming cocoon on the altar, and Ebolae snapped his fingers. Two of the cultists in the closest circle broke rank, carrying between them a huge clay jar sealed with wax and engraved with death's heads. The cultists placed the jar at the foot of the altar and re-joined the circle when Falciparum waved them away dismissively. Brother Pestis picked up the jar while Trypanos sliced into the cocoon. Black ichor bubbled out from the flesh.

"I hear death's wings!" Falciparum bellowed, spreading his arms wide.

"We hear death's wings!" the knights and cultists shouted back.

"Death is coming for everyone and everything," Falciparum declared. "Beneath the thunder of a thousand wings shall our work be done, and the earth shall know his glorious putrescence! Today, for the first time since the dawn of ages, the great lord Nergal will begin his rebirth, his path paved by the deaths of countless to his gifts!" The Blighted Brother pointed to the clay jar Pestis held in his hands.

"Beneath the thunder of a thousand wings!" the cultists bellowed in answer.

"Here he will grow strong, until his horde is ready to pupate." Falciparum continued his sermon. "They will complete their gestation in his presence, his power linking them to him, so that when the time comes and they emerge from the chrysalises we have made for them, every infection, every death they cause will feed the great one's power, and he will be strong enough to tear down the barriers between this world and What Lies Beyond! Desolated, your king and queen will return to the world that was stolen from their hands by the humans you detest, that you, like us, have abandoned in service to the true powers of this universe! United, we will usher in a new world!"

As the Desolated cultists roared their approval, Pestis lifted the clay jar above his head and smashed it against the altar. Wispy white forms flooded out of it, rising skyward, before, like iron filings drawn to a magnet, they were sucked into the wounds Brother Trypanos had sliced into the cocoon. The souls of countless men, women and children abducted, tortured, infected and killed to feed the hunger of demonic insects flooded it, and the cocoon swelled and began leaking stinking fluid. As the last of them were sucked into the pulsating white mass, a clawed hand, dripping in filth, tore its way out of the cocoon, and the Knights of Yersinia gave an ululating screech of joy.

Chapter 28: Recruitment Drive
Barracks at Dhekelia Cantonment, British territory on Cyprus

Captain Mark Talbot was a veteran of 23 SAS. He had served on infiltration and exfiltration missions, rescues of hostages and valuable targets, sabotage and destruction of valuable enemy facilities in Afghanistan, Iraq, Syria and Somalia, to name a few. He was calm under pressure and had remained clear-headed under enemy fire… but something about this mission was setting off every bad instinct in his body.

He'd known something was wrong when he saw the list of personnel he'd been assigned for the mission: all young lads, no families or dependents. That screamed high risk.

The team had left Hereford via private aircraft to Cyprus, where they would be briefed on the mission ahead. The moment he and his men had come to attention as the door to their quarters opened and a truly eclectic ensemble of people had walked in, Talbot's sense of unease about the whole affair went through the roof. His CO had indicated they would be briefed by a special detail from MI6, but he'd expected former public schoolboys in Savile Row suits, not… these.

A dark-haired young woman with facial piercings in black body armour, a lean man who looked more like a student than a soldier, a young woman with dyed purple hair, a man in his thirties—lean with curly dark hair, a broad chest and muscular arms.

"Gentlemen, good morning," the dark-haired young woman spoke. "My name is Lucy Murray. We are members of Argent Blade, a rather unique organisation within the intelligence gathering community. Whatever you may have heard, I advise you to forget it, because I can assure you the truth is far worse. All that matters is that for the foreseeable future, I am in charge of you."

"She can be in charge of me any time," one of the soldiers snickered under his breath, to giggles from two of his compatriots.

Captain Talbot was about to reprimand him, but Murray got there first.

"Something to say, soldier?"

"No, ma'am."

"Good," Murray said with a glacial look at the whisperer, before clearing her throat and continuing the briefing.

"You're probably wondering why I requested your CO provide me with a set of men with no family connections or close ties. The answer is simple: this mission is extremely high risk, and there is a good chance none of us will survive. I say this because I want you to know the risks first-hand; if any of you have qualms or would rather sit this one out, then you have my permission to leave. If you remain, then you do so in complete understanding of the consequences of that choice."

Talbot remained at attention. To his pride, the men did likewise. Murray nodded in satisfaction before motioning to the dark-haired man, who promptly killed the lights. A projector was turned on, and Murray pointed to the first photo slide: a ship marked with a red cross at multiple points along its hull.

"This is our target: the *Siren,* a former hospital ship licensed to the major medical company, Ouroboros Industries. Our most recent intel indicates the ship has fallen into the hands of this group, the Desolated." A photograph of the identified ship was replaced by a close-up of a graffiti tag of a horned skull.

"They're a terrorist syndicate that has been operating in secret for years, using proxies to fuel conflicts to serve their agenda. Last year's Halloween attack in Westminster was their handiwork. We have confirmed intelligence that the bioweapons attack in Bloomsbury earlier this month was their doing and that they are using this ship as a base to further refine and develop biological and chemical weapons. We have also intercepted communications that indicate they are planning another attack using a far more lethal bio-toxin, to be carried out in Athens within forty-eight hours."

"What is their end goal? Islamic extremism?" Sykes, one of Talbot's men.

"No, they only have one goal. Mankind's extermination. They're convinced mankind is a diseased species that needs to be purged from the world. They seek to elevate themselves above the rest, so they will be deemed worthy of survival. In short, they're zealots, dedicated to their cause, and completely devoid of fear."

"In short, no prisoners," Talbot noted.

Murray gave an approving nod. "Exactly, Captain Talbot. This mission is an extermination. The Desolated will take no prisoners, so you are fully authorised to use lethal force against them."

"What are our objectives?" Sergeant Michael Byrne, Talbot's right-hand man, chosen specifically because the captain knew he could be relied upon, enquired.

Murray moved onto the next slide, a detailed schematic of the ship.

"Our primary targets are located below deck; this is based on drone reconnaissance, but we don't have much to go on. My team's goal is to locate and destroy the laboratory facilities where the virus they've been developing is being manufactured, ensuring any and all elements of their work are destroyed. Your mission, Captain, is to support us in landing aboard the *Siren*. Once we break off to secure the Desolated laboratory and research facility aboard, your task will be to disable the ship's engines and secure a line of communication. Once we have confirmed any and all biological and chemical weapons are destroyed, you will contact HMS *Vengeance,* a Royal Navy submarine currently en route to the Aegean; her captain will be waiting for your transmission. Once they receive it, the *Vengeance* will sink the *Siren*, and any of us still remaining will have proceeded to the extraction point. Any questions?"

When none were forthcoming, Miss Murray motioned for the more muscled man to bring forward a large metal box. In front of the gathered soldiers, he opened it. They frowned at the gleam of silver hitting their eyes from hundreds, if not thousands, of bullets inside.

"Silver bullets?" Talbot picked up one and rolled it between thumb and forefinger, his scepticism clear. "I thought we were going after terrorists, not monsters."

Miss Murray was completely unamused. "You will encounter in that ship aberrations born from nightmare. You will need these to stop them; all such creatures have a weakness to silver."

"What kind of weakness?" Sergeant Byrne asked, picking up some of the bullets.

"All you need to know is that it can hurt them. Whatever experiments have been carried out on the people those things were, it's left them with a vulnerability to silver. Make sure you have as many as you can carry, and once we hit the deck, keep your eyes peeled. We," Miss Murray said, "have faced these terrorists and their aberrations before; they're adept at ambushes and they prefer to pick off isolated targets. So watch each other's backs in there. No man breaks off alone, and keep radio contact at all times. Any questions?"

The soldiers remained silent, and Lucy Murray nodded in approval. "Then I advise you to get some sleep and prepare yourselves for a battle unlike anything you'll have seen before. Wheels up at ten a.m."

***

"I'm sure you sounded very authoritarian," Gillian insisted.

A crescent moon illuminated the hotel room, where Lucy sat on the bed. She rubbed her neck as she continued her Skype call.

"Really?" she said doubtfully. "I thought I sounded like a kid trying to give orders while wearing her dad's clothes. Those soldiers were looking at me as if they couldn't believe their eyes. I suspect some of them wanted to get in my pants but if they took me seriously is anyone's guess."

"They will," Gillian said, toying with a lock of red hair. The colour was quite vivid; evidently time away in the countryside was doing her good.

At Lucy's insistence, Gillian had gone south to Cornwall, to try and come to terms with her regrets regarding her father, let her grieve properly, and more importantly, consult with the coven who had trained her, to try and make sense of why her powers were acting up—if it was some curse Echidna had cast with her last strength, or something else.

"Battle tends to make people forget their earlier perceptions and trust whoever makes sense, whoever shows they can direct when things fall apart," Gillian insisted. "For all your protestations, you keep a clear head and stay calm, even in trying situations. My father clearly thought so when he named you his successor…"

Gillian trailed off, the memory of her father still a bitter subject.

Lucy wondered if she'd ever truly forgive him for the secrets he'd kept from her.

Part of her wanted to, to remember him as her dad, the man who raised her, trained her, gave her everything she needed to become what she was… and another couldn't forget that he'd kept the existence of another woman's child hidden from her—not to mention the timing of revealing that.

"He did love you." Lucy tried to broach the subject. "He wasn't a perfect man, but he tried to give the best for all three of you. You, Valerie and Danielle. I don't think he honestly meant to hurt you, but… Maybe what happened to Valerie made him think he wanted to do more before it was too late, to not leave things unresolved."

"Well, he didn't achieve that, did he?" Gillian muttered sullenly, looking away.

Even separated by hundreds of miles, Gillian's anger and regret at not burying the hatchet with her father before his death were clear. The things she'd said that night they'd discovered Lawrence talking to Danielle, the angry words that had been exchanged between Lawrence and Gillian afterwards, the long weeks of awkward silence between the two and Gillian's refusal to reconcile with her father, all of it was playing on her mind now that Lawrence was gone.

"Life rarely goes the way we want it to." Lucy pressed her hand to Gillian's cheek on the screen, wishing she hadn't sent her lover away, even if she knew it was for the best. She would have liked one last night in her arms, getting up to all manner of things, just in case they never got another chance.

"All you can do is try and remember your father for the better aspects of what you had together. I know you're angry with him, and you have a right to be, but don't let it overshadow the good times, the happy memories you had with him. Hell, he may not have been a perfect dad, but at least you had a relationship with him. I envy you that a little."

Gillian gave a snort. "You'd have second thoughts if you knew him! Blimey, you would not believe the kind of things Dad got up to on our family holidays…"

"Well, tell me," Lucy said with a smile. "And then maybe, afterwards, we can make sure we don't leave anything unfinished ourselves." She raised an eyebrow.

Gillian shook her head in amusement and then rubbed her chin, trying to think of a good anecdote. After a few moments, her eyes lit up.

"Okay, so, when me and Valerie were seven, Dad insisted on us going with him on a holiday to Bath. Turns out, he had business to attend to, so we got dumped with his aunt while he got up to who knew what…"

***

In the hotel bar, Danielle Drake sat perched on a stool, nursing a glass of white wine before turning in for the night. She needed something to settle her nerves; Halloween had been a spur of the moment thing on her mother's part—the coven had been drafted and Danielle and her sisters had been running on pure adrenaline, with no time to think on it. Now, they faced heading into battle again, against a terrible and powerful enemy, and the anticipation was more terrible than the actual fight.

She took another sip of wine, trying to compose her thoughts. She wouldn't have another glass; the other witches her mother had sent over at Lucy's request had already turned in, and in her head, Danielle could already hear Angela's strident warnings about the fundamentals of casting spells.

I don't want my ability to cast being disrupted by a hangover or headache. I want absolute precision for tomorrow—

"Dutch courage?" a familiar voice muttered.

Danielle looked up as Charles sat down beside her. He looked a little bleary-eyed, and Danielle gave him a cold look as she noticed the pint of beer in his hand. *I doubt that's his first one.*

"I see you've found a bit too much," she said icily.

Charles shrugged. "Well, if what's been said is true, this could be our last hurrah." He took another swig of his beer. Danielle wrinkled her nose as he kept drinking. "You know, this could be your first and last battle. There anything you want to do before then?"

Danielle raised her eyebrows and gave him a look of utter disdain. "Not with you." She pushed her wineglass away, only to stop as Charles caught her hand.

"Come now. By tomorrow, that pretty face could be hanging from the claws of Falciparum, Ebolae or Trypanos. Surely one last night of pleasure just in case might be on the cards…"

Before Charles could embarrass himself any further, Danielle grabbed his wrist. *I'm not putting up with this.* She looked around to see if anyone was watching; fortunately, the few patrons and staff left in the bar had their attention elsewhere. Her palm started to glow as she channelled healing magic into the young Knight's flesh, burning out the alcohol. Charles gritted his teeth and glared at her balefully, but he knew better than to cry out and draw attention.

After a few moments, she severed the flow of magic, and Charles shook his head, blinking his eyes, feeling alert.

Danielle gave a smug little smile. She'd always been good at that. After nights out with her coven sisters, the next morning they'd be clamouring to Danielle to clear their heads.

"They used to call me the living hangover cure," she said, a little boastful, before turning her attention back to the glowering Charles.

"Go to bed, Charles," she snapped. "I'm not going to be your rebound girl, and I'm not going to watch you ensure the only thing you achieve tomorrow is a quick death. Go have a shower, get a good night's sleep and be ready for the fight. We're going to be plunging into hell tomorrow; we're going to have to rely on each other, and I don't want to get killed because you're nursing a hangover at a critical moment. Get yourself together. You might not be where you want to be, but you're still needed. Stop feeling sorry for yourself and live up to the expectations my father and the rest had for you."

Chapter 29: Dropping into Hell
The Aegean Sea, 25 miles off the Athenian coast

"Target in sight," the staff sergeant shouted as the rear of the C-130 opened, revealing the gleaming waters of the Aegean Sea miles below. They could see a long thin shape on the water, a ship slowly pressing on towards the Greek coastline.

"At its present speed, it'll make landfall in Piraeus within two hours," Captain Talbot shouted as the soldiers and their unconventional allies got to their feet, grabbing their weapons and parachutes, ready for the drop.

"Then we have our deadline. We know the Desolated and their allies are developing some form of bioweapon aboard that ship, most likely on victims of human experimentation." Lucy shouted to be heard as the rush of the wind came in. "If they get their weapon on the mainland, the death toll will be astronomical. We have our objectives. Captain Talbot, you and your men will make for the engines and the bridge, render the ship inoperable. The rest of us have two objectives: find wherever they're developing their pathogen, destroy all traces of it, then we make sure nothing gets off this boat alive. Assume all contacts when you hit the deck are hostiles. Shoot to kill. Any questions?"

There were none. All of them knew what they had to do, and the consequences of failure.

"Here goes nothing," Lucy muttered. "Geronimo!"

She flung herself into the void, followed by Charles, Liam—loaned to her by Moira, Edmund and Siobhan, since the daylight hours and the Mediterranean climate were inimical to vampires—Danielle, along with two other witches whose names Lucy had forgotten, and a squad of the British Army's finest soldiers.

May God grant it will be enough. I'd rather my first command not be my last.

The wind whipped past her head as they fell. The deck of the ship flew up to meet them, and Lucy's hand fumbled for the cord of her parachute. Black and green clad figures scurried about on the deck below like insects spilling from a disturbed hive, guns aiming to the sky.

"Incoming!" The wind whipped Lucy's words away from her, but as bullets tore upwards, she heard, faintly as if from a distance, the roar of gunfire as her own forces shot back.

Lucy pulled the cord, jerked back as her parachute opened behind her, and pulled her pistols. As she drew closer, she shot at anyone who might be aiming at her, either killing or forcing them to keep in cover.

Two cultists charged at her the moment Lucy's feet touched down, but before they got near, Charles landed on the deck, falx in hand. He swung upwards and one of the cultists fell, trying to hold in their guts. The second pulled out a knife, only to be sent staggering back as Lucy shot them in the belly. Charles spun on his heel and beheaded the cultist.

Screams came from above, and Lucy saw the cultists had claimed some casualties amongst the soldiers. Two men were drifting down, lifeless in their parachutes.

Danielle and her witches hit the ground like lightning bolts. As soon as they were down, the young women thrust out their arms, fingers contorted into claws. Lightning and flame speared from their hands, shocking or immolating any cultist in range. Some died as the electricity tore through their bodies, others as the heat ignited and detonated the ammunition in their guns. Yet others fell as Talbot and his men landed and dropped the cultists spasming in electrical-induced agony with clean, precise shots.

"I thought you said this lot would be a challenge!" Talbot shouted at Lucy as the cultists, caught off guard by the assault, fell back, retreating back into the depths of the *Siren*.

As they fled, one of the cultists kicked over a rusted metal barrel. Its contents of oily black sludge spilled all over the deck and began to rise up, taking on a humanoid shape...

"You want a challenge? Allow me to oblige!" came a wet and guttural snarl as the rising mound of slurry suddenly exploded.

The soldiers closest to it, pursuing the retreating cultists, were drenched in the sludge. They howled in agony as it burned through body armour, clothing and flesh like acid. Their screams were abruptly cut short as Brother Ebolae, drenched in the filth that had birthed him, slashed out with a rusted sword in each hand, beheading both men with a single stroke.

No matter how many silver bullets they shot into him, the Blighted Brother kept coming, rusted blades coated in diseased venom cutting down men with every stroke. As Ebolae charged towards Talbot and two more holding their ground, suddenly there came the crackle of flames, and the Champion's Blade sliced low. It bit into Ebolae's gut, sending fragments of rusted breastplate and chunks of diseased intestine spilling to the deck.

"Oh, I have had enough of your refusal to acknowledge your betters!" Ebolae bellowed.

Charles ducked under the swing of the left sword and parried the other. He rolled under a cut at his head and brought the Champion's Blade down in a two-handed grip, slicing off Ebolae's left hand. The rusted sword and severed hand clattered to the deck, but with a roar of fury, Ebolae jabbed the stump at Charles's face. He gagged and choked as he was blasted by a spray of black blood filled with squirming white maggots. Ebolae's rusted sword knocked the Champion's Blade from Charles's loose grip, and it went skittering across the deck.

A black blur flung itself at Ebolae. Liam snarled as he seized the Knight of Yersinia around the throat, dragging him away from Charles lying on the deck.

"Do what you need to!" Liam shouted as he wrestled with Ebolae.

His claws sliced off chunks of blubbery flesh and rusted metal, while Charles wiped the Blighted Brother's blood from his face and moved to support Liam. The Blighted Brother threw Liam off, when suddenly the front of his helmet exploded outwards. Ebolae pawed at the hole blown in his skull as Captain Talbot emptied his rifle into Ebolae's head.

Not one to miss an opportunity, Charles hefted the Champion's Blade and swung high. The Blighted Brother's armoured knees hit the deck with a loud clang, before his headless corpse pitched forward and dissolved into black, maggot-riddled slurry.

"It won't put him down for long," Lucy muttered.

"What the hell was that thing?" Talbot shouted over the racket as he reloaded.

"It'll take too long to explain; just know that's an elite enemy combatant. There are five more of them, heavily altered. They're priority targets and do not, *under any circumstances,* consider engaging them alone. They—"

Lucy's words were cut off as a fusillade of gunfire erupted. She was pitched on her back as several shots hit her in the chest; the Aegis stopped the bullets from penetrating, but she was still winded from the impact. Looking up, she saw the cultists were back.

Danielle and another witch—*Claudia, maybe?*—flung fireballs into the ranks of the cultists. Liam seized an oil barrel, tore it open with his claws and then flung its contents at the burning cultists, completing their transformation into human torches.

As the invaders pressed their advantage, Lucy shouted orders. "You all have your objectives, and we're running out of time!"

***

The Knights of the Order of the Argent Blade pressed on, shooting anything that moved. There were a fair number of the cultists, but more common were creatures like the living dead they'd battled in Bloomsbury. The Knights had taken the most direct route, hoping to draw the creatures off the soldiers, who were more at risk to the diseases they carried.

As they came to a corridor, Liam sniffed the air, his face contorting in a frown. "There is a powerful smell of rot coming from that direction." He pointed to the left. "Something lingers between life and death, held in stasis by powerful magic."

"We'll check it out." Lucy motioned for Danielle and her witches to fall in.

"We'll take the right," Charles said, just as a door opened.

All stood in shock as a quintet of figures emerged from what looked like a laboratory: two lab staff, two guards, and a familiar face.

"Make sure the additional samples are shipped to the American facilities; the Emissary will want them for the next stage of the operation after the European infections are in full swing..." Josef Mengele trailed off, his eyes going wide as he saw who was in the corridor.

His guards reacted first, raising their rifles and shooting. The witch beside Danielle collapsed, a hole blown through the centre of her skull.

"Claudia!" Danielle screamed.

The guards kept shooting, and two soldiers fell with their throats blown out.

And then with a roar, Charles was upon them. Lucy's eyes went wide—he was like a man possessed. *Something's definitely reinvigorated him… Well, I won't complain if it gets us out of here!*

The reborn Champion's Blade slashed out, and one of the Desolated guards screamed as his gun, along with both arms severed at the elbow, clattered to the ground. The second was trying to line up a shot when Charles kicked him back into the wall and swung low. The cultist dropped his gun to try and stop his intestines spilling out.

"Move it, you fools!" Mengele shrieked at his underlings, flinging them at the intruders to cover his escape.

Charles beheaded the assistant on the left, while the second dropped his notes and samples and tried to run for his life down the corridor, only for Lucy to fling one of her poisoned knives. It hit him between the shoulder blades and he collapsed, spasming briefly before becoming still.

A black blur darted after the fleeing Mengele. The undead Nazi was almost at the end of the corridor when Liam hit him with the force of a wrecking ball. Mengele collided into the wall with such force, even Lucy winced. The mad scientist hit the ground hard, but Liam wasn't done with him. His fingernails lengthened and turned black as, seizing Mengele by the throat with his left hand, Liam grabbed Mengele's leg with the right and pulled hard. Mengele shrieked as his right leg parted company with his body at the knee. Dust and grey fluid leaked from his veins in place of blood.

By the time Lucy and the others got there, Liam had torn off the left leg as well, and Mengele was thrashing on the floor like a marionette with its strings cut, howling profanities and improbable threats in rapid German.

"Hello, Josef! How've you been? Long time, no see," Lucy said with a poisonous smile, the sarcasm dripping from her lips. It rapidly fell as she drew another knife, jammed it under the scientist's chin. "Where are you keeping the hell-flies? I want all locations aboard this ship!"

The undead Nazi spat at her.

Liam stamped on his chest hard, cracking ribs, and snarled, "No way to treat a lady, that is! Now, care to answer the question?"

Mengele smiled at the werewolf, baring his rotted teeth. "As much as I'm sure you think you're in time to stop our little plan, I'm sad to say you're wrong. Our plan was to deploy once we made land in Greece, but we had a contingency in place. How do you think those soldiers you sent to cripple this ship's engines are doing?"

***

The heat and humidity were incredible as Captain Talbot and his men, accompanied by Lydia of the Camden coven, made their way into the *Siren*'s engine room. Fleshy growths of human proportions covered the walls, and a loud buzzing sound was growing louder and louder…

"This feels more like an insect hive than a ship… what the hell is this madness?" Sergeant Byrne raised his shotgun.

The interior workings of the ship were so encrusted with growths, it was impossible to work out where the engines were to place charges. It was anyone's guess how the cultists were preventing the ship from breaking down with the amount of filth coating the engines.

"It'll take too long to clear this out," one of the soldiers said, even as he tried to peel a resinous growth from a nearby pipe.

Lydia pushed her way through the soldiers, pulling off her gloves. The men raised their eyebrows as they saw her hold her hands out.

"Let me work my magic."

The air over her hands waved as the temperature rose and the resin retreated from the pipe, leaving the metal bare. The soldier who'd been complaining snuck up behind her.

"What other kind of 'magic' can you work?" the young man asked, looking over her shoulder.

Lydia rolled her eyes and kept focused on her work. "None you'll ever see."

"Less of the chitchat, Jenkins," Talbot snapped. "Sergeant Byrne, as soon as her... *talents* have cleared things up, start planting charges."

"Yes, sir."

The sergeant wiped a bead of sweat from his forehead. The temperature in the room was rising rapidly, more and more of the metal beneath the fleshy growths becoming clear...

Suddenly, a cacophonous buzzing erupted from all around them. Long claws of black chitin tore their way out of the growths on the wall. *Cocoons,* Captain Talbot realised, as insectile heads with snapping mandibles and gleaming red eyes, followed by hairy grey bodies, pulled themselves free of their pupae, awoken by the heat.

"Fall back!" Talbot shouted over the screeching of the newborn hell-flies as they saw fresh meat, and the screaming of his men and desperate gunfire as they realised their supposedly easy assignment had seen them walking straight into hell.

The heat radiating from Lydia's hands turned into lancing flames that immolated two of the monstrous insects trying to pull free of their cocoons. Several of the soldiers took advantage to shoot, but as Lydia advanced, Talbot saw movement to her left.

"Look out!" he shouted, a second too late.

Lydia screamed as a snapping head lunged. Mandibles clamped around her shoulder and arm, biting deep. Jenkins charged over to free her, but over the screams, crackle of flames and frantic gunshots, Talbot could hear clicking getting closer.

With the Desolated and their allies having spent weeks capturing and transforming refugees into hosts for hell-fly larvae, there were hundreds, if not thousands, of cocoons clinging to the walls throughout the ship. Most of the swarm had been placed in ways that would allow them to find their way to the upper decks. Once there, they spread their wings and took to the air, a gargantuan army of demonic insects swarming towards dry land and the unending tides of human flesh upon which to glut themselves and lay their eggs within.

Chapter 30: Legion's End

Hell-flies came swarming into the corridor. Mengele giggled dementedly as Charles and Liam slashed and clawed at the attacking insects.

"Get to the source of this!" Liam shouted over his shoulder as he wrestled with another hell-fly, the insect's mandibles snapping at his throat. With a roar, he twisted hard and tore the hell-fly's head off with his bare hands. Pale white ichor sprayed the walls and his face. Liam choked in disgust, but before any of the swarm could take advantage, Charles pushed the werewolf back. He sliced at any insectile claws that tried to reach Liam as he wiped his eyes clean. The swarming bugs tore through the group, forcing them to flee in all directions.

We can't kill them all, not without being torn apart, Lucy thought as she and Danielle ran down the corridor.

The sounds of battle faded as they pressed deeper into the ship. Looking around, they saw what looked like laboratories and hospital wards, now engulfed by mould, mildew and rot, cocoons long since torn open and their occupants gone, denuded skeletons protruding from the remains.

"How many people have died here?" Danielle whispered in disgust.

"Too many," Lucy spat.

"Tell me we're going to destroy this evil place and the bastards who made this happen," Danielle snarled. Embers kindled to life in the young witch's hands.

"Count on it!" Lucy said as they passed two deflated cocoons, their occupants having long since emerged.

All of a sudden, she heard something familiar, like a blade being drawn.

"Get out of the way!" Lucy shoved Danielle in front of her as a muscular arm covered in black scales burst from the cocoon on the left.

Lucy sliced out with her kukri. She grinned as the silver blade bit into the flesh, spilling dark blood across the floor and walls.

"Get out of here! Kill these at their source!" she bellowed as two Legionaries tore their way free of the cocoons and turned to her with a snarl.

She briefly thanked the gods Gillian was safely back in England, out of reach of these monsters, before she went on guard and bared her teeth in answer.

She flung an explosive knife at the closest Legionary. To her amazement, it leapt into the air and spun, kicking the knife away; it hit the wall and detonated harmlessly. One of the creatures saw Danielle running and turned to give chase. Lucy shot at the back of its head, but the demon easily ducked under the bullet.

Right, they get smarter with every incarnation, Lucy thought, only to hear claws clicking on the floor behind her. She turned, and her face fell.

"Oh, bollocks."

Six more Legionaries bared their teeth and snarled.

"My name is Legion, for—"

"Spare me the fucking Bible quotes!"

Lucy flung a smoke grenade at them. One of the demons batted it aside with a clawed hand, but the grenade started spewing oily grey smoke. She seized the advantage.

I can't kill all of them by myself, she knew instinctively as she pulled something from her belt and flung it to Danielle. *All I can do is delay them.*

Better work fast.

She turned on her heel to parry bone talons stabbing for her stomach, and retaliated with a slash at the closest Legionary's head.

***

At every door she passed, Danielle activated one of the explosive charges she'd been given at the briefing, setting the timers for five minutes. She had no idea what was being grown in these labs, but whatever it was, it would not survive being incinerated.

She heard the clicking almost too late. Just as the hell-fly dropped down from the ceiling, she leapt away and thrust out her hand to blast the demonic insect away with telekinetic force. The hell-fly collided with the nearest wall and lay stunned for a few moments, but then shook its head and got back to its feet, its mandibles clicking angrily as its red eyes narrowed.

Danielle broke into a sprint. The buzzing of the hell-fly's wings grew closer, and suddenly, the creature's head collided with the small of her back. Sent stumbling to the ground, Danielle rolled over and thrust out a hand in the nick of time. The hell-fly thrashed and snapped its jaws futilely as it hung in mid-air, suspended by unseen bonds.

"Fuck off!" Danielle snarled.

Her outstretched hand clenched into a fist, and she flung the monster away. It collided with the far wall, legs thrashing. Danielle followed up with a swiftly flung fireball. The demon rolled away, the fireball hitting the wall... and then the hell-fly growled in irritation when the sprinklers drenched it and the corridor in dirty water.

Danielle chanced a look away. The lights were on in the room at the end of the corridor, the only place in this part of the ship that still had them.

Clutching what Lucy had tossed to her, Danielle sprinted towards the light. The buzzing grew ever louder as the hell-fly pursued her down the corridor.

***

Backed into a corner, Lucy parried the claws stabbing for her throat. More scraped across her back and she staggered, though fortunately the Aegis stopped the bone blades from going into her spine. *Thanks, Dad*, she thought, grateful again for her father's last gift. The kukri in her hands spun and slashed. One of the Legionaries staggered back, clawing at the stump of its hand, before her next stroke punched through its throat.

It was a victory, but one Lucy knew she couldn't repeat. She was outnumbered six to one, and even with another Legionary crumbling to dust at her feet, she knew she'd never kill them all before one of them found a weak spot in her armour.

Then she heard something in her ear, a burst of static on the Order's private frequency. Lucy gave a feral smile as she got the message's meaning; Danielle had reached the target.

"COME ON, YOU UGLY BIBLICAL FUCKERS! WHO'S NEXT?!" she bellowed defiantly.

The Legionaries roared in fury and charged her en masse. Lucy's kukri hacked and stabbed out, punching through the meat of one demon's shoulder, slicing off the fingers of another's right hand, but she was dragged down. Two seized each of her arms and legs and pinned them down as a ninth demon straddled her chest, its pale eyes narrowed in contempt.

"You are one and we are many. You were a fool to think you could destroy the Legion by yourself. Let that folly torment you as your soul is rent apart in the void!" the closest Legionary snarled, pulling back the bone blade at its wrist for a slash across her throat.

"Oh, I didn't plan to kill you all singlehandedly," Lucy replied blasély, acting unafraid even though her heart was pounding.

The demon withheld the killing blow, its dark-skinned face contorted by confusion.

Lucy's smile became predatory as she leant forward. "All I wanted to do was keep you busy!"

And then the Legionaries fell to their knees, screaming. The ones holding Lucy down let her go as they clawed at their chests. White light bled from the spot where their hearts would be. The one who'd been about to slit Lucy's throat glared at her.

"That's the thing about leaving valuable things unattended. People are liable to do something with them."

***

Danielle shouldered her way into the room with centimetres separating her from her pursuer. She tripped as she stumbled in. A serpentine mess of cables crisscrossed the floor and plugged into various life support machines monitoring a body lying inert on a hospital bed.

Before Danielle could look closer, a triumphant screech and loud bang came from behind. The hell-fly was on top of her, and Danielle grabbed its neck, forcing its head back to keep its mandibles from her throat. Her palm glowed, and magic blasted the insect off her. Danielle rolled over and sliced one of the cables connected to the machines with the kukri Lucy had given her. The exposed wires spat sparks. Grabbing the cable, Danielle heard a snarl and turned back to see the fly crouching, its mandibles clicking furiously as it made ready to lunge.

I'm not dying here. Danielle beckoned the monster on. With a rattling screech, the demonic insect lunged at her. Its front legs smashed into her belly, knocking her off her feet. Its head descended, mandibles ready to bite.

"Go to hell!" Danielle snarled and thrust the cable in her hand into the hell-fly's closest eye.

The demon shrieked in agony as the water covering it conducted the electricity through its body. Its eyes burst, and it vomited black filth and sparks, before it gave a final keening wail and slumped forward, lifeless. Danielle dusted herself off and made a noise of disgust as the giant insect's carcass crumbled into inert ash.

"Revolting," she muttered, before racing over to her objective, hoping the insect's attack hadn't caused a fatal delay.

The body on the bed didn't even react as Danielle drove the kukri into its heart. She remembered what she'd been told: only by killing the host body from which Legion was spawning could the demon itself be destroyed for good.

"Red light, green light," Danielle muttered as she pressed the red stud in the dagger's handle. She grinned as it turned green, before bolting out the door, one hand thrown behind her, calling energy to herself...

"One, two, three..."

A shimmering blue barrier formed over the ward door as she dived through it.

"Four, five, six!"

Behind her, there was an almighty bang. Torn pieces of meat slid off the ward door and the barrier of energy she'd cast across it as the explosive charge inside the kukri detonated.

***

In the lower bowels of the ship, the Legionaries screamed simultaneously as their connection to the world of the living was severed. Their physical forms crumbled into black ash as the demonic entity was banished back to the nightmare realm it had been called out of. Lucy whistled a sigh of relief, her heart still pounding, and recovered her kukri from where it had fallen when the demonic body it had been lodged in disintegrated.

Me and Gillian are safe... from Legion at least. Safe is a debatable thing where I am now!

"Nice work, Danielle. You cut it a bit fine, though," she muttered to herself... and then a clawed hand sent her flying.

She hit the wall hard. Shaking her head to clear it, she saw the familiar figure of Nathaniel Danvers down the corridor, his face a mask of fury.

"You just can't keep your hands to yourself, can you?" he snarled. The demon within him broke through, tossing aside his sunglasses to reveal his mutilated face.

"I can't remember any Knight who's caused me so much grief as ones who have *your* family name attached to them! I only thank the Pantheon that you're the last!" Danvers seized her by the back of the head, intending to slam it into a nearby wall.

The blast of a gunshot came from behind. Danvers let her go, looking down at the bloody hole blown through his chest. Before he could recover, Lucy seized one of her knives and slammed it into the demon's groin. Danvers roared in rage, staggering back as red-black blood streamed from the wound. Lucy knew it wouldn't be fatal, but it gave her an opening.

Her hands flew to the gun at her waist, and Lucy emptied the magazine. Black blood sprayed the wall behind Danvers as bullets tore through his chest and erupted out of his back. Lucy got back to her feet and ran; she doubted her ability to come out alive against the Emissary, not without help. He roared in fury, the sound of pounding footsteps behind her as he gave pursuit.

Lucy raced down the ship's corridors, Danvers close behind. She tried not to touch anything; the ship's interior was crawling with vermin and filth, and Lucy didn't want to test how much the Order's mark could protect her from whatever demonic diseases infested the *Siren*.

As she turned a corner, Charles bellowed, "Lucy, hit the deck!"

Lucy didn't ask; she flung herself face first to the deck. She looked up to see that Charles, Captain Talbot and a group of his soldiers had formed a firing line in the corridor. The moment Nathaniel Danvers came around the corner, they started shooting. The Emissary came to the fore as the bullets tore into his flesh, roaring in fury, his features taking a more draconic cast, but despite the murderous fusillade, he kept advancing. Lucy grimaced. While her chances against him were slim, the soldiers would be helpless if Danvers got to them. As he stalked towards them, claws extended, Lucy pulled two of her knives out, crushed the glass beads at the centre of the blades and flung them. Danvers roared as they sank into his chest, flooding his veins with their toxins, and whirled back to face her, his eyes a blazing yellow.

"Try me, you overgrown iguana!" she snarled, giving Danvers the finger for good measure.

The Emissary roared in outrage. Lucy ducked, and his fist dented the wall on impact. The gunfire petered out as Lucy and the demonic herald battled it out, the soldiers fearful of hitting one of their allies.

As Lucy ducked under another punch, Charles snapped, "Captain Talbot, fall back and take your men to the secondary objective. This battle is ours."

Lucy smelt ozone and heard flames crackle to life along the Champion's Blade, but before Charles could get close, the Emissary swung out with the tail forcing its way out the back of Danvers's trousers and swept Charles's legs out from under him. Lucy charged to help Charles, but a clawed foot kicked her full in the chest. She went flying through the air, down the corridor. Metal creaked as railings gave way under her back, and she heard herself scream as she fell into the void that was the ship's hull.

Chapter 31: Revelation
Boscastle, Cornwall

Gillian Templeton breathed in the sea air as she sat down on the sun-warmed rocks along the coast, encircled by women of a range of ages, from teenage girls and young women in their twenties, to a few more matronly women of later years. The only other occupant of the circle was a severe-looking woman in her fifties, with a pentacle necklace and iron grey hair tied back in a bun behind her head, dressed in tight black clothing, trimmed with silver at the hem and sleeves.

I still remember when she had black hair, Gillian thought, suppressing a smile as she looked Agnes Poole, mistress of the Boscastle coven, her earliest tutor in magic, directly in her pale blue eyes.

The Boscastle coven had been instrumental in teaching a teenage Gillian how to properly conjure and wield magic after Zuberi had given her the rudiments following an argument between her and Valerie that ended with their bunk bed on fire. The memory of her sister brought a pang to Gillian's heart. While the fresh air and the respite from the constant fighting and grief in London had helped her calm herself, she was still on edge. The coven had insisted she would be safe if Legion showed its face in the area, that they would have an early warning for demonic incursions, so she wasn't afraid of that, but every night, her dreams were the same…

Valerie and her father dressed in white and gold, beckoning her to follow, Whitby Abbey in the distance, as it always had been when they'd gone on holiday… Then she was walking barefoot through a forest, coming to a clearing where a figure dressed in black and silver faced away from her, attending to matters on a stone altar. The figure set down her burdens and began to turn to face Gillian as thunder rumbled and the sound of swords clashing drew near...

That was when she always woke up.

"What you're describing, your hair changing colour in the wake of your magic, is unlikely to be a curse," Agnes explained.

The rest of the witches around them began to chant. The locals didn't seem particularly bothered. *No doubt, they think we're just a bunch of New Agers trying to find ourselves or get some kind of insights into our lives,* Gillian thought as she watched a couple of fishermen idly watch them briefly before returning to fixing broken nets. *Ignorance is bliss.*

Sometimes, she wondered what might have happened to her life if she'd been born in a different family, not one bound by centuries of duty to a war the rest of the world knew nothing about. *Maybe Valerie and Dad would still be alive, Valerie married with a couple of grandkids to keep Dad happy, both of them safe and far from the front lines... But would I have met Lucy? The magic, the war, they made me who I am... If my life were different, who's to say it would be better?*

Gillian shook her head to clear it and turned her attention back to Agnes. She was here for a reason: to find out what was happening to her, lest it prove detrimental to her ability to serve the Order.

"So what does it mean?" Gillian asked, toying with a lock of her hair. She hadn't used magic in a few days, so the red was back to its vibrant colour, but she wondered how long it would stay.

"Ancient covens thought it was a blessing from Hecate," Agnes replied. "Usually, it happened when a girl from the covens was in fear for her life. The magic would take hold of her independently and assail the threat, continuing until the witch was safe—"

"Yes, well, the more power I draw on, the greater the risk to my health," Gillian said. "If my magic is going to be intensifying without my say-so, I want to know the reason why."

"Which is what we're about to do." Agnes waved a hand towards the chanting witches.

She placed certain herbs into a silver bowl engraved with stars and moons, then pressed her finger to the bowl's contents. A spark leapt from her fingertip to ignite the herbs. The coven's mistress placed the bowl in front of Gillian. Fragrant smoke rose to her nose.

"Close your eyes and breathe in," Agnes urged her former student. "Journey into your own mind, face your ghosts, and know what is at the root of your predicament…"

***

She waved her arms to clear the smoke away. She was in the grounds of Whitby Abbey, the ruin looming over her. The sun was bright and vibrant, and Gillian looked down. To her surprise, she was dressed in red and black, looking like a priestess of old.

"Why Whitby?" she muttered as she walked towards the ruined abbey.

"It's familiar to you," a voice she'd thought she'd never hear again said from behind. "It's a place with strong memories attached to it, which will help make communicating easier."

Gillian's eyes went wide as she turned around and saw her twin sister dressed in white. Without hesitation, Gillian wrapped her arms around Valerie's waist, pulling her twin into a hug.

"Oh gods, it's so good to see you, Val!" Gillian squealed, crushing Valerie's waist. "Oh, I've missed you so much! I'm sorry, I'm sorry I wasn't there—"

"Relax." Val patted her sister on the head and wended her way out of Gillian's embrace. "I made the choice to fight that night, and I don't regret it. Come on, we always knew what we were risking in this life. You don't have much time; she needs to talk to you."

"She?" Gillian asked, confused.

Valerie motioned in the direction of the ruined abbey. "She's waiting for you inside. She's been trying to get your attention for a while—why else do you think you and the others have been hearing me out and about? Or your magic has been acting up? She needed you to speak with her, and you've been delaying it for too long. Time is almost up."

"Almost up for what? What's going on, Val?"

Her twin sister shrugged. "I was just the errand runner, the one to bring you here. Now get going—you were always running late!" Val insisted with a wry smile and a shake of the head.

Gillian began to walk towards the abbey, but a thought occurred to her.

"Will I ever see you again?"

At this, Valerie's expression became rather pensive. "I hope you will."

"You hope?"

Valerie's expression only grew grimmer. "I know what she's about to ask of you. I've no idea what will happen if you agree."

Gillian opened her mouth, but Valerie motioned towards the ruin.

"You really don't want to keep her waiting."

Gillian gave her sister one last hug, putting into it everything that had been left unsaid between them, every bit of regret for every sisterly argument, every night out and celebration that would never take place, and turned in the direction of the ruin. As she started walking, Valerie called out one last time.

"Oh and by the way, Lucy's done the world of good for you. Don't lose her. You might need her before the end."

"The end?" Gillian asked, but Valerie would say no more.

With a sigh, Gillian walked through the closest archway. At the far end of the ruin, where the altar would have stood in ages past, was a figure dressed in white with their back to Gillian. A man dressed in a pristine white suit stood between the figure and Gillian. He turned to face her...

"Daddy!" Gillian cried out, a genuine smile on her lips as she called her father by a term she'd only used rarely when she was a girl.

Lawrence Templeton—whether it was him, his soul, a ghost, she didn't know—turned to face her, his smile almost as big as his daughter's. He winced as she hit him like a charging bull and wrapped her arms around him.

"Easy, girl," he chuckled, patting her on the head as she hugged him tightly. "You're a lot stronger than you were doing this as a girl."

"I'm sorry, I'm so sorry." Tears ran down her cheeks. "Those things I said, I didn't mean them, I—"

"I know you didn't." Lawrence patted his daughter on the back. "The fault is mine. I know I wasn't exactly the best father when you and Valerie were children, and Danielle... that's a secret I'll always feel guilty for keeping from you. I took the easy way out to get rid of a problem, burying it under the carpet so I could keep you in the dark. I did it with the best of intentions; I didn't want you to have to deal with that on top of losing your mother, and when you were older, there never seemed like the right time to discuss it... and I must admit, it was easier to keep the secret and let you and your sister think I was without flaws..."

Gillian snorted. "Me and Val never thought that, Dad. Sorry to break your illusions..."

Lawrence scoffed. "Typical children, no respect for their elders these days!" he muttered curmudgeonly.

He allowed himself a warm smile as he placed a hand on his daughter's cheek. "I know you two thought I didn't value you as much as I might've if you were boys, but I was always so proud of you two, what you accomplished. For all the things I did during my time, you were always what I was most proud of. Never doubt that. Never." He kissed Gillian on the forehead. "I know, whatever comes next, you'll do me proud."

"What are you talking about? You and Valerie, you're being so final, like something is about to happen—"

Another person cleared their throat.

"I have waited long enough, and time is of the essence," the waiting woman interjected.

She turned to face them, and Gillian gasped. The woman seemed in her thirties, her face unlined and youthful, but her hair was as white as fresh snow and her eyes were the same, devoid of pupil and iris. Despite her seeming blindness, Gillian didn't doubt the woman could see her.

"I've seen you before, in my dreams. Who are you?" Gillian demanded.

The woman gave her an enigmatic smile.

"I am you. Or rather, like you," she replied. "I was the first. The first to hold the power and use it to defend, rather than subjugate."

"You're a spellweaver?" Gillian asked, genuinely surprised. The woman nodded.

"The very first. I and my brothers were all firsts. The first to wield the power. The first to wear the armour. The first to wield the blade. When darkness's children spilled forth to devour all mankind, we led those who would not kneel to the slavering hunger of the horde and be consumed like cattle. We gave our all to the fight... and yet it was not enough."

"The first... You were the original Knights?"

The woman chuckled.

"That word came into being long after we gave our lives, but we were the first to fight against the darkness you battle even now... the ones who battled at its source. As is often the case, history plays storyteller with truth, so now our battle has become the playground of gods and monsters, as have our lives. I must confess, in all my wildest dreams as a girl in Thessaly, I never thought women in Britannia would think of me as a goddess..." the woman opined with a chuckle.

"You are... Hecate?"

"Is that my name, or the one history gave me?" the woman wondered. "I no longer remember... Things grow so faint when you've been away for so long..."

"Where are you? The last battle against Typhon and Echidna... the first knights died in that battle. It was their disciples who carried on the fight against the creatures that continued to exist and emerge from What Lies Beyond..."

"No," Hecate, or at least the woman bearing her name, replied. "The last battle was a slaughter. We assembled a force like no other, of as many allies as we could muster, but it wasn't enough. Typhon and Echidna had torn a massive breach between this world and the other, and no matter how many demons we slew, more kept coming. Finally, we had only one recourse. Those who I had trained the longest, along with my brothers—legend has turned them into Zeus and Hermes—fought our way through to the breach the Father and Mother of Monsters had made, and forced our way inside, dragging them back with us."

"You actually went into What Lies Beyond?" Gillian asked, agog. "That's suicide!"

"No more so than fighting a hopeless battle," Hecate retorted. "Our hope was while the attention of the demons was focused on tearing apart the hoplites we put in their path, we could seal them off from their home world and the energy they needed from it to survive, both severing their flow of fresh reinforcements and weakening those already through enough for our forces to mop them up. Time flows differently in What Lies Beyond... and while for us, little more than a few hours have passed since we went through, it has been millennia on your side.

"For generations, we've helped minimise the damage that the hordes of What Lies Beyond have tried to do to the barrier, to breach through and resume the war that we interrupted... but their constant attacks have taken their toll.

There are only a handful of us left, and soon enough all of us, even myself, preserved in this half-life in the hell behind reality, will perish. We have had to retreat, keep moving as we fight to strengthen the barrier on this side—and since we can't be everywhere at once, Typhon and Echidna have had time to make breaches of their own. Their emissary is often in places we cannot hope to strike, working his way through to find gullible minds to widen the gaps he slips through... but now a storm is coming."

"What do you mean?" Gillian asked.

"The barrier is close to utterly collapsing. It has been for decades; it is the only way Echidna could make her way through to your capital, the only way Nergal even now places his feet on terra firma for the first time in centuries. We cannot hope to stop the onslaught that is coming. In the dark places of the realm beyond, an army is being assembled for a full-scale invasion. We won't be able to prevent them on this side. You must prepare."

"Prepare?" Gillian asked, agog. "If we tell the governments of the world a demonic army is about to enter reality, they'll think we're crazy, or on drugs! They'll want to know where this army will come from—come to think of it, so do I!"

"We won't know until it will be too late," Hecate said sadly, "and by then, I and my forces will have been wiped out. We will do what we can to slow down the attack, but we will have no way to tell you when the main thrust will come before it breaches into your world. You will have to react to the first attack. I suggest you build your armies, gather as much power as you can to you and your fellow Knights— strange word." Hecate's gaze trailed off, before she turned her attention back to her modern counterpart.

"You have the Aegis, the Blade and the power already. Now the blood is in your grasp, use it. Proliferate it. Find the Fang of Cerberus; it will be needed in the battles to come. Recruit from those who can believe and the Othersiders who wish their world on your side to survive. And gird yourselves for what is to come. Victory in the battles ahead will come at high cost, and you must be prepared to lose much, as we did the last time…"

"Are you saying we will die?" Gillian asked.

Hecate gave her a pitying look.

"In this war, there are always worse things than death… but we have all known we risk death in these battles. Think more of those we have sworn to protect from the first. Thousands will die to feed demonic hunger if you do not use the time you have been given wisely. I and what forces I have left beyond the barrier will buy you what little time we can. It likely will not be much, so use it wisely. War is coming… and it will be up to you to win it this time."

As Gillian looked back at her father and sister, both of whom had stony, regretful expressions, as if they'd already been told what was to come, that everything they'd done and fought for in their lives was about to put in jeopardy, she felt Hecate place a hand on her shoulder. She turned back. The woman had a slightly hopeful smile on her face, an encouragement from one spellweaver to another, separated by time, but united in purpose.

"I have more than just grim tidings for you, sister-in-arms. I have a gift for you."

"What kind of gift?" Gillian asked, suspiciously.

Hecate smiled, and suddenly it felt like electricity was coursing through her. She gasped in ecstasy; even Lucy's touch in the dark of the night hadn't made her feel so amazing. She opened and clenched her fingers, grinning as she felt stronger, fitter than she had in years. Even in its dream form, Gillian felt like she could tear the abbey apart with her bare hands.

"What is this?"

"All the power I can spare from my own battles," Hecate explained. "Use it wisely; the enemies you will face when we are no more and the barrier comes down will be relentless. And I have one last thing… If you are to play my part in the war to come, you will need your own Zeus and Hermes to help, and right now, they need your aid."

***

The smell of ozone saturated the air, driving the chanting women away from the rock with shrieks of dismay. Gillian's eyes were still closed, but her lips were moving rapidly, her fingers tracing a circle around herself in the dust that immediately erupted with glowing blue light.

As Agnes Poole and the women of the Boscastle coven watched in awe, the glowing circle around Gillian became an all-enclosing dome that swallowed her whole and then collapsed in on itself, leaving nothing but a few fading sparks and a rush of air, carrying their charge away to an unknown place.

Chapter 32: Nergal

Lucy came to groggily and shook her head to clear it. The stench of putrefaction was everywhere, and she thanked whatever gods were out there she was protected from supernatural contamination as her hands sank into the slimy morass around her: a fetid slurry of sea water, rotted meat and the contents of voided bowels. Suppressing the urge to vomit, Lucy shook her head to discourage the flies that had settled on her while she'd been unconscious.

"Ah, welcome," a gurgling burble of a voice called out. "Welcome to the garden. It's so rare to have such company in my home! Do you like what we have done with it?"

Lucy's lip curled in disgust. If this was meant to be a garden, it was one created by a truly demented mind. Human skeletons had been lashed to iron girders stood upright in the fleshy sludge coating the floor of the ship's hold, their flesh and organs draped about them in mockery of foliage and hanging fruit. All around the chamber, dozens of human-sized cocoons, torn open from the inside, clung to the walls, their former occupants even now flying towards the mainland.

The grotesque centrepiece of this macabre tableau was a squat, pallid figure sprawling on a makeshift throne of human bones and rusted iron girders. It was as big as a pre-teenage child, but with insectile features: multiple staring red eyes, clicking mandibles dripping with slime, and the beginnings of a glassine carapace forming about its shoulders and back. Cushions made from flayed human hide and stuffed with entrails rippled beneath the beast as it shifted its ample bulk. Long claws raked the fleshy mantle of human skin draped over it like a cloak as it watched Lucy advance towards it. All the while, it hissed and growled. Five of the Knights of Yersinia chanted and bowed before the bloated monstrosity while Falciparum, who watched as Lucy clambered her way through the rotting mire, idly tapped his sword against the marshy ground.

"My lord Nergal, may I present to you the new, and final, Grand Master of the Order of the Argent Blade." He dropped to one knee before his master.

The pallid demon sat on its throne quirked its head to one side, as if curious what all the fuss was about.

"Loathsomeness waits, and dreams in the deep, and decay spreads over the tottering cities of men," Nergal quoted. "Once this ship docks, decay will spread across the world of men, virulent, unstoppable, carried by my beautiful little children." Its voice was almost affectionate as dozens of flies crawling over its body flew off, disturbed by the brute's movements. "And only my faithful shall be spared its glorious ravages. When Typhon and Echidna come through into this world, after the sheer death and destruction shatters the barriers and the denizens of What Lies Beyond spill forth, they will find me in control of the only untainted meat left in this world, and they will have to give me my due! At long last, I will have my rightful place in the Pantheon, the respect I am owed!"

"Only if you succeed, and I plan to do something about that," Lucy snarled, drawing her kukri.

Nergal growled, his mandibles clacking angrily at the interruption to his sermonising.

"You *dare* speak?" the demon lord spat. "You dare to address your betters? Your only role is to die, since you cannot spread my glorious bounty to the rest of your kind!"

"What can I say?" Lucy said with a shrug. "I was never one for authority!"

She drew her gun and fired. Nergal bellowed as silver bullets perforated his swollen belly. Streamers of diseased blood spilled down his bloated front, but all she'd done was enrage him.

"Kill her!" the demon screamed, pointing a long talon at her.

Falciparum, Ebolae and Trypanos advanced, the others staying close to protect their master. Lucy took aim at the chains supporting one of the iron girders rooted into the slushy ground and shot twice. The bullets severed the chains, and like a felled tree, the girder came crashing down. Trypanos gave a roar of dismay just before it fell atop him, crushing him into the fleshy mire. The impact sent up gobbets of rotted flesh and blood; Lucy gagged as it splattered her face. She ducked to reload behind another of the metal mockeries of trees as Ebolae swung for her head, then darted away as his twin swords sliced through the girder she'd hidden behind. Spinning on her heel, Lucy shot Ebolae twice in the face, sending him staggering back, blood spurting from the hole blown in his helm.

All the while, Nergal wailed and roared in frustration. "You will pay for this desecration! I will flay you apart a nerve at a time, make vineyards from your spilled innards and let mushrooms grow through your skull while you draw your last breaths!" the demon lord snarled, his fury palpable.

Lucy shot a bullet at him, only for Pestis to smash it from the air with his rusted axe before he brought the weapon slicing down on the girder pinning Trypanos, freeing his brother. The five warriors advanced on Lucy, clashing their weapons together. Lucy aimed her gun between each of the monstrous knights.

I'll be lucky if I get to drop one, two at the maximum, before the others tear me apart...

And then a roar came as the bloated figure of Brother Paramyx lunged and tackled her around the midriff. Lucy's blade went flying from her hand, lost in the fleshy morass all around. She tried to aim at Paramyx's head, only for a gauntleted hand to smother her own. Lucy grimaced in disgust at clammy flesh bulging from the gauntlet, oily and festering, pressed to her own, before Paramyx ripped the gun from her grasp and crushed it into rusted metal. It fell as red-brown dust. The other knights laughed cruelly, accompanied by the raucous, chittering screeching that passed for laughter from Nergal.

Suddenly, the same hand that had disarmed her seized Lucy by the throat. She desperately kicked at Paramyx's bloated belly spilling out from the wreckage of his breastplate, but if he felt anything, the Blighted Brother gave no sign. He didn't even flinch from touching her, despite the burning of the Order's mark. With a growl, he flung her at the foot of his master's throne. Nergal's mandibles chittered gleefully as he glared down at Lucy. The Knights of Yersinia formed a semi-circle to prevent escape, keeping their weapons trained on her.

"Oh dear. Has your little plan to be a glorious hero, bearding evil in its den, gone horribly wrong?" Nergal's mandibles rasped as he spoke. "Falciparum, I see the Order your once-blood created remains as self-righteous, impractical and vainglorious as always! Always do the righteous seek to fight against the tide of the inevitable, to try and prevent the inexorable tide of decay that—"

Nergal's sermonising was cut short as Lucy began laughing. The insectile demon growled angrily.

"You find something amusing? Why not share it with us? A final amusing memory before you and your precious Order are consigned to the ashes of history where you be-long!"

Lucy raised her head from the muck, spitting at the would-be god's feet and baring her teeth in a mocking grin.

"Well, you're part right; this isn't how I planned to do this, but truth be told, I'm right where I want to be!" She grinned as she activated the GPS beacon at her wrist.

Nergal screeched in annoyance and pointed at her again. Trypanos seized the beacon off her wrist and crushed it under his booted foot, but Lucy laughed mockingly.

"Sorry, but all they needed was a few seconds. You want to know something that's good for dealing with bacteria, boys?" Lucy forced herself back to her feet, her smile dripping with sweet poison. "Salt water," she finished as an almighty explosion rocked the *Siren*, a chunk of the hull caving in from the impact of a torpedo.

As seawater flooded into the hull, another explosion shook the corrupted ship, and all six of the Knights of Yersinia were swept off their feet, their formidable strength and resilience worthless against the ocean. Nergal screeched and scrabbled up to the top of his malformed throne, the fly wings protruding from his back fluttering frantically in fear. Lucy, smashed into the throne by the flood, pulled herself up and grabbed the monster's bloated abdomen.

"Unhand me, apostate whore!" Nergal bellowed, trying to shake her off, but Lucy held on.

Suddenly, she felt a hand seize her waist; it was Falciparum. The raging sea had torn away the hood and veil of chainmail covering his face, revealing the emaciated skull beneath it, wild with rage and fear.

"No, we all die together!" Falciparum shrieked, trying to pull her under the water.

"Not here."

Using her right hand, Lucy pulled free one of her explosive throwing knifes and stabbed Nergal in the back. The demon lord shrieked as Lucy stabbed him again and again, his wings beating manically as he took flight, trying to escape the rising sea water and his attacker. Falciparum roared in frustration, desperately trying to hold onto Lucy, but she flung the knife back into his closest eye socket and he involuntarily let her go. The Knights of Yersinia tried to stay above the rising water, but the weight of their armour dragged them down as they cried out for their master's aid. Nergal didn't give them a backward glance, heading straight for the hole torn in the roof of the hold by his plague swarm.

Suddenly, there was an almighty explosion of blue light, and Nergal shrieked in pain. Lucy glanced up, shielding her eyes with her arm, expecting to see another appearance from Valerie, but what was there was far more welcome. Gently levitating down from a gaping portal in mid-air towards the rapidly flooding hold was Gillian, her red hair growing ever paler, her eyes a flawless white without pupil or iris, as she channelled her magic to keep her afloat. Lucy looked up at her lover in unabashed awe…

"You are a goddess," she whispered the words she'd spoke on Samhain again, eliciting a shriek of fury from Nergal.

"I AM THE ONLY GOD HERE!"

His rasping outrage was suddenly cut short by the staccato roar of gunfire. Nergal howled as several of his eyes exploded into mush. Lucy cast about herself, seeing Captain Talbot slamming a fresh clip into his rifle.

"There's only one God, pal, and he's a lot better looking than you!"

Nergal roared, and Talbot was forced to dive for cover as the demon projectile-vomited a greasy, stinking black slurry crawling with maggots. The walls behind the captain's position began to melt as if struck by acid, but Talbot, accompanied by his sergeant and several other soldiers, returned fire. Nergal shrieked as they tore apart his wings. Both demon and Knight dropped like stones, Lucy holding onto Nergal's back with one hand as her other desperately reached for any handhold as they plummeted towards the rising water.

Suddenly, a gust of wind smashed both Lucy and Nergal towards a metal staircase leading down into the hull. They landed hard on their backs, half-stunned. As Lucy shook her head clear, she chanced a look up, seeing Gillian, hands outstretched, drawing the elements into the ship's hold. Sparks flickered in her lover's hands, the signs of magic she had used before…

With a shriek of rage, Gillian flung two colossal lightning bolts, one from each hand. They speared into the rising water, and Lucy heard muted screams and wails as the diseased warrior brotherhood, in accordance with the requirement that all six had to die at once to destroy them for good, were destroyed not by valour on the battlefield, the sword of some brave and skilful knight, but the simple laws of nature they had tried to corrupt for their own benefit. A scummy brown slick rose to the surface of the water, all that remained of six once-noble young men who'd sold their souls to darkness in a desperate effort to cheat death.

Suddenly, a keening screech brought Lucy's attention back to her current predicament; Nergal lunged at her, and her hands seized the demon's mandibles just before they clamped shut around her throat. She pushed him away, but he attacked again, Lucy struggling to keep the snapping jaws away. All the while, the pallid, insectile demon shrieked and jabbered, trying to put Lucy between itself and Gillian's magic.

"You think you've stopped anything by killing those six fools?! There will always be weak, desperate men and women terrified of death; I will find more to make into willing servants. As for me, once my children reach the mainland and their infection spreads like wildfire, I will feed from every sickness, every death, every weakling human who succumbs and rises again, until the flame of health is no more—"

"Oi, ugly! You like wildfire?"

Nergal looked up, only to be hit full in the face by a torrent of flame blasting from Danielle's outstretched hand. Lucy kicked Nergal off her and rooted at her belt. She pulled out the syringe she'd saved for this, still miraculously intact, and uncapped it as Nergal flung a chunk of broken metal at Danielle, disrupting her casting as she ducked to avoid losing her head. Lucy pushed herself into a sitting position, spitting at Nergal to get his attention. The demon snarled and crouched, ready to spring…

Here goes nothing.

As Nergal leapt atop her, Lucy stabbed out, jabbing the syringe into the soft flesh between head and thorax. Depressing the plunger, she injected twenty ccs of Rosa's blood directly into Nergal. The demon reared up, shrieking as the Bane blood, completely anathema to him, began to take effect. Lesions opened all over his body as the blood ate him from the inside out.

With a disgusted snarl, Lucy kicked him away, sending him crashing into the rising water. Lucy and Danielle watched in revulsion as, thrashing and shrieking, Nergal dissolved into black slime spreading across the surface of the water. Suddenly, another round of magical lightning blasted down from on high, accelerating his disintegration. Flesh and skin sloughed off and turned the sea water into a slimy soup.

With a final, choking gurgle, Nergal tried to raise a clawed hand to the sky, only for the limb to snap off at the elbow joint, before the dissolving carcass sank beneath the water's surface and was gone, Lucy and the others vaguely hearing a faint howl of thwarted rage echoing around the ship's hold as Nergal was banished.

Chapter 33: Abandon Ship

"Time to go!" Talbot bellowed as the *Siren* gave a groan like a dying beast.

He tossed a line to Danielle and Lucy, who quickly hauled themselves up. The soldier pulled them up over the rail. As Lucy looked around, she saw barely a handful of soldiers with Talbot, and all of them looked like they'd taken a battering.

"Are you all that's left?" she asked.

Captain Talbot opened his mouth, about to say something, when there came a shriek of tortured metal from all around them.

"Best save it for later," the soldier remarked as Gillian floated down to their level, and he motioned for them to all to run.

No one protested, they just fled through the corridors. Talbot's shotgun banged repeatedly as they encountered cultists and ship's crew fleeing for their lives; he gunned them down without mercy. Few even bothered trying to defend themselves, and the other soldiers slew any who Talbot missed and tried to fight back. Another almighty explosion rocked the sinking ship.

"Christ, how many more holes do they want to blow in this thing?" Danielle shouted, then shrieked as the ship listed again and the nearest wall became the ceiling.

"What are you doing here?" Lucy asked Gillian as the press of the corridors brought them side by side.

"I was shown where I needed to be," the spellweaver replied enigmatically. "We'll discuss it when we're out of here. There's something you and Charles need to know—"

"Can… hear me? Come in, can you hear me?" Anne's voice came in over their earpieces.

"I read you, Anne," Lucy replied. "Where are you?"

"I'm aboard a couple of Royal Navy gunships heading your way. We're about ten minutes out from your location. You need to get to the upper decks, we'll extract you from there!"

"Yeah, that might be a bit of a problem…" Lucy said, only to be cut off as another impact caused part of the corridor to collapse.

Gillian and Danielle shrieked, while Lucy felt an arm wrap around her waist, Talbot dragging her back as the ceiling caved in. She muttered, "Thanks," negligently patting him on the chest.

"Lucy, what's happened? That sounded bad," Anne said.

"I think the Navy were a bit overzealous. Our path's been cut off, we'll have to find another way off this—"

A baleful roar came from behind them. All eyes turned to see one of Talbot's remaining soldiers arch his back and cry out as a bloody fist erupted through his sternum, punching through body armour like it was paper. The body collapsed, leaving an extremely enraged Nathaniel Danvers standing behind it, looking thoroughly bedraggled, as if he'd climbed out of the ship's flooded hull. His Savile Row suit was torn to shreds, though not just from being flung around by the sinking ship. Russet-coloured scales and spines pockmarked his face and limbs, and when he bared his teeth, they were the crocodilian fangs of the Emissary.

"You ruined *everything!*" Danvers howled, his expanding dentition distorting his voice. "It would have been beautiful; Nergal would have purified the filth of humanity with his pestilential gifts, and my master and mistress would have leisurely strolled through the broken barriers to claim their prize! My rewards would have been beyond measure, my past failures forgiven! Why do you insist on interfering?!"

Talbot shot him in the face. Danvers's head snapped back, his jaw broken by the gunshot.

"That," he snarled, his voice distorting as the Emissary pushed his way through to the fore, the demon's influence causing the broken jaw to reset, "was a mistake!"

"Anne, we may be delayed," Lucy muttered as Danvers's hair and skin continued to turn into reptilian scales and bony horns.

Gillian pressed herself against the heap of debris at the far end of the corridor.

"Buy me some time, and I'll get us out of here," she said, only for the Emissary to laugh.

"You won't get the chance, girl. I see Legion failed to kill you, so I shall have to just do it myself. I'm afraid this will hurt, but look on the bright side—once I'm done, you'll be reunited with your philandering father and your failure of a sister—"

Danvers's taunt was cut short as Gillian telekinetically threw a hefty chunk of broken steel plating at him, smashing him back down the corridor. Lucy, Talbot and two more soldiers charged and tackled the Emissary to the floor before he could rise again.

"Keep him down," Talbot bellowed as the reptilian demon tried to throw them off.

Lucy pulled out the last blood-filled blade, intending to bury it in his shoulder and send the Bane poison flooding through the Emissary's veins, when with a roar, the demon threw them all off. They smashed off walls and debris.

"I wish I had more time to deal with you pissants as you deserve, but needs must!" he growled.

A clawed hand darted out and seized Gillian by the throat. He gritted his teeth as her mark burned him. The soldiers and Lucy scrambled to their feet, but the Emissary's tail lashed out low, sweeping them all down again.

"I see if I want someone dead, I have to do it myself!" the Emissary growled.

A snake-like tongue ran up Gillian's cheek and slurped up blood from the long scratch there, when a roared battle cry came from behind him. Blinding white light filled the hall as the Champion's Blade sank into his spine. The Emissary roared in fury, but Charles tore the falx out, ducked under the swing of a fist as the demon whirled round, and then sent the sword slamming into the Emissary's chest.

"Do you never die?!" the demon bellowed, kicking Charles back against the wall.

The Emissary's claws came out, and Charles blocked the first swing with his arms. The Emissary kept raining blows down on him, though, and soon enough, Charles started to miss.

The demon is going to pummel him into submission, and then it'll rip him open like a side of beef!

Lucy reacted instinctively. Charles and she had their issues, but she didn't want to watch him die. She pulled out two of her explosive throwing knives and flung them at the Emissary's back. To her shock, the demon caught and flung them back. Lucy dived aside as they sank into the nearby wall, hearing the explosion and feeling the heat as the blades detonated. She heard a groan of pain from Charles, and then next thing she knew, a heavy weight stomped down on the small of her back. She tried to crawl away, but another kick to the ribs knocked her on her back.

"Bold as always!" the Emissary laughed in mockery. "Bold little Lucy Murray, always too stubborn to know when she's beaten!" He sneered as a tridactyl foot stamped down on her chest and she cried out in pain. "You know, with Lawrence gone, I almost want to let you get out of here alive, if only to watch the amusement of you trying to piece it all back together, make some glorious little effort to stop what is coming all by yourself. Maybe even leave you as the last human in the world when it's all said and done, just to let you see all your actions have achieved is nothing… but, no." The creature ran a forked tongue over its jagged teeth. "There is always the possibility that somehow, just somehow, you could find some way to undo our work, so as much as I would like to continue this game with you as my new opponent, perhaps it's better to end it now."

The Emissary crouched down. Lucy turned her head away in disgust as the carrion reek of its breath assaulted her.

"Would you rather I broke your neck or tore your throat out? Decisions, decisions!" The monster raked a claw along her cheek, just before it threw back its head and roared in agony.

Its clawed foot lifted off Lucy's chest, and as it spun round, Lucy saw that Charles had sunk the Champion's Blade once again into the Emissary's shoulder. The white flames burned as they tasted demonic blood. The demon threw Lucy aside with a snarl but Charles had expected that.

"Lucy!" he yelled, kicking the knife towards her.

The Emissary turned, but slowly, too slowly. Lucy slammed the blade into the demon's shin and depressed the stud in the handle.

"Is that the best you—" the Emissary began to sneer, only to freeze in horror and double over in pain. Fiery red lines were spreading out from the point of impact, and the monster was screaming, both in its true voice and that of Nathaniel Danvers.

"What have you done? What have you done to me?!"

"Ten ccs of blood taken from the veins of a Bane," Lucy taunted.

All over the Emissary's body, patches of russet scales fell out in bloody chunks, revealing patches of almost human skin. One of the horns atop his head snapped halfway along its length, clattering to the decking. The Emissary's face shifted, one half a reptilian monstrosity, the other half human, and both were twisted beyond recognition. Black patches of necrosis crawled all over his body. His right arm snapped off at the elbow, the limb little more than rotted black meat that withered into sludge.

With a roar of fury, Nathaniel Danvers, Emissary of the Pantheon, collapsed into a steadily dissolving puddle of bloody slime. Gillian extended her hands, but Danielle waved her back and blasted the disintegrating demon with streams of fire from her fingertips. What final words the demon or his human form might have said devolved into incoherent keening as the fire and Joshua's blood did their work. When only the upper torso of a malformed skeleton remained, the Emissary's disintegrating body pitched forward, and Lucy stamped on its horned skull, reducing it to fragments of bone and black filth.

"Thank you, Joshua," Lucy muttered, sorry the boy was not here to see this.

The ship gave another ominous creak. She didn't have much longer left.

"We need to get out of here now!"

"This way!" a familiar voice shouted.

Lucy looked down the corridor, seeing a bare-chested Liam, his chest and shoulders covered in bleeding wounds, holding a thrashing sack slung over one shoulder. He waved at them to follow him, but as two of Talbot's remaining men made to, there was an almighty crash from above and the ceiling caved in, crushing them under it.

"Liam, get out of here! We'll find another way out!" Lucy bellowed, even as Danielle gave a yelp and the water rose all around them.

"Gillian, we need a way out of here! Don't know about you, but I don't want to drown in this floating shithole!" Charles shouted.

Gillian quirked an eyebrow at him before she began chanting. Blue sparks danced in her palms as an ever-widening sphere of energy grew larger and larger between her hands. Over the growing roar as the power built up, Lucy heard the sound of Liam's footsteps retreat as he fled to find another way off the sinking ship. With a roared final syllable from Gillian's lips, the sphere of energy expanded outward, then collapsed back to its source. Lucy and

Charles were yanked off their feet and dragged back with it. Danielle shrieked and Talbot cried out in surprise as the spell transported them away.

***

Light returned to them with a flash. Lucy heard birds crying, wind rushing past her ears. She opened her eyes and saw herself falling, the Aegean Sea rushing up to meet them. She looked to her left and right and saw the others falling—and not just them. All around them, flies the size of lions plummeted towards the ocean, legs twisted upwards, nothing more than husks robbed of life now the power that had brought them through was gone.

"Oh this is perfect, just bloody perfect!" Charles shouted at Gillian as they plunged towards the water.

"I had a lot on my mind! I just thought outside—"

The rest of what she shrieked back at him was lost in the rush of air. Dead insects hit the water ahead of them.

"Oh, here goes nothing!" Lucy grimaced.

She straightened her legs and took a deep breath as she hit the water. She kicked upward, gasping rapidly as her head breached the surface, only to shriek and swim aside as another dead hell-fly plummeted towards her.

"Oh, that's disgusting!" Lucy spat in revulsion.

Looking around, she saw the others surface, and quickly took stock of their numbers. Herself, Gillian, Charles, Talbot and another of his remaining men, the sergeant Byrne.

Suddenly, they heard gunfire from behind them. Turning, they saw the *Siren* sinking, and a dark shape leaping from the side of the ship. Life rafts packed with Desolated cultists moved to pursue the newcomer who'd dived below the surface. Lucy wondered how long it would be before the cultists took notice of them floating helpless in the water.

A trio of dark shapes passed overhead with a roar.

"Alright!" Captain Talbot shouted at the three helicopters.

The cultists pursuing the figure who'd leapt from the sinking ship—who they could now see was Liam, clutching a bag between his teeth—turned their attention to the reinforcements, but their weapons did little more to the military helicopters than scratch the paintwork. The helicopters' response was a lot more effective. Cultists were gunned down, sinking beneath the water to join their lair at the bottom of the ocean.

As they floated helpless in the water, Talbot turned to Lucy and asked, "So is this a standard day for your organisation?"

"No, usually it's a lot smaller scale than this," Lucy admitted. "But if you're interested in finding out more, we do have a job opening or two. Pay's not great, but the work's always interesting…"

Chapter 34: Reforging
Temple Church, London

"Danielle Drake, Mark Talbot, Thomas Byrne, you have seen the truth of What Lies Beyond. You saw it and chose to stand and fight the spread of the evil that it breeds, the threat it poses to all those who live free and ignorant of its corruption. You have been made ready to fight the shadow war we have waged since time unremembered. You have been asked to join the ranks of the silent Order, to stand vigil in the shadows that others may walk in the light, but this is not a command to be followed blindly. To take up the Argent Blade and stand ready against what tries to slip out from the darkness is a calling, a choice we all make willingly, and now we ask it of you. Will you stand the long vigil at our side? Will you give all that you are, all that you have—your skills, your intelligence, your life if need be—to protect people who will never know what you've done for them?"

As the words left her, Lucy felt a strange sense of déjà vu. Less than a year ago, she would never have thought she would be in Lawrence's place, inducting new recruits. She knew there was still some disapproval of her election to the position of Grand Master, but the events aboard the *Siren* had more or less quelled the dissenters. Gillian, Anne and Claire were behind her all the way, and after the defeat of Nergal, Charles, while still resentful about being passed over, seemed to be willing to give her a chance now.

So long as he watches my back, I won't mind if he's only doing it to make sure he's still in poll position to take over if I fall in the line of duty!

"To the last ounce of strength. To the last drop of blood. To the last gasp of breath. As long as one of those is still in me, then I will fight to the bitter end. I will not break, I will not run. I will stand with those who hold the bulwark, who bear the shield, who stand in the darkness that the innocent may walk in the light. I swear it, in blood and upon steel," all three of those in front of her said.

Lucy wondered if they'd experienced the same internal conflict she'd felt when she stood in their place, if they felt the same uncertainty and hesitation at making such a monumental decision that would mark the rest of their lives.

Lucy drew her kukri from within her robes and walked over to each of them in turn, first slicing across the palm of Thomas Byrne, then Mark Talbot and finally Danielle Drake, giving her a small smile of encouragement. Charles helped them all to their feet and led them over to the font, where a young man with short blond hair in the robes of a Catholic priest, who she'd been introduced to three hours prior as Father Paul, stood reading from the same book Father Peter had at her own initiation, the holy invocation to bless them with the protection of the mark.

Father Peter's absence felt strange, but he was heading for the Vatican itself, accompanied by Rosa. Now that she had the unique blessing of a Bane in her blood, she was invaluable to those fighting the good fight, and a target for all those who served it. Joshua's tragic fate had made that unequivocally clear, and the priest reasoned that one of the holiest sites on earth would be the best place to keep her safe from those who would do her harm.

Lucy felt a great sense of guilt at the fact their shadowy war had robbed another young woman of the life she might have wanted, but Rosa had been fairly upbeat about it before she and Father Peter departed for Heathrow.

"An innocent boy died for no other reason than what was in his blood. I won't let him be forgotten. I will do something good with what I've been given, both for me and for him. I will live two lives, however I can, for myself and

Joshua, and I will make sure that his life, however short it was, is never forgotten."

Lucy had nodded in understanding and offered her hand to Rosa. "I hope we meet one day again, Rosa, in better circumstances."

"Don't take this the wrong way, but I'd rather we didn't," Rosa replied with a rueful smile. "I'm not sure I need that kind of excitement in my life again."

Lucy had chuckled at that, conceding the point.

Good luck, and safe travels to you, Rosa Tirelli, wherever fate takes you, she thought as all three of her new recruits winced when the holy water in the font burnt the fresh tattoos on their right arms, activating their protective aura, ensuring that they need never fear the touch of the demonic.

With the ritual nearly complete, Lucy nodded to Claire, who stepped forward holding a silver tray bearing three silver-steel kukris sheathed in scabbards of black leather. The three new recruits took one each, to wield until their fight came to its end.

And may that be a long time in coming, Lucy thought. *I'd rather my tenure as Grand Master—or should that be Grand Mistress? I don't know, that title sounds like it should belong to a dominatrix—not be a short one. I'd rather have a few years of quiet and easy victories against whatever's left or tries to take the place of the Desolated. I mean, I'm going to have enough of a battle convincing the old greybeards in the Ministry of Defence to give us proper funding when they see who's running the show now!*

Lucy walked up to her newest soldiers and clapped each of them on the shoulder in turn.

"From this day until the day you finally fall, you are one of us. You are forever a Knight of the Order of the Argent Blade."

***

The English Channel, eight miles off the coast of Dover

The small fishing boat came to a stop, dropping anchor in the calm waters. Edmund Dalton checked his pocket watch; the face read one a.m. More than enough time to get this done.

A small matter of justice, long overdue.

Edmund and Moira still had memories of comrades who'd been lost, either by his hand or the monstrosities he'd helped the Desolated and their Nazi allies unleash upon the world. They both wanted to see justice done.

The boat's captain, an old man in his late sixties, white-bearded and stony-faced, looked out from the wheelhouse, caught Edmund's eye and nodded, before turning his attention back to the distant French coastline. He was an old fisherman by the name of Tobias Morgan, but what many people didn't know was that he had been one of Moira and Edmund's foundlings, brought up and grown to old age. He'd never married, never started a family, and had lived a quiet life in obscurity on the English coast, but he remembered the kindness and duty the vampires had shown him in taking him off the street, and was more than happy to do them or their allies in the Order a favour when the time arose, but he preferred to remain ignorant of the Order's activities. For that, Edmund couldn't blame him. It was safer for Tobias—if he didn't know anything, he couldn't be coerced into divulging it.

"We're far enough out," Edmund said to his wife, his voice terse. "Let's get this done."

Tobias cut the engine, Edmund nodded and Gillian emerged from below deck, dragging a thrashing hessian bag behind her, its contents making muffled, profanity-laced shouts and trying to get free. Gillian gave its contents a kick for good measure before stepping back as Moira and Edmund came up from below, carrying a heavy industrial safe with them. Lawrence had left extremely specific notes about what was to be done if the Order or any of their allies captured this quarry. Neither of the Daltons could fault him for his anger; Lawrence had lost two family members to their captive—an aunt murdered by Nazi hands at Auschwitz, and a daughter who'd died because of the monsters the depraved mind they were about to destroy had unleashed… to say nothing of the thousands their captive's depravity had killed.

It's a pity he's not here to see justice done, Edmund mused sadly as he and Moira placed the safe on the ground. *His daughter must do it in his stead.*

"Get it over with," Gillian said. "This bastard has had this coming for a long time."

Edmund's claws extended and he ripped the sack open. The limbless head and torso of Josef Mengele spilled out onto the deck. The doctor's mouth was firmly wrapped with duct tape, so the best he could manage were muffled curses and threats that, in his current state, were pretty much impossible.

"You have the right to remain silent, Herr Doktor!" Gillian lifted Mengele up by the scruff of his neck and dragged him towards the safe. "For the love of Christ, do us all a favour and use it!"

When Mengele continued to rant on and on, however, Moira seized his face in her hand. Her claws raked deep furrows in the undead flesh, clumps of grey skin falling away as she looked the doctor in the eye and snarled in warning. "Keep mouthing off, boyo, and I'll send you to the Pearly Gates without any means of begging for your miserable hide!"

Mengele took one look at the baleful glare in Moira's pale blue eyes and, realising her last words hadn't been hyperbole, quickly shut up. There was no mercy or patience in her gaze, just a century's worth of loathing.

With Mengele mercifully quiet, Edmund promptly wrapped the undead madman's torso in several kilograms of steel chains purloined from a shipyard. He locked them with reliably durable padlocks before tossing Mengele none-too-gently in the safe and throwing a few lead weights in there for good measure.

The two vampires matched Mengele's look of impotent fury with one of deepest disgust as Edmund pulled back his sleeve, baring the sword and horned skull sigil tattooed on his arm.

"Josef Mengele, on behalf of the Knights of the Order of the Argent Blade, for the crimes of murder, treason to the human race, war crimes, crimes against humanity, partaking in magics prohibited by the Salem Compact, demon summoning and countless others, you are hereby sentenced to death."

Mengele cast a strange look at his current situation. While far from ideal, it hardly seemed a prelude to an execution. In answer, Moira gave the old Nazi a smile so reptilian one might have expected a forked tongue to dart from between her teeth.

Gillian stepped forward to loom over the captive Mengele, smiling poisonously at him. "You'll die for your crimes, Herr Doktor, but Mr Dalton never said you'd die today."

A booted foot stamped down on Mengele's chest, pushing the metal further onto the undead doctor's sternum. Ribs infused with dark magic began to snap under the weight.

"For my father, Lawrence Templeton. For my great aunt, Charlotte Elizabeth Templeton. For my sister, Valerie Meredith Templeton, and for all the others whose lives have been ruined because of you."

Gillian spat in Mengele's face before nodding to Edmund.

"Do it."

Mengele's final words were a cacophony of muffled shouts as he realised what was about to happen, before Edmund brought the safe door slamming shut. He ripped off the handle and wrapped it in more chains, condemning Mengele to his new cell. Without further preamble, Edmund kicked the safe over the side of the boat. It hit the water with an almighty splash and sank like a stone. With their enhanced hearing, the pair of vampires could hear muffled yells for freedom before the safe sank deeper, taking Josef Mengele to his watery fate.

Death was too good for such a monster. Instead, Mengele would reside on the ocean floor until the safe rusted away to nothing, and even when that happened, he would remain trapped and chained on the seabed until the fish consumed the rotted meat of his necromancy-tainted bones and the water pressure crushed his carcass into nothing, only then perhaps releasing his twisted spirit to whatever torment awaited him beyond this world.

Edmund stared out to sea as Tobias turned the boat back for England. Moira walked up to her husband and squeezed his shoulder.

"So, what next?" she asked.

"Well, we get home before sunrise, and wait and see."

The pair of them walked over to Gillian, staring at the distant cliffs of Dover, and Edmund gently touched her on the shoulder.

"Your father would be proud of you," he said. "You've done a great thing, given justice to so many who suffered at that bastard's hands."

Gillian allowed herself a wan smile at the thought.

"Thank you. I must admit, I know we weren't close when he died, but I like to think he'd approve of what I, and Lucy and the rest of us, have done this time. The Desolated are broken, perhaps for good this time—one of their greatest assets is now at the bottom of the Channel. Nathaniel Danvers is destroyed, and most of what they had is lying at the bottom of the Aegean Sea. In addition to failing Echidna on Halloween, now they've won the enmity of a powerful demon lord who is not going to speak highly of them to her and her husband. There will still be threats to come—Lucy is new and untested, and there will be other factions out there wanting to test her strength—but I think we might be able to rest on our laurels for a bit."

***

Mount Etna, Sicily

Lakshmi Varsani stalked up the slopes of the volcano, her temper seething at the latest failures of her brethren and the fact she was now forced to handle the aftermath of the newest disaster alone. The last transmission from the *Siren* had told her everything that had happened: Nathaniel dead, the Emissary utterly destroyed, the Knights of Yersinia obliterated, and the great plague they'd hoped to unleash thwarted.

In a fury, Lakshmi had killed any cultists who'd managed to escape. That they were alive when their betters had fallen implied incompetence or cowardice, and as such, they weren't fit to continue serving the brotherhood. They'd found her in a small hostel on Sicily, where Nathaniel had dispatched her with specific instructions, should the worst happen… which was why she was hiking up an active volcano in the dead of night.

Her fingers shifted into claws that raked a specific emblem into the wood of every tree she passed, as Nathaniel had told her, a pilgrim's cry for help.

Though the rest of humanity had forgotten, generations of cultists had come here and watered the trees with human blood, sacrifices to draw their imprisoned master's attention and maybe earn some small measure of his favour. Etna was the site of a battle that most of mankind had banished to the memory of legend, but Lakshmi and her brethren had never forgotten, and still planned for the day when its outcome was undone.

With every rune she carved, Lakshmi sliced open her own finger and let blood slide into the grooves carved in the wood. Her tainted blood's scent filled the air, a plea for help to her master, anything that might turn the tide. The thought of the Order of the Argent Blade resurgent sickened her.

"Well, we can't have that," a sepulchral voice growled in the back of her head.

Lakshmi spun round, but there was no one there. She was alone.

Suddenly, she heard stones being kicked aside. She spun around and saw a broad, muscular figure stalking towards her. He had the look of a soldier in the Italian Army, wearing dark camouflage, a pistol holstered at his hip, but Lakshmi could *feel* he was like her, touched by What Lies Beyond. His fingernails were black claws, but most striking were the two yellow, slit-pupiled eyes tattooed on each cheek below his real eyes. As she watched, he inclined his head to her and motioned for her to follow him back down the mountain.

"It is time we left this place, Lady Lakshmi. Let our enemies have this temporary victory. We will retreat into the shadows, build a new army, one worthy of our master when he is at long last freed, and set the true order in place. The time of shadow games and subtlety is over. When we are strong again, when we are ready, this time it will be open war."

Who are you? Lakshmi signed.

The newcomer smiled, and Lakshmi saw his teeth were crocodilian fangs. He blinked, and her eyes went wide. He had blinked with all six eyes, two flesh and blood, and four inked upon his skin.

"My name is Geryon. And I am the one who will lead you to victory."

Acknowledgments

I must confess, there were times I thought I would never make it to this point. This is the first time I've completed a sequel to one of my novels, so this is quite an achievement for me. Like Lucy, however, I didn't complete this task alone; there were plenty of amazing men and women who played their part in bringing this story to completion, so let me acknowledge and thank them. They're knights in their own way, helping me slay the demons of uncertainty and self-doubt, as equally terrible as any monster from What Lies Beyond.

First, to my lady love, Becky Finch, who's been nothing but supportive every step of the way, letting me bounce ideas off her, reading chapters, making suggestions of her own to improve the characters and plot, and just letting me rave when I couldn't see the next step forward. Thank you so much for putting up with the perfectionist writer who loves you, sweetheart, particularly when everything has been so chaotic this year.

Next, to my parents, Robert and Ashley Courtney, for giving me the beginnings of becoming a writer by surrounding me with so many stories throughout my life, all the support, advice, love and just tolerance for putting up with me moaning and groaning about writing all the way through lockdown, and to Becky's mum, Connie, for supporting her perfectionist of a future son-in-law when he's in angst because his current chapter is being so uncooperative.

To my amazing beta readers, Sean Donovan, Roger Sandri and Katherine Graham, a massive thank you for taking the time to read through *Plague Carrier* and give me your thoughts; the story is so much stronger for it, and I really appreciate you offering to beta-read. Also, I want to give a massive shout out to The Writer Community on Instagram, whose support and enthusiasm for my work in progress, as well as your love for *Argent Blade*, were a great motivation to see this through to the end. I hope you'll all enjoy what I have planned for the finale of the *Argent Blade* series.

Next, a huge thank you to the amazing team at Rowanvale Books. All of you, at every step of the publication process, were so helpful and supportive; you completely rewrote my opinion on self-publishing my work and helped make every stage of the self-publishing process so straightforward and easy for me to understand, and the gorgeous cover art your team created is as amazing as all my previous books published with you.

Finally, a huge thank you to you, the reader, for staying with the story of Lucy Murray and the Knights of the Order of the Argent Blade. Without you, I wouldn't have a reason to write, to pursue my passion that is telling stories, and I hope you fully enjoyed *Plague Carrier* and will return for the grand finale that will be *Argent Blade: Endwar*!

Until the next time…

Author Profile

Luke Courtney grew up surrounded by books, and that inspired him to start writing his own stories to hopefully inspire others the same way his favourite authors had for him. Being surrounded by the rich history and vibrancy of the city of London, as well as his lifelong fascination for history and mythology, helped inspire and set the Argent Blade novels to paper. He is the author of the Argent Blade and Phoenix Saga series, as well as the children's story Two-Horn, and is working on a number of other stories for the future.

Luke divides his time between writing the next instalments in both series, working in a small military museum in London, telling stories about the men, women and horses of the Household Cavalry, and spending time with his amazingly supportive wife, Becky. When not writing, he enjoys reading, gaming, painting and anything to do with animals or history.

www.instagram.com/lc90authorhub
Luke Courtney (Author of Argent Blade) | Goodreads

***

What Did You Think of *Argent Blade: Plague Carrier*?

A big thank you for purchasing this book. It means a lot that you chose this book specifically from such a wide range on offer. I do hope you enjoyed it.

Book reviews are incredibly important for an author. All feedback helps them improve their writing for future projects and for developing this edition. If you are able to spare a few minutes to post a review on Amazon, that would be much appreciated.

Publisher Information

Rowanvale Books provides publishing services to independent authors, writers and poets all over the globe. We deliver a personal, honest and efficient service that allows authors to see their work published, while remaining in control of the process and retaining their creativity. By making publishing services available to authors in a cost-effective and ethical way, we at Rowanvale Books hope to ensure that the local, national and international community benefits from a steady stream of good quality literature.

For more information about us, our authors or our publications, please get in touch.

www.rowanvalebooks.com
info@rowanvalebooks.com